ARTIFACTS

NATALIE LEMLE

SIMON & SCHUSTER

New York Amsterdam/Antwerp London Toronto
Sydney/Melbourne New Delhi

Simon & Schuster
1230 Avenue of the Americas
New York, NY 10020

First Simon & Schuster hardcover edition May 2026

Interior design by Carly Loman

Manufactured in the United States of America

1 3 5 7 9 10 8 6 4 2

Library of Congress Control Number: 2025936657

ISBN 978-1-6680-6834-2
ISBN 978-1-6680-6836-6 (ebook)

For E and S

"I shall never rest until I know that all my ideas are derived, not from hearsay or tradition, but from my real living contact with the things themselves."

– J.W. GOETHE, *Italian Journey*

I.

MARCH 7, 2022

NEW YORK CITY

People with bad blood like us shouldn't procreate. Jinny said that to me once when we were little, and I never forgot it.

She did, though. Which is to say, Jinny's pregnant—by choice. *Arrangement* was the exact word she used last night as she was shoving clothes into her backpack, avoiding my wide-eyed stare. I imagine her now on her flight back to LA, taking a pause from grading her students' midterms to gaze out the window at flat clouds like in the O'Keeffe skyscape at the Art Institute, the one I loved as a kid because she did.

My thoughts are interrupted by an unfamiliar, genderless voice: "It's a shakedown."

I'm in the client-facing kitchen on the fifteenth floor, the only one in the firm with an espresso machine—and I'm startled, not because I can map any significance onto these words, but because it's seven thirty on a Monday and the labyrinth of cubicles I walked through to get here was deserted as of five minutes ago. I open a drawer and tune in as I dig for dark roast.

"They want everything back," the voice says, quieter now. "*Tutto. Si, tutto.*"

I peer around the corner, momentarily locking eyes with a bright-eyed older woman pressing a cell phone to her ear. I'm pretty sure

I've never seen her before, but she turns away before I can get a good look at her face. As she makes her way down the corridor, I take in her tweed jacket, the seam in her pantyhose, and the way she's ever so slightly favoring her left leg.

Americano in hand, I head to the elevator bank, clocking the unoccupied reception desk. I feel an impulse to turn back and ask the woman who she is and how she got up here, but then I remember about Jinny and catch the elevator.

BACK AT MY DESK, I sip coffee and stare out my window at the steel-gray Hudson, ruminating on last night's sequence of events. Jinny across the table from me at dinner, drinking water instead of Sancerre; Jinny explaining after she vomited back at my apartment that morning sickness is a misnomer for the constant nausea of early pregnancy; Jinny insisting she was doing this on her own when I asked who the father was.

I'm refreshing my inbox for the tenth time when there's a knock at my office door. "Yeah?" I call, glancing at the time in the upper right corner of my laptop. It's 7:46. I got in early so I could proof and revise the second draft of a complicated estate plan, but I haven't even opened the document. I should have gone to the gym, which is where I go when I really need to get something done. Nothing makes me more productive than the threat of exercising.

Emmanuel Reyes, the chair of the firm's litigation practice, sticks his head in. "Got a minute, Lena?"

"Sure," I say, getting to my feet when he signals for me to follow him. "I just need to—"

He cuts me off. "I'll be brief."

Emmanuel, who is not my boss—but whose advocacy would go a long way with the other equity partners at my annual review—is a good guy, deep down. I've heard him talk about his childhood in

Rhode Island after a few drinks at work functions, the one-bedroom Section 8 apartment that housed him and his mother and his two brothers. When he clears his throat, I put the estate plan out of my mind and follow him.

Emmanuel's office window is at least five times the size of mine, and as he gathers up a stack of papers at his desk, I take a seat at the round table in the corner and look out into the building next door, where a man on a headset is pacing around a conference room.

"Am I remembering correctly from that recruiting event way back that you speak Italian? You studied abroad or something?"

I straighten my spine and nod. "It's rusty, I'm sure," I say. "But yes." I look up at the white grid of his dropped ceiling and calculate: eighteen. I was in Italy eighteen years ago. Incidentally, there are six rows of three large squares in the ceiling—I'm no numerologist, but this synchronicity feels somehow meaningful. I smooth my bangs as I try to picture myself back then: center-parted ash-brown hair down to the middle of my back, wide eyes, slack jaw.

"My granddaughter picked it out this morning," he says, catching me eyeing his graffiti-print tie as he pulls out the chair next to me. "She spent the night."

"How old is she?" I ask, out of politeness rather than genuine interest.

Emmanuel smiles and shakes his head. "Four. We gave up and put a sleeping bag on the floor of our room."

I nod, thinking of how I slept on Jinny's bedroom floor throughout our childhood, and then commandeered the whole room when she went to college. Other than my *Romeo and Juliet* movie poster, which I taped to the back of her closet door so I could doze off to the sight of Claire Danes kissing Leonardo DiCaprio, the room remained a shrine to my sister. My sister, who is now ten weeks pregnant.

He opens a manila folder. "Italy is accusing Fordham University's museum of housing looted art. The report that came out of NYPD's investigation is pretty brutal."

I open my mouth to ask what this has to do with trusts and estates, but I change my mind and nod.

"We've been retained to represent Fordham in the case."

This is a single-office corporate law firm; we're less hierarchical than most big firms, which means that while it takes longer to make partner, it's also easy to keep up with cases outside my practice area. But I've never heard of litigation working on a cultural heritage case, or any art law case. "They don't have their own general counsel?"

"They do, but she doesn't want to touch this."

"Why?"

"She's a higher ed attorney. She doesn't know anything about looted antiquities—"

"Sorry," I interrupt. What does *Emmanuel* know about looted antiquities? "Since when do we do cultural heritage law?"

"My team won a case a few years ago," he says impatiently, "brought against an art dealer who was implicated in selling Nazi-looted paintings to some oil family in the fifties. I obtained a complete dismissal of all claims against the client."

"He didn't do it? The art dealer?"

"The case fell under government enforcement and compliance. The court was determined not to have jurisdiction," Emmanuel says. "The claims were dismissed."

So Emmanuel *has* practiced art law here. And now my skepticism is replaced with the energizing realization that this conversation must be about bringing me on to his new case—it's not unheard of, after all, for litigation to pull in support from trusts and estates, especially during discovery.

"The museum only collects ancient art," he continues. "Everything Italy wants back is fifth century or earlier. They don't have great evidence for all of it. Most of it, actually. But this one, this cup—this is the smoking gun."

He slides a photograph of a bas-relief glass cylinder layered into an ornate metal casing toward me. It looks like a cup made from stained glass with its green glow. I spot a winged figure holding up a bow and arrow. "It's Cupid," I say.

"Yeah," he says. "Amor and Psyche, that's how they have it catalogued. There's something, some kind of metal—silver maybe?—mixed in with the glass, which makes it green." He shuffles around his papers and pulls out another photograph. "If the light shows through the other way, it turns red. Dichroic glass, I guess it's called."

"Why is it the smoking gun?" I ask, noticing another vignette on the cup, in which a woman with butterfly wings—Psyche—holds up a torch to sleeping Cupid's face.

"The Italians have Polaroids of it from a Swiss warehouse raid in the nineties. The dealer, this Italian guy, Valerio something, was arrested for illicit antiquities trading. Most of what he was dealing in was looted."

My throat spasms, and I start coughing as Emmanuel opens his laptop and pulls up a document that shows a series of scanned blown-out Polaroids of the cup at different angles.

3–4 sec vetro—? is written in Sharpie on the central photo's bottom white border.

"You okay, kid?"

I clear my throat and nod. "So this guy was just keeping Polaroids of all the things he sold?"

"Apparently it was part of an inventory system. The text down here is—"

"The origin date, right? Their guess. And material."

Emmanuel grins. "See? I knew you could help."

My cheeks warm at this validation, and I try to sound as nonchalant as possible when I ask, "Where in Switzerland was the warehouse?"

"Chiasso. Right over the border from Italy, in the Alps. Near Lugano."

A warehouse near Lugano. Giamma. My eye twitches, and suddenly I'm in a wind tunnel with Giamma on one end and Cyrille on the other. I can practically feel Cyrille telling me—what is he telling me? He's moving his mouth, he's saying something, but I can't hear it, and I can't read his lips.

Emmanuel regards me impatiently. "What's wrong?"

"Nothing," I say with as much confidence as I can muster.

Thankfully, Emmanuel forges ahead. "The Italians haven't shared all their evidence. But in advance of that, I need you to go through the paperwork. I know it's not your wheelhouse, but this is too complicated to assign to someone who doesn't understand international tax law. And a lot of it is not in English. Hence my question about whether you speak Italian."

A sudden calmness comes over me. Some part of myself, I understand, is being unearthed. An old drive, an old yearning, and for a moment I can imagine a world in which I'm not locked away in my office drawing up estate plans and red-lining paperwork and editorializing wills according to my clients' verbal tics. A world in which I am an active participant, doing work that matters.

"You'd be doing me a huge favor," he adds. "And I checked, trusts and estates leadership is good with it."

"Right," I say, returning my gaze to the window. The man in the headset, the one I saw in the building next door when I first sat down, has disappeared. Cyrille was there too—up at the dig site in Orbagne that dark August morning—and then he was gone.

I take a deep breath, cringing at the sour smell of my now-cold coffee. I cover my cup with my hand and refocus. "So I'll start with the policy docs?"

Emmanuel relaxes into his chair. "There's a lot to wade through. State, national, international—there's UNESCO's charter, and then there are all the Italian policies. I'll give you access to the folder on the drive."

"Okay," I say. "Next steps?"

He looks at his watch, then gathers up his papers. "Actually, the curator from Fordham will be here in about an hour for deposition prep. You wanna sit in?"

"Sure," I say, putting the will I came in early to revise out of my mind.

BACK IN MY OFFICE, I call Lakshmi. She picks up on the first ring. "I have five minutes," she says.

"You want to call me back later?"

"No, now is good." She's breathing audibly; I can tell she's on foot.

"Are you on your way to a meeting?"

"I took my morning call from home so I could do Ovid's walk. Iñigo left for a board meeting in San Francisco at the crack of dawn."

A visual of the husky mix they rescued a month ago, which I've only seen in photos, comes to mind. For as long as I've known Iñigo, I have a harder time picturing him; he's always traveling for work lately. "Maybe he crossed paths with Jinny at security."

"How did it go with her this weekend?"

I decide to wait until Lakshmi has more than five minutes to get into it. "I'll tell you later."

"Tell me now!"

Outside my office, two first-year associates erupt into unselfconscious laughter. I watch them for a moment, telegraphing my disapproval, then I get up and close my door. It's better to keep work relationships professional. Also, your twenties are not for socializing—they're for building your career. I spent those years billing ten-hour days, then eating takeout at my desk while I caught up on non-billable to-dos. I always had Lakshmi, but we only ever saw each other on the weekends when we were finished with the work we'd brought home with us.

"She's pregnant," I say.

"Oh, babe."

Hearing the empathy in her voice, I feel a wave of affection for Lakshmi, because it is such a relief not to have to explain. That with the little information she has absorbed about Jinny and me over the years, she can fill in the blanks and issue an appropriate response.

"Listen," she says. "I'm just getting to work. Come over tomorrow. You can finally see the new place."

In general I prefer to self-soothe with reality television and peanut butter and jelly on weeknights, but I should go. I should be with my friend, meet the dog, see her new place in the West Village, furnished by Iñigo's IPO windfall and Lakshmi's recent promotion to partner. "Yeah, fine. Thai?"

"I'll make us something."

Lakshmi never cooks. "Will I like it?"

She laughs. "Just come over at eight. Okay?"

"Wait," I say. "Remember our professor Cyrille? From that archeology seminar sophomore year?"

There's a long silence. And then, "Why are you thinking about him?"

Despite the wariness in her tone, I press forward. "The head of litigation just pulled me into this case against Fordham's ancient art museum. Apparently they have all this stuff that Italy wants back. And I just—we never—" I hesitate, recalibrating. Then I decide to go ahead and come out with it. "Remember how Cyrille's dig was looted?"

"Lena," she says slowly, "the last time we talked about this, it did not end well."

She's right; the last time we talked about Cyrille, it led to the first and only fight of our nearly twenty-year friendship. We got past it, but I'll never forget the betrayal I felt when Lakshmi said to me, eyes pleading in exasperation, *only* you *can get over whatever you think happened.* I didn't talk to her for almost six months after that.

"You're right," I say. "Never mind. I'll see you tomorrow."

When we hang up, I open a new tab in my browser and search for Cyrille DuPuy, which I haven't done in a decade. Nothing comes up except an old academic profile on the Université de Lyon website. Next, I google *archeologia Orbagne.*

My mouth floats open as I click into a press release announcing that the Roman villa I spent a summer excavating—my Orphean summer, as I've come to think of it, because at a certain point I started to get the sense that looking back on that brief period meant relinquishing something important about the life I'd managed to create for myself—has been granted UNESCO world heritage status.

I scan the photos of *La villa del frutteto,* which is now a fully excavated, multibuilding stone compound. There are images of elaborate interior floor mosaics: some are abstract geometric patterns, and then there are figurative ones that illustrate the workings of a farm—an apple orchard, a wine harvest, a field of roses—and finally, the mountains, with their ancient roads snaking up and around them. I breathe in audibly.

After I look at the images, I read the accompanying text. Cyrille's name is nowhere to be found, and the site's discovery is fully attributed to Dr. Pietro Botti. Which probably means what I think it means: Cyrille never came back.

I was once someone who believed that unearthing something from the ground, holding it, turning it over in my hands, would somehow teach me something about my place in the world. Maybe I am still that person. Because in this moment, I want nothing more than to run my hands over the rough surface of this alpine mosaic, to understand in a practical sense how thousands of tesserae came together to form an accurate image of the magical mountains rising around it. Something tells me that if I could do that, I might finally fill in the lacunae of my summer in the Alps. I might even start to understand the person I have since become: a risk-averse, paper-pushing attorney who keeps her office door closed.

Italy wants Fordham to return antiquities that belong to them. But cultural heritage is, in a way, a myth: a story conceived in retrospect to explain what to do with the things we have inherited. After my summer in Orbagne, I came to understand that ancient objects belong only to the past, which will always try to reclaim you. And to fixate on the past, I remind myself, is to sabotage the present.

AT NINE O'CLOCK I GRAB my laptop and make my way to the small conference room next to Emmanuel's office. The *daisy room,* we call it, because of the framed print on the wall adjacent to the floor-length window. Whoever picked out the firm's art back in the nineties, before we moved from Midtown to Hudson Yards, must have been inspired by a hospital waiting room. Or maybe just the culture here. If we had decorative pillows, they would be embroidered with phrases like *Let's take a surgical approach* and *We need to stop the bleeding.*

"Lena," Emmanuel says when I walk in, "this is Dr. Boswell."

I recognize Dr. Boswell immediately, but she looks different here than she did in the context of the kitchen downstairs. More grandmotherly, maybe—I notice now the oversized flower brooch on the lapel of her tweed jacket and the pink tone of her dyed blond hair.

"Caroline," she says, studying my face.

Emmanuel pours Caroline a glass of water from the carafe on the center of the table. After a few minutes of small talk, he opens his folder.

"Let's start from the beginning," he says. "The cup was a donation from a company called—" He looks down at the museum's provenance report. "Creon, one of your vendors. Can you walk us through the accession process?"

"Yeah, so this was part of a group donation," Caroline says with a flippancy that counters her buttoned-up appearance. "From Creon, as you say. They manufacture the glass display cases we use throughout the museum—"

"And to clarify"—Emmanuel interjects—"this was a donation, not an exchange of some sort? Was there a conflict-of-interest clause in your vendor agreement with them?"

Caroline clears her throat. "Most of our vendors make generous annual cash donations," she says. "The president of the company made a gift of art in lieu of a monetary donation. This was a one-off in 2007."

Emmanuel looks up from his papers. His silver eyebrows are knitted together. "Sidebar," he says. "And this is not an accusation. I get that it's standard in your world. But it sounds like pay to play. Obviously this is not a government case, but it's a political one, and it's higher ed. So we need to be careful with the verbiage you use to describe your relationship."

Caroline narrows her eyes and nods. I open my laptop as inconspicuously as I can and google *Creon museum cases.* The website is in English. They have sophisticated branding and high-res photos of artifacts in glass cases on their home page. I navigate to the *About* section. None of the leadership team's bios are accompanied by headshots.

"Let's keep going," Emmanuel continues. "How did Creon's president determine what to give the museum? Were you involved in that decision?"

Caroline breathes in deeply, and I get the feeling she's told this story a hundred times. "Creon holds and displays an important collection of imperial Roman objects," she says. "In their Turin office."

"Wait," I say, glancing up from my laptop. Emmanuel shoots me a look. "I'm sorry to interrupt, but Creon's website has them based in Rome. With offices in Los Angeles and Seoul."

Caroline regards me quizzically. "Their unofficial headquarters are in Turin. And the gallery is open by appointment."

I type *Creon gallery* into my notes document and nod at her. "Got it, okay."

"The gallery is small, and it doubles as a showroom for their products—their display cases. And I knew—I'd always known—that Filippo has a ton of stuff in storage at the office."

At this I straighten up. "Filippo Dalmasso. Creon's president?"

Caroline nods. "We're talking rare sculptures, sarcophagi, papyrus fragments—incredible stuff. Anyway, in 2006, we were on a museum patron trip, this was with Oliver—"

"Oliver?" Emmanuel asks.

"Oliver Clive, Fordham's director of planned giving."

I tilt my head to the side as an image of a solicitous, well-groomed man flashes in my mind's eye. "I know Oliver," I say to Emmanuel, who nods back at me. To Caroline, I clarify, "I've worked with him on a few estates I represent."

She looks surprised. "Really?"

"For the university, not the museum. Fordham alums love giving back to Fordham."

Emmanuel shuffles through his papers. "I don't see him on any of these witness lists."

Caroline shrugs, and Emmanuel nods at me. I type Oliver Clive in the *to-dos* section of my notes.

"So anyway," Caroline says, "one night we're at dinner and Oliver starts telling him about the tax breaks if he donates through the American office. When the works were last appraised, all that, and whether they're promised to any other institutions.

"And then the Greek and Roman galleries reopened at the Met a few months later," Caroline continues after a brief pause. "Filippo came in for the opening. This was when the Rothschilds' collection was getting a ton of press. And that's when he committed to making the donation. I was thrilled, obviously."

"But the donation was anonymous?" Emmanuel asks.

"Correct," Caroline says. "Very common for a gift of that magnitude. They don't want the other museums they work with coming after them with requests."

"Did you have a role in selecting the objects he was donating?" Emmanuel asks again.

Now Caroline leans forward. "Look. I'm a papyrologist by training. I wanted the fragments. The cup, it's special and everything, but we're small. We're not super focused on late Roman stuff. We've got one in-house conservator for the collection, which encompasses the entire ancient world, and she doesn't do glass. I actually had to outsource conservation for a lot of what he donated. Though I will not deny that the cup raised the museum's profile. There are only two complete figurative dichroic glass cups in the world. The other one is in the British Museum."

"Okay, so you outsourced conservation," Emmanuel says. "Who did the cataloguing?"

I raise my eyebrows, impressed with Emmanuel's museum-speak. Caroline hesitates.

"I guess what I'm asking," Emmanuel adds, "is who verified the provenance? Was that you?"

"Provenance is a judgment call," she says. "And this was a group donation. And it was before all the drama of Marianne's indictment. The aftermath of it, I mean."

"Marianne?" I ask.

She pauses. I examine her face. She looks either exasperated or indignant, or both. "Marianne Flynn," she says.

I look over at Emmanuel, who gives me a minute shake of his head.

"The point is," Caroline continues, "it was a different time. It's not like now, when there's a microscope on everything we do."

Emmanuel clears his throat. He's losing his patience, I can tell.

"What you have to understand," Caroline says, "is that most of these so-called 'looted antiquities' are being repatriated on a moral basis." She looks at Emmanuel and me expectantly. "It's good PR."

"And so this document—" Emmanuel holds up a scan of the provenance from the original accession file. "Who composed this document?"

"I did," Caroline says with a trace of resentment. "Based on the information that Filippo provided, which I took at face value. And the collections committee ratified it."

"Who sits on the collections committee?" I ask. Emmanuel shakes his head at me again, this time vigorously. "Sorry," I say. "Not relevant."

"It might be relevant," Emmanuel says. "But let's stay on track."

"Look, there's nothing nefarious going on here," Caroline says. "I'm not an idiot. I've been in the field for decades. I've seen sketchy deals, and trust me, this was not sketchy. There was no reason to think anything from Italy was unearthed after 1939. This cup, for example—it's glass. The condition is too good for it to have been looted. There's a fragment at the Met with the same dichroic properties—go look at that. *That* was probably looted."

Caroline delivers these words with such force that for a second I'm utterly convinced there's no reason for us to be sitting here, questioning her. But then her eyes glaze over, as if she's making a calculation of some sort. "Why?" I hear myself ask.

Caroline and Emmanuel exchange a glance. "What do you mean, why?" she asks.

I close my eyes hard, picturing the dark mountains surrounding Giamma's car on the road from Orbagne to Saint-Marcel. *Italians would never dig holes like that,* his friend said from the back seat when

I asked them about the looting at Cyrille's dig that winter. Even looters in Italy care about the art, was the implication.

When I open my eyes, Caroline is searching my face. I can't tell if she's challenging me or reconsidering me. But I decide to disengage; I don't want to give either one of them a reason to take away my seat at this table. "Forget it."

Emmanuel gives me a quizzical look, then asks Caroline more questions about her current relationship with Filippo Dalmasso, which she tells us is ongoing and good; Creon just provided six new cases for their Etruscan gallery renovation. I stay quiet, silently berating myself. I haven't lost my composure like this in a client-facing meeting since I was an associate.

"Last thing," Emmanuel says. "What have Creon's people said about all this?"

For the first time in our conversation, Caroline deflates slightly. "We haven't been in contact."

She's lying. I feel it in my bones. Caroline was speaking in Italian this morning. She must have been on the phone with Filippo Dalmasso.

"So your relationship is 'ongoing and good,' but you haven't discussed the charges?" Emmanuel presses.

"I'm not sure he knows about them at all," she says. "Though every time Italy makes one of these requests it seems to end up in the press over there. But I have not brought it up, no."

Emmanuel watches Caroline for a long moment, then puts his pen down. "All right. Let's leave it there."

On our way out of the conference room, Caroline hesitates, then reaches into her bag and pulls out a postcard. "The cup will be on view for the next few weeks for an exhibition—" She pauses, registering Emmanuel's alarmed expression. "I know, I know," she says. "But the show has been in the works for years, long before any of this. *The Many Faces of Aphrodite.* There's a VIP opening tonight, just for our top-tier patrons. You're welcome to stop by."

"I'll be there," I blurt, as Emmanuel simultaneously says with feigned regret, "I wish we could make it."

Caroline looks amused and takes her leave. I walk Emmanuel back to his office.

"Were you just trying to be respectful of my time, or do you not want me to go to the opening?" I ask.

"Go if you want to. But bill the hours and take notes. She's slippery. I can't put my finger on it, but something feels off about the sequence of events. We should talk to this Oliver guy. And maybe the conservator she mentioned. Can't make it up, huh?"

Now would be the moment to tell Emmanuel about the phone call I overheard this morning, but I decide not to. It's as if I want to preserve the curiosity I'm feeling in this moment, to keep it for myself. "Do you think Filippo Dalmasso knows it was looted?" I ask.

Emmanuel shrugs. "I don't see what changes if he does."

When he closes the door to his office, I stand there in the hallway, examining the Cupid and Psyche cup on Caroline's postcard, trying to call up as many details as I can about the myth, which I knew well at one point in my life. Venus sending Cupid to mess with the mortal princess Psyche, whose beauty rivaled hers; Cupid falling in love with her instead; Psyche disobeying when he told her never to look at him, holding up a torch to his beautiful sleeping face in the middle of the night after she realized she was pregnant. Psyche atoning for this betrayal and then marrying Cupid in an apotheosis blessed by the gods, just in time to give birth to their daughter.

Mainly I recall the solitude of navigating noun declensions, conjugating verbs, grasping for English equivalents to the Latin. Words can only take you so far, I remember thinking. Maybe they can get you out of your own head, but they can't bring you into the past. Not like artifacts can.

II.

JANUARY 9, 2004

NEW YORK CITY

The Romans wanted Aosta for its roads—the roads the Gauls were blocking. That was one of the big things I took away from my initial encounter with Cyrille, perhaps because I myself felt stuck at an impasse of sorts.

I was hanging around the Classics Department on a bleak day toward the end of winter break, perched on the chintz arm of a sagging couch, waiting for the professor who had been supervising my independent study on spoken Latin, when Cyrille wandered into the department looking like a lost mountain climber: rosy cheeks, Fair Isle wool sweater, earmuffs holding back shoulder-length hair.

He introduced himself and showed me a printed email. I led him to his office, a windowless hole occupied only by an enormous high-resolution scanner—the height of early aughts technology and the pride of our department administrator. Cyrille was gracious about it, but I would have been disappointed. All the way from Lyon to New York City for a fluorescent-lit closet?

"So, Lena," he said, getting the pronunciation of my name right when I told him it was short for Maddalena. "What do you study?"

He was examining my face in a way that made me think he cared about my answer. "Ancient civilizations," I said, not mentioning that I was a sophomore transfer student, an undergrad.

He dropped his backpack on the floor. "You will participate in my seminar, I think?" He cocked his head and smiled, still wearing those earmuffs. I smiled back; I couldn't help it.

"What's it on?" I asked.

That first conversation would have been much easier if I had known then that he spoke Italian in addition to French. "My dig," he said, "is in the mountains. Near the Petit-Saint-Bernard Pass—that is, where Hannibal made his crossing with the Carthaginians. We will discuss the archeology of this region starting from the age of Augustus."

I knew about the Punic Wars, about Hannibal charging over the Alps with his elephants—but I knew nothing about ancient life in those mountains: the stone monuments that the Romans went on to destroy and replace with their amphitheater, villas, and temple to Jupiter.

"Several objects from our last dig season will soon be on view at the regional museum in Aosta," he said, his gray-brown eyes shining.

"Wow," I managed. It did sound thrilling, pulling ancient objects out of the ground. But something about Cyrille and his dig eluded me. I didn't know anything about archeology, not really. Whatever combination of nature and nurture I possessed drove me to seek out facts, the certainty of authority, names and dates. I knew what other people had written in history books. I didn't know that history was subjective, biased—in the eye of the beholder, so to speak. I didn't know then what I would come to understand, that archeologists are the beholders.

I liked who I seemed to be in Cyrille's eyes: a worthy vessel into which information could be poured. He was doing most of the talking, but I felt unearthed, held, sensing his voice as a vibration rather than hearing it—understanding, maybe for the first time, that human existence was more than a linear march toward some arbitrary goal, that time could be bent, that the past could be readily accessed and recast.

This line from Erasmus, recently translated for my independent study, came into my mind: "It is the main and essential part of happiness to desire to be no other than what we already are." Meeting Cyrille, seeing myself reflected in his eyes—it was the first time I ever wanted to be who I was.

ON A COLD WEDNESDAY IN January with the sun low in the sky, I walked up Broadway and across Columbia's quad to the brick building that housed the Classics Department for Cyrille's first seminar.

I was wearing the new red parka my father had sent me for Christmas, a curious choice for someone who lived in San Diego and hadn't spent a holiday with his daughters in over a decade. I hadn't called him on Christmas Eve, and I hadn't called my mother, who was presumably home alone in Wilmette. I was alone too. Other than a handful of international students, the dorms were deserted over the break, and I'd used the phone in the lounge to call Jinny, who was in California working on her doctorate in German Studies.

Now I walked through the stale hot air of the foyer and up the stairs, pausing to dislodge the snow-caked fray of my jeans from my boots. On the second floor, a few faceless graduate students were sitting on worn sofas in the department lounge, balancing books on their laps.

Cyrille was in the lounge's adjacent copy room humming with his back toward the door, and he didn't hear my footsteps over the roar of the machine. I fished out a Werther's from the candy bowl on the coffee table and glanced at the clock above the department administrator's door. It was 4:13—I had seventeen minutes until class started.

In the empty classroom, I unzipped my parka and took a seat in the back. The smell of chalk prompted me to look up at the board, which contained a diagram of the players in *Antigone* left over from a prior class. Everyone thought Antigone's misstep was speaking truth to power, but that wasn't the problem. Her mistake was being loyal to people who couldn't protect her, while openly disagreeing with those who could.

Cyrille finally appeared in the doorway and smiled at me, then looked around the room. He was wearing a cable-knit sweater and pleated pants. He'd cut his hair and grown a beard, which drew attention to his upturned eyes. "This won't do," he said, dragging a desk toward the middle of the room.

I rose to help him configure nine desks into a circle. I couldn't think of anything to say and was relieved when he volunteered that in the two weeks since his arrival in New York, he'd been up to the Cloisters three times.

"Lena," he said with a focused intensity, like he was about to ask some high-stakes question. I braced myself. "What is your interpretation of the tapestries?"

I knew he was referring to the ones with the unicorns. I'd seen them during my transfer student orientation the previous August and had barely paused, walking quickly through the dark gallery with its floating dust particles and rosiny smell. I thought about the one panel I could recall, a despairing fenced-in unicorn surrounded by a field of wildflowers.

I'd been eager not to repeat an embarrassing incident from earlier that week with the same group when, standing in front of Sargent's *Madame X* at the Met, I'd felt what Madame X, whoever she was, felt—a longing, an emptiness, a sense of power being relinquished—and I'd head-to-floor fainted.

The painting had called to mind a photo I had of my mother from when she still brushed her hair and put on real clothes. My father had taken it on the Chicago premiere night of the one film he ever managed to make; I was four, Jinny eight. I can still see her now—

the long black dress, luminous skin, swept-up hair—descending the carpeted stairs of my childhood home, resigned sadness spreading over her face.

My father was there next to me at the bottom of the stairs with the pocket Canon he was so proud of—I'll never forget the sound the zoom made when it emerged like a telescope, those little zipping warbles. He snapped a few photos, then consulted with the babysitter. When I looked at Jinny as they walked out the front door, she was holding back tears too. We always felt uneasy when we were away from our mother. A therapist we saw in the aftermath of my parents' separation asked if we—Jinny and me—felt responsible for her. I didn't know how to answer that, which was okay, because Jinny always spoke on my behalf.

"They're medieval, right?" I finally managed.

Cyrille launched into a theory about what the unicorn symbolized—it was either Christ or someone's lover—and I was relieved when students began to trickle in. He greeted them warmly, then left to retrieve his photocopies.

A girl with glowing skin and an optic-white ski jacket—Lakshmi—sat down next to me. "I've seen you before," she said in a soft British accent, putting her bag down next to mine.

I attempted a smile. I didn't recognize her, but I didn't want her to think I didn't want to know her. "Probably," I said.

"Is this your first seminar?"

Her tone was kind, but I felt self-conscious. The class was supposed to be for French-speaking graduate students, but between my Latin and Italian I'd managed to pass the prerequisite language proficiency exam. The truth was that I wouldn't have understood most of what we were learning in English either. There were a lot of technical terms—*flange, stratigraphy, tumulus.*

I admitted that yes, it was my first seminar. She made an impressed face and told me that we were the only undergrads in the class, then offered up small talk about the weather. She was from Bangalore but had gone to high school in Switzerland, so she was used to the snow. "The dorm!" she interrupted herself to exclaim. "That's how I know you."

I had a single in an all-girls dorm and didn't know the names of the young women whose rooms abutted mine. They gave off an axe-grinding energy, like they'd been left out or bullied in high school and were now seeking a role reversal of some sort, maybe even revenge. In my class of a thousand at New Trier, I hadn't been homecoming queen—but I'd had friends, I'd had boyfriends. Now I went in and out of my room with my eyes on the floor.

I started digging in my backpack on the floor between my legs, trying to look busy, desperate for Cyrille to reenter the room and get started. I pressed a button on the side of my Nokia for the time: 4:31 p.m. "Do you guys know Lena?" Lakshmi said.

I popped my head up and met a trio of second-year PhD students from Lakshmi's Aeschylus class. "We're Greek," one of them said. "Well, Magna Graecia. We're here so we can spend summers digging in Selinunte."

I'd seen photos from this university-run dig in Sicily on the bulletin board in the department hallway; I knew it was one of the reasons the PhD program was renowned. But I was more interested in the Romans than the Greeks.

"This guy," the grad student continued, lowering her voice. "He wants us to call him by his first name, right? Cyrille—his thing is the Salassi. They're a footnote. You can barely even classify them as Gauls. I mean, let's be honest, they were alpine Celts." She glanced behind her at the door. "This seminar is so random. It's like, not a single person that finished last year got a placement and *this* random guy gets a visiting professorship?"

Cyrille finally came in—danced in—because that's how he was at first, always with some happy song in his head. But there was something false about the lightness he seemed to be making a big effort to convey. It was an act, I suspected.

"Take one and pass," he said, dropping a stack of packets onto my desk, each of them two fingers thick and composed of disparate pages from various books in French and Latin. He'd apparently made good use of the scanner in his office.

He took a seat at the empty desk to my left, greeted us, and asked us to turn to page three in the packet, which showed a map of the Roman Empire as Caesar Augustus came to power. He lapsed into French and I made out what I could, the map speaking for itself, as it were, with respect to the strategic location of Aosta—its enclosure within the Alps and above the Apennines. The streams that fortified the city and connected it to the gold mines in what was now Ivrea, and to the Po River, which provided access to the whole ancient world through the Adriatic Sea.

I glanced out the paned classroom windows at the purple and orange sunset over Amsterdam Avenue. "Why did Augustus need *this* particular territory?" Cyrille asked in English. "Lena?"

I felt my ears get hot. "Uh . . ." I started, scanning my packet for an answer. Suddenly, our first encounter from a few weeks prior came into my mind. "Oh—the roads?"

"*Exactement.*" He nodded energetically and added, "The region offered many opportunities for Roman traders and investors."

Lakshmi elbowed me, and I met her eyes briefly before turning back to my packet, to the map of Roman territories under Augustus at the end of the first century BCE, which included large swaths of North Africa, much of what is now Greece, Turkey, Armenia, and Syria, and almost all of modern-day Spain and France.

"*Tournons la page,*" Cyrille said, and papers swished. "*Et voilà,*" he added in reference to a hand-drawn map of Augustan-era Aosta and its surroundings. "*Vallée d'Aoste.*" There was a star next to a town on the left side of the map called Orbagne. "Who has read *Les Metamorphoses de Apuleius*?"

Eight arms floated into the air. I knew the novel by its alternate title, *The Golden Ass.* It was in fact fresh in my mind, having just translated it for my fall Latin class.

He smiled. "*Alors.* You will recall the wholesalers who are traveling through the countryside, reselling cheese they have purchased from farms to the inns. Try to imagine something similar in the Alps, and deeper integration with the Roman economy after the founding of Aosta."

The Golden Ass was the only complete Latin language novel to have survived antiquity, which was why it was important to read despite having been written not as high literature, but for the entertainment of the masses. In class I'd rolled my eyes as the boys kept tricking our professor into analyzing the part when Lucius, transformed into a donkey, agrees to sleep with a kinky rich lady. I never would have thought there were clues about the Roman economy to be gleaned from the book. The only section I'd taken seriously was the imbedded myth of Cupid and Psyche, which Lucius hears from an old woman in league with the bandits who have kidnapped him.

But I understood the point Cyrille was making, even though I'd been convinced of an opposing view by the philologist who taught my freshman year ancient civ survey. He believed that the markets of the Roman Empire were not centrally integrated but fractured—and that the main reason Rome ultimately fell wasn't because of the Goths' invasion in 476, but because as their coercive capacities weakened over time, the Romans had become vulnerable to inconvenient costs, like transporting supplies to distant military outposts. I'd been fascinated by the idea that something as banal as the cost of transport could influence a historical outcome of that magnitude.

Now Cyrille launched into a long speech in French. Over and over, I heard him say "*Col du Petit-Saint-Bernard*" and "*Col du Grand Saint-Bernard*," which corresponded to two labeled routes on the map.

From what I could piece together, the Salassi had controlled the two most efficient modes of transit over the Alps: the Great St. Bernard Pass and the Little St. Bernard Pass. Their small population was thus able to block the flow of trade from Rome itself to France, Spain, and by extension the whole western side of the empire in both directions. For centuries—*siècles*—they had undergone periods of truce and war with the Romans.

Cyrille switched back to English. "When Augustus eventually overtook the Salassi, the forty thousand who were not killed were sold into slavery."

I narrowed my eyes, letting this sink in. My understanding of slavery in ancient Rome was that it was a social class one was born into. I'd been taught that conquered peoples were eligible for Roman citizenship; thus, there were Romans representing every nationality in the Mediterranean, all the way to Asia minor.

"The Romans succeeded," he continued, "because they were highly organized—" He searched for the right word. "—administrators."

I knew the Romans weren't exactly peace-seeking, but Cyrille was the first Romanist I'd met who didn't glorify them. I looked around the room. The grad students exchanged glances, but Lakshmi kept her eyes on Cyrille and raised her hand. "Wasn't it inevitable? The demise of the Salassi? I mean, I'm looking at this map—they were surrounded on all sides."

"Ah-ha," he said, nodding. "A very good point. What do others think?"

Cyrille always seemed to be trying to admit that we knew better than him. I guess that made him a good teacher in my mind—he never acted like he was above us. And I appreciated that he didn't try to pass off archeology as reverse divination, the way my Latin professors made it seem like language was the only way into antiquity. In Cyrille's seminar, the historical record was open to interpretation—it was as if the way we perceived an event or an object was just as valid as what Strabo had written in his *Geographica.*

For weeks I would find myself returning to Lakshmi's question about the inevitable demise of the Salassi. The idea of fate had always terrified me—what was coming for *me,* when? It felt innate, this sense of dread I'd always known. But sitting there that night between Cyrille and Lakshmi, instead of an unfurling of possible threatening scenarios, what I registered was an unfamiliar sense of safety. I knew well enough not to trust such a feeling, but I tried, just for the moment, to relax into it.

AFTER CLASS, LAKSHMI INVITED ME to dinner. I usually used my points to get takeout and snacks from the on-campus convenience store, which I ate in my dorm room alone, but I agreed, somewhat reluctantly, to join her in the dining hall.

In the four months since I'd been at Columbia, the extent of my social life had been a handful of fall frat parties. On these occasions, I'd stood at the periphery of dark rooms, waiting for a girl from my transfer student orientation group to come back from wherever she'd gone—to the keg, to the bathroom—thinking about how all of these people were being gaslit by an imitation of Big Ten culture in New York City. Back at University of Chicago—where I'd spent my freshman year, and where social isolation was the norm—when I'd thought about what college would be like in New York, I'd imagined that my classmates would be sneaking into clubs with fake IDs and dating much older men. I never predicted that hundreds of high school valedictorians would be clamoring for the approval of recruited athletes.

"What'd you think?" Lakshmi asked as we made our way across the quad.

"Of the seminar?"

She turned to me and smiled genuinely, and a node inside my chest I hadn't been aware of loosened and dissolved. "I was worried about the French, but I don't think I missed too much," I said.

"Anyone who knows Latin can figure out French," she said, breathing out steam. At her boarding school in the Italian part of Switzerland, she'd studied Latin, Greek, and French. She'd picked up Italian from the locals. And with her parents she spoke Kannada and Hindi.

I was impressed, and slightly threatened. I only had three languages. The German my mother had taught Jinny and me as kids had made high school Latin seem easy, and when Magister Rizzi, my high school Latin teacher, noticed my interest in Italy, he'd offered to teach me Italian. He was from Verona. Privately, I thought of him as a descendant of Romeo Montague; I loved his low, gentle voice, and the way he would nod patiently as I tried to express myself in a language I came to love mostly because my mother and Jinny had no interest in it.

At the dining hall, Lakshmi and I handed our IDs to the attendants, then picked up trays and split up. I'd grown up with microwave dinners and fast food and cereal with skim milk, and I was so overwhelmed by the choices at the hot food stations in the dining halls that I always stuck to the salad bar. I got a cup of chicken noodle soup and spooned cottage cheese into a separate bowl. Then I found Lakshmi at the stir-fry line and waited with her until it was her turn to order.

We found two seats on the other side of a round table where a girl and boy were gazing into each other's eyes, deep in conversation. Lakshmi shot me a look, and I smirked.

"I'm happy for them," I whispered. But mostly I was happy for me, because I was pretty sure that Lakshmi wanted to be my friend.

"Same," she said sarcastically, then: "What are you doing for the summer?"

I knew I should be applying to internships and jobs, but I had no idea where to start. My parents weren't paying my tuition; it was only thanks to financial aid and the help I got from my grandparents that I would graduate without crippling debt. But I needed to figure something out, because there was no way I was spending a summer riding out the ups and downs of my mother's moods.

"I'm applying to the Sicily dig," she said, taking a sip of Sprite. "They sometimes take undergrads."

Lakshmi was—is—as her name would imply, very beautiful. She never wore a stitch of makeup back then. She sometimes does now, but she doesn't need to. And yet I couldn't imagine her wielding a pickax in a trench on a dusty dig.

"Because I definitely can't go home," she added. And she gave me the outline of her parents' impending divorce, which had seemingly been catalyzed by her return to New York the previous fall. Her mother was making plans to move out while Lakshmi's father was away on business.

I appreciated that Lakshmi was being open about what she was going through; it endeared her to me, and I tried to convey empathy with my eyes. But I couldn't find it in me to reciprocate. I guess what Lakshmi was describing, difficult as it may have been, seemed completely in the realm of normal.

I told her my parents had separated when I was five and Jinny was nine—that they lived as if they were divorced—but I didn't say why it was so hard to go home. I don't think my body would have given voice to the actual words. At that point in my life, I'd never said anything about my mother's increasingly frequent breaks with reality to anyone except for Jinny. I guess I was ashamed of what whatever was wrong with her implied about me.

* * *

TIME SEEMED TO SPEED UP as the semester progressed. I struggled through Cyrille's packet, I completed my other schoolwork. I did my work-study shifts at the library. I ate my meals with Lakshmi and called Jinny in California on the weekends and was amazed to eventually realize that I almost never felt alone anymore.

"I heard Cyrille's dig is looking for American participants," Lakshmi said before class one night in March. We'd walked over together from our dorm and had arrived early enough to get the seats closest to the windows. She gave me a look that implied I should consider this for myself.

"Oh yeah?" I replied, keeping my tone as neutral as possible. I felt immediately suspicious, because I connected her statement to a confusing interaction I'd had with Cyrille at his office hours earlier that week.

We'd been reviewing my midterm paper on the various ways the Duria River had been used by the Romans in the wake of their victory over the Salassi. But he poked holes in every point I made, especially my argument that the struggle against distance was enemy number one of civilization. At first I wasn't insulted, because there was something playful in his tone, and I could feel my ears reddening as it occurred to me in his cramped office that he was treating me more like a friend than a student. At a certain point I got flustered and asked him flat out what my paper was missing. In response he motioned for me to pull my chair close to his. He'd been waiting for me to ask, I realized. He'd been waiting to show me.

I looked over his shoulder as he turned to his desktop monitor and double-clicked on an application called ArcView. "This is Ostia Antica," he said as a black-and-white map loaded onto the screen. "Augustan Rome's biggest port, yes?"

I'd heard of Ostia—I knew it was where the Tiber met the Mediterranean—but I hadn't studied it in depth. I nodded, archiving this new fact, that it was Rome's biggest port.

"I worked here for four seasons during my doctorate. We developed a digital model of the terrain from the port all the way to here"—he indicated an area north of the city, outside the walls—"where many Roman senators owned estates. In this way we discovered evidence of a river basin, which was unknown to archeologists despite hundreds of years of excavations. It was dried up, buried under significant sediment cover. With the discovery of the river basin, we were able to understand more about ancient trade as it related to the area's immediate surroundings, which gives us clues about the rest of the empire. This same framework can be used to analyze strategic rivers in the Alps."

"How did you do that?" I asked. "Identify the river basin, I mean."

He shifted his weight forward. "For this work we used a cesium magnetometer. It is a new technology."

The term *cesium magnetometer* was completely foreign to me; it sounded like something out of a Roald Dahl novel. "How—"

"It's a form of survey work. You attach a sensor to a cart, which sends data back to a base station magnetometer that corrects for global-scale magnetic fluctuations. With the cart, you walk the site. And with the data, you create a map a like this." He pointed to his screen.

I nodded, afraid he would get even more scientific if I asked for further clarification. But as I gazed at the black-and-white map on his screen, I thought of my ancient civ professor, who was building a visual model of Roman trade with the computer science department. *Geospatial modeling will transform the way we think about the ancient world,* he'd said.

"The main requirement for any strategic outpost was access to a reliable water source," Cyrille continued, "like the Duria in the Aosta Valley. Which could be used for transport, irrigation, even for mining. As you point out in your paper. But we know this region had big estates, not all of them accessible by the river in its current form. Similar to what we see in the area immediately south of Ostia Antica." He paused, maybe expecting these words to trigger a realization on my part. I racked my brain.

"What about tributaries?" I offered, thinking about the spindly offshoots of the rivers on the maps in our packet.

He kept going. "*Oui, mais* tributaries can dry up over time. What did Pliny say, do you recall? In Book Eighteen of *Natural History*?"

I knew who Pliny was, but I'd never read more than a few passages from *Natural History*. Cyrille hadn't assigned it to us; why did he expect me to know? I shook my head.

"*A country house ought not to be located near a marsh or facing a river.* So we can conclude—" He pointed his index finger at me and wiggled it around.

I shrugged, annoyed at him for putting me on the spot, and for assuming a level of knowledge I didn't have. I was his student; he was my teacher. I was there to learn what I didn't know—from *him.*

"Aqueducts."

I sighed. I should have been able to get that one. But now I felt defensive. "Didn't you say specifically there were no notable aqueducts in this region?"

"I said there is nothing like what we see elsewhere in Gaul. Nothing like the Pont du Gard, for example."

I let this sink in. It was a matter of semantics, I concluded.

"Most aqueducts were underground," he added. "The Romans came up with ingenious ways to get water where they needed it to go. Claudius drained the Fucine Lake by enlisting an army of laborers to spend eleven years digging a hole through a mountain in total darkness."

"So did the Romans do something like that with the Duria?"

He shrugged. "*Aucune idée.* It's interesting to think about."

When I stood to go, exasperated and weirdly drained, he asked if I had ever considered pursuing archeology in practice rather than in theory. I took the question as a condescension—it was now painfully obvious to both of us that I knew nothing technical or practical about archeology—and pretended not to understand him.

"You can definitely get credit for it," Lakshmi said now, bringing me back to the current moment. "Plus, they have a grant from the Italian government that gives free room and board to students. And then we'd both be in Italy!"

Lakshmi had been accepted to the Selinunte dig; I'd been rejected from three stipended museum internships—I could only swing an internship if it was paid.

"Interesting," I hedged, tuning in to a conversation between two grad students who'd just entered the classroom.

"And you know they're just taking things from museums now too," one of them said, a twentysomething with a receding blond hairline and wayfarer glasses. "While the Americans watch. This fucking administration."

Lakshmi told me after class they were referring to the looting of the Baghdad Museum, but I'd never heard about it. I knew about the Iraq War—I wasn't living under a rock—but no one in my family ever talked about politics. My mother was the daughter of Mennonite pacifists, and my father's parents were homesteading artists before they died. Growing up, my mother had subscribed to academic journals, my father had watched obscure independent films, and Jinny and I had watched MTV whenever the cable bill was paid. None of us consumed the news.

"Hey James," Lakshmi called, interrupting them. "What's it like on a dig?"

James still seemed pretty worked up about the war, but he smirked, breathing heavily in and out of his nose. "It's freedom—freedom mixed with authority. It's the antithesis of being in a classroom learning about archeology. Which is a joke. Learning about archeology might as well be . . . history." He erupted into high-pitched laughter. Lakshmi shot me a look.

"You can't *really* learn anything about archeology outside of an actual trench," he added when he caught his breath.

I felt I understood what he meant. When I went to museums, I always had the sense that the antiquities were out of place—estranged, even. They were vulnerable, the way they were forced to bare themselves unnaturally in sterile glass cases, completely removed from their intended origins and uses.

Cyrille entered the room then. He was quiet, and his shoulders were hunched. An uneasy feeling came over me.

He sighed and took a seat. "I'm sorry," he said in English, covering his face with his hands.

"What is it?" I blurted. I could feel Lakshmi's eyes on me. But I was too distracted by the cloud of nausea spreading in my stomach to care.

"It's late in Orbagne." He looked up at the ceiling. "I learned just now on the phone that my site has been . . ." He trailed off, searching for the word he wanted. "Vandalized."

Someone, or a group of people, he explained, had burrowed into the snow at the winterized site, removed the tarps, and gouged violent little holes in the meticulously back-filled trenches. "We'll never know what they took," Cyrille said, rubbing his hands on his corduroys.

I looked around the classroom. Lakshmi's brow was furrowed. The grad students were shaking their heads. But no one said anything.

I opened my mouth in outrage but managed to stop short of asking questions Cyrille wouldn't be able to answer, starting with: Who were these people, these thieves? What did they think they were doing, violating an important archeological site?

"What did the police say?" was what I eventually came out with.

He smiled weakly. "I should not say more. But thank you for your concern."

At this I felt the warmth returning to my face, and I pressed the backs of my hands against my cheeks. I was relieved. I understood now that this intense, distraught man was who Cyrille really was. I'd been right—his levity was a cover. And now that I recognized him, I felt an urgent calling to help him.

The next morning at work, I launched Internet Explorer and asked Jeeves about the looting of the Baghdad Museum. Fifteen thousand ancient objects had been taken within thirty-six hours a year prior, in April of 2003. "Stuff happens, and it's untidy, and freedom's untidy, and free people are free to make mistakes, and commit crimes, and do bad things," Donald Rumsfeld had said in response to the incident.

I looked away from the computer screen, trying to make sense of what I was reading. Those ancient objects were worth something; wasn't that why they'd been stolen? But some things were right, and some things were wrong. This—stealing the remains of ancient Babylon, stealing ancient objects in general—was wrong.

Then there was an article about a book published ten years ago, *Art Crime* by John Conklin, which stated that art theft was the third-largest area of international crime, after drug smuggling and arms trading. I found the book at the end of my shift and read the introduction. "Yet the plundering of ancient sites for artifacts comprises nearly 90 percent of all art theft transpiring in the world today," it said. *Ninety percent.* My breath caught in my throat.

That night at dinner, I showed Lakshmi the book. "Who would buy something *stolen*?"

She seemed unfazed as she picked at a grilled cheese sandwich. "You should see the people I went to high school with. Lots of people who want beautiful things don't care how they get them."

I thought about a high school acquaintance of mine who'd been caught shoplifting at an Abercrombie & Fitch. "You mean—"

"I actually feel sorry for the looters," Lakshmi mused. "Think about it. Most of these sites are in postcolonial countries." She paused for a beat, her eyes brightening. I loved Lakshmi's theories about the way the world worked, especially when I got to watch her invent them in real time. "The looters are basically victims of colonialism. They have their power taken from them, so they lose their connection to their own cultural heritage." She paused for dramatic effect. "You could even take it a step further. You could argue that the West set this whole dynamic up, and now they're trying to 'protect' the culture they ruined. It's pretty hypocritical when you think about it like that."

It was hard for me to fully grasp what she was saying, which didn't stop me from attempting to refute her. "I don't know if that applies to Italy."

Lakshmi raised her eyebrows at me. "Really, Lena?"

"Italy wasn't colonized."

"What were the Romans doing?"

"Oh," I said, mulling this over. I didn't want to disagree with her—I also wouldn't have even known how to—but I felt defensive, because she wasn't getting my point. "I'm talking about now. Why are people taking things now? And who does ancient culture belong to?"

"You know what I think?" she asked. When I looked up at her, she grinned. "I think you're an archeologist."

THE NEXT WEEK, when Cyrille explicitly advertised an opening on his dig, Lakshmi elbowed me and mouthed a reminder about the free room and board.

I was surprised to feel my heart pounding in my ears as I looked at the raised veins in my right hand. But I didn't hesitate—I flung it into the air. I wanted to know what they knew, the archeologists. I wanted to see history for myself.

III.

MARCH 7, 2022

NEW YORK CITY

By the time I get to Fordham's campus in the Bronx, I'm so curious about the Cupid and Psyche cup that I'm undeterred by how frustrating it is to locate the museum, housed on the fifth floor of an imposing academic building.

When I finally find it, the first thing that occurs to me as I take in my surroundings—a series of conjoined galleries lined with cases, yellowing wood floors, and overhead track lights on full blast—is that I am underdressed, even taking into account the navy blazer under my damp parka, and the youngest by at least two decades. A woman in a floor-length gown leans one elbow on a high-top table, champagne flute in hand, and nods at a man in a bow tie.

I spot the Cupid and Psyche cup in its own freestanding case on the other side of the room. It's smaller than I imagined, the size of two fists stacked on top of each other, but it's impossible to miss its vivid green glow.

As I make my way over to get a better look, a cater waiter approaches me with a tray of bacon-wrapped dates drizzled with some kind of syrup. "Is this honey?" I ask as I attempt to pluck one off the tray.

He offers me a cocktail napkin. "Balsamic glaze."

I pull harder, but the date doesn't give. The waiter stares down at the tray, and I can feel his rising discomfort as other attendees start to gather around, waiting for their turn. But I can't abandon ship now; too many people are watching. I give it a final, firm tug, which sends the entire tray flying. There is a collective gasp as it crashes to the floor.

"I'm so sorry," I say to the silent, blinking faces around me. And then, nodding at the Cupid and Psyche cup, "Good thing it's in a case, right?"

"Step away," the waiter says to the crowd, extending his arms like a referee. I shove the date in my mouth and drop to the floor to help him clean up the mess.

A few minutes later, in line at the coat check, my cheeks are still burning when some instinct—a feeling in my body, an abstract sense of recognition—compels me to turn around and identify the source of a male voice.

He's tall, the man whose voice caught my attention. At least six foot three. His eyes are semi-concealed by the gray of his photochromic glasses, apparently activated by the gallery lights.

"I—um," I stammer when he clears his throat, my gaze resting on the marble baseboards of the foyer-like room we're in, overcome by a sense of déjà vu. But I've never been to this museum before; I'm certain of it. I didn't even know it existed until this morning.

He raises his eyebrows. "Can I help you?"

The voice—I know it, but I can't place it. "Sorry. You look like someone."

He watches me for a long moment, which gives me time to register that he didn't pronounce the *h* in *help*. And when he opens his mouth to respond, I catch a glimpse of his crowded bottom teeth, and now my eyes are widening in perplexed fascination, because I understand suddenly that I am not having déjà vu. I do know this man. This is Giamma.

"Lena?" he asks, squinting incredulously as he removes his glasses. Now I can see his eyes, which are reddish brown, same as his hair.

My jaw tightens. It's not the fact of running into Giamma at an ancient art museum—it's the timing. It's running into him the same day that I was assigned to an Italian restitution case.

He shakes his head and breaks into a smile. "I almost didn't recognize you."

I laugh awkwardly, my hand springing up to the deepening lines in my forehead, partially concealed by my bangs. I didn't have the bangs back then, or the dense blond highlights I've been getting since I started going gray a few years ago.

A young woman in a fitted black dress appears at his side. When she smiles at me, I'm taken aback to recognize myself in her approval-seeking, heart-shaped face.

"This is my wife, Eva," Giamma says. "Eva, this is—"

"Lena Connolly," I say, suppressing the urge to recoil. "Caroline Boswell invited me."

Giamma's eyes narrow slightly. "How do you know Caroline?"

"I'm one of her lawyers."

Eva pulls her glossy dark hair to the side of her neck. "Why does Caroline have lawyers?"

I decide to tell them the truth, unprofessional as it may be—I want to see Giamma's reaction. "There's an investigation into this collection."

Giamma nods neutrally, but he's smoothing his eyebrows, a nervous tick I remember from the summer we were together.

"Rome is prosecuting," I add in an attempt to further provoke him.

He crosses his arms over his chest. "Prosecuting—Fordham?"

I shrug. "Caroline can probably share more with you than I can."

After a long silence, Eva clears her throat. "Remarks are starting soon," she says to Giamma. "I came to get you."

I follow them out into the main gallery, where a mahogany podium emblazoned with Fordham's red crest has been set up next to the Cupid and Psyche cup. Caroline stands at the microphone, surveying the crowd, eyes equally bright as they were this morning, seemingly unfazed by the restitution case.

"Thank you all for being here on this drizzly, and frankly depressing—" She pauses for effect, and a few of the patrons chuckle in response. "—March evening." She takes in a breath, then resumes. "It goes without saying that this rather encyclopedic exhibition, almost a decade in the making, would never have come to fruition without your support. As you know, we are the little engine that could, and we've been able to do so much incredible work with this small but mighty collection—in large part because of you. So *thank you*, truly, for helping to sustain us, and for enabling us to make this show a reality."

The room erupts in applause.

"I also want to extend a very special thanks to Eva Reilly, who was my curatorial fellow in the early days of planning the exhibition."

I look over at Giamma as the audience claps for Eva. He seems genuinely proud of her. He never responded to the emails I sent in the years that followed my summer in Orbagne, and this is why: he met and fell in love with another smarter, more accomplished American girl.

"Turning now to the woman of the hour," Caroline continues. "Most people know Aphrodite—Venus, to the Romans—as the goddess of beauty and love. But she is much more complex, much more *contradictory* than that. She was the goddess of political harmony, agricultural fertility, seafaring, and military victory. To the Julio-Claudians, she was the source of all life: Venus Genetrix, the mother goddess. To that end, she shares much in common with her further afield counterparts, which is strikingly apparent in the group in this case"—she motions behind her—"where we've lined up a series of Aphrodites, along with examples of her Mesopotamian counterpart Ishtar, and her Egyptian counterpart Isis."

She gestures toward the case from behind the podium. "We're very lucky to have in our collection this fascinating example of Isis nursing Horus, which is shown next to a similar sculpture of Aphrodite and her son Eros. You might notice a similarity to another famous pair from Christian iconography: Mary and the infant Jesus. In many ways, these were the original *maestas.*"

The audience murmurs and nods. Caroline smiles back at them in self-satisfaction. "As Claude Lévi-Strauss, may he rest in peace, once said: 'Imported ideas take root only if the importing culture needs them.' No matter what you believe in, every culture needs a divine mother, am I right?"

The audience laughs, right on cue.

She turns her attention to the Cupid and Psyche cup next to her and continues: "Out of all of Aphrodite's children, it is Eros who most captivated Greek and Roman artists. And it is Eros—or Cupid, I should say—who we see depicted on this incredible late Roman dichroic cup, one of only two complete figurative examples in the world. What you're seeing here is a visual translation of the myth of Cupid and Psyche, amplified in the second century—though we know this myth dates to at least the fifth century BCE, possibly earlier—by the only complete Latin novel to have survived antiquity, *The Golden Ass,* by Apuleius."

She gestures to the scanned lines of Greek that have been enlarged and printed on the wall behind her.

"I hope you'll take the time to look at some of the additional primary texts we have juxtaposed with this cup, which was not known to have been made of glass until the second half of the twentieth century, and almost certainly served as a vessel for wine in a religious context, either for ritual feasting, or general ceremony—"

Caroline is looking right at me when she says this. Why? What is she trying to convey? Then I realize that she's not looking at me so much as she's looking through me. I glance around and notice a woman a few feet behind me in a tailored suit, hands in her pockets. She must feel herself being watched, because she looks over at me, and when I absorb the recognition on her own face, I place her immediately. Simone.

Neither of us acknowledges what we've both clearly just realized, and Simone turns her attention back to Caroline. I cross my arms in an effort to contain myself, but this action has the opposite effect, and my pulse echoes throughout my entire body. I bend my neck from side to side, which only magnifies the sound. I'm not listening to anything Caroline is saying; for all intents and purposes, I've left the room, because now I've completely lost the plot, and all I can see are flashes of my summer in Italy—Giamma ducking into his car the first morning I was in Orbagne, the little boys circling him on their bikes. Simone reading Thomas Mann in her bed. Pietro and his father standing in Simone's cataloguing shed, and Cyrille at the summit of a mountain pass.

When the audience starts clapping, I turn toward Simone. Before I can say anything, Caroline appears at my side. "Si," she says breathlessly. "This is one of the lawyers I was telling you about, Lena Connolly."

"Nice to meet you," Simone says, clearing her throat. Her hair is even shorter than it was the summer we were in Orbagne, her eyebrows thick and untamed. She's not wearing any jewelry, apart from a Cartier Tank watch on her right wrist.

I decide to play along. "You too," I say. "Si, like *sigh*? Is that short for something?"

"Like S.I. Newhouse. Or Cy Twombly. Who Newhouse collected," Caroline interjects, chuckling to herself. "Si is the conservator I mentioned earlier this week, who restored the cup. We outsource a lot of our Roman stuff to them."

I nod. "So you run your own—" I search for the right term.

"Conservation studio," Si says. "Excuse me."

Caroline and I watch as Si makes their way to the other end of the gallery. "They hate small talk," Caroline says.

"You know, we should get Si in for a formal deposition," I tell her.

"Why?" Caroline asks, her voice jumping an octave. "I can get you the conservation report."

I decide not to press; after all, Caroline can't prevent me from reaching out myself.

Caroline's countenance suddenly morphs from panic to relief as her eyes dart around the gallery. "Speaking of depositions. I did want to make sure you chatted with Oliver tonight. I caught up with him this afternoon, and—ah, there he is." She points to the opposite end of the room and waves.

"Great job up there," Oliver says to Caroline when he arrives at her side.

She kisses him on both cheeks and nods at me. "You already know Lena."

"It's been a while," he says, giving me a one-arm hug. "Since your Limoges guy, I think?"

He turns to Caroline and lowers his voice conspiratorially. "A few years ago, one of her clients wanted to bequeath an absurd collection of book-shaped Limoges snuffboxes to the library; you wouldn't believe the hoops I had to jump through to get them to green-light it—"

"Oliver, those were *mine,*" Caroline says, swatting his chest in mock irritation. Red blotches climb his neck.

I fight back laughter. "Are you thinking of the trustee who endowed that decorative arts position in the art history department?"

Oliver shakes his head apologetically. "You're so right. Yes."

"Honest mistake," I say. And to Caroline, "My client had a collection of Limoges enamels that went to the Frick."

Ever since the tax code was changed in 2018, I've been advising my clients to donate valuable artworks within their lifetime in order to reap maximum benefits. Years of working with estate appraisers have taught me that contrary to auction house headlines, most art—even expensive, blue-chip art—does not fare well on the open market. Which is precisely why it's advantageous to donate it. My client with the Limoges enamels, for example, a retired banker with his own private equity fund, reduced his tax bill by 60 percent the year he donated to the Frick.

"I'll set up some time for us to talk about the Creon gift," I say to Oliver, who nods agreeably before drifting away.

I turn to Caroline, only to discover she is now deep in conversation with none other than Eva, Giamma's wife. "So how do you know John?" Caroline asks me.

Eva regards me expectantly. "John?" I echo.

Caroline nods at Eva. "She just told me you knew him."

"John," I repeat, my mind swirling. It's true that like me, Giamma had a complicated relationship to his name, an elision of Gian Maria. It's possible he changed it from Gian Maria to Gian, and then to John—but I can't think why he would have.

I need to keep it together; I need to be strategic. I don't want to give Caroline a reason to request my removal from her defense team. "I went to Columbia for undergrad," I say, a clear deflection, though to my relief it seems to satisfy them. "Small world."

"Yeah, really. He was one of my research fellows too. Back when he was at Columbia. Great guy. I actually set these two up."

I feel a ping of recognition. Giamma worked for a curator—no, he was trying to help a curator. Or rather, a curator helped him get into grad school—that's what it was. It was Caroline.

"Would you believe I thought about setting her up with my son first? But I came to my senses. My kid's a terror. Major abandonment issues. Probably because I was always leaving him with a nanny to go on digs. Anyway, this one"—she gestures to Eva—"deserved better. They just got married at Eva's grandparents' place outside Chicago. Fitzgerald used it as the basis for the house in *Tender Is the Night.*"

"Are you from Lake Forest?" I ask Eva.

"Partly," she says. "I grew up all over."

The smile slips from my face, and now I'm desperate to talk about anything else, because even though I've never read *Tender Is the Night*, I know the house Caroline's talking about—Lake Forest is near Wilmette—and now I've identified exactly the type of person Eva is: privileged, cultured, worry-free. I'm overcome with enmity that this is the person Giamma chose. This is the person he chose over me.

I think of my last serious boyfriend, a Machiavellian scientist who couldn't have cared less about the research on plasmonic nanostructures executed by undergrad assistants that landed him on the cover of *Nature* and a fellowship at the MIT Media Lab. We were long distance for a while after he moved to Cambridge, taking turns on the Acela for weekend visits, but the relationship grew strained, and I started dreading our weeknight phone calls. The thing he talked about more than anything else was meeting with the Lab's celebrity donors. When we broke up, he was unfazed and quickly moved on with a twenty-something MIT fundraiser. I subsequently deleted Instagram.

You never remember what someone says, the saying goes. You remember how they made you feel. The scientist made me feel superior, if anything—and not in a good way. Superior because the things he cared about were so superficial and inconsequential. Giamma, on the other hand, had loved the ancient and beautiful things I loved. He'd made me feel like an equal. I didn't love him, I don't think—but I loved who I thought I was to him. I haven't had that feeling since, I now realize.

Eva excuses herself and disappears into the crowd. I'm seized by the urge to leave this place, these people. I don't belong here, even if part of me wishes I did.

Caroline will be threatened if I bring up Si again, but Giamma seems to be fair game. "So you and John worked together?" I ask.

"We still do, sometimes. He's very well-connected."

"What do you mean?"

“What do you mean what do I mean? He knows a lot of people. Donors, art collectors, academics. He’s well-connected.”

“Is he connected to Filippo Dalmasso?”

A series of expressions sweep over her face. “Why do you ask?”

I shrug. “He’s Italian, right?”

Caroline nods slowly. “For the record. It’s almost impossible for an object to come on the market now with a completely clean provenance. Filippo’s collection might as well be a museum collection.” She pauses. “His donation—this cup—it honestly might be the thing I’m most proud of in my career.”

Now I seriously consider telling Caroline that I majored in Classics, went on a dig, and know exactly what she’s talking about. But Emmanuel’s warning is echoing in my mind: she’s slippery.

“If you’ll excuse me, I need to work the room.”

“One quick thing before you go. About Simone—”

Caroline gives me a look. “Si?”

“Right, I mean Si.”

Caroline studies me. We’re about the same height with my two-inch boots, so she’s looking right into my eyes. “It’s very disrespectful to call them Simone, you realize.”

I close my eyes and shake my head. “Sorry, yes—”

“Where’d you even come up with Simone, anyway?”

If there’s a moment to tell Caroline that I knew Si before, it’s now, but I can’t seem to find the words. Maybe it’s less about Caroline and more about what it would mean for the case if it got out that I have connections to these people. I very much doubt a judge would see any of it as a coincidence. “I, uh—” I stammer.

Caroline’s phone starts to vibrate. She holds up a finger and turns away to answer it.

I need to talk to Si—that’s what I need to do. About the case, yes, but also about Orbagne. I need to know if they remember.

I make my way to an adjacent gallery where attendees are hovering around a table covered in elaborately composed charcuterie platters. As I gaze at the spread, my vision starts to blur. I think of my ex-boyfriend, the scientist, who peered through microscopes at minuscule organisms jerking around in a petri dish. I roll my neck around and close my eyes, but when I reopen them, nothing has changed. My shallow breaths are coming faster and faster, and when I look down, the floor seems far away.

I scan the gallery for a place to sit down, and I spot Giamma and Eva chatting with a few of the attendees. Giamma's hand hovers over the small of her back.

I take out my phone and draft a text to Jinny, realizing that she never messaged to let me know she landed safely. I write "hey," then delete it. When I look up, Giamma is standing in front of me.

My shoulders shoot up to my ears. But then the static in my vision dissipates, and when I draw in a deep breath, the unsteady feeling passes. "You scared me."

"You need to be careful," he says in a low voice.

There's something condescending about both this admonition and the tone with which he delivers it, and I reply without considering a strategic angle. "Actually, you need to be careful," I say. "You can marry an American, anglicize your name, try to hide your accent, but I know exactly who you are."

He examines my face, and to my surprise, breaks into a smile. He nods toward the figurines in the display case a few feet away from us. "And I know who you are," he says.

But Giamma does not know who I am. He never did. I never showed him my whole self.

"If you need to talk," he says, handing me a business card, "call me on this number."

Later, on the subway ride back down to Chelsea, overwhelmed

with the cognitive dissonance of being simultaneously weighed down and buoyed by the evening's events, I drop the card on the floor. Despite my curiosity, I do not want to talk to Giamma—it's Si I want to talk to. Si is the one who restored the Cupid and Psyche cup. But an eager young man standing next to the door picks it up. He's quite handsome, actually, with his wild hair and full lips. I could see myself ending up with someone younger than me, now that I think about it. Someone deferential and unjaded, with a rich inner world.

"Miss," he says, waving the card. I smile at him and gesture at the open seat next to me. I'll tell him to cross out Giamma's number and write down his. He sits, and we start talking, my pen at the ready. But when I mention the exhibition at the Fordham Museum, he tells me, straight-faced, that the pyramids at Luxor are portals to other dimensions. He's experienced them, the portals; he's traveled through time. The multiverse is full of love and light, he says.

I stuff the business card in my bag along with the pen and turn away.

I'm angry, I realize, as I stare out the window at the blur of advertisements lining the tunnel walls of the D train, and not just about the boy, who is now describing the pyramids' uncanny alignment with various celestial bodies. I'm angry about Caroline's alignment with these ghosts from my past. It's not shocking that Giamma and Si are in New York—they were both New York–bound the summer we were in Italy. I've always known—sensed, rather—that they were here. Can it be that all these years I've been subconsciously working to advance their reentry into my life? Is it possible that I would have reencountered them at some point even if I hadn't attended this opening tonight?

But I did attend the opening. Giamma seemed genuinely surprised to see me; Si did not. And even though I didn't see them together earlier, Si and Giamma know each other. They weren't exactly close the summer we were all in Orbagne, but they definitely know each other.

Caroline Boswell, my new client, works with both of them. This is the part I'm angry about: it's too uncanny to be a coincidence.

IV.

MARCH 8, 2022

NEW YORK CITY

Lakshmi and Iñigo's new penthouse on Hudson Street has pale oak herringbone floors, a veiny marble kitchen, and a direct-access elevator. When I arrive, Ovid nips at Lakshmi's heels as she greets me with a hug. I bend down to pet him, but he barks and repairs to a white love seat.

"Red or white?" Lakshmi asks as I follow her to the kitchen.

I've never understood people who say alcohol helps them escape themselves; for me it has the opposite effect—like I'm in a small cell with a recording of my thoughts blasting over a loudspeaker. Lakshmi knows that I'll only ever have one glass, which I'll sip slowly all evening. "Red," I reply.

Lakshmi pulls out the top drawer of her wine fridge, and I take a seat on a barstool. "I can't believe this is where you live."

"It makes me a bit sick when I think about it, to be honest."

She doesn't have to say more for me to understand what she's getting at—the contrast of her life to the lives of the refugees and asylum-seekers she spends her days advocating for. I could never do what she does. It's too depressing, and Sisyphean, and the reality is that helping the weakest and least powerful members of the human race means not being able to look away from the horrible things that have been done to them. At least my job, for all its tedium, doesn't prevent me from sleeping at night.

Until now, that is. I didn't sleep at all last night after I spent some time on the Fordham Museum website and discovered that John Piromalli is a member of Caroline's "Curator's Circle," and sits on her collections committee. *He's well-connected,* Caroline said, bristling unmistakably when in response I asked whether he was connected to Filippo Dalmasso.

"What are you making?" I ask Lakshmi.

She hands me a glass of translucent red wine, then goes back to stirring her sauce. "So I have a new client. New *clients.*"

I relax onto my stool. "You seem excited," I say.

She leans her elbows on the counter. "Okay, get ready. Confidential, of course." Even though there's no one to witness our conversation but Ovid, she lowers her voice. "This is straight out of a soap opera. So there is an Italian—Calabrian—mafia called the 'ndrangheta. Which, by the way, comes from the Greek word *andragathía*—"

My shoulders stiffen and I put down my glass.

"Just wait," Lakshmi says, clocking my discomfort. "They are the world's biggest traffickers of cocaine and heroin—not a joke—and over the past twenty years they've expanded from Italy to all of these American and Canadian cities. Including New York. They're doing all the things you'd expect organized crime to do—laundering money, loan sharking, arms smuggling—but that's not why we got hired. We got hired because this group of women, wives and children of the men in charge, living on Long Island of all places, say they've been exploited, and they want to come forward with information about the organization."

I nod slowly, searching Lakshmi's face for her motivation in telling me all of this. We talk about work all the time, but she rarely divulges specifics about her clients. Is it possible she doesn't remember that I dated someone from Calabria the summer we were in Italy? Then again, I can't remember what exactly I told her about Giamma back then.

"Look it up, it's crazy. En-dron-ghe-ta. They do blood pacts, they speak this obscure dialect, they are inducting children into what's essentially a cult of violence when they're twelve or something. Anyway, this recipe is from one of the women. She made it for me last week and I had her write it down. It's kind of a pasta alla norma but with— Why are you making that face?"

"Sorry, I'm just taking it in, what you're saying." I shift my weight and tuck one leg underneath me. "You know the guy I dated in Orbagne was Calabrian?" I venture.

Lakshmi suppresses a laugh. "Lena. I think you would have known it if you were sleeping with a mafioso. That's like me saying Iñigo is a terrorist because he's Basque."

I stifle a gasp when I hear the elevator door open. But it's just Iñigo with a pizza box in hand. He looks the same: wiry, rumpled, thumbprints on his glasses. Ovid yelps and runs over.

Iñigo unshoulders his laptop bag and bends down to nuzzle the dog, and I catch Lakshmi cringing. "I thought you were taking the red eye," she says.

"Did you walk him?" he replies.

"Yes," she says, and I can hear the irritation in her voice. "What about 'hi darling, how was your day?' You didn't even say hello to Lena."

Iñigo winces and comes over to kiss me hello. "This place is incredible," I say, attempting to diffuse the tension permeating the room.

"I agree," he says with a sad smile. I take in his unshaved face and the way he's bowing his head, trying to make himself smaller.

Lakshmi carries our wineglasses to the dining table, and Iñigo follows her with his pizza. When we sit down, Iñigo realizes there isn't a wineglass for him, and silently heads back to the kitchen.

"I swear, he's obsessed with the dog," Lakshmi says. Her voice drops to a whisper. "*I'm* the one who wanted the dog in the first place. But now it's just work, and Ovid. I would have obviously made enough for three if he'd told me earlier today that he'd be home. He never tells me anything anymore."

I shake my head in solidarity, but Iñigo comes back before I can say anything.

As we eat, I feel the impulse to direct the conversation toward her case, because some latent instinct is telling me there's something relevant to uncover. But I ignore this urge, and instead, Iñigo tells us about his board meeting with the blockchain technology company that bought his gaming start-up, where he spent a decade developing video games that leverage real-time geographic information. "You can do anything with blockchain," he says. "Everyone knows about crypto. But you can use it to build marketplaces, databases, inventory systems, social networks. Collaborative video games." I nod along, remembering the first time I met Iñigo in Selinunte, where he was working as a GIS analyst on the Columbia dig with Lakshmi.

"Would you ever use it on a dig?" I ask.

Lakshmi shoots me a sharp, questioning look—she's worried I'm going to bring up Cyrille again, I can tell.

"I was just thinking about the first time we met," I say to her. "How Iñigo explained GIS to me."

She relaxes back into her chair. "Feels like a lifetime ago."

"For sure," Iñigo says to me, ignoring Lakshmi's comment. "You could use it to catalogue the finds. That way no one could doctor the provenance."

After a beat, he changes the subject to their upcoming trip to Bilbao to visit his family, but Lakshmi's gloominess only intensifies.

At the end of the evening, I tap the face of my phone and see three missed calls from Jinny.

It occurs to me now that Lakshmi didn't raise the subject of Jinny's pregnancy at all, which is a relief. After we hug goodbye, I weigh whether or not I should take off my coat and lead her to the couch so I can tell her about reencountering Giamma last night. But then it would be impossible not to bring up Cyrille, and there is no part of me that wants to disrupt our current dynamic, or to change the way she is looking at me right now: gratefully, nonjudgmentally. I need her on my side. More than anyone else, I need her.

OUTSIDE ON THE SIDEWALK, even though there's no one I'd rather talk to less right now, I call Jinny back.

It's immediately apparent that something is wrong—that I've done something wrong. "Hey," she deadpans.

"How was the flight?" I ask in as neutral a tone as possible.

"Not bad," she says. Now I realize that she sounds distracted, not offended. Worried, maybe. If I could see her face I'd be able to read her. Jinny's eyes are two different shades: one is a blue-gold, veering toward brown, and the other is straight cerulean. When she looks at you from the brown side, she has the gaze of an innocent, but on the bright blue side, she always looks slightly sinister, like she's scheming.

"Class was okay?" I ask.

Jinny took an early flight yesterday so she could make it back in time to teach her afternoon class at Pepperdine, where she's a tenure-track professor of comparative literature. I try to imagine her now in Malibu, the radius window of her book-lined office that opens out onto a verdant lawn that gives way to the Pacific. In general, I don't like to think about her work too much, because I know that deep down she thinks her translations and *TLS* book reviews are more important than anything I'll ever do in my career. She's made it clear to me in many ways over the years that she thinks my decision to go to law school was a cop-out, a choice I made on impulse to somehow spite her. Which is ridiculous. If anyone influenced my decision to go to law school, it was Lakshmi, whose father threatened to stop paying her tuition junior year if she didn't agree to follow in his footsteps. Academia was too political for her anyway, she said at the time—plus, she had the etymologically relevant languages, an intimate familiarity with Cicero, and a preternatural ability to absorb and regurgitate names and dates. I had all of those things too. Law school made sense.

"I had to come down to San Diego," Jinny finally says.

My stomach fills with dread. There's only one reason she ever goes down there. "What happened?"

Jinny sighs. "He's fine. He had an enormous kidney stone. They put him under so they could blast it with some kind of laser."

I'm aware that I should feel some degree of sympathy for my father, but I can only think about Tonya from *The Real World: Chicago*, who was always leaving her Alka-Seltzer all over the house and calling in sick because of her kidney stones. I almost mention this to Jinny—I know it would make her laugh—but I'm too disoriented by the revelations of the past two days.

Jinny misinterprets my silence. "Hey," she says. "He's okay. He just came out of surgery."

Now it occurs to me that Jinny might be sitting in a hospital room next to our dad. I might even be on speakerphone. "Oh," I manage.

"I'm in the waiting room, don't worry," she says, reading my mind.

I don't say anything, and what feels like a full minute of silence passes.

"He did ask about you, and how you are," Jinny says. "He was all stressed about the anesthesia, talking about his will and whatnot."

I've asked her countless times not to talk about me with him, but this doesn't seem like the right moment to point that out, or to ask her what she said on my behalf.

"You're in it, if you're wondering."

"I'm not," I say quickly. Beyond the fact that I would never accept anything from my father, I can't imagine that there's anything to be distributed, besides the proceeds from his dead parents' house, where he's been living alone for thirty years. His only income, to my knowledge, consists of residuals from the Claymation film he made—the only film he ever managed to make.

Even though Jinny can't see me, I can practically feel her blue eye on me, judging. And given the circumstances, I'm not feeling particularly patient. I let the silence go on for a while, but then I can't stop myself. "I know you hate it," I blurt. "That I don't talk to him."

"What does that have to do with anything?" Jinny asks, which, notably, is not a denial.

A sound from the back of my throat escapes my lips. I bang the crosswalk button with my fist. I'm at Twentieth and Ninth. Finally the light turns, and I cross the street.

Jinny waits for me to respond, and when I don't, she adds, "Lena, I don't hate anything about you."

I consider that and decide I'm not going to let her avoid addressing this. "You do, though. You disapprove, at best."

Jinny exhales audibly and slowly. "If anything, it makes me sad," she finally says. "Not for him, but for you. I hate that you have to carry it with you, this anger toward him."

"Why can't you just support me?" I ask, at which point I realize that I am almost in tears. This is what one glass of wine does to me. Also, I've passed four pregnant women since I started walking home.

"Lena, what the hell are you talking about?" Jinny asks me now. "What makes you think I don't support your boundaries? Of course I do!"

"Okay, okay, don't yell," I say, startled by Jinny's intensity. I feel like changing the subject, or even ending the conversation altogether, but I take a deep breath, and the pressure behind my eyes subsides. "I will just never forgive him for leaving us with her."

"I get it," Jinny says. "I obviously understand more than anyone. But Lena, let's be honest, he was never going to get custody of us back then."

"I disagree," I say. I can back this up with numerous case studies from the family law class I took in law school. But I don't mention that because this argument is shaping up to be the most direct confrontation Jinny and I have had in years, and I'm not sure how things have gone off the rails so quickly.

When Jinny speaks, it's with an aggressiveness I can't remember ever hearing out of her. "Let me ask you something, Lena," she says.

I stare down at the sidewalk, steeling myself against Jinny's emotions and the sudden, intense smell of Marlboros, which brings me right back to my stilted conversation with Giamma last night. So much has happened in the span of three days—too much. All of this is too much.

"Who is more guilty—the person who doesn't protect you? Or the person who actually hurts you?"

"Stop," I say. I know what *she* thinks the answer to that question is, and I know she knows that I can't answer it. I am going to hang up on her if she doesn't stop, I decide. I'm only a block away from my apartment now.

"No," she says shakily. "Why do you think I wanted to have a kid, Lena? Do you even care?"

When she told me about the pregnancy after I overheard her vomiting in my bathroom, I was only thinking about nature versus nurture, and inheritance, and of Jinny and me cowering on the beige living room couch in our childhood home during our mother's paranoid tirades.

"I want to do it over," she says. "I want to give my daughter the childhood we didn't have."

"It's a girl?" I say. I know this to be an incorrect response, but I won't take her bait.

For a long time, Jinny says nothing. And then, "You know what your problem is, Lena? You only ever think about your own pain, what other people are doing to *you.*"

At that, I tell her I'm headed into my elevator and hang up without waiting for a response.

Later that night, when I finally fall asleep, I dream that Jinny and I are in Orbagne. I'm showing her the dig site, and she takes a trowel and starts hacking at the fresco we've uncovered. *You're ruining it,* I scream, but my voice is hoarse, and she can't understand me. *Stop,* I scream, *leave.* Cyrille appears from out of my peripheral vision and shushes me. *Let her,* he mouths.

I HAVEN'T BEEN TO COLUMBIA since my graduation, despite having lived in the city ever since. Now, trudging through the quad's slush under Alma Mater's bronze gaze on my lunch hour, I remember why I never come up here—it's too unnerving to recall myself as the transfer student who thought trading a Classics department in Chicago for one in New York would be the solution to her problems, real and imagined.

At the entrance to the library I fall into step with a young man straining under an enormous backpack. When I spot a glassy-eyed security guard keeping watch over an ID sensor inside, I stick close to the backpack and take the stairs to the second floor.

As I approach the information desk, the site of my undergrad work study, I'm pleasantly surprised to see my old supervisor behind a monitor, clicking her mouse incessantly. Her crow's-feet have deepened, but other than that she looks the same: long gray braid, Coke-bottle glasses magnifying watery hazel eyes. She senses my presence and looks up. "Lena Connolly," she says, mirroring my smile. "How long has it been?"

I lean on the counter and tell her everything that I can remember about the program Cyrille showed me at his office hours eighteen years ago.

"Well, you didn't need to come all the way up here," she says, interrupting my rambling. "All that GeoData stuff is hosted on the cloud."

"Here," she says, waving me over in response to my blank face. I step behind the desk and look over her shoulder. She clicks her cursor into a search bar on a web page with a GeoData@Columbia logo in the upper left corner. "You said his research was about a town called Orbagne?"

I nod. "He also published research on Ostia Antica and some famous villa to the south of it. He was there in the nineties."

"Let's see what we can find." She squares her shoulders, then drums her fingers on the keyboard. "Here we go," she says about thirty seconds later. "Hydrography of Central Europe. Drainage, territorial boundaries, shoreline features. We can zoom in to Italy, here—" She cuts herself off and looks up. "I'll be right back."

Back when I was working for her, my supervisor would make a beeline for the bathroom every time she got excited about something. It would usually be at least ten minutes until she returned. I take a seat at her desk and play around with the map, trying and failing to locate the river basin. "That's why," I whisper, noticing that this map is dated 1725.

I click back and do another search for *Cyrille DuPuy*; in the results, I find a set of maps produced from a 1996–1999 survey in Ostia Antica. I click into a map, but it doesn't look anything like what he showed me on his computer all those years ago. I zoom in on the mouth of the Tiber, searching for the hidden river basin—but I have no idea how to read this black-and-white image, its dotted lines and gray variants.

I take a deep breath and zoom out; now I can see all of Ostia Antica. On the left side of the screen is a clickable list labeled *Layers*. I click at random until the view is as minimal as possible—a real map with clearly identifiable features. This looks familiar; yes, this is what Cyrille showed me in his office eighteen years ago. I locate the Capitolium, the Curia, the Baths of Neptune, and the Forum. To the west of the city center are the waterfront and the port.

The port—Rome's biggest port. Cyrille taught me that when he showed me this map.

I look down at the keyboard, unzipping my parka as I remember the rest of the conversation I had with Cyrille back then. He told me his team worked from the port all the way to the senatorial estates outside the city. The *senatorial* estates.

This memory swirls in my mind for a few moments until, in a flash of sudden recognition, I connect it to the present.

I open a new tab and search for *Botti Italian senator.* A familiar man smiles at me in an image at the top of the results. In another photo, he points a stern finger at someone outside the frame, a microphone clipped to his white collar.

According to Wikipedia, Andrea Botti has been the federal secretary of Italy's Lega Nord since December 2003 and a senator since April 2006. This is it—this is the connection. Giamma grew up with Pietro and his father; he was close with the whole family. Which would explain his awkwardness when I told him about the investigation into Fordham's collection the other night: he already knew. His friend's politician father is behind the restitution request.

When my supervisor returns, I thank her for her help and wander out of the library in a daze, images flooding my brain: patches of melting snow on a mountain summit, the inchoate stone outline of a Roman villa, my gloved hand holding a trowel, the vivid red of an ancient fresco, a ziplock bag of pottery shards, and of course: Cyrille. As I descend the stairs, I can sense him right behind me. I try to keep my eyes forward, but when I stop hearing his footsteps, I hesitate. And just like Orpheus, I'm a coward. I look back.

V.

JUNE 8, 2004

ORBAGNE

On the train ride up and into the Alps, I never had a linear sense of altitude—there was only the feeling of pressure in my ears, the blur of green and blue and gray. When we reached Orbagne, I alighted at a stony platform with no accompanying station. The train groaned off behind me as I stood there, dazed from my thirty-six hours in transit and still reeling from a dream I'd had on my flight from Rome to Torino: that the plane had gone down in a fiery crash, and that I'd died. It had been so real—my fear, the sense of actual physical pain—that when I awoke to the plane's gentle landing, I'd enthusiastically joined the Italians' puzzling round of applause and hadn't been able to stop touching my limbs since.

The sun was descending toward the mountains, which still didn't look real, even now that I was off the train. I'd never seen natural beauty like that in real life—to comprehend it, I had to think about the whole scene as a reproduction, as if I was looking at a photograph instead of the real thing. Which was maybe related to the way I viewed myself in the world—superimposed. I felt like I could never figure out how to fully be in a place.

As I dragged my suitcase over cobblestones, referencing the hand-drawn map Cyrille had included in the orientation email I'd printed, I was oblivious to all the details of that small town, which I would later discover: the faded pink stucco of two- and three-story buildings, white-against-blue street signs, the hole-in-the-wall fruit stand that sold cleaning products and cigarettes, the lone bar with its pensioners and freezer full of Magnum ice cream bars, the defunct fountain in the center of the town's small piazza with its Bacchanalian motifs.

I located the centuries-old palazzo that served as the dig's dorm and entered its unlocked double doors. In the foyer, pale light shone through an adjacent room's window and illuminated cracked terrazzo floors and utilitarian furniture. Voices echoed from somewhere deeper in the house, mixing with the sound of clinking dishes and running water.

"Lena!" I heard Cyrille exclaim as a light flicked on at the top of the wide staircase. I watched as he descended the stairs, hand skimming the wrought iron handrail. When I saw his face, I registered that he was worried, and to my horror, my eyes started to sting.

A young man appeared on the landing at the top of the stairs. "Pietro!" Cyrille called up to him. "*Puoi aiutarla con la valigia?*"

"Of course," Pietro replied in English. He flew down the stairs and put his hand on my suitcase handle. He was even shorter than Cyrille, with sandy curls partially obscured by a paisley bandana. There was a bump in his nose like the ones I'd seen on faces from Roman coins. His blue eyes were cold.

"Are you hungry?" Pietro asked me in English, which through the filter of his accent I mistook for "Are you angry?"

"No, no," I said, suddenly remembering a passage Cyrille had read to us in his seminar from Julius Caesar's *Bellum Gallicum* about the Gauls' blue eyes, which the Romans associated with inferior intelligence and cruelty. "Why do you ask?"

Cyrille searched my face. "You look tired."

I was tired. I'd known when I purchased the cheapest plane fare I could find with my grandmother's credit card on a computer in the Columbia library that the trip would entail two layovers—one in Detroit and another in Rome—before landing in Torino. A train from Torino would take me the rest of the way to the dig site in Orbagne. But I hadn't looked at the length of the layovers, and so I'd waited six hours in Detroit before boarding my flight to Rome, at which point I'd understood what the Alitalia rep had meant when she said, "A long journey, eh?" at check-in. I arrived in Rome in the evening, but my connecting flight to Turin didn't leave until the next morning; I was stuck at Fiumicino Airport for the night.

At Fiumicino, the first non–US airport I'd ever set foot in, I wandered around the terminal, eavesdropping on conversations, smiling to myself when I overheard a middle-aged man passionately discussing Tuscan pecorino cheese. "The thing you have to understand about pecorino Toscano," he was saying in Italian, "is that it is the only version of pecorino with the correct balance of salt. You understand this, right?" A woman, elegantly dressed and open-faced, was nodding her head energetically. "Yes, yes. Let's find our gate."

I found these initial exchanges to be thrilling, innocuous as they were—I felt like I'd entered another dimension. It wasn't just the fact of understanding the Italians; it was that I immediately perceived a particular energy in their comportment. It made me think of Magister Rizzi, the way his irreverence was tinged with gravitas.

At a certain point the shops closed, the lights dimmed, and I stretched across a conjoined pod of fiberglass chairs, resting my head on my sweatshirt and hugging my backpack, exhausted but unable to relax my eyes. As I drifted in and out, I remembered how my mother used to lie next to me on the floor of Jinny's room and read Goethe's *Italian Journey* to us at bedtime. In the book, Goethe had visited the museums in Rome by torchlight; he'd described all the figures I'd come to learn about: Laocoön, Apollo, Pyrrhus, Juno. Maybe this was the origin of my fascination with Italy, of my fixation on ancient things in general.

Now Pietro grabbed my suitcase and led me up the stairs. "You and Simone have the best room," he said.

On the second floor of the palazzo, the walls were yellowed and decaying, and there were no overhead lights. I followed Pietro as he ambled down the hallway with more confidence than I'd ever encountered in a man who was so much smaller than me. He stopped at a tall, narrow door with a cast-iron handle and knocked.

"Yeah?" a voice called from behind the door.

In the bedroom, which was bigger than the dining room downstairs, a rickety chandelier hung from the ceiling between two twin brass-frame beds. A young woman was perched on the edge of one of them, reading a book. "Hey," she said, standing up as we entered. "Lena, right?"

I nodded, feeling relieved—Simone felt immediately familiar to me, with her Meg Ryan haircut, thin arms, and nervous energy.

"Sorry for the mess," she said. The contents of her open suitcase littered the room. "I'm just getting organized. We can share that." She nodded at an oversized armoire at the far end of the room.

"Did you get here today?" I asked when Pietro left the room.

"Yesterday," she said. "I think you're the last to arrive."

"There's only one working toilet in this whole house," she continued. "For us and twelve dudes. Well, ten. Pietro and Cyrille have their own apartments in the building next door."

"What's with all the guys?" I asked her.

"That's archeology, man."

I thought of Lakshmi and all the other female students in Cyrille's seminar; we'd easily outnumbered the guys. "But there were tons of girls in the archeology class I took."

"I don't know what to tell you. I've been one of a handful of girls on all three of the digs I've done. My classes were all girls, too, but anyway—most Classics students don't go on digs," she said, smirking. She'd just graduated from Mount Holyoke.

Simone told me she was starting a master's in conservation at NYU in the fall. "I can't wait to be in New York," she said. "I've only ever lived in small towns."

I nodded. The polite thing to do would have been to ask her where she was from—central California, I later learned—but what I really wanted to tell her was not to get her hopes up, that people were the same everywhere. Except maybe in Italy. "We'll be in the same city, then," I said instead.

"Oh yeah, Pietro told me. Columbia, right?"

I nodded. "What's his deal?"

"Pietro? What do you mean?"

"Does Cyrille report to him, or does he report to Cyrille?"

"They're co-directors. Cyrille's in charge of survey and Pietro's in charge of the finds."

"But Cyrille was the one who discovered it, right?"

I glanced over my shoulder, following Simone's eyes. Pietro had returned with my backpack.

"Oh, thanks," I said, my cheeks burning at the thought that he might have overheard our exchange.

"No problem," he said in a neutral voice. "See you in the morning."

When he left, I tossed the backpack on my bed and sat down next to it. I told her about my dream on the airplane.

"Death in a dream means rebirth," she said.

I eyed her skeptically. "But I was definitely dead. I exploded; I was in pain."

"How do you think babies feel when they're being born? Why do you think they scream when they come out?" She raised her eyebrows, then smirked. "My parents are Jungian psychologists."

As I was considering this, a strong and familiar smell prompted me to look over at my suitcase on the foot of my bed. "Do you smell something?" I asked Simone. "Like laundry detergent?"

She shook her head.

I unzipped the suitcase and groaned. My shampoo was seeping through the seams of the plastic bag that contained my toiletries. Everything smelled like syrupy roses.

"Yikes," Simone said, rising to her feet. She looked genuinely disappointed for me. "Hey, you can use my shampoo. You can borrow anything you need."

I looked up at her, the full weight of the day gathering behind my eyes. But something pushed it out as I took in the kindness in her face, a sudden lightness. Simone didn't know me. I was far away from everyone I knew. Cyrille and I weren't much more than acquaintances. To Simone, to Pietro, to anyone I met in Orbagne—I didn't have to be the version of myself I'd always been. I could be someone who discovered things, someone who was capable of shaping the narrative rather than yielding to it. This was a profoundly comforting revelation.

IN THE MORNING, Simone's bed was empty. A strip of light shone through the clay-colored shutters and onto my starched white sheets. I walked over to the window.

When I opened the shutters and let in the morning light, my whole body hummed. I stuck my head out into the cool air, which smelled like the water from the jaw-shaped sprinkler Jinny and I ran through as kids, back when the lawn still got mowed. And the mountains, with their snow-covered peaks: *imposing* was not the word that came to mind, though people often describe mountains that way. *Imposing* was too pejorative. The right word was *numinous*, from *numen*.

On the street, a gang of boys on bicycles circled a man with a cigarette between his lips as he loaded duffel bags into the trunk of a silver sports car that looked too small for his body. He was clean-shaven with ear-length copper hair and wore a white polo shirt.

He was smiling at the kids as they goaded him—"*daiiiii,*" they kept saying.

Just as he was about to get into the driver's seat, he stamped out his cigarette and glanced up in my direction. I withdrew my head and shut my eyes hard in embarrassment.

I changed into a T-shirt and shorts and headed downstairs, my feet bare on the terrazzo floors, following the sound of voices to the big room off the entryway, where two long side-by-side tables were filled with young men devouring hard-boiled eggs, slices of focaccia, cold cuts, and cheese. I didn't see Simone or Cyrille anywhere.

Pietro spotted me. "*Oi, tutti,*" he addressed the room between mouthfuls of bread. "*Vi presento Lena.*"

They looked up at me and waved. I couldn't tell one face from another in the mass of dark hair and red cheeks. "*Benvenuta,*" one of them said with his mouth full. His face was creased like he'd just slept hard on it. I waved back.

Pietro stood and led me into the kitchen, where a woman was loading moka pots with ground espresso. She was petite, about a head shorter than me, and the linen tunic she wore over her enormous breasts revealed two full sleeves of nautical tattoos. Pietro introduced her as Martha, the cook. She was from Wisconsin of all places.

"What are those?" I asked her, nodding at five identical dark glass bottles on the shelf above the stove labeled GENETRIX. The gold Art Nouveau font reminded me of the Metra entrance next to Grant Park in Chicago, where Jinny and I had seen Radiohead perform right before she left for grad school. Underneath GENETRIX was a glowing moon encircled by a dense yellow bough dotted with white berries.

"It's a famous amaro from here," she said, wiping her hands on a towel and nodding at Pietro. "They make it at the vineyard."

She must have read the confusion on my face and added, "You drink it after dinner. Supposedly it's a very ancient recipe."

"It *is* an ancient recipe," Pietro said, reaching into one of the lower cabinets for a shot glass. "Here, she can taste."

I took the shot glass from Martha and examined the inch of honey-colored liquid she'd poured. It smelled like pine needles. I managed to choke it down, wincing as it burned my throat and gave way to an unexpected head rush. It was medicinal and sickeningly sweet, with a bitter aftertaste. "Is this alcohol?"

Pietro and Martha burst out laughing, and after a disoriented beat I joined in.

"*In bocca al lupo* for the first day," Martha said once we caught our breath.

"Oh," I said. "*Crepi il lupo.* Right?" I said, recalling a moment of panic from the previous day's journey, when I'd realized I needed to change trains at the Aosta station in order to reach Orbagne.

I'd been fortunate that a kind-looking middle-aged couple who had been eyeing me throughout the duration of the trip took mercy and helped me lug my suitcase down the stairs, through the tunnel, and back up more stairs to another set of tracks.

"*La valigia piu grande dalla signorina,*" the man said in mock concern, looking from me to my enormous suitcase.

I cursed that pre-Italy version of myself, the naïf who overpacked with full-sized toiletries in ziplock bags. The dig season was nine weeks long; it had seemed so important to have enough of everything. It never occurred to me that I could simply buy what I needed when I got there.

"*Dove vai?*" the woman asked me, tucking her bobbed hair behind her ear with one hand and reaching out for my train ticket with the other.

I cleared my throat. "*A scavare,*" I told them, for some reason. I guess maybe I thought if they knew I was going to a dig, it would justify the outsized suitcase, of which I was becoming increasingly self-conscious.

Something about that response gave me away. "*Apperò! Sei americana?*" the man said, and I felt exposed and relieved at the same time.

"*Si,*" I said.

He hiked up his pants with his belt loops and nodded enthusiastically from behind his thick mustache, as if he'd somehow been validated by this revelation. The woman looked embarrassed. "*Vai,*" she said to him, nodding toward the train. He hoisted my suitcase up into the cabin and skittered back to her side.

"*In bocca al lupo,*" she said to me, grabbing her husband's arm. I knew this expression from Magister Rizzi, who'd said it to us every time we were about to take a Latin exam.

"*Grazie,*" I said. "*E grazie per l'aiuto.*"

"*Crepi il lupo,*" the man corrected me. "*Si dice 'crepi il lupo.'*"

"Ah, okay," I replied. I knew *lupo* was wolf, but I had no idea what *crepi* meant.

Now, in the kitchen at the palazzo, I turned to Pietro. "What does *crepi il lupo* mean?"

"It means, *practicamente*—" He considered his response. "Let's hope the wolf dies."

"Huh," Martha said, frowning somewhat. "Never knew that."

I processed this. "In the mouth of the wolf" is the call; "may the wolf die" is the response. Later I looked up *crepi* in my Italian-to-English dictionary. It's subjunctive, from *crepare,* a verb that means, colloquially, "to keel over." The wolf isn't going to release you, you're not going to actively escape; the wolf would literally have to croak in order for you to make it out alive.

THE EXCAVATION SITE WAS THREE kilometers uphill from the outer edge of Orbagne and accessed by a gravel road that narrowed as it gave way to a forest, which thickened as the road inclined. On that first morning trek, I lost my breath almost immediately. The air warmed rapidly, and by the time Simone and I reached the dig site, I was drenched in sweat.

Back in our room, Simone had evaluated my footwear—an Herbal Essences–soaked pair of Nikes I'd had since eighth grade—and frowned. "A nail would go right through those soles," she said, handing over her backup work boots, which were too big for me. Within ten minutes, I'd felt the skin on my heels start to scrape off.

We finished our ascent and passed through a copse of pines and into a shaded clearing. Light flickered from above, but when I looked up and around, I could only see oblique patches of open sky through tree branches.

I spotted Cyrille. He was wearing a tool belt that contained a trowel with a bone-white handle, a small pickax, a paintbrush, and a magnifying glass. Pietro was bent down on one knee next to him, bouncing and nodding. The rest of the guys from breakfast sat cross-legged in a cluster in front of them.

"Half of them are Cyrille's students from Lyon, and the others are Pietro's contingent from the University of Turin," Simone had told me on the walk up to the site.

"Huh," I'd breathed out heavily, looking over at her. She wasn't winded at all.

"So you took a class with Cyrille or something?"

"Uh-huh," I said.

"My advisor knew about the dig. That's how I ended up here."

I managed a nod.

"So you probably already know about the papyrology thing," she said.

"No," I said breathlessly.

"Really? You never heard about how they found the site?"

I thought about it. In class, Cyrille had only talked about the site itself—its strategic location on a hill outside Aosta along the Little

St. Bernard Pass. He'd said nothing about the specifics of how he'd discovered it—or if he had, I'd missed it. "No," I repeated.

"So *my* advisor—well, she's not my advisor anymore because I graduated, obviously—she's a papyrus specialist. She's a big deal. She's actually leaving Mount Holyoke for a museum job." Simone glanced at me, and I tried to look impressed.

"I guess Cyrille was still a doctoral student in Lyon when he heard her give a paper at an archeology conference where she talked about a trove of papyrus receipts that she connected to an epithalamium by some poet in Alexandria."

"What's an epithalamium?"

"A wedding poem, basically. Invoking *Venus*, not Aphrodite, so it must have been for a Roman couple."

"But what does that have to do with the location of the site?"

"Oh right. So the receipts were for a bunch of stuff going to a villa in Augusta Praetoria. Wedding gifts, my advisor said. Porphyry, herbs, some kind of perfume. They were in an ancient Egyptian trash heap. The receipts, I mean. This was for a book she was writing about trade between Alexandria and Rome."

"Wow," I said, pausing to catch my breath.

Simone walked ahead and called back, "Kind of a big deal, right? So I guess Cyrille had already had this hunch about a Roman villa in this area, kind of like that place in Sicily, Piazza Armerina. The one with the girls in bikinis."

I recalled a set of slides Cyrille had shown us in his seminar, visual reference points for what his site might look like when fully excavated. In an image of a floor mosaic, a group of women were wearing bandeaus and underwear as they exercised with balls and weights.

Simone continued: "And then Cyrille started asking around the towns near Aosta, knowing that he'd never be able to get a permit to survey without an Italian counterpart. He came to Orbagne and happened to meet Pietro. And the rest is history."

"Wait," I said, clutching my side as surreptitiously as possible. "But how did they know—it was—here? Like, in this spot?"

Simone stopped, waited for me to catch up with her, then pointed downhill to the right of where we stood. "The Romans planted that vineyard."

I regarded the clusters of grapes emerging from the rocky soil, camouflaged by the wildness of their context. If Simone hadn't said anything, I don't know if I would have noticed the cascade of overgrown vines in irregular rows stretching into the distance. But now that I saw the vineyard, I couldn't unsee it. "Pietro grew up there. It belongs to his family," Simone added.

"So Pietro knew the Romans were here before he met Cyrille?"

Simone nodded. "Martha said they grow one of the oldest and rarest grape varietals in the world. Oh, and you see that little chapel over there?"

I followed Simone's gaze to a small stone building with an A-frame wood roof, a white cross at its apex.

"*Apparently* Mary Magdalene stopped here on her way to France. That's why their main wine is called La Madeleine. And some of her relics are in there, or used to be. Very Dan Brown, right?"

I was less captivated by Mary Magdalene than the rest of the world, even though I'd read the *Da Vinci Code* the year before like everyone else. I liked the idea that Constantine had excised the Gnostic Gospels in favor of the New Testament as a political strategy, even though it wasn't consistent with what I was learning in the Byzantine history class I was taking at the time. Constantine had worshipped Apollo publicly until at least 324, as indicated by the *sol invictus* coins that had been issued throughout the empire until then. His conversion to Christianity may have been politically motivated, but only in the sense that his various religious allegiances justified his military victories. Also, the empire was too vast and fractured in the fourth century, my professor contended, for

Christianity to have spiked as rapidly and decisively as the modern church wanted us to believe.

"And Cyrille had apparently already known that the villa he was looking for was along the Little St. Bernard Pass," she continued. "I guess it was just serendipity that he met Pietro, who was finishing his doctorate in archeology in Torino. Pietro's dad knows people at the Italian committee on cultural heritage or whatever—whoever gives out permits to archeologists. He's some politician."

My mind turned to Cyrille's story of the looting from a few months prior. I wanted to ask Simone whether she knew about the whole debacle and, if so, whether she had any guesses as to what they might have taken. But she launched into a speech about the pros and cons of carbon-dating papyrus—a pro being that it enabled you to authenticate something ancient, a con being that the date range was often too wide to be useful—and I nodded along until we reached the clearing.

Now we sat down with the rest of the guys. Cyrille was talking about the layout of the villa, which he stressed was no normal country estate; it had been built as a grand working farm and likely housed several generations of a family and hundreds of enslaved people. Its gardens had contained fruit trees—apple, quince, and pomegranate, as indicated by dozens of carbon-dated seeds—and an abundance of valuable indigenous herbs. The farm's yields were valuable Roman exports, and the family who lived here was likely among the wealthiest in the Empire. As he talked, I recognized vocabulary words from the time in high school Latin when we'd had to label the floorplan of a *villa rustica* with terms like *cubiculum, atrium, triclinium,* and *balenium.*

What Cyrille was describing was exciting, but it was a major departure from what I could see with my eyes. I guess I had been expecting grandeur of some sort, but looking around, there were just some rocky crenellations and a grid of trenches backfilled with wet dirt. I didn't see any porphyry anywhere. There was only the fluorescent pink of twine tied to stakes in the ground demarcating individual trenches.

I thought about the slides Cyrille had shown us in his seminar, the cleaned and catalogued artifacts that had been handed over to the regional archeological museum in Aosta: a lapis intaglio ring, an orange-yellow glass bowl, a gold bulla that would have held up a boy's toga. It seemed impossible that such delicate and precious things had been discovered here.

Eventually we were assigned our trenches for the week, and we set to work removing backfill. In my trench—where three French students smiled and nodded politely but didn't say a word directly to me—this entailed shoveling dirt into a wheelbarrow, pushing it up a narrow path, and dumping it in a pile that grew over the course of that first week into a full-on knoll. By Friday, there were angry red blisters on my hands and feet. I didn't mind. At night I fell asleep easily. I was happy to have something so tangibly external to focus on.

ON SATURDAY, SIMONE, MARTHA, AND I went to dinner at the café in the bed-and-breakfast down the street from the palazzo. We sat at an outdoor picnic table and nodded gratefully at the *nonna* who brought us plates of prosciutto, rye bread with lard, and slices of polenta loaf.

Martha, who had been in Orbagne since May after completing a master's in gastronomy at the University of Parma, explained that the bed-and-breakfast mostly housed rock climbers and hikers. This was substantiated by the French couple at the table next to us wearing dongled-out harnesses. She said that the handful of locals in Orbagne bought most of what they needed from the little grocer I had initially mistaken for a fruit stand, and that the bar sold beer and liqueur in addition to espresso starting in the afternoon. There was a single five-table restaurant housed in a stone domicile near the church.

It occurred to me then that Cyrille had only dined with us at the palazzo one time that first week. I'd tried not to say too much when he asked how I was doing. I didn't want to accidentally mention that I hadn't grasped that the dig would involve so much literal digging—that I'd envisioned myself dusting things off gently, maybe crouching down and troweling from time to time. That I had definitely *not* pictured myself pushing wheelbarrows full of dirt and detritus up a hill.

The *nonna* brought us a carafe of the house red, produced at Pietro's family vineyard, along with three jam jars.

"This wine was more popular than Barolo before World War Two," Martha told us as she poured.

The wine was translucent red with white bubbles and tasted to me the way wet rocks smell. But I didn't say that aloud because Martha seemed like an expert, and this was my first sip of wine. Neither of my parents were drinkers—I hadn't grown up around it. I'd had plenty of beer, even a Negroni once at a grad student party I'd attended with Lakshmi, but never wine.

"What happened in World War Two?" Simone asked. "Besides the obvious, I mean."

"Probably something similar to Burgundy. I'm guessing they couldn't get copper to make copper sulfate after the Germans confiscated all the metals in France."

Simone leaned forward at this. "What did they use copper sulfate for?"

Martha shrugged. "Pesticide, I guess? I know they treated the wine with it. Burgundy came back, obviously, and so did Barolo—but I think Pietro's vineyard is one of the only ones in the Aosta Valley that really recovered."

I felt warm and relaxed in the cool alpine air, a jean jacket draped over my shoulders, and I let my eyes wander past Simone and Martha as they kept talking about wine to the road behind them, cobbled with stones that threatened the tires of the little cars that navigated the same roads the Salassi had once governed. There was such a purity to things—every edifice had a patina, but nothing looked dirty. And I registered, in that clean air that smelled like nothing, that I never wanted to go home, whatever home was. I guess in a sense I felt, for the first time, like I *was* home, surrounded by all that history, the ghosts of everyone who'd ever shared this exact view of the mountains at twilight.

The sound of snapping rubber bands prompted me to examine the windshield of a familiar silver car. It was the same man I'd seen from my window the first morning in Orbagne, pulling into a parking spot next to the church. Simone turned around, following my gaze.

"What's *this* guy's deal?" she asked me. I shrugged. She went back to talking about the problem with the way artifacts from the site were being catalogued. "They have no *system,*" she was saying. "They're just taking photos and uploading them to some random computer. It's really bizarre. And they have no inventory code! Even a pottery shard needs its own inventory number with letters *and* numbers. Like that one I found today; it smelled distinctly of *merum.* I want to get it to the lab, but—"

She kept talking as I watched the man from the car, who appeared to be headed in our direction. He was in a gray T-shirt, and his copper hair was wavy and loose instead of combed back, the way it had been on that first morning. Our eyes met, or at least I thought they did, and a moment later he was in front of our table. I could smell him, cigarettes and cedar, and some other unnameable human essence. "I heard you speaking English," he said.

Simone and Martha just stared. "Yes," I said reflexively. "We're from the US."

He broke into a smile. "It's nice to hear American English. I'm working on my PhD in New York."

"Where?" I asked. "And in what?" Simone and Martha were glaring at me, but I didn't care.

"At Columbia. Art history," he said.

I stared at him, trying to square the surprising revelation that we studied at the same university with his physical appearance. There was something familiar about him—and by that I mean he had that vague recognizable quality of a person who is instantly attractive—but I'd never set foot in the Art History Department at Columbia. I didn't like looking at simulacra of art, which is what I understood art history to be—a dark room with a projector illuminating specters of the real thing.

"Anyway, I'm sorry to interrupt your dinner," he said, rubbing the back of his neck. "Have a good night."

His legs were so long that within a few seconds he was several yards away from the table.

Without consulting Simone or Martha, I got up to follow him. What made me do this, I don't know. It felt very much out of my control, like pulling your hand away from a hot surface.

When I caught up with him, there might have been a trace of relief on his face. "I saw you in the window," he said.

I smiled. "Those kids love you, huh?"

"They're refugees," he said. "From Albania. I try to bring them *regalini* from Torino. I come back and forth."

"What's here?" I asked.

"My parents have a summer place. It's a big empty house that never gets any use, so I come on the weekends. I still have friends here who never left."

He didn't break eye contact. And as I looked at his face—his square jaw, the dimple in his chin, the freckles on his lips—I wanted to know everything. About those childhood summers, about his parents, about the friends who'd never left Orbagne.

"I'm picking up my friend," he said, gesturing to the row of buildings beyond the bed-and-breakfast. "For the *festa del prosciutto.*" He raised his eyebrows, maybe inviting a comment or a critique. But I took it another way, and I stood there, still nodding, not wanting our exchange to end. I kept looking at his face, noticing now the bald slash in his left eyebrow, the freckles along his hairline. He was the tallest person I'd ever met. When I looked back at the table, Simone and Martha were staring openly at us.

HIS NAME WAS GIAMMA, short for Gian Maria. "It's a difficult name when you grow up in the north," he told me that night. His father was from Reggio Calabria. He looked like he wanted to tell me where his mother was from, too, so I asked him. "New York," he said.

"So you're half-American?"

"She's Italian."

He didn't elaborate, so to fill the silence I volunteered that my mother was German and my father was Irish. He nodded politely and didn't ask me anything about them, which I appreciated.

Giamma's friend was a compact and jocular twentysomething named Marco. His family owned the bed-and-breakfast and had been in Orbagne for generations. He was next in line to run it.

"I told my parents, we need to turn this into a youth hostel!!" Marco exclaimed, gesticulating wildly with his hands. "We need to take advantage. While there are archeologists here every year."

This was on the way to Saint-Marcel, from the minuscule back seat of Giamma's Porsche. Marco leaned forward, gauging my reaction to his theory, his elbows on the shoulders of the two front seats.

"If the site ends up being what my professor thinks it is, the archeologists will be around for a long time, and you'll have tons of tourists," I said, by way of a response.

"So maybe we expand *and* convert some of the rooms to dorms," he mused.

"You're here in the winters, right?" I asked him, identifying an opportunity to gather information. "What happened when the site got looted?"

Marco rolled his eyes. "A disaster." And he explained how the Carabinieri TPC had descended onto the town, the Monza and Torino offices fighting over who would handle the case. "The one thing I know is that Italians are not stupid enough to dig holes like that. I told that to the officers." The officers had interrogated Marco and his family about guests they'd had who could have been connected to the crime. "We told them everything we knew. I hope they find the crooks, I really do. My money is on the Albanians. Those guys are desperate."

I only thought of it later, as I was recounting this whole thing to Simone, that Giamma hadn't said anything; he'd just stared ahead at the mountain-engulfed roads, black against the navy sky, the stars like little pin lights poking through, no moon.

When I tiptoed into our bedroom at dawn, Simone sat straight up in bed. "What the hell, Lena?"

"Sorry," I whispered, stepping out of my Dansko sandals and climbing under my sheets. But I wasn't sorry. I was the happiest I'd ever been in my short life.

I told her about the towers of prosciutto in Saint-Marcel and Marco's plan to expand the bed-and-breakfast. But I didn't tell her everything, about the light that triggered on in Giamma's glove compartment after we dropped Marco off, the way it bounced off the gray metal of an object I'd only ever understood in a semiotic sense: pioneers living on a savage frontier, citizens rebelling against the tyranny of government. It couldn't have been anything other than a gun, and yet I didn't connect with it literally, barely even processed what it represented—death, violence, force; but also, protection.

My mind wouldn't—and couldn't—have gone there, because my body had taken over, and I was making my way through some sort of narrow canal, neither descending or ascending, just pushing instinctively toward sound and light, the logistics of physically navigating that little space the furthest thing from my mind. When Giamma kissed me, I remembered all the times I'd been convinced that Magister Rizzi wanted to kiss me, and how he never had; how I would lie in bed at home on school nights, practically exploding with desire, the way it was such a relief to finally locate the source of that feeling in my body. And so when Giamma reached for a condom in the glove compartment, I could only feel his warmth blurring into mine, a rush of adrenaline as he undressed me, and an overwhelming sense of safety. I hadn't been nervous or fearful—yielding control of my mind to my body had made me into a placid version of myself that I'd never known. When it was over, we kissed for several long minutes, and I breathed deeply for the first time in what felt like years.

"I'll take care of you," he telegraphed to me as I climbed out of the car. Through the open passenger window, he handed me a night-dark BlackBerry.

VI.

MARCH 12, 2022

NEW YORK CITY

Having spent every window of my free time this past week on the policy docs Emmanuel assigned to me, I call Lakshmi on Saturday morning and give her the broad strokes of the case. She agrees to come with me to the Met to look at the dichroic glass fragment Caroline mentioned at our meeting on Monday.

In the Great Hall, two enormous vases of lilacs frame the front staircase. Lakshmi's firm has a corporate membership—she shows her work ID to the man behind the ticket desk, who hands us two *M* stickers.

I haven't been to the Met since college; I almost never come to the Upper East Side. But I feel calmly attentive as we wander through a light-filled indoor courtyard, trying to let my eyes slide over freestanding sculptures without focusing too much on the fact that they've been bleached into oblivion by ignorant Victorian-era conservators—a fact I learned from an old Christopher Hitchens essay on the Elgin Marbles in the Fordham case file.

We locate the dichroic glass fragment in a dark gallery off the far end of the sculpture courtyard. It's underwhelming compared to the Cupid and Psyche cup, mostly because of its poor condition. I can understand now why Caroline said it looks like it was looted, but still, I study the half figure protruding from the glass scrap's surface in fascination. A satyr, or possibly Dionysus, the label says. I scan the rest of the text, which describes dichroic cage cups as the rarest variant of luxury glassware produced in Ancient Rome. This one is a pale brown that appears olive green in reflected light. It dates to the third or fourth century CE, same as the Cupid and Psyche cup.

The fragment is brown right now. But where is the light coming from? I look around and above me, noticing the track lights in the ceiling. I turn back to the case. Nothing—not the track lights, not my face, not Lakshmi's face—is reflected in the glass. Intellectually, I know that there is actual glass separating me from the fragment, but my hand reaches out to confirm what I think I know. Hand pressing against this cold barrier, my eye catches on a minuscule CREON logo at the edge of the interior of the glass case.

"You okay?" Lakshmi asks.

I shine my phone's flashlight at the case, dismayed that I can't get the fragment to deviate in any way from pale brown. The glass case must be doing something to filter out the light. "How did they know this was Bacchus?" I ask.

"They're calling it a satyr," Lakshmi says, referencing the label. "*Possibly* Bacchus. But see the thyrsus?" She indicates the mottled staff the figure is grasping in his hand.

"I forget what that is."

"It's like a wand made of fennel or something. Sometimes there's other stuff wrapped around it, vines, grapes. Usually there's a pine cone on top. It's associated with Bacchus."

"How do you remember that?"

"It says it right here, see? Thyrsus."

I smile and shake my head. Of course Lakshmi has retained the details of Bacchus's iconography. "Never mind."

Then it occurs to me—there are vines on the Cupid and Psyche cup too. The label at Fordham said that it was likely used in religious ceremonies as a vessel for wine. I procure Caroline's postcard from my bag so I can look for a thyrsus, or some other evidence of Bacchus. But I notice something else instead: a border of hand-shaped leaves looping along the top and bottom edges of the cup.

"I think I saw these exact garlands in there," I tell her, nodding toward the atrium.

A minute later we're standing in front of a sarcophagus that features the same leaves as the cup—oak leaves, I learn when I consult the label. I'm flooded with validation as I scan the rest of the text and process that the subject of the sarcophagus is Cupid and Psyche. On the left side, Cupid pierces Psyche with an arrow; on the right side, a dove watches them embrace. I show Caroline's postcard to Lakshmi. "Look," I say. "The garlands are really similar, right? The cup just doesn't have these pine cone things."

Lakshmi looks back and forth from the postcard to the sarcophagus.

"Are they pine cones or are they grapes?" she asks, squinting.

She's right—pine cones come from pine trees, not oak trees. They must be grapes. I scan for other similarities between the cup and the sarcophagus, but apart from the fact that both works feature oak garlands and Cupid and Psyche, they have no other visual similarities.

My mind turns back to the Bacchus fragment. "The Fordham curator said the cup's condition was too good to have been looted. But the thing is, looters could 'loot' from a crypt, or even a museum. Right? Like the looting of the Baghdad Museum, remember? The prosecution just needs to prove it was in Italy."

"Didn't you say they had proof it was there?"

"Switzerland. But the guy who had it was arrested for dealing in looted antiquities. He was Italian."

Lakshmi considers this. "They must have more evidence," she says. "By the way," she adds, lowering her voice, "one of the women in my case was talking to me the other day about the 'artifacts.' She told me that for a while the Islamic State was using antiquities from Libya to pay the 'ndrangheta for weapons. The 'ndrangheta turns around and uses the antiquities as collateral. It's a vicious cycle. And they try to sell this stuff too. I guess a few years ago a journalist from Turin posed as a collector in a group on Facebook and set up a meeting with an 'ndrangheta guy, who offered him some looted statue."

"Wait." My heart is beating in my ears.

Lakshmi looks at me with alarm. "Yeah?"

"Why did you tell me that?" I ask, reeling from the hunch that something important is being revealed to me too late.

"I thought you'd find it interesting," she says slowly. "It's not privileged information or anything. You can google it."

"Sorry," I say, confused as to why Lakshmi's mention of an Italian journalist is making me feel like this. I start walking, grasping for a rationale. "It's just—the donor from the Fordham case has a gallery in Turin," I say. "They make museum glass. They made all these cases."

"I'm talking about an undercover journalist."

I have a sudden flash of the art-filled rooms at Giamma's family's summer house in Orbagne. The bronzes, the tapestries, the oil paintings in gold frames. A memory is pushing through, but it's like trying to remember a dream—I can only grasp pieces of it. There's a crate; a man who doesn't speak English is wedging it open in front of me. Then an image of a thick envelope in my hands. Suddenly I feel lightheaded, because I understand now—not fully, but abstractly—what Giamma meant when he told me to be careful. Filippo Dalmasso could have been buying artifacts illegally, not just from some crooked dealer, but directly from the 'ndrangheta.

"Lena, are you okay?" Lakshmi says. "You look pale."

I clear my throat. "Do they have a café or something?"

We consult a museum map and walk toward a coffee stand. Lakshmi orders us croissants and lattes and we sit down at a round white table. I try to ignore my racing pulse and ask her if she's excited about the trip to Spain.

"Remember that movie we saw at the Angelika forever ago?" she asks, looking slightly uncomfortable. "The Chilean one about the guy with the bonsai trees? I think it was actually called *Bonsai*."

I don't remember. "I probably fell asleep," I say, watching her fidget with the pop socket on the back of her phone.

"On my way home I passed a plant store and bought Iñigo a bonsai tree. You know, to symbolize our love or whatever, like in the movie."

I stir sugar into my coffee. "Okay."

Lakshmi pushes her phone away and sighs. "I'm not going to Spain," she says. "I haven't told him yet, but I'm not going."

"Work stuff?" I ask.

"He let it die, Lena. The tree. Less than a week."

I can see that Lakshmi is upset, and I agree it's upsetting that he let the tree die, but I can't figure out what this has to do with skipping the trip to Spain.

"Things are not good between us," Lakshmi clarifies, this time without emotion.

I nod, because it won't do anything to point out what was obvious to me the other night at their new place—her tone, his hunched shoulders, the general vapors of discord.

"Maybe it'll be good to have some space?"

"When he leaves, I'm moving out," she says.

I stop chewing my croissant and try to get control of my face, which I can feel is twisting into an expression that could easily be interpreted as judgmental. Consciously, I don't judge Lakshmi. But she's been with Iñigo for almost as long as I've known her—since the summer we were in Italy—and it's hard for me to imagine how she'll backfill her life in his absence. Also, I'm wondering how long ago she made up her mind.

"I got a transfer to the London office. It's a step up. And when they told me, this strange thing happened. I just wanted it for myself. I wanted *something* for myself. Iñigo, I mean—it's been different ever since he made all that money. Instead of working less, he works more, and I don't know if he's changed, or if my perception of him has changed, or if my perception of *myself* has changed, but—he'll never leave. He can be miserable and stay. I can't."

I nod and attempt to mirror the matter-of-fact expression on her face. "London, wow," is all I decide to say.

I'm aware that it's ridiculous to think of myself, that I won't be able to call Lakshmi in the middle of the day or go to her apartment for dinner, that I already feel deserted.

"I'm sorry I didn't tell you earlier," she says, seemingly reading my mind, or maybe just my face, because I can feel that now I've lost control of it. "I truly didn't know if I'd be able to even go through with it until yesterday."

"I'm—happy for you," I say, as tears pool in my eyes.

She reaches across the table for my hand and squeezes it. "You're the first person I've told."

When our eyes meet, I try to force a smile, but I can't do it. I'm relieved to be her primary confidante, but that relief doesn't cancel out the painful reality that she is leaving me.

"Speaking of telling," I say, taking in a deep breath. I pause, and then tell her about encountering Giamma at the Fordham opening on Monday. I tell her about how he sits on the museum's collections committee, and how he's a member of Caroline's Curator's Circle.

Lakshmi listens without interrupting me. When I finish, she nods slowly. "Giamma is the Calabrian guy, right?" she asks.

I stare at her incredulously, then remember that earlier this week I mentioned him in the context of *her* case. "Yes, and I've always thought he knows more about the dig in Orbagne than he ever admitted to me." I drop my voice down to a whisper. "What if he had something to do with the looting?"

"So you're saying, what—that Cyrille was somehow involved with the black market or something?"

That hadn't actually occurred to me. I close my eyes, trying to come up with a linear articulation of the theory that's taken root in my mind. I hesitate, then push forward. "Okay, so the site was looted. Cyrille told us in March, I think. Sophomore year. There was still snow on the ground in New York. And then that summer, my roommate at the dig, who you never met—overheard a conversation about the looting between the Italian dig director and Cyrille. And when I asked Giamma about it back then, he just—I know he knew something."

I regard Lakshmi expectantly, but her face is blank. "The conservator who repaired the Fordham cup, here in New York—that was my roommate in Orbagne."

Lakshmi puts her phone face down on the table. "Seriously?"

"I'm trying to figure all of this out—but Lakshmi, I don't think it was random that I got put on this case."

"What do you mean?"

I draw in a deep breath and decide to go ahead and just say it. "Cyrille's Italian co-director, this guy Pietro—his dad is a senator. I think he might be behind the restitution request."

Lakshmi processes this. "Sweetie. I want to say this nicely—"

I lean away from the table, and her face changes, as if she's just realizing something. "Hey," she says gently. "It's totally possible. It's all possible."

I decide, maybe because I desperately want to be understood by her, that she's being sincere. "Thank you," I say.

We sit in silence for a while, and when Lakshmi picks her phone back up, I stand abruptly. "Can we get out of here? This smell is making me nauseous."

"What smell?"

"It smells like burnt coffee in here."

"It does?" Lakshmi asks. She's still sitting down, scrolling. "Just give me a sec."

I feel a wave of despair—this is the smell of my childhood home, a place where I always felt powerless. "Seriously, I need to go. It's making me sick."

Lakshmi stashes her phone in her purse and pushes back her chair. "I honestly don't smell anything, Lena."

We walk back toward Art of the Ancient World, but my stomach continues to churn. "I think I just need to go home."

"Sure," Lakshmi says.

When we exit the museum and walk down the front stairs, Lakshmi suggests we walk over to Madison to grab a cab.

"I want to walk through the park," I say.

"I'll walk with you."

"I don't really feel like talking, though."

Lakshmi shrugs, and we walk in silence toward the exit. I think about the Afrofuturism period room we peeked into on our way to the café, an imagined simulacrum of a house from Seneca Village, the nineteenth-century settlement of Black landowners that was seized and leveled by the city in order to build Central Park. There are still patches of snow along the path we're walking, and I try to picture the homes and churches of Seneca Village among them. But I can only think of all the knickknacks in the period room—the "house"—and how, according to the wall label, the curator who designed the room rejected the notion of one historical period because of her belief that the past, present, and future are interconnected. Informed speculation, the label said, can illuminate many possibilities. I keep turning that sentence over in my head as we walk: *informed speculation can illuminate many possibilities.*

"Are you feeling better?" Lakshmi asks when we get to Eighty-First Street.

I nod. "Just needed some fresh air."

She hails a cab, and I get in with her. When I walk into my apartment a half hour later, I sit down on my couch, a low mid-century sectional I found online a few years ago, and stare at my framed poster of *The Feast of Achelous.* In college I visited the original at the Met at least once a month; I should have gone to see it today. Every time I look at it I notice something new: a shell in the lining of the cave walls; a detail in one of the ancient vessels on the ground; a new facial expression on one of the figures facing Achelous the river god, who gestures to the water where his lover Perimele has been turned into an island by Neptune so he can hold her in an eternal embrace. Now I notice the leaves on the big tree at the left side of the painting—they're oak leaves, just like on the Cupid and Psyche cup.

I wander into the kitchen and open my fridge, which is empty except for a bag of slimy spinach, a block of blue-tinged parmesan, and a door full of old condiments. Then I stand in front of the kitchen window, which looks out onto PS 33 on Ninth Avenue. Sometimes I see parents dropping off their kids on my walk to work, which triggers a tender feeling that invariably gives way to a painful ache. It was always Jinny who walked me to my line at our elementary school every morning before getting in hers. I have no memory of any adult ever dropping us off or picking us up.

My phone rings. It's Jinny. The synchronicity startles me, and I silence the call.

In my room, the bed is unmade. I crawl in under the covers and stare up at the ceiling, thinking about Giamma, and Caroline, and the Cupid and Psyche cup. The main thing looping in my mind from the Cupid and Psyche myth is how everything changed when Psyche got pregnant. That was when she started to get nervous about the fact that she'd never seen her lover's face. If she hadn't gotten pregnant, her sisters never would have pressured her to bring that torch in and look at Cupid when he'd explicitly told her not to, and she never would have had to go through all of those trials and tribulations at Venus's jealous hands. I was so unsatisfied with the ending, when she makes it out alive and marries Cupid just in time for their baby to be born. After all that suffering, it was a total Pyrrhic victory. Psyche is supposed to represent the anguish and triumph of the soul, but if not for the pregnancy, she never would have had to suffer. No one would have had to suffer.

VII.

JUNE 14, 2004

ORBAGNE

"I figured out what to do about the cataloguing system," Simone told me Monday morning on our walk up to the site, our shadows hovering ahead of us.

I looked over at her. "Oh yeah?" By some miracle, the blisters on my heels had healed, and I was nearly matching her pace.

"So we're looking for evidence of the Augustan Age Romans—obviously—also, anyone who may have inhabited the site in the late Roman era. Have you ever heard of Melania the Younger? Apparently, Pietro thinks it was a family like that—maybe even *her* family—who expanded the villa . . ."

I tuned out, thinking about the messages Giamma had sent me on the BlackBerry that morning, which I'd read while Simone was in the bathroom. One, a line from *La Vita Nuova,* roughly translated to: "I have set foot in that region of life where it is not possible to go with any more intention of returning."

If quoting Dante was some kind of move, some manipulation, I never would have known, because I was reeling from the validation of requited infatuation. This was probably what drew me most to Giamma, at least initially—being desired by him based on whatever assumptions he was making. He hardly knew anything about me, but he was echoing back my own intensity. It was being wanted physically, possibly for my looks, that moved me the most after a year of feeling invisible at Columbia. I liked Giamma, but more than that, I liked who I was to him. We barely knew each other, but he didn't question that he was drawn to me, the same way I hadn't questioned his gravitational pull.

The day after our first night together, Giamma had brought me to *pranzo* at Orbagne's small restaurant in the building next to the church. All six tables were occupied when we arrived, so the owner, a friend of Giamma's family, led us upstairs to his own kitchen table. We took small sips of water while we waited for our *primi* and watched each other, alone in the apartment, hearing only intermittent sounds from the street outside. It was easy to be around Giamma, and when he reached across the table for my hand, I felt myself beaming, unable to disguise my happiness.

Giamma told me that he was leaving early the next morning for Torino, and that he'd be back the following Friday. "So we'll see each other then?" I asked, and he nodded, pulling my chair over to his and tucking my hair behind my ears. We kissed slowly, for a long time, and his hands were just starting to inch up under the hem of my dress—a sleeveless collared one I'd thrifted in New York a few months prior—when we were interrupted by the owner of the restaurant, who had brought two shallow bowls of gnocchi and a bottle of white wine. "*Scusa,*" he said, his face reddening.

We apologized and straightened up, but kept our chairs close together as we alternated between gnocchi and wine. For me, this sense of mutually felt ease, of being in sync, was superior to what I'd previously known in any relationship. Only family members had ever expressed love to me, and with the exception of Jinny, it always rang somehow false, because it usually came after they had done something wrong.

"I'm gonna run this by them," Simone said now, jogging to catch up with Cyrille and Pietro, who were a few meters ahead of us.

We were still on the straight part of the gravelly road that led to the site, and Cyrille slowed his pace to walk with me. His tool belt clanked with each step, and I felt a warmth emanating from his bare arms. "*Ça va?*" he asked.

"Pretty good," I said, wondering if he knew about Giamma, if he could tell that something was different with me.

"What do you think of all this," he said, nodding up toward the hill ahead. "Are you happy to have come?"

"Yes," I said honestly. "But it's different than I thought it would be."

He nodded thoughtfully. "I understand."

We walked in silence for a few minutes.

"My parents own a small market in Dijon, where I grew up," he offered. "And from when I was this tall"—he motioned to his waist—"I would work there after school, and in the summers. It was dull, very dull. But we had a magazine stand, and we kept in stock a few comic books. The best ones were about two Gauls, Asterix et Obelix, who fight against the Romans in the time of Julius Caesar. I read them over and over."

I raised my eyebrows, intrigued by this unsolicited glimpse into Cyrille's childhood.

He kept going. "In the comic, the advantage the Gauls have over the Romans is their magic potion, brewed by a Druid priest. It gives them their superhuman strength. I think this is where I got the idea to do archeology. When I read *Natural History,* Pliny described the exact same rites from Asterix. The priest, wearing a white robe, uses a golden sickle to cut the mistletoe, which is then used to make an antidote for all poisons."

I laughed. "So you thought Asterix was real?"

"I wanted to find evidence, evidence there was really a magic potion. On weekends I would go to the antiques market in Dijon, looking for a vessel that might have held such a potion."

"Did you find one?"

He shrugged. "I was young. But I believe here in Orbagne there is magic, in a sense. Magic that predates the Romans, and maybe also the Salassi. Though I imagine the Romans would have considered it to be a place blessed by the gods. By Venus."

"Why Venus?"

"The orchards. The apples. Their products were marketed as *sacré*, maybe. Because wherever they were getting their water from is not clear."

I thought back to when we'd talked about Claudius draining the Fucine Lake to bring water to Rome, and how the majority of aqueducts were underground.

"You think there's a hidden water source here?"

His eyes shone. "You are in the right place. I promise. You can believe me when I say that we are at the beginning. There is still so much to discover."

I WAS ASSIGNED TO A trench in the far west corner of the north wing, an area that according to Cyrille's estimation had most likely been a courtyard housing various fruit trees from throughout the Roman empire.

Simone told me on our midmorning break that Pietro was supportive of her cataloguing plan, and that he'd instructed her to start managing the dig's context sheets. Once the system was formalized, she'd transition to cataloguing full-time. Seeing the disappointment in my face, she hurried to add that she'd still be up at the site some mornings.

"Pietro seemed really excited about my new system," Simone continued. "He said it was *molto* innovative."

"Of course it is," I said.

"I already started sending things to the lab. Oh," Simone said, nodding up. Pietro had climbed up on top of a bench and was clapping to get our attention.

"*Oi, tutti,*" he called out. The room quieted down. I looked over at Cyrille, who was leaning on the table with his elbows, watching Pietro.

"Welcome to week two," Pietro said. "When the real fun begins." Everyone clapped. I hadn't ever seen Pietro look that animated, and the more we clapped, the more he lit up. I saw him glance over at Cyrille, who nodded curtly. "The wheelbarrows have been full for a week, it's been hard work, but you've all helped us get to this point."

I looked over at the Frenchies, as Simone and I had started calling them—the five male students from Cyrille's home university in Lyon who spoke in hushed tones and mostly kept to themselves. I had barely learned their names, keeping my eyes down as I exited or entered the bathroom, where at least one of them was always inevitably waiting for his turn. Now they were nodding vigorously, clinking their cups of water.

"This week will be important because we will—*magari*—start to uncover some of the key features of the site. And I am happy to share that we will have a visitor as well, a journalist from *Correiere della sera.* He will join us at the site tomorrow."

I looked over at Simone, who shrugged back at me.

"There is a lot of interest in this site," Pietro said. "And I hope you will help us share it with the world. Signore Valenti, the writer, may want to speak with you at a certain point, and those conversations of course are permitted, but we—Cyrille *ed io*—should be present for any interviews."

We nodded and blinked at him. "And that's it!" he concluded. "Anyone who is coming to the café tonight can meet outside at seven." Pietro stepped off the bench and returned to his seat, looking satisfied with himself.

Pietro had devised a sign-up system for the internet café one town over. His BMW hatchback could fit five of us, and the plan was to go twice a week, on Mondays and Wednesdays. I'd signed up right away because I needed to check for an email from Lakshmi, who had offered to research the best way for me to get down to Sicily for a visit.

At the end of the meal we piled into the car, and to my surprise—no one at the dig had treated me like I was deserving of any kind of special treatment thus far—the Frenchies offered me the front seat. Pietro's car was a stick shift, and as I buckled my seat belt, I noticed his white knuckles on the clutch and the way he sat up straight in his seat, glancing repeatedly in the rearview mirror. Once we were on the road, he handed me a black leather portfolio of CDs.

"Choose one," he commanded.

I flipped through pages of meticulously labeled mixes, thinking he must have used one of those fine-tip Sharpies to write the song titles separated by decorative bullet points. "Wow," I said. "You made all of these?"

"You know LimeWire?" he asked. I knew what it was but had never actually used it, because a high school friend of mine had gotten sued by a record company for pirating. Her parents had had to pay something like five thousand dollars to settle the case out of court. I couldn't imagine the scene that would have ensued with my mother if I had asked her to come up with that kind of money.

"I haven't bought music in three years," Pietro said proudly.

Pietro's music collection—it was a lot of Iron Maiden and Megadeth—called to mind a boy from high school whose neighboring locker had been covered with pictures of those bands. I'd been fascinated by his confidence; I couldn't imagine going through high school like that, with black lipstick and a spiky dog collar around my neck. But that night, in Pietro's car, I understood him. He'd elicited so many stares, and yet I never knew what he really looked like. Kind of a genius way to go through the world, hiding yourself in plain sight while simultaneously commanding attention.

I finally found something I recognized, loved even: The Strokes'

"Is This It," which had come out around when I got my driver's license. I slid the CD out of its plastic sleeve and inserted it into the player—I don't think I've ever wanted to hear an album more. But instead of the opening hook of its first song, what came on was the seventh song, "Last Nite."

"Ugh," I breathed, crossing my arms and glaring out the window. My reaction was disproportionate to the situation, but I was disappointed; I couldn't help it.

"What?" Pietro glanced over at me, nodding his head to the beat. The Frenchies were silent in the back.

"The songs are out of order," I said.

"My girlfriend burned this for me," he said defensively. "She organized all my music."

This was an interesting development, the fact of Pietro having a girlfriend. It explained the handwriting on each CD. "That was nice of her," I said.

The rural road we were on was starting to look commercial, with low buildings housing cafés, clothing stores, and the bright green plus sign of a pharmacy. I had no idea what town we were in, but it was significantly bigger than Orbagne.

"I'll tell her next time to check the order of the songs."

This response, for some reason, horrified me. Here was this person—named Benedetta, I later learned—who had selflessly taken the time to organize her boyfriend's ripped-off music collection, and he was going to give her *feedback* on the way she'd done it?

"Oh no, I don't think you should do that," I said, in Benedetta's defense.

This must have come out harsher than I meant it, because he whipped his head to look at me; and his face, in that split second, revealed so much about him—he looked pained and disgusted, as if I had stooped to some low level and kicked him when he was down—when our exchange, at least on its surface, couldn't have been more innocuous. He didn't say anything, and neither did I, but my mind was making silent, uncontrollable calculations. There was something vaguely threatening about Pietro; I felt it in my body.

When we got home at the end of the night, Simone was lounging in bed with her Discman.

I sat at the foot of her bed. "What are you listening to?" I asked her.

"Rachmaninoff," she said.

I told her about Pietro's CD collection.

"Yeah, he has an edge," she said.

"Why do you say that?" I asked.

She took off her headphones and sat up. "I overheard him and Cyrille arguing earlier, before dinner," she whispered.

I scooted closer to her. "About what?"

"Cyrille doesn't want that journalist to come."

"Why not?"

"Pietro said it's a favor to him, but Cyrille said that the site doesn't need any more attention. Because of the looting. Which, by the way, Pietro thinks was no big deal? He just kept saying, 'They didn't take anything else.'"

"*What?*" I hissed, incredulous.

Simone's face lit up at my reaction. "Yeah, and then he started telling Cyrille to be quiet. '*Stai zitto! Stai zitto!*' Like that."

"I knew it," I whispered.

Simone burst out laughing. "You knew what?"

"What else did they say?"

She shrugged. "The rest was in really fast Italian."

"We have to help him. Cyrille. We have to figure out what happened. What did Pietro mean by anything *else*?"

Simone kicked me playfully. "Go to bed, Lena. This isn't whatever soap opera you think it is."

* * *

AT FIVE IN THE MORNING, I woke up and couldn't fall back asleep. I got up and rummaged around in my backpack, then tiptoed down the stairs and took a one-cent euro to the silver wax coating on a calling card.

With the seven-hour time difference, it was just after ten o'clock at night in Wilmette, and Jinny picked up as I was leaving a voicemail.

"How's the proposal going?" I asked her.

When Jinny had applied for her PhD in German Studies, she'd already had an idea for her dissertation, a continuation of my mother's unpublished graduate research. I could never fully understand what they were talking about when they lapsed into a mix between English and German to discuss the relationship between a literary text and its audience. They talked a lot about the idea that an individual's experience with a work of literature was central to its cultural purpose, or something to that effect. I always had to feign interest, and luckily this was easier to do over the phone.

Jinny told me she was in the middle of translating some lyrical poems by an obscure nineteenth-century German writer who was imperative to understanding twenty-first-century life. "I'm talking Cervantes-level importance, Lena," she said.

I really couldn't fathom her obsession with my mother's research. Also, I felt excluded; but I couldn't admit that, even to myself. Back then, when it came to Jinny, I submitted to my emotions without interrogation, letting them pull me along like a piece of refuse in a rushing stream.

Which is probably why I asked, "How's Mom?" I knew it couldn't possibly be going well.

Jinny cleared her throat. "Want to say hi? She's right here." She put the phone on speaker before I could protest.

"Hi, sweetie," my mother said. She sounded like she was shouting into a tunnel. "It's going well?"

"Yeah, yeah," I said. "Jinny can tell you. The actual digging is hard, but good."

"Have you met any locals?"

"A few," I said. "How are the summer session students?"

My mother was teaching a German language bootcamp at a community college in Skokie, a job Jinny had found for her through an online newsletter from the German Cultural Center in Chicago. It had been over two years since she'd lost her job in the middle of my senior year at New Trier. She snorted a laugh. "Most of them are pretty dead behind the eyes."

I could hear Jinny laughing in the background. The transference of my mother's emotions was always heightened in person; even across the ocean I felt I'd been given permission to relax.

"I'm heading out for a drive," my mom said. "Call us again soon, okay?"

And then I heard Jinny's thumping footsteps and knew she was running up the stairs to the phone in her room.

"Hey," she said. "So things are not good here."

I winced. "But we knew that, though. I mean, you knew what you were getting into."

"She thinks she's being poisoned, Lena. She's not eating anything. She's out driving every night."

My mother's habit of driving for hours after I went to bed had started the year Jinny moved out. I'd mentioned it to Jinny when she first started doing it, but Jinny had hardly reacted at the time. It was oddly gratifying to hear the anxiety in her voice now.

"I mean . . . who does she think is poisoning her?" I mustered.

"She just says 'they.' *They're* out to get me. I mean, it's absurd. She's mentioned her colleagues, she mentioned Grandma. One time she mentioned Dad. If I wasn't so broke I would buy a flight and go stay with him. I shouldn't have sublet my room in Palo Alto. It's awful here."

The phone at the palazzo was housed in a room off the kitchen where Martha, who got up early to organize breakfast, stored the coffee and bags of pasta and rice she bought in bulk. I looked up at the door to make sure I'd closed it behind me. I had.

"What about bonding over your dissertations?"

"Her research is a mess," she sighed. "I should let you go. I need to get up early tomorrow and read."

"I should go too," I said. "I'm sorry about Mom."

"I'll keep you posted."

After we said goodbye, I stayed put and looked out the window. It was starting to get light, and bees buzzed around a wild tangle of purple flowers growing out of a crack in a boulder. The boulder was covered by a thin film of pollen. Maybe it meant something—the flowers muscling their way into existence, the shroud of pollen—but who could say? I waited there for a while, then went out of the room and walked up the stairs to my bed, where I dozed dreamlessly until Simone woke me up at six.

IT WAS THE ITALIAN CONTINGENT, to Pietro's delight, that discovered the fresco in the *triclinium* on Friday. They'd been troweling, having just cleared one more stratum, and had hit upon something hard—the top of a wall. We gathered around, elated someone had discovered something beyond the endless pottery shards we'd been pulling up.

Pietro jumped down and snatched the trowel out of one of the Italians' hands. He quickly became so absorbed in his work that he couldn't be bothered to scold us back to our trenches. And within minutes, we gasped as a shock of red, bright enough to have been painted yesterday, revealed itself against the brown dirt. He sat back on his heels as if kneeling at an altar.

"Valenti," he said, to no one in particular. "We need to call Valenti right now."

Cyrille nodded curtly. He seemed proud, but in a resigned way, like he'd known about this fresco all along and had simply been waiting for the moment it would be revealed.

Simone was on lunch duty at the palazzo. I missed her; she, more than any of us, deserved to share in the collective joy and awe that came as we watched Pietro slowly reveal a sliver of red across the entire trench, which spanned nearly twelve feet. It was decidedly magical, and like nothing I'd ever seen reproduced in my textbooks.

"It's the moisture in the soil," Cyrille said. "Ancient pigments love moisture."

Simone and Martha emerged from the pines with bags of sandwiches and fruit. I motioned them over wildly, and they gazed at the trench in awe. Simone took several steps back and shaded her eyes. "I can see it," she said, sounding like she was on the verge of tears. "I can see the villa."

LATER THAT NIGHT, when I told Giamma about the fresco, a look of recognition crossed his face, and he sat up a little straighter. "Cyrille is right, at least about the soil," he said.

We were eating dinner at Giamma's house—his family's summer house—which I could see from my bedroom window at the palazzo.

It hadn't been obvious from the outside that the house was sprawling, with a walled garden and an internal courtyard filled with potted herbs. "It's ridiculous," he'd said the previous Sunday when I slept over, his voice echoing in the atrium. "Completely inappropriate for the Alps." I'd nodded, trying not to look too impressed with it all, even though I was swooning internally. He'd pointed to the elaborate drainage system—discreet apertures in the ground that led to a collective gutter of sorts—for the melted snow in the courtyard. "We only ever came up here in summer."

Now my mouth was full of the porcini risotto Giamma had prepared in the terracotta-tiled kitchen, where we were perched on stools at the end of a tall farm table. I took a sip of wine. "What do you mean, 'at least'?"

"My guess is he knows very little about Roman wall art. Neither does Pietro."

"And you do?"

He smiled. "My dissertation is on a Roman painting cycle. Not fresco, but similar."

And he told me about the murals uncovered at Dura Europos, a city that the Romans used as a military outpost until it was abandoned after a Sasanian attack in the third century. It was in modern-day northern Syria. "They could have disintegrated in that arid environment, the paintings," he said. "Miraculously they survived. Only to be destroyed as soon as they were discovered."

I listened in fascination as he explained that British troops had accidentally found them in 1920 during the Arab Revolt, and a few months after the initial discovery a team from University of Chicago spent a single day excavating and photographing. But the Americans left the frescoes without adequate cover, and they were largely destroyed by the elements. The few from the synagogue that survived were installed in the Syrian National Museum in Damascus. The rest of the city was excavated in subsequent years by a team of French archeologists, and eventually a group from Yale brought most of the finds back to the US.

"Is that why you wanted to study in the States? Because they were at Yale?"

He looked vaguely uncomfortable when he said, "I'm writing about the synagogue paintings, which are now in Syria. There are almost no good images of them."

He hadn't answered my question, but I let it go. "Why'd you choose the ones that are so hard to get to?"

His eyes sparkled. "They are the best paintings from Dura. The largest, the most interesting. You want to see?"

He wiped his mouth with a napkin, then disappeared and returned with a large blue clothbound book. He set it down on the counter and flipped open to the bookplates at the back. "Here," he said.

I looked over his shoulder. Two men, one in a toga and one in a red tunic, flanked a winged woman in a yellow dress who was bent down over three figures. Three smaller winged women hovered in the sky. In the upper left corner, a large hand reached toward the man in the red tunic. "That's the hand of God reaching toward Ezekiel."

"And these," he said, indicating the winged women, "are Psyches—"

I nodded in recognition, feeling proud to know what he was talking about. "Like Cupid and Psyche?"

"Somewhat. Here she is more general. And you see, she is helping these souls"—he pointed to three flying winged women—"enter these three bodies."

"So what's your dissertation about?"

He drew in a deep breath. "The artist used a Psyche—a personification—as the livening agent. To illustrate a passage from the book of Ezekiel. Scholars are still divided as to why. Politically I think it's difficult for some historians to acknowledge that both Jews and Christians were influenced by the same common pagan traditions. But for me it's simple. There are many examples of this type of Psyche on Syrian sarcophagi. So I am analyzing visual precedents and influences."

"Have you seen it in person?"

He nodded. "It's like this, more or less. The color is slightly less saturated. But you can only see them by request; they don't appear in the museum map. Even in foreign guidebooks they are censored. In theory this protects them."

From what? I wanted to ask, but then I remembered about the looting of the Baghdad Museum. Being in a museum didn't necessarily protect something from being taken. "What is Damascus like?" I said instead.

He winced. "I don't know. Beautiful. Tragic. And it will get worse."

I didn't want to reveal how little I knew about what was going on in that part of the world, so I changed the subject. "What will you do when you finish the PhD?"

He shrugged. "It depends."

"On what?" I pressed, hoping that his decision had something to do with me—with our relationship.

"It's complicated."

A current ran through me as I imagined what it would be like to have Giamma in New York for the upcoming school year. He was ABD—an acronym I recognized from the way my mother always talked about her graduate studies whenever anyone asked, implying that she would at some point complete her PhD—and could technically finish his dissertation from anywhere. How often would Giamma and I see each other in New York, I wondered, if he did end up coming back? Would our relationship progress into something serious? Would he get along with Lakshmi?

"I want to show you something," he said, handing me my wineglass.

He led me across the courtyard and into a large dark room with wood floors and no furniture. When he flicked on the lights, I blinked in disbelief. The ceilings must have been twenty feet tall to accommodate the monumental tapestries installed on all four walls.

"What *are* these?"

"They're Flemish." He paced over to the far end of the room, the echo of his leather shoes muted by the fabric on the walls. "Each one represents a month of the year, May through October. This one's May."

In the tapestry, women were walking through a garden against the backdrop of a stone castle. Two girls in the foreground threaded roses into chaplets. I thought of the Unicorn Tapestries at the Cloisters.

"I feel like I'm in a museum."

He led me through a low doorway and into the next room, with the same sconce-dim lighting. I had to refocus my eyes to understand that I was seeing paintings in gold frames, at least twenty of them: portraits, landscapes, seascapes. Giamma walked over to a pedestal, which displayed two blackened bronze figures. I followed him, captivated.

"Here," he said, offering me one of the sculptures.

I looked up at him to make sure I was understanding correctly. He nodded.

I held the bronze, looking into the wide face of the figure, whose resigned features made her look wise and wearily alive, like she had a secret she was going to take to her grave.

"Heavy, right?" Giamma said.

"But what is this?" I asked.

"She is from Nigeria. Sixteenth or seventeenth century."

When I put the statue back on the pedestal, her eyes were saying something—it seemed as though she were pleading with me to pick her back up. She had mistaken me for someone who understood she didn't belong there.

THE NEXT MORNING, I stopped for an espresso on my way back to the palazzo to change clothes. A trio of old men sitting outside the bar at a red plastic table tapped their cigarettes into a full ashtray and nodded torpidly at me.

It was always the same man behind the counter at the bar—another one of Giamma's childhood summer friends. He was the only one out of four siblings who had never left Orbagne, and thus had inherited the bar from his deceased parents. Soft-spoken and gentle, he had a deep tan and rimless glasses, which he removed to go rock climbing. He only ever met my eyes briefly—out of respect for Giamma, I imagined.

"*Caffé*?" he asked quietly as I made my way past two Albanian boys digging in the ice cream freezer.

"*Grazie*," I said. He gave me a nod, then turned around to pull the espresso. The green pendant lights above the counter were turned all the way up. For the first time, I realized that there were no windows in the bar. The only decoration on the walls were old black-and-white photos of the mountains in crooked frames.

I pushed a one-euro coin across the counter. He shook his head. "*È pagato.*"

My brows knitted together in confusion, but before I could protest, his eyes flicked up and he came out from behind the counter and sprinted out of the bar. The ice cream freezer was open, and the boys were gone.

I stirred a packet of white sugar into my espresso and looked around. Through the open door, I smelled the men's cigarettes, and I could hear their laughter.

I sipped my espresso. Giamma's friend hadn't indicated that the coffee was on the house—he'd specifically said it was *pagato*. Paid for.

As I was taking my last sweet sip of espresso, he returned, panting and muttering. The only word I caught was "*cazzo*." I asked him what happened.

He slammed the freezer door shut. "*Non ti preoccupare*," he said. "*Anzi*—"

After a brief hesitation, he told me in Italian to tell Giamma he needed to talk to him as soon as possible.

VIII.

MARCH 14, 2022

NEW YORK CITY

On Monday, Emmanuel's assistant gives me the green light to interrupt him during one of the open blocks on his calendar.

I open his office door and peek in. He's at his desk wearing noise-canceling headphones, bobbing his head as he types. He seems like someone who could work while listening to a podcast at 2× speed. But I won't ask, I decide, just in case it's Kara Swisher. For some reason, he thinks we share a mutual love of her.

"Sorry," I say when he looks up. "I can come back, if you want—"

"No, all good," he says, removing the headphones. Adele's voice sounds in the speakers. "I'm actually working on a joint communication to the Italian Ministry of Culture and the Manhattan DA for the Fordham case."

I take a seat at one of the leather chairs in front of his desk. "You didn't want me to draft it?"

"This stuff is fun for me," he says. "I was in law school in Boston when the Gardner theft happened. I would have killed to work on a case like that. I knew—I just *knew* it was organized crime, even back then. I grew up around guys like that. Anyway, what's up?"

I sit up straight. "So I was thinking over the weekend about how the Italians must have more than just that series of Polaroids. Of the cup. You know, evidence-wise."

Emmanuel hesitates, then looks at me and says, "I'm starting to wonder if we should advise Fordham to return all of the requested objects to Italy. Including the cup."

I collapse my shoulders. "Wait. What? It's been one week."

"It turns out the Italians aren't ruling out the possibility of individual accountability," he adds.

"What do you mean?"

"Caroline's been on their radar for a long time."

"Really?"

Emmanuel clears his throat. "I did some back-channeling before we agreed to take on the case. My buddy at the DA's office warned me that she was named in a high-profile case—sealed—over a decade ago that an Italian suit brought against a curator from the Getty. Marianne Flynn. My motion to unseal the records finally came through on Friday."

I nod slowly. After Caroline mentioned Marianne Flynn last week, I proceeded to read every article the *New York Times* published on the disgraced curator's trial. But there was no mention of Caroline in anything I read. "What exactly did they accuse Caroline of?"

"As a collaborator in—hold on, let me find the exact wording." He turns to his computer and scrolls. "Furthering the black market for looted antiquities," he reads.

"Can I see that?"

"Everything is on the—"

"Drive. Right." I rack my brain. "So you think because of what happened at the Getty they're going after Caroline personally?"

"They're not ruling it out. Secondhand information, by the way. The guys at the DA's office gave me a heads-up."

"So then are the Italians also prosecuting Filippo Dalmasso?" I finally ask. "For buying looted stuff in the first place?"

"Who knows. The Italians won't tell us anything. They invited me to a 'colloquium' in Rome, to talk about this whole thing. But I get the sense they're not looking to have a real dialogue. If we can convince Fordham to give everything back, it'll be done."

"I don't think Caroline's going to do that," I hear myself say.

He searches my face. "And why is that?"

"Wouldn't it be an admission of guilt? Implied?"

"We'd structure the deal in a way that would protect her. It might be our one shot at getting her completely exonerated. Or at least avoiding a trial."

"But if Fordham gives everything back—I mean, it's a tiny museum. She said the cup raised the museum's profile. She also said objects are being repatriated on a moral basis. So even if she gets exonerated, she could be out of a job."

"Look. I'm not the morality police. But she doesn't look good. At the moment I can't picture her holding up under cross-examination. If we're going to properly defend her, we need to figure out how to—"

"Wait," I interrupt, thinking of Si.

"Yeah?"

"I—I mean we—should talk to the conservator. You know how Caroline said she had to outsource conservation of the cup? I met the person who did it at that opening last Monday. Don't you think we need to figure out what they know?"

He nods. "Good call. See what you can find out."

I get to my feet quickly, energized by our exchange. But something keeps me from moving toward the door. "Maybe I could also go up to Fordham and have Caroline show me the rest of the objects from the Creon donation—"

"Hold on, hold on," Emmanuel says, blinking rapidly. "I don't want to put you in an ethically compromising position. There's an argument for keeping some distance from her."

"You think I'll find something incriminating?"

"Let's just play it safe. For now. You've been helping me navigate all this stuff—I don't want to put us in a position where you'd need to bow out."

I recognize this as a polite refusal of my idea, but my breath catches in my throat because what he's saying is patently untrue. All I've managed to navigate are my own practically inconceivable personal ties to this case, the extent of which I haven't uncovered yet.

But I decide to leave Emmanuel alone and track down Si. Si was the one who restored the cup; they must know more about its provenance, or at the very least why the Italians are so confident it belongs to them.

SI IS NOT EASY TO FIND. The main problem is that I can't, for the life of me, remember their last name. I tried googling *Si antiquities conservation,* but that turned up nothing. This is the first time in my adult life that I've regretted deleting all my social media accounts, because I'm certain that at one point in the early days of Facebook, Martha tagged us in some old photos from our summer in Orbagne.

I'm supposed to be billing hours to a complicated inheritance case involving a deceased matriarch who watched *The Aristocats* a week before she died and subsequently named her cat the sole heir to her estate—although animals can't legally inherit, the estate is now stuck in probate, and my clients, her adult children, are fuming. Normally I live for any opportunity to delve into the bizarre world of pet trusts, but I can't stop thinking about my conversation with Emmanuel yesterday. I don't disagree with his instinct to facilitate the return of these objects from a legal strategy standpoint, I've decided. The main issue, apart from the fact that it feels wrong to capitulate so swiftly, is that now I have less time under the auspices of Caroline's defense to get to the bottom of why Si and Giamma have simultaneously reentered my life.

Giamma's card, which I made sure to fish out of my workbag the day after the panel, catches my eye. I need to move quickly, and given Caroline's reluctance to connect me to Si, Giamma is likely my best bet at getting to them.

He picks up on the first ring: "This is John."

"It's Lena."

There's a long pause, and I can imagine him on the other end of the line rubbing his eyebrow. "Hello," he says.

"I'm not calling to ask for your help, or your protection, or whatever."

"I have no idea what you're talking about."

"I need to talk to Si."

There's silence. And then, "We should talk in person."

I MEET GIAMMA ON WEDNESDAY at a wine bar a few blocks from my apartment in Chelsea. I'm sitting at a high-top next to the window in front of a club soda with lemon, and when he walks in I stand to greet him.

"Lena," he says, removing his coat. I can't read his expression. And it dawns on me: if any part of me is drawn to Giamma now, it's not because he is objectively attractive. It's because he has remained an enigma to me. I never understood him then, and I certainly don't understand him now. This must have been part of his appeal all those years ago, I realize—my own longing to decode a cipher.

"So," I open, reminding myself of my end goal: I am here to get Si's contact information. Nothing else.

He slides an envelope across the high-top. "Here."

"What is this?"

"Open it later."

I clear my throat. "Look, I just need their phone number. Si's. Or email, or whatever."

“I don’t have it,” he says, flat out.

I’m opening my mouth to protest when a waitress interrupts us. Giamma glances at the menu and orders a glass of pinot noir. I ask for another seltzer.

We watch each other for a while. Giamma taps his phone, then folds his hands and turns his attention to me. For an instant, I’m nineteen again, sitting next to Giamma in the apartment above Orbagne’s tiny restaurant. But there is wariness in his eyes now, not infatuation.

“My boss wants Fordham to repatriate everything,” I say.

Giamma’s eyes betray nothing, but he flinches slightly when he says, “I don’t know what you mean by ‘everything.’ I don’t know anything about this lawsuit.”

“I am going to track down Si with or without you,” I say evenly. “So you should probably just tell me what you know. About how Filippo Dalmasso obtained the antiquities he donated to Caroline.”

“Lena,” he says, a look of resignation on his face. “This has nothing to do with me.”

Now I’m winging it, but I have no intention of letting him off the hook. I decide to try a different angle. “Remember the night we first met all those years ago?”

“Of course,” he says gently.

“I asked you and your friend Marco about the looting that happened at the villa that winter. And Marco told me—do you remember what he told me?”

Giamma’s face changes—it darkens, unmistakably—and he crosses his arms.

“He said: ‘Italians would never dig holes like that.’ And that he thought it was the Albanians. And you didn’t say a word.”

Giamma clears his throat and leans on his elbows. “Look—”

“And I was remembering you with those little boys on bikes. You said they were Albanian, that people treated them badly. But you were nice to them."

"That was a long time ago."

We watch each other for a long time. I'm determined to wait him out. But the silence drags on, and I eventually lose my patience: "I can't believe what Pietro has accomplished. UNESCO, huh?"

Giamma smooths the slash in his left eyebrow. Finally, I've managed to make him uncomfortable.

"Are you still in touch with him and his dad?"

"Lena, where are you going with these questions? What do you want to know?"

I respond instinctively: "Why did you pursue me back then?"

The waitress brings Giamma's wine. "You can bring the check," he says, and I wonder for a second if the edge in his voice might belie a lingering sense of tenderness for what we had.

Which is not what this is about. This is about artifacts. This conversation is about tangible ancient objects and the people who have power over them. A sudden wave of desperation comes over me. "What happened with the looting? What did they take? And what happened to Cyrille?"

Giamma's face reddens. I stare at him, feeling energized for having come right out with these questions, which, now that I've asked them, I realize have been latent in my psyche for almost two decades.

He shakes his head and murmurs something, but I can't understand him. I forge ahead: "This is why I *need* to know why you're suddenly back in my life—"

When he lunges across the table, I recoil in surprise, not fear—despite his large build, Giamma is anything but intimidating, even when he's upset. "I did not look for you," he hisses. "Do we at least agree on that?"

I glare at him.

"You asked me why I pursued you back then," he says. "But the truth is, you came after me; you followed me—"

"I was nineteen. And if you didn't actually care about me, then you're a liar. You were a liar then and now you're—" I search for the right word. "Phony," I conclude. "You are a phony."

"And you're crazy," he says, exhaling loudly. He stands and puts on his coat. "I hate to be the one to remind you that you were the last person to see your professor before he disappeared."

My shoulders shoot up to my ears. Who is Giamma to call me crazy? I reach for something—anything—that might hurt him. "Does Eva know about me?" I ask. "Does she know what you used to do for work?"

He stands, takes out his wallet, puts a twenty-dollar bill on the table. "Just leave me out of this."

"Out of what?"

"Out of whatever mystery you think you're solving."

"I remember everything," I tell him, as he turns and heads toward the door. "Everything."

"Goodbye, Lena."

When the door closes behind him, I tear open the envelope, my eyes stinging with indignance.

It's a photo of four formally dressed people, torn out of an Italian magazine. Second from left is a jovial man with white hair and a deep tan. To his left is Pietro, and to his right is a familiar-looking young woman. And to *her* right is none other than Si.

Filippo Dalmasso e sua figlia Benedetta, the caption says. My mouth drops open, and not because of Si, who, notably, is not identified in the text. I recognize Filippo. I've met him; I've been inside his house. He was friends with Pietro's father. And his daughter was, maybe still is, Pietro's girlfriend.

* * *

LATER THAT NIGHT, I pull up the New York Department of State Division of Corporations website. Under search criteria, I select Limited Liability Company and type in *art conservation.* The search returns thirty-four possible matches, and I start with the ones in New York County. Though I'm not really expecting to find anything, it's worth trying, because the Si I knew was a rule follower who would definitely be paying their annual LLC fees.

All of the businesses have vague names like "Art Conservation Limited" and "Art Conservation Solutions." But halfway down the page, there's an outlier: "Artemis Antiquities LLC." I click into it, and whisper *Zimmermann* in recognition when I see the name under the Service of Process Name and Address section. Si Zimmermann owns Artemis Antiquities, a Sole Member LLC.

I do a regular search for *Si Zimmermann Artemis Antiquities.* Google returns a few results, including a *TechCrunch* article from 2015, which details a million-dollar seed round for a cloud-based art inventory platform called Artemis, developed to "foster international museum collaborations and dialogues." I read the article three times, but I can't figure out what the company does, exactly. Also, Si's name doesn't appear anywhere. All the quotes are from either "a representative from the start-up" or an "anonymous angel investor."

There's no phone number, but there is a street address.

WHEN I WAKE UP, I cancel my internal morning meetings and take the A all the way up to the top of Manhattan. My plan is to scope out the studio first and then figure out my next step. The address on Si's business filing is on Thayer Street, and I get off at the 200th Street Station.

I follow the map on my phone, and within moments I'm standing in front of a moss-covered limestone apartment building. It's 8:46. I double-check the address. This is definitely it. The front door is unlocked, and I enter a dusty lobby with a pink marble floor and an empty doorman desk.

When I hear the ding of an elevator, I feel suddenly exposed. This is very clearly a home address. It was a mistake to come here—there's no doubt in my mind that Si would hate to be caught off guard by an unexpected visit from me. I retreat toward the door, and just as I'm about to walk out, a voice croaks behind me: "Can I help you?"

A dignified man in a faded, oversized suit is emerging from what appears to be a mail room, his arms full of packages.

"Oh," I say. "No, I was just leaving."

He shrugs and takes a seat at the desk. I watch for a moment as he arranges the packages in front of him. ZIMMERMANN is Sharpied onto the side of the one closest to me. I step closer to look at the box, which is about twice the size of my head and coated in layers of FRAGILE tape. The return address is in Italian. I take this as an omen and lean my hip against the desk.

"Actually, can I leave a note for Si Zimmermann with you?"

I tear a page out of my gridded Moleskine and write *Please call me,* along with my phone number and initials.

On my way back to the subway, a sign for the Cloisters points up a sloping park path. I check my work email; there's nothing urgent, so I head into the park.

The winding path is steep, and eerily deserted. I pause at one of the turns and gaze past bud-sprouting branches at the Hudson, unnerved slightly to see no evidence of New York; to realize that I could be anywhere.

The museum's wooden double doors are locked. There are no signs, so I pull out my phone and look up the hours: 10:00 a.m. to 4:30 p.m. on Thursdays. It's 9:34 now; I decide to wait.

When it opens, I wander into the gallery that houses the Unicorn Tapestries. I gravitate to the panel that made an impression on me when I first moved to New York—the one of the unicorn fenced in. I examine the woven blood dripping from the unicorn's wounds. The museum is empty save for a few gallery attendants, but I can practically feel Cyrille in the gallery with me, asking me what I think. I don't know what to tell him, so I look around for a label. The red stains on the unicorn's body represent pomegranate juice, it says, not blood. The unicorn's constraint isn't secure, the gate is open, and he could escape if he wanted to.

IX.

JULY 3, 2004

TORINO

On the eve of the Fourth of July—a Saturday—Giamma picked me up at the palazzo to go shopping in Torino.

Earlier that week, when he'd asked me to accompany him to *aperitivo* with his friends, I'd hesitated. When he pressed me, I admitted that I didn't know what I would wear. To which he'd replied: *a problem we can solve.* I loved that Giamma was interested in clothes; it seemed to signify how comfortable he was in his own skin.

As we drove into the city center, I stared in awe at Torino's wide boulevards, cream-colored buildings, piazzas, and porticoes, understanding now why Lakshmi had said this was her favorite city in northern Italy. "It's modeled after Paris," Giamma told me. "The same urban planner."

I nodded absently, thinking about how Torino got its name from the Taurini, who Cyrille had said would have been contemporaries of the Salassi during the Age of Augustus had they not already been destroyed by Hannibal in the Second Punic War. Taurini was derived from the Latin word for bull—which made Torino the city of bulls. "Later I'll show you the Porta Palatina," Giamma added, reading my mind. "The Roman gate."

We parked and walked up a stone arcade and into a boutique, where we were greeted by a lanky green-eyed man dressed in cotton-linen pants, a close-fitting button-down, and leather shoes. A delicate gold watch dangled on his wrist as he extended his hand to greet me.

The boutique initially appeared to be only slightly bigger than the room I shared with Simone at the palazzo, with a single gold rack lining its periphery. A polished terrazzo floor peeked out from under a white rug, reflecting light from the crystal chandelier, which illuminated a vase of peach roses on the front table.

I reshouldered the cheap leather purse that I'd bought at a sidewalk sale in New York, feeling mangy and out of place while Giamma chatted with the man with the green eyes. I had to strain to understand them—they were cutting off the ends of their infinitives and speaking with a cadence I couldn't place. It was Italian, and yet it wasn't. They were talking about their families, I think, but at one point they may have been talking about me, because Giamma nodded my way and I caught the word "*lingua*," which he pronounced "lenga."

The man sized me up and shepherded me through a doorway and into another, larger room which contained an off-white sofa, an expanded trifold mirror, and an empty rolling rack. He motioned to the sofa and asked in perfect English if I'd like any water or coffee.

"A coffee, sure," I said. He gave a single nod and turned away.

Giamma appeared in the doorway and smiled at me. "We're going to get you something perfect," he said. I smiled back, thinking about how no one besides Jinny had ever watched me try on clothes in a fitting room.

The man returned, an espresso in one hand and three dresses on wooden hangers in the other. I stood up to take the cup from him and glanced over the dresses he'd brought, with their dark and silky fabrics.

I ended up with a bow-neck black dress, which hit just below my knees, and a pair of gold heeled sandals, which Giamma assured me would be more comfortable than they looked. He was wrong, and

I had to work hard to conceal my discomfort as we walked to the bar. Though when we crossed a piazza, I was momentarily distracted from the pain by the way the buildings were illuminated in orange from the sun, which was now low in the sky. *This* was a scenic beauty I could process—unlike the mountains, Torino was completely man-made—and I squeezed Giamma's hand.

He pushed open a massive door, which gave way to a courtyard buzzing with young, attractive people drinking cocktails at round tables. "Here we are," he said, surveying the crowd. "My friends are over there."

As we approached our table, I slowed down and let go of Giamma's hand in dismay. Seated at the table, among the couples, was Pietro, dressed in real clothes: a yellow sweater and white linen pants. I'd never seen him without his bandana. It was unnerving—almost embarrassing—to see him with his blond curls exposed.

He caught sight of me and did a double take. I stared back at him. Giamma noticed what was happening and grinned. "You already know Pietro, of course," he said.

I nodded silently and gave the two of them a weak smile. Giamma seemed to think that Pietro's presence would come as a pleasant surprise to both of us. In fairness, I hadn't said anything to Giamma about my mixed feelings toward Pietro; apart from notable findings, we hardly ever discussed my days up at the dig at all.

I sat down next to a young woman who introduced herself as Benedetta. This was Pietro's girlfriend, the one who had organized his music collection. Giamma leaned in and named everyone else at the table, then ordered me a white wine. The group was talking a mile a minute—I could barely keep up.

"*Prendiamo qualcosa?*" Benedetta said to me, nodding toward the edge of the courtyard where there was a large wooden door.

I glanced at Giamma. He was nodding intently at the guy to his left, whose name I had already forgotten. "Uh, *sì*," I said.

I followed her into the building and understood then what she'd meant by "take something"—it was impossible to miss, an L-shaped table overflowing with all kinds of food: meats, focaccia triangles, peppers and eggplant in olive oil. Suddenly I had the sensation of being watched, and when I looked up, a bartender averted his gaze.

I gestured to the Genetrix bottle on the glass shelf above the bar. "That's from Pietro's vineyard, right?"

Benedetta's hair was light brown like mine and pulled back in a low ballerina bun, exposing her long neck and face, which was skeptical, or maybe disapproving. But when she spoke—in Italian—her voice was kind. "His father thinks it's an old marketing scheme, but I think it goes back to the Gauls. I really do. So does Pietro."

If Genetrix's Gallic roots were part of a marketing scheme, what did Benedetta mean by "old"? Was she saying the same thing Cyrille had said to me about the villa, that he imagined the Romans may have marketed the villa as blessed by the gods, Venus in particular? Venus, Genetrix—those two words went together, I realized. There was a temple in the Roman forum dedicated to Venus Genetrix—Julius Caesar had built it as a testament to his descent from Aeneas, the son of Venus.

"You know Giamma from the art world, then?" she said, or something to that effect, because I wasn't sure exactly what she meant by "*mondo dell'arte.*"

"*L'archeologia,*" I clarified, watching as she filled up her plate.

She looked impressed. "*Davvero?*"

I smiled and relaxed my shoulders, thinking that maybe she was someone who romanticized archeology the same way I had.

I asked her if she had gone to university with Giamma, mainly because I wasn't sure how to construct the question "how do you know Giamma?" in Italian.

"We did study together, yes. A long time ago." Then Benedetta told me that her father, a collector of antiquities, was friends with

Giamma's father. "His mother too," she added. "But not as much anymore, ever since she left."

"Where did she go?" I asked.

Benedetta gave me a sharp look and said nothing.

I asked her if she—Benedetta—lived in Torino. She said she studied in Torino but lived in Aosta. I nodded. No follow-up questions came to my mind, and we returned to the table. Seeing our plates, the others got up for their own, leaving me, Giamma, Benedetta, and Pietro alone at the table.

Benedetta reached around me to punch Giamma playfully in the arm, and said something like, "*Che bella fidanzata che hai.*" Giamma kissed me on the cheek.

"How did you and Lena meet?" Pietro asked a bit skeptically, if I was interpreting his tone correctly. But I reminded myself what Benedetta said about Pietro believing that the amaro dated back to the Gauls, and I remembered his elation when we discovered the red frescoes—we cared about the same things, Pietro and I. Giamma too.

Giamma shrugged. "I heard her speaking English at Marco's, and I introduced myself."

I gnawed on the pit of an olive. I couldn't think of anything to say, and I couldn't decipher the expression on Pietro's face as he nodded slowly. I exhaled in relief when the others came back to the table, and the topic of conversation switched to August *ferie.*

As the evening progressed, I had the growing sense that *this* was the reason I had come to Italy—not to pull objects out of the ground or to be mentored by Cyrille, who was for the most part off in his own world, but to meet Giamma. And I had a flash of my future, living in Torino, or back in New York with Giamma, leaving behind all the people who had ever let me down. I loved him and he loved me, I thought to myself, drunkenly.

* * *

TWO GLASSES OF WINE AT *aperitivo* led to another three at dinner, and when we finally stumbled back to Giamma's Torino apartment, he led me to his bedroom.

He flicked on a lamp in the bedroom and playfully removed my new dress, then watched me slowly unfasten my bra and slide my underwear down my legs. I liked having his eyes on me; I touched myself so that he wouldn't look away. Maybe it was the alcohol, or perhaps the particular way he looked at me—but in that moment I was proud of my small breasts, and the swell of my hips, and all the aspects of my body I'd always felt ambivalent about.

Walking over to him where he was, perched on the edge of his enormous antique bed, I paused briefly before pushing him down onto his back and climbing on top of him. Our lips met, and his eyes rolled back into his head, but I kept my eyes open, watching him transform into a vulnerable, almost desperate version of himself. His desire went beyond want—he needed me; I recognized that he needed me, possibly more than I needed him. And an image of one of those sharks, the ones who go around with the little fish attached to their underbellies, came into my mind—but I wasn't sure, when it came to Giamma and me, who was the shark and who was the little fish.

When I came to on Sunday morning, Giamma was still sleeping soundly. I rolled out of bed and recoiled when I glimpsed myself in the mirror above the fireplace in his room: my skin was blotchy and creased, and gluey mascara lined my eyes.

I hadn't brought anything with me, not having understood that we would not be returning to Orbagne at the end of the night. I crept out of the bedroom, closed the door quietly behind me, and made my way to the bathroom. In the hallway, light poured in from the opposite end of the apartment. The place had probably been constructed around the same time as the dig's dorm, but it looked like it had been maintained in a way the palazzo in Orbagne hadn't.

My eyes swept up to the high ceiling's elaborate crown moldings and back down to the braided stone floor.

I pushed open the bathroom door and collapsed onto the toilet in relief. When I glanced down between my legs, I caught sight of bright red blood. A sudden urge to get back to Orbagne, where I had a box of tampons stashed in my suitcase, came over me.

I ran the faucet and splashed my skin, watching the water in the sink as it turned black from my eye makeup. The hand "towel" on the counter—it had the feel of a dinner napkin—was white and embroidered. I ran my fingers over a swirling cursive *P*, wondering—not out of suspicion but out of curiosity—if Giamma lived in the apartment alone, or if this, too, belonged to his parents. And then I remembered what Benedetta had said about his mother having left, and I weighed the risk of bringing up the topic with Giamma—how likely was he to reciprocate, to ask me about my own mother?

With one eye open and my face dripping, I opened the cabinet next to the sink and peered in for something that wouldn't turn black with the residue of my mascara, but there were only more of the same white dinner-napkin towels. I pulled out a stack and placed it on the counter so I could look deeper into the cabinet.

Eventually I gave up and dabbed at my eyes with toilet paper. Then I opened the medicine cabinet. I found a face cream, pumped a small amount onto the toilet paper, and worked it carefully around my eyes. I moisturized my skin and squeezed some toothpaste onto my finger, then located a comb in a drawer and ran it through my hair.

I restacked the towels in the open linen cabinet, standing on my tiptoes to make sure the pile was even. That was when I noticed a latch: a cabinet within a cabinet.

A childhood road trip from my grandparents' house to the historic mansions outside Philadelphia came back to me. Of the three we saw, it was Fontill—built by an archeologist, I recalled—that I'd been most intrigued by, with its hidden doors and concealed dumbwaiters. It was a home where children could easily escape their parents, unlike the one I'd grown up in.

I didn't think; I reached into the back of the cabinet, lifted the hook out of the eye, and pulled the little door open. I don't know what I was expecting to find, if anything; I was operating on pure impulse. The open door gave way to a spacious compartment, and I hoisted myself onto the counter to get a better look. I couldn't get much closer, so I reached my hand inside, and immediately, just to the right, I felt a plastic-encased mass.

As I squinted into the darkness, a stack of white bricks came into focus. It was insulation of some kind, was my initial thought. The bricks were just beyond reach, and in the few seconds it took me to think through why there would be insulation inside an interior bathroom wall of an apartment, I remembered the little bag of white powder I'd found in my freshman year roommate's desk back in Chicago when I was looking for the stack of Post-its I'd loaned her, the way she jeered at me when I confronted her, asking if I wanted a bump. My jaw went slack.

"Lena?" Giamma said from the doorway.

I froze and turned to him robotically. "I—I just—" I stammered, managing to get something out about the towels.

He let me go on for a while, then extended his hand. "Here."

I didn't take his hand; I was too embarrassed, too shocked by the whole thing. I jumped down and stood there in my underwear and bra, staring at him.

"Come. Let's take a coffee."

I crossed my arms and followed him down the hallway, dipping into the bedroom to put on my black dress. My hands trembled as I zipped it up.

A few minutes later, I watched him load a moka pot with espresso grounds in the kitchen.

"Look." He cleared his throat. "I know you saw something—that might have scared you."

I sat down at the small table in front of the window, clocking how far up we were from the ground. It was only one or two stories.

"There is nothing to be afraid of."

I wasn't exactly afraid of the situation I'd found myself in; I was stupefied by it. So much so that when I opened my mouth to speak, nothing came out.

"Listen, people work," Giamma attempted. "Everyone has to work, right? And okay, yes, I might not have the most—conventional job. But it's a job."

And it was then, only then, that I realized I had no idea how Giamma spent his time during the week. When I'd asked him, he'd said he worked for his father's company. But I hadn't asked what he *did* for his father. He'd implied, or maybe I'd assumed, that given his studies in the US, whatever he was doing was temporary. "So you're a drug dealer," I said.

Giamma looked at me quizzically, then appeared to register something as he studied my face. "Yes," he said. "Yes, exactly."

He took a seat at the table and poured espresso into two little cups. "I'm not proud of it, but yes, I sell drugs. You know how it goes."

"I mean, not really!" I blurted.

"It's common here," he said, nodding vigorously. "Very common."

I cleared my throat, trying to let some of the tension melt away from my face as I stirred sugar into my espresso. "Common to sell drugs or to do drugs?"

He thought it over. "It's just a job."

I noted the gentle tone of voice and reminded myself that I hadn't ever observed anything threatening or violent whatsoever in Giamma. I felt safe with him; I had no reason not to believe the things he told me. "You said you worked for your dad."

"My father owns a few restaurants and nightclubs here, in Torino. I help with the operations."

I eyed him. He nodded insistently. "What about your father?" he asked.

I cleared my throat, caught off guard. "He's dead." This was true in a way; he was dead to me.

Giamma nodded sympathetically. I was afraid he was going to press me for more information, so I added, in an effort to divert the conversation: "My grandfather runs a business. His sons—my uncles—work for him."

"What kind of business?"

My maternal grandfather had turned the modest Mennonite workshop he'd inherited into a successful kitchen cabinet business. Interior designers all along the East Coast paid hundreds of thousands of dollars for his custom work. "He's a carpenter. A builder, I guess. Or he used to be. Now he just oversees everything. His company makes kitchen cabinets."

Giamma looked interested. "Wood, really?"

I averted my eyes, unnerved by an image of my grandparents' kitchen in Pennsylvania that was pushing into my mind, of Jinny and two of my older cousins frantically snatching up cards on the cherrywood table in a late-night game of Dutch Blitz. Jinny shoots me a look, which I ignore. I'm emptying my pile faster than anyone else; I have a shot at winning. I feel Jinny's eyes on me, and when I look up, I see my mother moving through the kitchen in a silent rage. She stomps out into the cold, slamming the door behind her.

I closed my eyes, willing the memory to go away. But it didn't, and I remembered the rest: Jinny leading me by the hand over patches of black ice to the car. The two of us pretending to sleep in the back as my mother fumed in the driver's seat. The car sputtering to a complete stop on the shoulder of the highway a few hours later.

We'd run out of gas in the dead of winter on the highway in rural

Ohio. My mother was shivering as she instructed me to steer while she and Jinny pushed us to the exit. I opened my eyes, rattled by the memory, thinking about the kind stranger who pulled over to help us; he could have been a serial killer. But he wasn't, and we'd survived that night. We'd survived our whole childhood. Compared to my mother, Giamma was safe.

"How does he source it?" Giamma asked.

"I'm sorry?" I said.

"Where does he get the wood?"

"I guess, probably—in Pennsylvania. Where he lives."

"I have some sources in Long Island," he said. "If he ever needs them."

"For . . . wood?"

He absorbed my confusion and shrugged. "Anyway, the place we were last night is one of my father's."

Then it dawned on me, looking at him: he was *embarrassed* to be working for his father. Maybe the cocaine was an extension of the restaurant business. Here was Giamma, who was working on his PhD in art history at an Ivy League university in the United States, and he had no choice but to aid in the family business, which had nothing to do with his interests or potential. I felt a surge of compassion for him.

"Benedetta was asking me last night how I knew you," I offered. "She asked if I knew you from the 'art world.' I didn't know what she meant."

He brightened and nodded for me to follow him. In the front room, which had a larger and more ornate fireplace than the one in the bedroom, Giamma walked to the mantel and picked up a small stone figurine of a nude woman, roughly truncated at the neck. "You saw some of my father's collection in Orbagne. He is an art dealer too. I help him occasionally. But look." He handed me the sculpture. "She is Venus, I think. Possibly Isis." He gestured at the orb in her hand. "It's almost exactly like an example of Venus from Dura Europos. But it's impossible that she came from there."

I cleared my throat. This new development was consistent with my perception of Giamma, something I might have guessed myself: that he was sophisticated and wealthy enough to spend time buying and selling art. "How do you know?"

He hesitated. "Many headless female figurines like this have been found throughout Gaul. But her identity depends on how you interpret what she's holding in her hand. If she's holding an apple, she is probably Venus. If it's a patera, she could be anyone. She could be Isis. She could be a Gallic goddess who was never Romanized."

My eyes shifted from the sculpture to the rest of the room. There was a high, stiff-looking couch, a seascape in a gold frame over the fireplace, and three large windows framed by velvet curtains. It didn't look like a place a twentysomething would want to spend time in. I was out of my depth, on every level.

I changed the subject. "How come you never told me you were friends with Pietro?"

Giamma looked genuinely confused. "What is there to say? We grew up together, and then we studied together at university. Benedetta too."

I narrowed my eyes. When he'd mentioned studying archeology as an undergrad, he could have told me that he'd gone to school with Pietro and Benedetta. "You studied together?"

Giamma made an exasperated expression. "Lena, what's the problem?"

I recalibrated. I could see that it was useless to try to get him to understand that withholding information was a form of lying. "Never mind. I'm sorry."

"No, *I'm* sorry," he said, approaching me and reaching in to uncross my arms from my body. I playfully resisted him, which he interpreted as an invitation, picking me up and turning toward the bedroom. He looked hurt when I wriggled and told him to put me down.

"It's just that, I—I need to get back to the house. Martha's doing a barbecue for the Fourth of July."

He deflated slightly. "Also, I need a tampon," I added. I was afraid he was making his own mental calculation of what danger I represented to him, now that I knew his secret. But to my relief, his face relaxed in understanding.

He handed me the sculpture. "Here. Take it. It's yours."

The figure seemed to tingle with an ancient energy, and I felt a jolt of adrenaline as I held it in my hands. In the rough part, on the neck, I could see some kind of residue. This had come out of the ground, maybe even recently. "What do you mean?"

"It's a gift. For you."

I suppressed a laugh at the absurdity of his offer. "I can't accept this."

"Of course you can."

"What would I even do with it?"

His eyes shone. "I'm sure you can find someplace to put it."

I was flattered to realize that he was seriously offering the sculpture to me; that he thought I should have it. Any skepticism I might have felt was pushed out by the sense of adulation I felt in that moment. "I live in a dorm," I said.

"Leave it with your mother. Or your grandfather."

I handed the figure back to him. "You're very generous, but no."

Giamma shrugged and put it back on its stand on the mantel. "*Siamo pronti*?"

WHEN I WALKED INTO THE palazzo around noon, Cyrille was standing in the entryway.

"You look nice," he said.

"Oh—" I uttered, looking down at my new dress.

"Do you want to go for a drive?" He looked at me intently, just like when we'd first met on that winter day in the Classics Department.

"Sure," I said. "Can I change quickly?"

"Of course. I'll wait here." He leaned against the iron balusters in the staircase and gave me a tight smile.

I had the sinking feeling I was in trouble. Sleeping away from the palazzo wasn't explicitly against the rules, but I had the sense it was frowned upon, based on Simone's reaction every time I came home from Giamma's at dawn.

I ran upstairs, dug for my tampons, and threw on a T-shirt and shorts. Then I stopped in the bathroom before I jogged back down.

Cyrille and I walked to the piazza, where he unlocked a black Peugeot.

"I'm going to show you the summit," Cyrille said. I knew he must be referring to the Little St. Bernard Pass, which the Salassi had governed and taxed, antagonizing the Romans for generations—until Augustus emerged from his triumvirate and made an example out of them. Thinking about Augustus made me remember how frequently that spring Lakshmi had asserted that he was a much more brutal emperor than people wanted to believe; and suddenly, even though I was with Cyrille, I felt intensely lonely. I missed Lakshmi.

As we drove up into the mountains, I asked him what he'd been up to over the weekend.

"Writing," was all he said.

I gazed out my window and tried to appreciate where we were, the magic of being in those mountains. My ears clicked as we ascended, and I caught glimpses of snow holdouts on the brilliantly green grass. The Duria River rushed on beside us until, at a certain point, it diverged from the road.

"Okay," Cyrille said, as he eventually slowed the car. I looked around. We'd been driving uphill for almost an hour, and yet the mountains continued to rise around us.

"This is the summit?" I asked.

He parked the car on the shoulder of the road and unbuckled his seat belt. "*Ouai.*"

We walked for several long minutes, and then I breathed in sharply, because I recognized where we were from one of Cyrille's slides: the stone outline of the Roman *mansio* that had housed travelers going over the mountains and to Rome in the early part of the first millennium.

"France is right there," he said. "We are almost standing on the border."

We kept walking, and soon we came upon the stone circle that predated the Salassi, a Neolithic site that had been deemed holy thousands of years prior. "Imagine there would have been a megalith here in the center," he said.

We were standing on the side of the road in front of the stone circle, completely alone. The sun was high in the sky.

"The first time I came here, it was rainy—a lot of clouds and fog. Not clear like today. Today it is clear enough to look down and feel *l'appel du vide.*"

I looked at him in confusion.

"To imagine jumping off the edge," he clarified with a mournful smile. "*C'est normal.* But we should not look down. Just in case."

I disagreed; this was not normal, looking down from a great height and feeling an urge to jump.

"Simone said that you found the dig site after you heard her advisor giving a paper on papyrus receipts," I said to Cyrille.

He nodded. "Partially true."

I regarded him expectantly.

"Her advisor's research was very interesting. It was the mistletoe in the poem that took my attention, because it does not grow in Egypt. But it grows in abundance in the Aosta Valley."

This made sense; Simone had said that her advisor's research was about trade between Alexandria and Rome. And Cyrille had mentioned mistletoe in the context of his love of Asterix comics, the day he'd said that the villa we were excavating was somehow magical.

"It was an important ingredient in Gallic religious rituals," he continued. "And it is the principal ingredient in the Botti vineyard's famous amaro. Which I have known about since I was small. We sold it in my parents' market."

I pictured the label on the bottles of Genetrix in the kitchen back at the palazzo, the golden bough encircling a glowing moon, the word ORBAGNE printed in red below it. And suddenly I recalled the sequence from *The Aeneid*, when the sybil tells Aeneas that if he wants to see the ghost of his dead father, he needs to retrieve a golden bough for Proserpina, who would grant him entry to the underworld in exchange for it. *Viscum* was the word used to describe the bough that Venus sent two doves to help Aeneas find, I remembered. It was the word for mistletoe. Mistletoe came from oak trees.

But why, if Cyrille was so interested in the Gauls and their rituals, had he been looking for a *Roman* villa? "Were the Salassi on the vineyard before the Romans got to Orbagne, or something?"

He gestured to the *mansio* behind us. "Inside is a *fanum* dedicated to Epona Augusta. The only goddess from Gaul to be incorporated into the Roman pantheon."

I nodded, recognizing *fanum* from Cyrille's seminar. I'd looked it up in my Latin dictionary after class one night and learned it was the etymological root of the word *profane*. A *fanum* was a Roman temple built over a Gallic sacred place. Something that was profane was not sacred, because it was *pro*—outside of—a *fanum*.

"The Romans adopted Epona because she was useful to them. They did not yet have a goddess dedicated to horses and donkeys. And the Roman cavalry were very present here. But they erased all the other deities worshipped by the Salassi."

I thought about the statue Giamma had tried to give me earlier that morning—he'd said it could have been a Gallic goddess who was never Romanized. "Like who?"

His pupils looked big and dark. "*Dur* is water in Gaulish. I suspect the Salassi personified the Duria River as a goddess, the same way the Parisii worshipped the Seine as Sequana.

"And I believe we are excavating inside a sacred grove. That we will find a *fanum* inside or near the villa at Orbagne. It could provide unprecedented insight into the culture of the Salassi, which the Romans exploited and erased."

So Cyrille wanted to uncover the Gallic origins of the site—this was the narrative he wanted to find evidence to support. But why had he brought me all the way up here to tell me that? Suddenly I realized—he hadn't explicitly told anyone else. Or maybe he had, and he'd been met with disagreement. "What does Pietro think?" I asked, testing this hypothesis.

Cyrille winced as if I'd pressed on a bruise. "Pietro told me. About Gian Maria."

"Giamma?" I clarified, caught off guard. He hated being called Gian Maria.

"Lena, this is uncomfortable to say," Cyrille said. "But he is not someone you want to confide in."

Cyrille was probably ten years older than me, and he was the most open and curious person I'd ever met. I felt I understood him, and I was therefore inclined to trust him. But in that moment I felt judged, and it wasn't right for him to judge me.

"What did Pietro tell you, anyway?"

Cyrille sighed, and a long moment passed. "Pietro and his father know him well. The more they know, the more vulnerable the villa is."

Now I was confused. Was he talking about Giamma *and* Pietro? What did he mean by "they"?

"Marco knows something about the looters," I blurted. Whether this was an attempt to protect Giamma, or to defend myself, or if it was an act of genuinely trying to be helpful to Cyrille, I didn't know.

"Marco—at the inn?" Cyrille asked.

"I wanted to tell you earlier. But it sounded so ridiculous. He thinks some Eastern European gang looted the site in the winter. He said Italians wouldn't dig holes like that."

Cyrille didn't laugh like I thought he might; he nodded thoughtfully, as if Marco's theory somehow tracked.

"You should talk to him," I said. "Marco."

"I will," Cyrille said, and when he patted my back, I sensed that there had been some subtext to our conversation that I hadn't gotten. It was only later that night, in thinking back on our conversation, that it occurred to me that maybe Cyrille's original direct object when he was telling me who not to confide in wasn't in fact Giamma, but Pietro.

What I sensed from Cyrille on that day, standing in view of that millennia-old holy site, was a yearning to make sense of something. And if I had paid closer attention, if I had really tried to listen to the words he was saying and to imagine what he might already know, I might not have miscalculated so fatally; I might not have made it about me.

ON THE RIDE BACK TO THE VILLAGE, we took a different route. At a certain point, the road narrowed and we approached a small commercial center—Toulet.

I saw the internet café. Just past it was a billboard of sorts, with large, garish green words at the top. The only word I recognized was *vota.* Underneath the text, a smiling man leaned against a purple Corinthian column.

"He is the reason we are allowed to excavate," Cyrille said when he saw me gazing out the window. "You know him?"

I shook my head.

"Pietro's father, Andrea," he said. "He will be elected to the Italian Senate."

Cyrille explained that Andrea had agreed to the excavation because of the porphyry recorded on the papyrus receipts Simone had told me about. The presence of imperial porphyry—the rare, red-purple variant of the stone reserved for emperors at the height of the Roman Empire—on Andrea Botti's vineyard would validate his political ambition and signal a return to the lost power of the Caesars.

"But you don't care about the porphyry, you care about the mistletoe?"

Cyrille's eyes softened as he pursed his lips into a faint smile. He looked over his shoulder to check his blind spot, then changed lanes.

WHEN WE GOT BACK, Martha used a stove-top grill to make sausages and hamburgers, and we all sat on folding chairs outside in the weedy yard drinking bottles of Moretti until the sky started to turn pink.

Later that night, I walked into the kitchen to find Cyrille helping Martha with the dishes, singing "God Bless America" at the top of his lungs. Martha shook her head and laughed. There was something about the way she was laughing, the light in her eyes, and the way Cyrille was reflecting her own joy back to her—they were flirting.

I smiled and leaned against one of the wheeled tables Martha used for food prep. Cyrille didn't look worried at all; it was as if our conversation that afternoon had never happened. But my levity was suddenly replaced by a vague sense of betrayal. He had secrets, I realized. And the ability to hold on to them.

"Lena!" he said when he saw me. "Come, sing with me!" But I shook my head and made my way to the phone room on the other side of the kitchen.

I returned to this moment over and over in my mind in the weeks that followed. I couldn't stop wondering what might have been different if I had stopped to interrogate the real emotion underneath that impulse to withdraw: fear. But I wasn't afraid of Cyrille. So what, or who, was I afraid of? Cyrille deserved my loyalty, not my distrust. If I had put my feelings aside and sung with him, or stood close to him—if I hadn't walked past them to the phone room to call Jinny at that moment—maybe everything would have been different.

I CLOSED THE DOOR BEHIND ME and dialed home with my calling card. It was nine in Orbagne, so two o'clock in Wilmette, and I was hoping that my mother, who often slept most of the day on the weekends, would still be in bed.

Jinny picked up on the first ring. "Hello?"

"Hey! I'm glad—"

She cut me off. "Why did it take you so long to call?"

"Uh—it's been a week?"

Jinny's voice got high. "It's just that mom is—"

"What? Is she sleeping?"

"No," she said. "She's gone."

My initial reaction in that moment, as I processed the worry in Jinny's voice, was relief. Profound relief that I wasn't there, that I'd be able to control my exposure to this situation, however it unfolded. "What do you mean, gone?"

"I was at the restaurant yesterday for a double shift, and when I got back to the house, she wasn't here. No note, nothing. Her car was gone. And I didn't think anything of it, she's been doing her night drives all summer. But this morning she still wasn't here, which is weird."

"Did you try calling her?" Our mother had a beat-up Motorola that she often forgot to charge.

"Of course I called her. The voicemail box was full. And I called the police, and I called Grandma." Jinny sounded distraught.

I scratched my neck as my mind raced, but I couldn't think of what to say. I looked at the bags of rice and pasta and tins of coffee and wondered about the original function of the room I was in. Had it always been a pantry? What family sagas had transpired in this house, here in this picture-perfect village in the Alps? Maybe—probably—they hadn't fought about anything. They'd probably sat around, worry-free, in front of roaring fireplaces, snacking on speck and fontina cheese.

"What's wrong with you?" Jinny asked.

"I—what?"

"You really have nothing to say?"

Jinny must have known this question would trigger me; she knew I got upset when either of our parents recounted the story of my delayed speech, how I hadn't uttered any intelligible words until I turned three. And so maybe my tone was more acerbic than I meant for it to be when I said, "Honestly, Jinny, what can we do? What can anyone do?"

Jinny expelled a sharp breath. "You know, Lena, that's the difference between you and me. I don't just sit back and let things happen—I *do* something in a crisis. I don't push the hard things off on everyone else. And by the way—"

I stopped listening and pictured Jinny, glasses slipping down the narrow bridge of her nose, her straight auburn hair falling into her face. She was probably sitting on the beige love seat in the living room among piles of my mother's ungraded student exams, books, magazines, and binders. When we were little, Jinny and I would huddle together on that couch as my mother tore around the room looking for her car keys, enumerating all the ways we contributed to her suffering. I would inch my way into the couch's corner, and Jinny would sit in front of me, a human shield. What I tried to convey with my eyes on those nights was betrayal—the genuine feeling of betrayal at having a mother who didn't know how to mother.

What I had most held against my mother, though, was that she taught me to feel what she was feeling. Which, I realized in that moment, letting Jinny's voice wash over me, was fear. She had been afraid, and she'd taught us to be afraid.

When Jinny stopped talking, I hung up. Whatever abstract worry I'd felt at the beginning of our phone call had been replaced by indignance. I was an entire ocean away from my mother, and I didn't need to be made to feel guilty for having escaped her, especially not by Jinny, who had left me alone with her for three whole years. Had Jinny been more present during that time, had she bothered to come home at all, she would have known that my mother had disappeared overnight countless times, and that she'd always come home.

X.

MARCH 22, 2022

NEW YORK CITY

"It's *super* sad," the new paralegal tells me, in a tone one might use to comfort a small child whose ice cream scoop has toppled from its cone.

I wave her into my office. "Wasn't he ninety-three or something?"

Her young face lights up. "Totally."

"Did you print the bequests?" I ask, leafing through the folder she's handed me. "The development person at MoMA already called twice. Didn't even wait until the body was cold to find out if he changed his mind about restrictions while he was on his deathbed."

"Oh . . ."

"They say you can't take it with you, but that's what a trust is for—to make sure no one else takes it either."

She nods vacantly. Maybe she doesn't get the joke, or maybe she's afraid to laugh. I make a mental note to work on my delivery. Then my phone buzzes, an unknown 212 number. I decline the call. "Let's just start with all the gifts of art—"

The phone rings again, same number. "I need to take this."

The paralegal stays put. "Of course."

"You can close the door on your way out," I clarify, reaching for my phone.

"Lena?" a familiar voice asks on the other end of the line.

I'm barely able to contain my excitement, but I wait until my office door is fully closed to respond. "Is this Si?"

There's a long pause, and then: "Can you come up to Inwood?"

AN HOUR LATER, I'm back in front of Si's moss-covered building on Thayer Street. I make my way through the lobby and present myself to the doorman. He looks past me, and when I turn around, I see Si's blond head peeking out of an open door. They wave me in.

"Is this an apartment?" I ask, taking in the kitchenette to my immediate right, the hall tree of coats in the entryway, and the three closed doors beyond where we're standing.

"This is my studio," they say. "I live upstairs."

I'm suddenly conscious of my full bladder. "Can I use your bathroom?"

"Of course," Si says, nodding to the farthest door.

The bathroom is spotless, but when I close the door behind me, I nearly gag from the smell inside. It's unlike anything I've ever encountered—something approximating a mixture of Windex and minty urine. As I sit down on the toilet, I follow the penny tiles on the floor to where they meet the edge of a cracked bathtub almost fully concealed by a closed shower curtain. From my seated position, I pull it back and peer in. A marble sculpture of a little boy is in the tub, soaking in a clear solution. When my eyes start to water, I yank the shower curtain closed. As I wash my hands, I glance up at the mirror and shake my bangs out of my eyes.

When I reemerge, Si is in the sliver of a kitchen next to the front door. "Want something to drink? Water? Tea?"

"Sure," I say.

I watch as they spoon matcha into two cups and flick on an electric kettle. "I have macadamia or oat milk," they say.

"Whichever," I say.

Matcha lattes in hand, Si leads me into the room next to the bathroom. It has parquet floors, high ceilings, and closed blinds. They sit down at a wheeled chair in front of a desk and motion to a futon. I scan for evidence of the work Si does, spotting a wooden box on the desk and a few vaguely dental-looking tools resting on a paper towel. Other than that, it's a regular office, with a double computer monitor setup and three towers of filing cabinets.

Si nods at me. "So," they say.

I push up the sleeves of my turtleneck and rub my arms. "You're not easy to find. Which is by design, I assume."

A look of recognition flickers across Si's face as they sip their latte.

"Do you mainly work with museums?" I offer.

"Museums, art dealers. I do some inventory management too. Occasionally I work with private collectors."

"How'd you start working with Caroline?"

Si gets up, walks over to one of the windows, and twists open the blinds. "I've known her forever."

I wait as long as I can, but Si stays silent. "How did you meet?" I ask.

"She was my advisor in undergrad."

I tilt my head in confusion. "Didn't you go to Mount Holyoke?"

"She left for Fordham after I graduated. So she could get back to curating."

"*Back* to curating?"

Si returns to the desk chair and crosses an ankle over their thigh. "Aren't you her lawyer?"

"I mean, yes—"

Si's eyes widen, and I recognize their conspiratorial tone when it drops down a register: "She was a curatorial assistant at the Getty in the nineties."

I nod, waiting for them to say more. "And?" I finally ask, taking a sip of the matcha, wondering why a drink that tastes like dirt is so widely revered.

Si narrows their eyes. "Come on, Lena. Does the name Marianne Flynn ring a bell?"

My conversation with Emmanuel about the unsealed documents from the Getty suit floats back to me, and I wonder if Si knows Caroline was named in the Italian suit against Flynn. "Caroline worked with her."

"It scared the shit out of Caroline."

"What, the indictment?"

"Well, yeah. But also, she was blacklisted. No museum was ever going to hire her."

I'm skeptical of Si's fatalistic take on things—when Marianne Flynn's trial came to a head in 2007, Caroline was at least a decade removed from her time at the Getty. And having gone through all the unsealed documents, there's nothing to indicate that Caroline was anywhere as close to the illicit objects in question as Marianne Flynn was. "Why?"

Si examines their fingernails. "I need to know something."

I sit forward and clear my throat. That Si would have an agenda is probably something I should have foreseen. "Sure."

"How bad is it?" they ask.

I close my eyes. This is exactly why I shouldn't be having off-the-record conversations with witnesses. I have always felt completely transparent in Si's presence; they will know right away if I obfuscate any details of this situation. "You mean—"

Si cuts me off with a look of exasperation. "How bad is it going to get for Caroline?"

"I don't know," I tell them honestly. "I'm just assisting. But I know that the Italians weren't ruling out the possibility of individual accountability. At least as of a week ago."

Si nods, looking unsatisfied. "Caroline always says that Marianne wanted collaboration between American museums and archeological countries. All those new global exchange initiatives that happened after her trial, she'd actually proposed in the nineties. When Caroline was working with her."

I study the grid of Si's bare parquet floors, processing this information. "Did they fire Caroline?"

"She left on her own."

I nod slowly, thinking about Si's assertion that Marianne wanted what was the best for the objects. What does it mean to want the best for an ancient, inanimate thing? How can anyone, even a curator, really know? "How did that whole thing start?"

Si groans, but their eyes are bright. "Lena, really? This is common knowledge."

I feel a smile spreading over my face; it's invigorating to be reunited with someone who only ever knew the version of me that was captivated by the ancient world. Someone who would contend that an Italian restitution lawsuit is common knowledge. I can hear my tone shift from guarded to open when I exclaim, "Just tell me!"

Si smiles back. "A lot of people would say it started with J. Paul Getty himself. He started collecting right before World War Two, around the time that Mussolini launched his cultural heritage campaigns. He was definitely buying looted stuff. Everyone dealing in the black market knew who he was. Guys would come to him directly. It's crazy—in the seventies, they even kidnapped his American grandson for this huge ransom. And then there was the Getty bronze. A statue—a full male figure, except for the feet, and lost wax, so it was Greek—that got caught in an Italian fishing trawler, but in international waters. The fisherman sold it to some Italian art dealers, and it got passed around and then acquired by the Getty in the late seventies. The crazy thing is that it probably came from an ancient Roman shipwreck of a boat that was bringing back looted Greek statues to Italy. That's why there are so few of these Greek bronzes, because the Romans stole them and melted them down."

"So the Getty had it, and Italy wanted it back?"

"They wanted dozens of things back. And they eventually got a lot, but not the bronze. My point is that the Getty had been on Italy's radar for decades. The year before Caroline left, there was a raid on a Swiss warehouse. The guys running it had Polaroids of stuff the Getty had bought. Including the bronze. But the Italians couldn't figure out the paper trail, and eventually the statute of limitations expired."

The taste of dirt—matcha—lingers in the back of my throat, and I scratch my neck. "So Caroline left, and Marianne stayed."

"Right."

"But why? And why was she blacklisted?"

Si looks away. "None of this is documented," they say. "But she took the fall. That's what I think. I think she took the fall for the department and bought Marianne more time."

The warehouse Si just mentioned has to be the same warehouse where the photo of the Cupid and Psyche cup was found. Which would mean that Caroline knew the dealers running it.

My heart pounds in my chest. "Where was the warehouse?" I ask urgently. "The one with the Polaroids?"

This is clearly a spell-breaking question. Si's eyes flash, and they shake their head. "Look it up if you want. That part is well-documented."

I fight the urge to narrow my eyes. Between media coverage and unsealed documents from the Marianne Flynn case, the only art warehouse related to the Getty I've read about was somewhere near Geneva. Si knows more than they're willing to say right now, I'm certain of it.

"Anyway," Si continues. "It worked out for Caroline in the end, going into academia. She's a big deal, you know. Her work on papyrus receipts changed the field."

I straighten my spine at Si's description of Caroline, because it's dislodging a memory: the skin scraping off my heels on my first morning in Orbagne as Simone tells me how Cyrille found the location of the villa—it was thanks to her college advisor, a papyrologist whose research Cyrille had encountered at a conference in Rome. Cyrille telling me later at the Little St. Bernard Pass summit that it was the mistletoe in the poem she was studying that had piqued his interest. *It doesn't grow in Alexandria,* he said. *But it grows in abundance in the Aosta Valley.*

Caroline was Si's original connection to the dig in Orbagne. "She knew Cyrille," I hear myself say.

"I don't think she *knew* him, knew him. She knew the dig."

The photo from Giamma of Si posing with Pietro, Filippo, and Benedetta flashes in my mind. "Are you still in touch with Pietro?" I ask as nonchalantly as possible.

They look down, and I'm not sure if they're nodding or shaking their head no. "Here and there. We had a bit of a falling-out, unfortunately. Or maybe not so unfortunately."

I know it won't do any good to pick an old scab and make an enemy out of Si. But I can't let it go.

"I googled the site," I say. "The Villa del Frutteto."

Si stiffens. "Yeah. He got what he wanted."

"UNESCO?"

They scoff. "*I* was the one who pushed for UNESCO."

"So what did he want?" I ask, at the risk of looking too interested.

"To confirm his theory of the site," Si says matter-of-factly. "That it was one of the estates owned and abandoned by Melania the Younger."

"And to keep his dad happy," they add.

A rush of affirmation shoots up my spine. "His dad?"

"I spent six more summers there. The finds were incredible," Si says. "But Pietro was going too fast. Not fully destroying the stratigraphy, but almost. I couldn't keep track of everything. Sometimes things would go out to the lab for analysis and never come back. Or his dad would ask me to do appraisals without telling me what they were for. I refused, obviously. He had his own theory about the villa."

"Which was?"

"Glory of Rome, full stop. He wanted to prove it was used as an *imperial* country house, like an alpine version of Tivoli. And to be fair, that wasn't out of the question. Everyone agreed on those carbon-dated papyrus receipts, even Cyrille—despite the fact that papyrus is notoriously difficult to carbon-date. We're talking margins of plus or minus a hundred and fifty years, best case. Anyway, it was physical evidence. Pietro's dad wanted to get down to the end of the Augustan strata so we could 'finally unearth the imperial porphyry.' But the poem didn't mention *imperial* porphyry, only porphyry."

"So he thought you guys were going to find, what, the Pantheon floor?"

"I think he honestly thought we were going to find an imperial sarcophagus. That he could bury himself in, like Napoleon tried to do. I kept telling them we weren't going to find anything like that in the Augustan strata—the timing didn't line up. Obviously historical texts aren't always accurate, but the first written mention of imperial porphyry wasn't until 18 CE, which is about forty years too late for our timeline. If we were going to find imperial porphyry, it would have been in the *late* Roman strata, which had already been excavated by Pietro and Cyrille. And I was right. They found zero imperial porphyry."

I want to ask Si about Cyrille, but I'm not sure if I'm ready to hear what I know in my bones to be true—that he never returned to the site. That no one in Orbagne ever heard from him again.

"For a while I rationalized being there, because it looked great on my CV, and Pietro kept giving me more responsibility. Oh, and he started paying me."

"Right," I say, covering the top of my cup to prevent the matcha's dirt smell from wafting up. I refocus my gaze, determined to keep it together.

"Hey," Si says gently. "It was a long time ago."

Their tone is resigned; there's no trace of accusation. And I get the sense that I've just avoided a potentially dangerous confrontation, so I nod solemnly, breathe in, and change the subject. "What's your take on all this repatriation stuff?"

"I'm torn," they say after a thoughtful pause. "On the one hand I think these objects are for everyone, and that's the purpose of museums, right? To provide access. And I mean, we went to that museum in Aosta together."

"Yeah," I say, thinking of our visit to the archeological museum so many years ago, the way Si surveyed the dusty galleries with their exacting and disapproving eye.

"Everything was dirty and scattered, all the cases were scratched. Except for that one with the stuff from the villa—which was probably donated by Filippo. And anyway, who's going all the way to Aosta to see art in a regional museum? People complain that it costs twenty-five dollars to go to the Met now, but that's much cheaper than a plane ticket and the wherewithal it would take to actually get to the Italian Alps. Also, a lot of these regional museums don't even have the resources to keep objects on display. Like the Nostoi collection, the one that was returned to Cerveteri in 2017. The museum there is so understaffed that it's literally never open. Anyway, in my opinion—if museums open the floodgates, they'll have a hard time justifying keeping anything ancient. Some provenance that checked out twenty years ago but turns out to have been forged—we can't go back. But we can do better now. A group donation of the scale of what Filippo gifted to Fordham—there were hundreds of items, most of them fragments. I don't blame Caroline for not digging into every last thing. She didn't even catalogue everything on arrival. I did a lot of it as a contractor, but that was almost five years after the initial accession."

What *Filippo* gifted, is what Si just said. But the gift came from Creon, not Filippo. Did Filippo Dalmasso lie about the ownership structure of his collection? "So you worked on the gift in what, 2012?"

"Something like that." Suddenly Si's expression changes, and the number eleven between their brows deepens. "Are you lawyering me?"

"What does that mean?" I ask.

"You being here. It's about the case, right?"

I'm quiet for a long time, trying to determine the question underneath this question. "A little, but I'm also really happy to see you, Si. It's been a long time."

Si breathes in and out, watching me.

They're still with me, I decide. Gently, I change gears. "When you kept going back to Orbagne summer after summer—how did you deal? With all the destruction, or whatever you said Pietro was doing? How did you stomach him just plowing through?"

Si thinks it over. "Honestly?" they say eventually. "That's *why* I stayed. I salvaged as much as I possibly could. I was a cataloguing machine those six summers. I can't even imagine how much more would have been lost if I hadn't been there."

"So it wasn't just about your CV, like you said before?"

Si smirks. "Give me some credit, Lena. I mean, don't get me wrong, I care about my business, I care about making money. But I care about the objects more. That's why I was pushing for UNESCO. At a certain point I realized that if I didn't leave I was basically enabling him to keep doing what he was doing. And it worked. Eventually Pietro came around on UNESCO, so now the site is subject to their international regulations. And monitoring."

Si's brown eyes stay fixed on me. I believe that they care about the objects; it's consistent with the Si I knew the summer we were roommates. But what I really want to know is where everything Si worked on in Orbagne ended up. I try to get at this indirectly: "Out of curiosity—and I'm asking as Lena, the person, not Lena, Caroline's lawyer—how do you think Caroline would react if the Italians proved stuff was looted?"

"In public or in private?"

"How about private?"

"She would say it's irrelevant. The artifacts she's in charge of are safe, insured, publicly accessible, blah blah blah."

"But—" I start, feeling insulted by this flawed logic. Present conditions don't cancel out a history of wrongdoing. *All's well that ends well* is not an argument that would ever hold up in court.

"Anyway, they'll never get the Cupid and Psyche cup back," Si interjects with a shrug.

This comment seems to precipitate a shift in the atmosphere of the room. "Because of the statute of limitations?"

"There's no statute of limitations on looted antiquities in the States."

"But isn't that how Marianne Flynn got off in the end? The statute of limitations expired?"

"Only because they couldn't prove that the objects were stolen. Even now, if someone can definitively prove the Getty bronze was stolen, there would be legal grounds to return it." Si's eyes glaze over, as if they are making a silent calculation. "For all we know, the Cupid and Psyche cup legally belongs to France."

I squint. "What do you mean?"

"That kind of glass came from Alexandria, and there was a single workshop in Rome we know of that worked with it. A *vasa diatreta* was made to be ceremonial—to be on display and used only occasionally, even back then. When Napoleon's army raided Rome in 1796, they took anything and everything of value that was out in the open, which this probably was. So theoretically it's been on the black market since then."

I look down at the floor again. "But Italy was its country of origin."

Si raises an eyebrow. "Was it? Italy wasn't Italy until 1861. When it was unified. We have to accept history for what it is," Si adds, reading the skepticism on my face. "And then go from there."

To accept history for what it is—how is this possible if no one can agree on what happened? But right now I don't want to disagree with Si, about the past or the present, and so I rack my brain for a safe subject.

"Are you still in touch with Martha?" is what I come up with.

To my surprise, a trace of disapproval crosses Si's face. "She never left."

"Orbagne?"

"No, I mean, she's still in Italy. She married an Italian chef, had kids. She lives in Mantova."

"Huh," I say.

"After the whole thing with Cyrille, she said she was done with the mountains."

"What 'whole thing'?"

Si narrows their eyes. "She was in love with him."

Cyrille was in the kitchen at the palazzo in Orbagne, I remember, washing dishes and singing while Martha looked on in admiration, the night Jinny told me my mother was missing.

"Kind of an asshole move, when you think about it. Like, I get that you can't get along with your co-director or whatever, but here's this girl you've been sleeping with, you've made promises to her, and you ghost her?"

"You think he just left of his own volition?" I ask, somehow managing to control the waver in my voice.

Si looks at me straight on. "Look, I get what you're saying. He was embarrassed, he was scared, whatever. After the article came out and stuff. But I'm sorry, professional humiliation is no reason to just disappear completely on your girlfriend."

When Si says this, I want to ask about *their* love life—their fingers are ringless like mine—but what comes out is, "Girlfriend is a strong word."

"Why? Because you never heard him call her that? Let's remember that you were basically MIA for most of the summer. Off with your *boyfriend.*"

Si's sarcastic tone doesn't match the blank expression on their face. But this accusation is so unfair that I snap. "You're the one who's still friends with him."

"We're not friends," Si says quietly. "Giamma and I have done a few projects together. That's it."

"He wouldn't give me your number. Why?"

They look down at their watch. "I should—"

"Wait. About Pietro. I mean, about his dad. Do you think—" I hesitate. I want to be direct; I want to float my Andrea Botti theory, to confirm it. But it feels too risky. I can't figure out if I trust Si, or for that matter, if Si trusts me.

"I need to get back to work."

At the mention of work, I reach for my phone, but it's not in my back pocket. Or my purse. I barge into the foyer in search of my coat.

"Wait—" they say sharply, too late. I'm already frozen in the doorway of the wrong room, staring in awe at floor-to-ceiling shelves lined with meticulously organized objects: marble sculptures, bronzes, and pottery. In the center of the room are boxes and crates in various packing states and sizes.

Si nudges me out and pulls the door shut. "It's in there," she says, nodding to the other door. Their pale face is flushed. But this is Si's conservation studio; why are they embarrassed? As in, why wouldn't a conservator have a room full of ancient objects?

I locate my jacket in the closet. Si hovers next to me as I fumble in the pockets. My phone is nowhere to be found. "Was someone else here while we were in the other room?" I call as I head back to Si's office. "Can you check the bathroom?"

"Sure," they say flatly.

I wander back over to the desk, where a pile of appraisal documents printed on Artemis Antiquities letterhead catches my eye.

"No luck," Si yells from the bathroom. "Want me to call you?"

"Yeah," I say, turning around to watch the futon. A muted buzzing emanates from the desk behind me. I'm instantly vindicated—Si *did* take my phone. I turn around and survey the desk, following the sound to a wooden box next to one of Si's monitors. It's an old-school BlackBerry, lit up and buzzing.

Si reappears, iPhone to ear, to find me holding up the BlackBerry, an unknown number beginning with +39 blinking on its screen.

Si's tone is neutral: "I use it for work."

"Okay," I say, reeling, thinking—and how could I not?—of Giamma, how he refused to put me in touch with Si. "Do you need to take this, then?"

They pocket the BlackBerry. "I'll call him back."

Si stalks over to the futon, lifts a throw pillow, and seizes my phone. They raise their eyebrows at me. "Here you go."

"So weird," I say. "It didn't buzz when you called." I look at the face of my phone. Sure enough, there's a missed call from Si's phone number.

"You should go, Lena," they say curtly.

XI.

JULY 7, 2004

ORBAGNE

"So you're a detective now?" Pietro asked me in his BMW on the way to the internet café. I looked over at him, annoyed that no one else had signed up to go that night. He smiled tightly at the road ahead.

I knew he was referring to my conversation with Cyrille from the day before, but I feigned confusion. "What do you mean?"

"Come on," he said. His tone cut into me. "An Albanian gang?"

I clenched my jaw. Now that I knew he and Giamma were friends, I needed to be careful. "It's just something I overheard at the bed-and-breakfast," I lied. "When I first got here."

"You realize I'm the reason this dig exists, right?" Pietro said sharply. "There is no villa if not for me."

I understood this to be a warning of some kind. "Cyrille is lucky to have you," I said, in an impulsive appeal to his ego.

Pietro's shoulders relaxed down. "Do me a favor," he said, glancing in his rearview mirror. "Don't indulge him. He is completely paranoid. He doesn't need any more theories."

I was relieved when in response to my silence he turned and headed toward the renovated low stone building that housed the internet café.

Inside the now familiar space, the jewel-toned couches were vacant—no one was waiting for a turn ahead of us. Only one of the eight desktop computers was occupied, by a middle-aged woman drinking a Coke Light. A petite twentysomething wearing a T-shirt with the word *WHATEVER* emblazoned across the chest greeted us from behind a desk.

I took a seat at my assigned computer, launched the little blue *e* icon, and logged into my Columbia email. Lakshmi had written in response to the details for my upcoming trip to Sicily. The Ryanair flight was shockingly cheap at eighteen euros, round trip—from Torino to Trapani.

Pietro was in the row behind me, his serious face illuminated by the glow of his screen. I turned back to my inbox. One of the emails had an exclamation point next to it. It was from Financial Services with the subject line *URGENT ACTION REQUIRED*. It had been sent the week prior. "Shit," I whispered.

As I skimmed the body of the email, a knot formed in my chest. In bold at the end of the last paragraph I read, **if we do not receive 2003 tax return documentation by July 15th, your financial aid will not be renewed.**

Since they were technically still married, my father filed a joint tax return every year for himself and my mother. Earlier that spring, I'd asked Financial Services for an extension on the paperwork I owed them when I hadn't been able to pin down my mother on the subject. But then I couldn't bring myself to call my father in time for my June extension deadline, and Jinny had promised she would take care of it while I was in Orbagne. Now I forwarded the email to Jinny, adding a line of question marks before the original message, reminding myself that she had always done what she said she was going to do, regardless of whatever was going on between us. Then again, her voice on the phone the other day had barely even sounded like her.

On the way back to Orbagne, I stared out the window at the mountains in the distance. Whatever I was picking up from Pietro, whatever danger I sensed—it paled in comparison to the threat of losing my financial aid. After my last conversation with Jinny, I'd decided I wouldn't—couldn't—go back to Wilmette, maybe ever. And so if my financial aid fell through, I wouldn't just lose my education; I'd lose my home.

I snapped out of my anxiety spiral when I realized that we were back in Orbagne, but that Pietro had driven past his usual parking spot near the church. "Where are you going?" I asked.

"I need you to meet someone."

My heart thudded in my ears as he looped around to the back of the palazzo, then pulled up next to Simone's cataloguing shed and turned off the car. I froze in my seat, bracing myself for whatever was about to happen. As inconspicuously as I could, I felt for Giamma's BlackBerry in my pocket, thinking about the sequence of buttons I would need to press in order to reach him. But then Pietro clapped his hands together, which startled me, and when I managed to look over at him, he was smiling genuinely.

"What's wrong?" he asked.

I shrugged and shook my head in dismay. *So many things,* I didn't say.

"Let's go, then."

I opened the car door slowly and followed him. The night air was cool on my bare arms. He opened the back door to the building next to the palazzo, the one that housed the bar where I bought coffee on the weekends with Giamma. Inside, a single bare bulb illuminated moss growing out of the cracks in a stone staircase. "Where are we?" I asked as he led me up the stairs.

"This is my apartment," Pietro said, opening an unlocked door. He led me through a small, windowless living room and into the kitchen. "*Ti presento Signore Valenti.*"

I took in the small man at the table in front of me, the infamous reporter Cyrille and Pietro had mentioned a few weeks prior. I instantly relaxed. Signore Valenti couldn't have been less threatening, with his delicate nose and bright eyes. He was also younger than I'd expected for someone we were calling *signore*. "*Piacere*," I said.

Pietro's kitchen looked makeshift—its appliances were collaged in arbitrarily, mismatched in terms of both vintage and scale. The fridge was about a third smaller than the one I'd grown up with, and the microwave sat on top of a front-loading washing machine opposite a stand-alone stove.

"*Piacere*," he replied. The way he said the letter *r* in the back of his throat struck me as somehow effeminate; I'd never heard an Italian word pronounced like it was French. Pietro gestured to a chair at a round table covered with a waxy floral tablecloth. I sat down. A lit cigarette was resting in an espresso cup next to a notepad and a small digital recorder.

Valenti nodded back at me. "*Pronto*?" he asked Pietro.

"Signore Valenti has a few questions for you," Pietro explained. "For the article he's working on about the dig."

I nodded gamely. "Sure."

"*Allora*," Valenti opened, again with the soft *r*. "You are Cyrille's American student." He took a drag of his cigarette.

The corners of my mouth tugged upward. It made me feel special being referred to as Cyrille's American student, as if I were some apprentice, some important mentee, when in reality I'd been the least-active participant in his seminar. "Yes," I said, sitting up a little straighter.

"What was it like learning from him in the classroom?" he asked in English. Pietro took a seat in the chair next to me.

"He's an incredible teacher," I said. "The class was in French, and I don't speak French. But I probably learned more from him than from any of my American professors."

Valenti nodded and scribbled in his notepad. "And—eh—the course he taught; it was about this pah-ticular site?"

I looked over at Pietro, who kept his gaze trained on Valenti. What were they getting at? "Sorry," I said. "Is the article about Cyrille's class or the dig?"

Valenti glanced at Pietro.

"I'm sure he'd give you his syllabus," I said, remembering what Pietro said back when he announced Valenti's arrival—that both Pietro and Cyrille were supposed to be present for any interviews about the site. "Isn't Cyrille's apartment in this building? Maybe you should ask him directly," I added.

"Of course, of course," Valenti said, exchanging another glance with Pietro. "We will speak to him. And, eh, what is your sense of the American interest in the site?"

I stifled a laugh. I had no idea what Americans thought of the site. I only knew that this was a niche subcategory of Roman archeology the graduate students in Cyrille's class had barely studied.

"I mean, Columbia hired him. So my sense is that, yes, American academics are interested in the site—right?"

They nodded back at me. Pietro muttered something under his breath.

"*Allora,*" Valenti repeated, keeping his eyes on me. "When you studied with Cyrille in the States, did he ever show you any computer-generated visualizations of the site?"

I looked at Pietro. "What does that mean?"

"Exactly what it sounds like," he said.

I did vaguely remember something from that thick packet, a digital aerial view of the site. But I wasn't going to give out information on Cyrille without context, especially since Pietro and Valenti clearly had some kind of hidden agenda. "Why do you ask?"

Pietro crossed his arms and let out an exasperated sigh.

"I don't think so," I said pointedly.

Valenti moved on and asked me some other basic questions about my experience as an American up at the dig site. After about ten minutes, he clicked his pen and stuck it in the spiral of his notebook. "*Grazie.*"

"*Niente,*" I said. It really had been nothing, the interview.

BACK AT THE PALAZZO, I ran up the stairs to retrieve my calling card. Simone and Martha were in our room watching *Almost Famous* on Simone's MacBook. They waved me over and asked what had taken so long.

"I just talked to that reporter, Valenti."

Simone paused the video. "At Pietro's *apartment,*" I added.

Martha sat forward. "He's still here?" she asked. "What did he ask you?"

"Just random questions about Cyrille's seminar at Columbia. He seemed fixated on me being American."

"I don't think you should tell Cyrille," Martha said.

My conversation with Pietro about Cyrille's paranoia in the car on the way to the internet café came back to me. "What's going on with him?" I asked Martha. "Is he okay?"

"They're waiting for some funding to come through," she said.

I nodded, thinking how uncanny it was that I was in a similar situation. In a way, it made me feel less alone. It also reminded me that it was two in the afternoon in Wilmette, and that I needed to try to catch Jinny before she left the house for her shift at the restaurant.

"I'll be right back," I told them.

I went downstairs and closed the door behind me in the room off the kitchen where the phone was. The line rang and rang and then went to voicemail. When I opened my mouth to leave a message, nothing came out. Everything was fine, I told myself. My mother had disappeared countless times, and she'd always come home.

THE FOLLOWING SATURDAY, Simone and I took the first train to Aosta. By then I'd tried to reach my mother and Jinny five times, and had managed to leave a sheepish, rambling voicemail only once. I attempted to put the whole ordeal out of my mind as Simone and I stood and had coffee at a hole-in-the-wall bar near the train station in Aosta before walking over to the museum.

The archeology museum was housed inside a yellow palazzo dotted with small windows, and the entrance hall echoed with our footsteps as we approached the admissions desk, where Simone announced that we were guests of Pietro Botti. A fair young woman slid two tickets toward us.

"Let's go right away to the objects from the site," Simone said, trying to decipher a sign at the bottom of a staircase. Simone didn't know much Italian, but she had said more than once that she was having no issue picking it up. "It's a kindergarten language," was her take. I didn't agree with her. I'd tested out of Italian grammar and into literature classes at Columbia, but I still missed things all the time.

We entered a gallery featuring an oversized open-shelving system crowded with Roman-era pottery. "So this is why all of the shards we find are meaningless? Because if they were worth studying, they'd be more complete?" I said to Simone.

"Correct. Though the fragments can still tell a story," she said. "Or they can be reassembled. Which I'm going to learn to do in grad school." A faraway look spread over her face. "That's why we need to catalogue everything. I told you that pottery I said smelled like merum came back with a range that's consistent with Augustus, right?" She meant the carbon-dating range, which she had taught me was accurate but not an exact science—you only ever got a window of dates, which could span centuries.

"No," I said. "You didn't tell me. But what does it mean?"

Simone shrugged. "It's just good to have all the information. If Pietro is right that the site was continuously inhabited throughout early Christianity, I find it interesting that there are Augustus-era shards in the strata we're in."

"Hey, look," I said, stopping in front of a stone slab I'd seen pictured in Cyrille's packet. "This is that famous *incolae* inscription."

Simone stood next to me and peered at the stele's Latin words. "'*Salassi incolae qui initio se in colonia contulerunt*,'" she read. "*Contulerunt*—what verb is that?"

"*Conferre*. I had to look it up. The Salassi helped bring the new colony together, it says."

I told her how Cyrille had talked about it in the context of the Romanization of Aosta, how he'd said the inscription seemed to indicate that not all surviving Salassi had been sold into slavery as Strabo had recorded in *Geographica*. *Does the physical artifact supersede the historical record?* Cyrille had asked. *Or can two things be true?*

"Of course two things can be true," Simone said in response to that.

Now that I knew him better, I sensed Cyrille would have disagreed—that in his view, the artifact did supersede the historical record. He had emphasized, in our conversation at the summit, that he believed we would find *evidence* of the Salassi at the villa. "And when it comes to the villa?"

"What do you mean?"

"You said, 'if Pietro is right that the site was inhabited continuously throughout Christianity.' Does Cyrille disagree with him?"

Simone considered this. "I think they disagree about how and why the site was abandoned. I know Pietro thinks it might be one of the estates abandoned by Melania the Younger."

"I don't even know who that is," I admitted.

"She was this rich Christian zealot," she said. "Fourth century. Her fortune came from her grandmother, Melania the Elder—and Melania the *Younger* got everything when her father, Melania the Elder's son, died. A bunch of grand estates all over the Roman Empire. She tried to get rid of everything, you know, to live for Jesus or whatever, including everyone who worked for her, but there weren't enough people who could afford to buy the estates. The ones she couldn't sell she abandoned when the Goths invaded Rome in 408."

"So Pietro thinks the villa was abandoned by her and Cyrille disagrees?"

"I don't know if Cyrille disagrees so much as he's unconvinced. Pietro thinks it was an act of God that destroyed the villa, some natural disaster. Like a lightning fire. Which would explain that burn layer you guys found in your trench. *I* think her slaves burned it down. The slaves Melania tried to free. I mean, it makes sense. They depended on her for their livelihood. They had nowhere to go, and they were mad."

We wandered into the next gallery, which housed a reconstructed *thermopolium*—a Roman kitchen. Here the pottery increased in variety: a cooking pot on a reconstructed stove, spice jars, utensils, cups, and oblong amphoras that would have stored wine.

"So she abandoned them when the Visigoths invaded—wouldn't it make more sense if the *Visigoths* burned the villa down?"

Simone shrugged.

We made our way to the case that displayed the objects from Cyrille's first dig season, which stood out compared to the others because it was new and sleek. We put our faces up to the glass and examined an ivory comb, two rings, the mustard-colored glass bowl I'd seen on a slide back in New York. I zeroed in on one of the rings, which was gold with a big, round piece of lapis lazuli on its face. Etched into the blue stone was a delicate bird. The label identified all the objects as third or fourth century CE and described the villa as an active local archeological site.

"Do you remember that Catullus poem about the bird?" I asked Simone.

She smirked. "Haven't thought about Catullus since Latin AP."

"That's why I remember it! It was on my exam."

"The one where Lesbia is torturing the sparrow and Catullus says he wants her to torture him instead, right?"

I burst out laughing, and Simone's eyes lit up. "What?" she said. "That's what it's about."

"She's just playing with the bird," I said. "And he wants attention from her. Anyway, he probably gave her a ring like this."

"You are such a nerd," she said, smiling.

"You're the one tracing merum on pottery shards! We're the same."

"Lena, you and I are not the same," she said softly. The smile slipped from her face.

And on some level I must have understood then what I know now, because they were telling me as explicitly as they possibly could—but whether out of ignorance or discomfort, I didn't know how to acknowledge what was being communicated without words.

Maybe it would have been different if I'd simply asked them to say more, or if I had nodded, or put my arm around them and said, "You're perfect as you are." Because to me, in that moment, they were. But I was too unaware of who I myself was, to think that someone else might be beyond the surface of what I saw in them. You can't make sense of other people when you don't understand yourself.

WHEN WE GOT BACK TO the palazzo around one, Martha was smoking a cigarette in the kitchen. "Are you guys hungry?" she asked. "I can throw in some pasta."

"I'm just going to show Lena something," Simone said, "and then we can have lunch."

I made a face at Martha, who rolled her eyes back at me.

The garden behind the palazzo had become increasingly wild, and the moss growing in the cracks between the stones of the shed's damp exterior walls had proliferated aggressively. The door was open. "What the hell?" Simone said.

We stood in the doorframe and took in the scene: Pietro was rifling through one of the bins as Benedetta and a silver-haired man looked on.

I knew right away that the old man was Pietro's father—I recognized him from the campaign billboard Cyrille had pointed out to me. He had the same cold blue eyes as his son.

"Ah, *ciao*," Pietro said, looking back and forth at us. "What about the museum?"

"We went," Simone said, scanning the shed's interior, which she had completely transformed since the last time I'd been there: now the bins were labeled, there was a desktop computer, and the folding table was lined with thick brown paper. "Thanks for the tickets."

I watched Benedetta, whose gaze was as intense as the night we'd met. Her white sheath dress was a sharp contrast to the dirt floor we were standing on.

Pietro introduced his father as Senator Andrea Botti, the *sindaco*—mayor—of Toulet. The next town over, where we went to the internet café.

I tried to read the expression on Pietro's face. It was as if he was trying to express appreciation for some healthy food that tasted awful. He'd eat it because it was the polite thing to do, but not without betraying his disgust.

Simone and I nodded vaguely as he described us in Italian as the American girls on the dig, mentioning my background as Cyrille's student and Simone's American advisor at Mount Holyoke.

"You have an Italian name," Senator Botti said, addressing me as *Lei,* the polite "you."

"My mother named me after a woman Goethe loved. That's what she always told me."

When I was little, teachers would look at me skeptically on the first day of roll call. *Really?* they seemed to be saying, as if I'd been the one to choose my name. I would shrug in response and nod. That's when I first understood that I'd have to absorb the consequences of my parents' choices. As soon as I was old enough, I would clear my throat and clarify right up top: "It's Lena."

But Pietro's father wasn't skeptical; he seemed to approve. "The German writer?"

I nodded, then glanced at Simone, who looked hopeful, like she was waiting to be asked to give a speech.

"May I?" she said. She stepped toward the folding table, where a few larger fragments of pottery were laid out. She picked up a loupe, handed it to Pietro's father, and gestured to one of the fragments. "Now everything is organized with a new system—"

Andrea held up his hands and gave Simone a patronizing smile as Benedetta simultaneously stepped forward and took the loupe.

A minute later, Pietro looked at his watch. "*Allora,*" he said. "We can't be late for lunch."

"*Grazie,*" Benedetta said kindly as the three of them edged past us.

I was relieved to see them go. "Thank you for what?" I said to Simone. "How weird was that?"

"It's nice," she said. "He's showing them around."

"Don't you think it's odd that he brought them on the day you asked for tickets to the museum? He didn't give you any credit for all this, by the way."

Simone shrugged. "He helped me set the whole thing up. He's the one who got me all this stuff—the new bins, the acid-free paper, the archival ink pens."

"Right, but he wouldn't have known to do any of that if not for you," I said.

"It's his family. If he wants to impress them, who cares."

She was right; it didn't matter if Pietro wanted to show off to his father or his girlfriend. But there was something suspicious about the way Pietro had dismissed us—I knew *I* wasn't important, but Simone had completely overhauled the way they were handling and cataloguing our finds. She was making Pietro look good, and she deserved credit.

Pietro was much more legible to me now that I'd met his father—as in, it made sense that he had been raised by a condescending politician. Even if Pietro had primed his dad to look down on Simone and me, Andrea Botti seemed like a disapproving, smug man who never gave anyone the benefit of the doubt.

"Didn't you say his father was the reason the dig got funding in the first place?" I asked, thinking of the campaign billboard I'd seen in Toulet with Cyrille. "Can he help with whatever funding they're trying to get now?"

"Not, like, *proactively* I don't think. He's just a politician with good connections."

I nodded, logging this as a subject to carefully bring up with Giamma when I saw him later that night. "What did you make of Benedetta?"

Simone shrugged. She had slipped on a pair of white gloves and was carefully returning the artifacts to their bags. "She seems nice."

"I can't tell if he deserves her."

Simone turned to face me. "Come on, Lena. He's not evil."

BACK IN THE KITCHEN WITH MARTHA, my BlackBerry pinged with a message from Giamma. *Stuck in Torino. Call me? I need a favor.*

"A BlackBerry, huh?" Martha said. "You're fancy."

"Uh, no," I said between bites of penne with roasted tomatoes. "This isn't mine."

Martha put down her fork. "Whose is it?"

Her enthusiastic interest stopped me from telling her the truth. "It's my sister's," I said.

"Oh," she said, turning back to her pasta. "That was nice of her to let you borrow it."

She launched into a summary of her relationships to her two younger sisters, who both lived in the same neighborhood in Milwaukee where she'd grown up. Her parents helped them with their kids. The problem with three siblings, she explained, was that one person always got left out. In her family, that person was her.

"Is your sister older or younger than you?" she asked.

I felt a pang. "Older."

I could tell from her expression that she wanted me to say more but I was afraid I would get emotional if I did. It was dawning on me, perhaps abstractly, that my mother's absence back in Wilmette was not the routine behavior I'd initially assumed it to be, and that something might actually be wrong—with my mother, with Jinny, or both.

UP IN MY ROOM, I called Giamma, who asked me to go over to his house around four o'clock to receive a crate. I looked out the window. The street was quiet; all of Orbagne's little businesses were closed from one until three thirty in the afternoon. "Isn't the door locked?" I asked.

"There's a key behind a loose stone," he said, then proceeded to tell me exactly where to find it.

I was to let myself into the house, then wait until I got a *squillo*—a missed call—at which point I was to open the outer gate. "Keep the front door open and tell him to put the crate in the gallery."

"Okay," I said hesitantly.

"He needs to open the crate in front of you," he said. "Have him show you every surface."

"Wait," I said. "What am I checking for?"

"Defects."

"What kind of defects?"

"It's a bronze shield."

Giamma had said that his art dealing was a hobby. But the edge in his voice conveyed the opposite, that this was in fact a high-stakes situation. For as intrigued as I was about the shield, I didn't want to mess up something important. "I don't know," I said.

"I'll be there before it gets dark," he said. "It's not a big deal."

"What if something goes wrong?"

"It won't."

"What if it does?"

He sighed. "I will make it worth your time. How does that sound?"

I hesitated, thinking of the sculpture Giamma had tried to give me, the dirt that coated the rough truncation at the figure's neck. Maybe I should have taken it, given my now tenuous financial aid situation.

"Lena, please. It's a favor to my father," he said.

Now I felt emboldened. This was supposedly Giamma's *family's* summer house, but I'd never met either of his parents, and he was an only child. I felt defensive on Giamma's behalf—I didn't think anyone owed their father anything. "He can't come and check it himself?"

I felt Giamma's exasperation through the phone. "No, he can't."

This made me think immediately of Jinny, and where things stood with us, and I felt a wave of anxiety that quickly gave way to a surge of self-loathing I had to twitch to shake off.

The reality was that I had nothing to lose. It wouldn't cost me anything to help him. "Fine," I said. "I'll do it."

* * *

BY THREE FORTY-FIVE I WAS at Giamma's. I located the key behind the stone in the wall and let myself in. The BlackBerry buzzed fifteen minutes later.

I opened the outer gate and glanced out at the street. A teenage boy in the passenger seat of an idling black SUV stared me down as a familiar-looking figure pulled a large crate on a dolly through the courtyard. It was the green-eyed man from the boutique in Torino, I realized.

I led him to the gallery as Giamma had instructed, thanking him clumsily in Italian for his help with the dress the week before. When he gave me a blank look, I second-guessed myself—*was* he the same man from the boutique?

In English, I told him that Giamma wanted me to inspect every surface. He nodded and wrenched open the crate. My eyes widened as I processed what I was looking at: a metal shield, about four feet in diameter. Its rough brown surface was dotted in sea green. This was bronze, definitely.

"What is this?" I couldn't stop myself from asking.

"*Lo scudo di Polinice*," he said.

Scudo was shield in Italian; I knew that. But I didn't know who or what he meant by *Polinice.* I looked for identifying clues. One side of the object bore a simple design, a laurel crowning a sun. Running my fingers lightly over the remnants of paint in the grooves of the laurel, I wondered whether someone had actually used the shield for protection, or whether it had been decorative. It seemed to hum with vitality, and when I was done with the inspection, I was sad to see it disappear back into its crate.

He looked at me expectantly.

"*Grazie*," I managed, though it came out with the intonation of a question, not a statement. He nodded and departed silently.

Later that evening, Giamma returned. I showed him the shield. He nodded his approval and hugged me, then led me up to the bedroom. We kissed in the starched white sheets of his bed for a while, the sun casting a dark yellow rectangle on the wide wood planks of the floor. He slid his hand up my tank top, then pulled down the cups of my bra and held my breasts in his warm hands—and though I could feel the heat in his body when he pressed up against me, my mind wouldn't shut off. I was thinking about everything that had happened that day: the visit to the museum with Simone, the encounter with Pietro and his family, the call from Giamma, inspecting the shield.

"What's wrong?" he murmured.

I propped myself on my elbow and looked at him for a long moment, observing the way the red-gold edges of his hair framed his handsome face. I reached out my free hand and stroked his clenched jaw, then turned and wedged the back of my body into his torso, draping his arm over my rib cage.

My eyes floated to the stack of faded magazines on the nightstand. For the first time I noticed the word *Asterix* on a red spine in the middle of the stack. "What's this?" I asked, reaching for it. On the cover, two men, one big, one small, surveyed a village surrounded by rivers from a mountain lookout.

"Do you know Asterix?"

I paged through the comic. The words inside were Italian, but this was definitely the comic Cyrille had told me about back in June. "Cyrille told me that this was his favorite. That it made him want to become an archeologist."

Giamma sat up. "Really?"

"Yeah, he said that in the comic they do the same rituals that Pliny describes in *Natural History*. Something with mistletoe and a magic potion."

"What else did he say?"

My hackles went up; the only other time I'd seen Giamma this enthusiastically interested in something was when he'd offered me the Venus figurine at his apartment in Torino. "Why do you want to know?"

He relaxed onto his back, and I lay down next to him.

"You can tell me," I said.

He was quiet for a long moment. "What do you mean?"

"I mean, you can trust me. What are you doing with this stuff?"

He sighed. "Don't worry about it."

I looked over my shoulder at him. "I'm not worried," I said truthfully. "I'm curious."

"It's better if you don't know."

I flipped onto my stomach. "Then why did you ask me to inspect the shield? Did you not think I was going to ask about it?"

He was silent for a while, but I waited him out. "I need to bring it to Switzerland tomorrow," he finally said. "And I'd really rather not."

"Why not?"

He closed his eyes and shook his head. "It's complicated. My parents are complicated."

I felt a rush of compassion for Giamma. In his own indirect way, he was confiding in me. And he'd implied earlier that he couldn't ask anyone else to receive the crate. "I could go with you," I offered. "To Switzerland."

He squeezed my body gently into his. "Yeah?"

"But I don't think that thing is going to fit in your car," I said.

"Pietro is lending me his."

Before any questions or suspicions could come into my mind, he turned on the television. Rai was airing *L'ultimo bacio,* a movie about a married man who has an affair with a teenage girl when he finds out his wife is pregnant. I was mesmerized by it, maybe because of the score, which lodged itself in my brain and remained there for the rest of the summer and years afterward. My favorite part was the wife's rage when she found out about the affair. It made me think of Juno's wrath in the *Aeneid,* except it was completely justified.

I'd been wronged too. All I needed from my parents was their tax return—that was it. I never asked them for anything. And all I needed from Jinny was for her to make good on the promise she'd made to help me with this. Everyone who should have been taking care of me had chosen not to. I had absolutely nothing to lose. That was how I saw it.

XII.

JULY 11, 2004

LUGANO

On Sunday morning, we drove three hours east in Pietro's BMW hatchback, the back seat flattened to accommodate the crate.

I recounted to Giamma how I'd seen Pietro slipping into the church from the window after he stopped by to hand over the car keys. "I haven't seen anyone coming or going from that church the whole time I've been here."

"A priest from Toulet does an early service a few times a week. I think it is just the old people and Pietro."

"That's kind of weird, right?"

He smiled. "We have very deep Catholic roots here."

"No, I mean—" I reached into the glove compartment for Pietro's CD collection and held it up. "In the US, people think this kind of music is satanic."

Giamma shrugged, apparently unfamiliar with the link between death metal and the devil. "Pietro is, I think, the only one I know who really believes in God."

When I studied Dante's *Inferno* in an Italian literature class, I understood for the first time why people believed in God—it wasn't for the sense of community, or the love and mercy he supposedly emanated; it was out of a need for protection. From that vantage point, there was no harm in believing in God. I was not like my mother—who hadn't actively attended church since she was a child, yet thought God was communicating with her directly—but maybe I was like Pietro. Maybe I believed in God the same way he did.

"Are we here?" I asked as Giamma pulled into a space near the front of a large, nearly empty parking lot. I spotted a single-story gray building about a hundred feet away. He killed the engine, by way of response.

All morning I'd been pushing up against Giamma's aura of anxiety—telling him everything was okay, smiling more than I normally did. But now, the empty space between the warehouse and mountains in the distance felt deeply foreboding. I reminded myself that I trusted Giamma, and that he'd only included me on this errand reluctantly.

A man emerged from the building pulling a steel handcart behind him. He stopped, shaded his eyes, and waved at us. A breeze blew a wisp of his thin blond hair out of place.

"Who's that?" I asked.

"Wait here," he said, opening the car door.

Giamma walked over and shook the man's hand, then took the handcart from him. He wheeled it over to the car, at which point I got out. Even from where I was standing, I could see the surprise that registered on the man's face as his leathery skin transformed into a grimace.

"Do you need some help?" I asked in a low voice as Giamma pulled the packing blankets the crate was sitting on toward him, letting the crate slide onto the metal cart.

"Just follow my lead."

As we approached the entrance of the building, the man nodded at me but didn't introduce himself. Then he led us through a lobby with matted carpet and into an office with blank walls, filing cabinets, and a closed ThinkPad on the otherwise bare desk. He opened a drawer, procured two bottles of water, and motioned to a chair. "You're welcome to wait here," he said slowly to me.

I was startled—not by being relegated to the office—but to realize that he was speaking with an unmistakable Midwestern accent. "Are you American?" I couldn't stop myself from asking.

He looked just as surprised to hear me speak, his face illuminating with recognition as he looked from Giamma to me. "You hired an American?" he asked Giamma.

Giamma smoothed his eyebrow.

"Where are you from?"

"Chicago," I said. "Outside Chicago."

"I grew up in Indiana," he said, smiling. "Small world."

I glanced at Giamma. "I'm Lena, by the way."

"Quentin," he said, nodding toward the door. Apparently, now that he knew I was American, I was invited to join them.

The warehouse reminded me of the Home Depot where Jinny and I had bought last-minute Christmas trees a few times. It had the same high ceilings and endless rows, except that here they were populated with crates containing—I assumed—works of art.

I tried to keep the awe from my face when we approached two large tables filled with sculptures at the end of a wide aisle. "You can unpack it," Quentin said to Giamma.

Giamma laid the cart down and pried open the top of the crate. He slid out the shield, which we had rewrapped in the muslin it had arrived in. Quentin helped Giamma lift it onto an empty spot on one of the tables.

He gazed at the shield in awe. "I don't know how he did it, but he did it."

I kept trying to catch Giamma's eye, but he was watching Quentin look through a loupe at the shield's dark surface.

"Do you know what this is?" Quentin asked me.

I looked at Giamma, sensing that this was some kind of test. His chin shifted minutely to the right. I shook my head no.

After a few minutes, Quentin pocketed the loupe and clapped his hands together. "Lunch?"

Giamma exhaled audibly.

THE GROTTO—which Giamma had told me in the car was just another word for restaurant in this part of Switzerland—was cool and windowless and built into the side of a mountain.

We'd parked along the road, and as we were walking over, I was reminded of my daily walks to the dig site. Ascending while still being surrounded by other, bigger mountains; it was a feeling I'd begun to enjoy, the sense of being constantly dwarfed.

"What does our American friend think?" Quentin asked with a smile as we sat down at the table. There was something disarming about him—in spite of myself, I smiled back.

"Of Lugano?"

"Sure," he said.

I glanced at Giamma, who nodded at me. "The lake is beautiful." On our walk to the grotto, I'd had to stop and refocus my eyes when I caught sight of Lugano's bright blue lake, which seemed to have leaked out from the base of the surrounding mountains. It was nothing short of magical, that view of the mountains pushing mist around a glowing pool of water.

"A step up from Lake Michigan?"

"Definitely," I said.

Quentin craned his neck to look around the restaurant. I regarded the menu in front of me, which was in Italian with French, German, English, and some other language I'd never seen. "What's this?" I asked Giamma, pointing to the one I didn't recognize.

"Romansh," he replied. "It's vulgar Latin."

"Who speaks it?"

Giamma shrugged. "No one. Maybe a few holdouts in the mountains."

A waiter in a white button-down tucked into black jeans approached our table and set down two large plates of cured meats and cheeses, tonged a warm hunk of bread onto each of our plates. I felt utterly transported by the idea that there were holdouts of people who spoke Latin; it made me feel like time was being bent in some way, like I could access the past more readily.

"Giamma tells me you are working on the *gâche* in Orbagne," Quentin said.

I squinted—this was Cyrille's word for the site, a Lyonnaise term I understood to mean "place" or "spot." I'd never heard anyone else use it besides Cyrille, and I was certain I'd never repeated it to Giamma. I shifted in my seat, sensing Giamma's eyes on me as I nodded.

"Have you been to the site?" I heard myself ask. And before Quentin could answer, I turned instinctively to Giamma. "Actually. I don't think you've told me—have *you* been up to the site?" I tried to keep my tone light and agreeable.

"Not recently. When I went there at the beginning there was nothing to see yet," he said coolly. "And Quentin never comes to Italy."

I helped myself to a slice of prosciutto, thinking about how I'd meant to bring up the subject of the dig's funding with Giamma. But I tuned back in as I chewed that salty, melty ham, registering a strong undertow of tension between the two men in front of me.

"How's he doing?" Quentin finally asked. I sat up straight, recognizing a particular look on Giamma's face, the same one I'd seen the morning after the *aperitivo* in Torino. The "he" was Giamma's father, I suddenly understood.

"He's okay," Giamma said. "Counting down."

Quentin nodded, piling slices of cheese on top of his bread. "And Iris?"

Giamma shrugged awkwardly. I looked from Quentin to Giamma and back again. Was Iris Giamma's mother?

Sensing danger, I decided to intervene. "So how long have you lived in Lugano?" I asked Quentin.

He gave me a slightly patronizing smile. "Longer than you've been alive."

The waiter returned to the table with a plate of skewered and sliced meat, and plates of *contorni*: polenta, zucchini, and potatoes.

Quentin passed a plate to Giamma, who served me, and as we ate, I stayed quiet. They talked about the upcoming *ferragosto,* during which Quentin would be at his home in Montenegro. "And will you go to Puglia?" he asked Giamma.

I felt a pang when Giamma nodded without hesitation. We hadn't talked about what would become of our relationship when the dig season ended—would he invite me to join him in Puglia? If not, what would I do at the end of the summer? I had a return ticket to JFK for August 9, my birthday, but the dorms didn't open until the end of that month. Jinny and I had talked about meeting up somewhere between New York and Chicago, but that felt increasingly unlikely.

"And you? When do you return to the States?" Quentin asked me.

"I'm not sure yet," I said. I didn't want to dissuade Giamma from inviting me to Puglia with him. But no invitation followed; the subject was dropped, and we ate in relative silence for the rest of the meal.

After lunch, Quentin kissed me on both cheeks outside the grotto.

Back in the car, I replayed our conversation in my mind. "Was Quentin asking— I mean, is Iris your mom?"

Giamma nodded—despondently, it seemed to me.

"Where is she?" I asked gently, recalling what Benedetta had told me about her leaving.

He sighed. "She's in New York. It's better for her there."

"Why?"

I felt compunction the moment this came out, because now there was the possibility of him reciprocating and asking me about my mother.

But he looked relieved by the question. "Her father—my grandfather—was the Consul General of Italy in New York. His term ended soon after she was born, and they came back to Torino. She married my dad when she was young; she never finished school." He paused, taking one hand off the wheel and wiping it on his chinos. "I think she spent her whole adult life regretting the decision to marry my father, and to become a mother."

I nodded vigorously, recognizing myself in his situation. He was right: it was about regret. My mother had regretted marrying my dad and having Jinny and me. But she couldn't take back her decision; she couldn't unbirth us. What happens to children who inherit their parents' regret? Was this the root of my hypervigilance—the transference of my mother's regret?

Maybe, on some level, I'd always understood—albeit in an abstract, subconscious way—that my mother's regret was imprinted on me. But sitting next to Giamma in Pietro's car on that Sunday in July, driving back from Lugano to Orbagne, it occurred to me that the undercurrent of regret was, in some ways, a kind of nostalgia. Not for good times past, but for things that hadn't happened. Nostalgia for the possibilities that were no longer. Motherhood opened up a portal that closed behind you as soon as you walked through it. And even though I'd never been able to articulate it, I'd always sensed that my mother was feeling her way around in a dark tunnel. It was difficult for her to keep moving forward, and impossible to go back.

I looked over at Giamma, at the freckles dotting the outline of his bottom lip, and reached for his hand. He enclosed my hand in his and squeezed.

"She has her American citizenship," he said. "My mother. I'm trying to get back there."

"To New York?"

"When I get back, I can finish my dissertation, I can stay with her. I can get back to real life, to the things that matter. I won't have to do"—he gestured to the back of the car—"this."

I blinked, trying not to read too much into the fact that he hadn't mentioned me in the context of his return to New York. "So why did you even come back here?"

He glanced in his rearview mirror again. "I owe someone a favor."

"Who, your dad?"

"A curator in New York. She helped me get into Columbia. She got me out of here."

At the mention of Columbia, I felt a sudden pressure behind my eyes. Without financial aid I'd have to drop out.

When we stopped at an intersection, he handed me an envelope.

"What's this?" I asked.

"I told you that if everything went well with the shield, I'd cut you in."

I opened the envelope. My eyes widened.

"It's eighteen thousand," he said.

This time I didn't turn him down. I was taken aback by the relief that flooded my system as I dropped that heavy envelope into my purse. It was the weight of my fate, it seemed to me.

* * *

A FEW HOURS LATER, we arrived in Orbagne. Pietro had texted Giamma to say he was at his parents' house for Sunday dinner; we would return the car to him there.

When Simone had pointed out Pietro's family vineyard that first morning in Orbagne, the only structure she'd indicated was the off-limits chapel that supposedly contained Mary Magdalene's relics. So there were other buildings on the Botti vineyard—of course there were—I just hadn't seen them yet.

Giamma turned right at the halfway point of the route I walked every morning to and from the dig site, near where the road morphed into a wooded path. By living at home, Pietro could have saved both time and money, but he'd instead chosen to rent an apartment in the center of Orbagne.

The car strained up the wildflower-lined dirt road. When we eventually reached the house, the first thing I noticed—apart from its impressive scale—was the roof, constructed with thousands of scallop-shaped stone tiles. I'd seen similar tiles on other roofs in Orbagne, but none with this reddish-purple hue. Giamma pulled up to a garden shed, where three other cars were parked.

Pietro's mother answered the door in a blue housedress. She looked nothing like her son. With her dark, down-turned eyes and elongated chin, she looked, I thought, strangely like my mother.

She greeted Giamma with a kiss on each cheek and opened the door wider. "*Prego.*"

The house's interior smelled gamey and was unlike any of the other buildings I'd entered in Orbagne—the beamed ceilings were low, and in what looked like the living room, rough ivory walls were interspersed with paned stained glass windows. White sheets covered the furniture.

In the kitchen, Pietro and Simone were hunched over a MacBook at a table to the right of a cavernous hearth. I located the source of the smell—it was coming from a simmering cast-iron pan on the stainless steel stove, an anachronism in a house full of things that looked old. A white-haired woman with enormous hands was at the counter scooping the seeds out of a halved cantaloupe.

Pietro got to his feet, looking back and forth between Giamma and me in apparent confusion. But he didn't ask any questions; he just pocketed the BMW key and sat back down next to Simone, who hadn't looked up yet.

I tiptoed over to the table and saw that she had her digital camera plugged into the laptop—she was examining a photo she'd taken of the lapis bird ring at the museum the day before. "Boo," I whispered.

Simone's shoulders shot up to her ears. "Why, Lena? Why can't you say hello like a normal person?"

"Sorry," I said with a smile. "What are you doing?"

"I'm just making some back-records," she said once she'd recovered. "Pietro was giving me details on the objects from the museum. He made the point that this is probably a dove, not a sparrow. Which is most likely why it was found early on in the excavation, because yes, a dove symbolizes Venus, but it also can symbolize the Holy Spirit, or the soul in general—"

She noticed Giamma hovering behind me and cut herself off. "Where have you guys been all day?"

"We went to Lugano," Giamma said. "*Grazie ancora,*" he added, looking at Pietro.

"You should stay for dinner," Pietro said. "We have enough. Benedetta is with her parents in Aosta." He gestured toward an adjacent room whose walls were lined with book-filled shelves. "And my father left for Rome this afternoon."

Giamma wandered over to the stove to see what the woman was cooking, while I peered into the study. There was a mahogany desk with an ergonomic leather chair in front of the fireplace. Two additional smaller desks were pushed against the wall. One held a hulking desktop computer and a blinking modem; on the other one, a pile of oversized envelopes sat next to an industrial printer. A folding table in the center of the room displayed an assembly line of posters, flyers, and buttons, all bearing the name Botti in Kelly green. Maybe this was why Pietro didn't want to live at home—it was Andrea Botti's campaign headquarters.

"Braised *coniglio*," Giamma said, his eyes bright. "Rabbit. This was my favorite when I was small. Do you want to join?"

When Simone chimed in to say she was staying, I nodded.

The white-haired woman placed a plate of sliced cantaloupe wrapped in speck on the table. Pietro whispered something to her, and she nodded and disappeared down the hall. Based on her silent, perfunctory movements, I gathered that she was staff, not family.

A few minutes later, she returned with a bottle in her hand and a corkscrew in the other. Simone intercepted the bottle as Pietro was reaching for it.

I looked over Simone's shoulder at the bottle's faded label. The word *Monteleone* was foregrounded in cartoonish block font against a grayscale image of the house we were now in, stone roof tiles and all. On the upper right of the label was a red-and-white crest with an image of a horned man—it looked like a satyr—in the center.

"*La* 1942, *davvero*?" Giamma said to Pietro. "What will the senator say?"

Pietro smirked. "He hates these old vintages."

"So this place used to be called Monteleone?" Simone asked.

"The vineyard belonged to my mother's family before my father bought it from them."

In the dining room, a massive table had been formally set with porcelain plates. Pietro's mother was seated at the table, browsing a newspaper. She looked up over her reading glasses when we sat down, and I saw her eyes soften at the sight of the bottle.

We clinked glasses. The wine was a deep, nearly purple ruby, and tasted almost leathery; I had to work hard to keep my mouth from betraying the ambivalence I felt to such a foreign flavor. But when I swallowed, a memory of Jinny and me dipping strawberries into a bowl of powdered sugar at my mother's kitchen table flashed in my mind. I took another big sip and replicated the flashback. I liked it, I decided.

Giamma put his nose in his glass. "*Pazzesca*," he said with reverence.

Pietro's mother smiled at him and uttered something in Italian about the "old way" of making wine.

"What's different about how you make it now?" Simone asked as dinner was served.

"After, I will show you," said Pietro.

His mother raised her eyebrows but stayed quiet.

As we ate, my eyes traced the elegant design of the table's inlaid stones. In the center, a cluster of off-white rosettes carved out of what looked like alabaster was encircled by green medallions. Along the perimeter, I counted twelve apples, which were the same color as the wine in our glasses.

"This was a wedding gift for my parents," Pietro's mother said in perfect English when she saw me examining it. "From my Sicilian grandmother."

Giamma put his fork down. "I never knew you had family in the south. Where in Sicily?"

"Vittoria," she said. And to Simone and me, "The southeast of the island. Where they make many good wines."

"So you are descended from winemakers on both sides," Giamma said.

She pressed her lips together and nodded. Then she opened them as if to say something, but stayed quiet. We watched her expectantly.

After a long silence, Pietro pushed back his chair. "*Andiamo*?"

* * *

THE WINERY WAS A FIVE-MINUTE wooded downhill walk from the main house. I refocused my eyes in disbelief as we approached a clearing where an impossibly contemporary, barn-sized structure had been erected near the edge of a ridge. At the door, Pietro hesitated, then input a code on a device that looked like an alarm clock my father had once gifted me from Sharper Image that woke you up with the smell of citrus.

The overhead lights activated automatically to reveal a room as jarringly bright as an operating room, filled with steel tanks and conveyor belts. Pietro clapped his hands together. "This is where they make the wine."

Simone was already on the other side of the room, having noticed that part of the floor was comprised of a thick plexiglass. "I've been talking about the merum on that pottery fragment for weeks, and you didn't think to tell me about these?" she called out.

When we walked over to her I saw the mix of wonder and scorn on her face. "Well?" she said to Pietro, gesturing to the six enormous clay dolia imbedded in a stone platform about ten feet below the plexi floor where we stood.

He sighed. "You were carbon-dating it."

"Have you carbon-dated *these*? Why are they down there?"

"They are safe."

I glanced at Giamma, whose cheeks were flushed—whether from the wine or the confrontation, I didn't know.

Simone's eyes darted around the room.

"We can't go down there," Pietro said preemptively. "It's sealed."

She stalked toward the closest door.

"*Aspetta*—" Pietro attempted; but Simone was already gone.

Outside, she was standing on the level part of the glade behind the building, breathing heavily. Her hands were on her hips. "How many were there?" she demanded.

"How many—" Pietro repeated, stalling.

"Dolia. How many dolia were there? How big was this vineyard, exactly?"

I looked around. A stone-lined enclosure, about the size of the trench I was working in at the dig site, abutted the building. Next to it was a sarcophagus-like stone basin, connected to the enclosure's grated floor by a wide ramp.

"We don't know," he said quietly.

"How about a guess?"

He shrugged. "One hundred?"

"One *hundred*?" Simone shouted.

Giamma stepped forward and placed his hand on her left shoulder. "Okay, okay. *Tranquilla.*"

She recoiled. "You're how old—thirty?—and no one has ever told you that telling someone to calm down always has the exact opposite effect?"

The whole scene felt dreamlike. To ground myself, I raised my eyes to the sky. Day had turned to dusk, and big clouds were racing above the mountains in the distance. Simone pulled me to the side to ask if I knew what we were looking at, and I shook my head no. She explained that the enclosure was the winery's treading area. Grape juice flowed into the collection basin, which upon closer examination, bore five carved faces—one in each corner and one in the center. The four in the corners were either women or cherubs, with their round cheeks and flowing locks. The one in the center looked just like the satyr from the wine label.

Simone wasn't actually mad at Pietro, she confessed. She was happy he'd brought us here.

When we reconvened at the edge of the clearing, Giamma was lighting a cigarette. After he'd taken a few drags, he offered it to Pietro. Pietro took a turn and then offered it to Simone, who offered it to me.

Every time someone had offered me a cigarette that summer, I'd waved them away. But this time I put it between my lips and breathed in. My throat spasmed, and I practically vomited out the smoke I'd inhaled, my eyes burning with tears. Giamma took the cigarette, laughing sympathetically and rubbing my back. I turned away from him, hacking continuously into my elbow. "You're okay," he said.

When I finally caught a deep breath, I wandered over to the edge of the ridge and looked out at the mountains, which seemed to be pulsing with a primeval life force. The incline of the vineyard was inconceivably steep; it would have been a perilous endeavor, harvesting those dark purple grapes threaded in and among pergolas made from tree branches. My eyes followed the vines to the valley below, and I recalled a moment from a childhood road trip to the Grand Canyon: clutching Jinny's hand at a lookout, watching a pack of mules with eager tourists on their backs descend toward the Colorado River. Here there was no river—it was also greener, and much smaller in scale—but the sense of grandeur was the same.

My eyes fell on the Mary Magdalene chapel that Simone had pointed out on my first morning in Orbagne. How had anyone ever accessed it? As I surveyed the area for a path, I caught sight of the pink twine on the stakes that demarcated the trenches at the dig site on the other side of the valley, fluorescent against the dusky sky.

In all those long days up at the site, the possibility that someone might have visual access to us as we worked had never occurred to me. And all at once I was filled with a combination of doubt and hope, a feeling governed by a strange emotional logic, which was somehow connected to love. The world was vast and unknowable. Though I was fixated on accumulating truths in the form of facts—I could recite the first fifty lines of the *Aeneid* and the names and dates of all the Roman emperors—the reality was that I *knew* very little. Most of what I understood about the world I'd taken on trust.

XIII.

MARCH 25, 2022

NEW YORK CITY

On Friday, I'm at work when Emmanuel calls me into his office. "The plot thickens," he says as I take a seat at the round table in front of his windows.

He has a mischievous look in his eyes that I've never seen before. "Tell me," I say.

"The Italians were apparently trying to prosecute Dalmasso years ago. But they backed off because . . . drumroll . . . he had ties to organized crime."

Something catches in my throat, and I shield my face awkwardly as I process this new information.

Emmanuel furrows his brow. "You okay?"

"How do you know this?"

"I had a heart-to-heart with my buddy from the DA's office last night over drinks. He spilled that they want to get Caroline on willful ignorance. In vino veritas, I guess. He said, 'produce the evidence that exonerates her, or hand over the objects.'"

"Willful ignorance—as in she knew the provenance was sketchy?"

"Right. She turned a blind eye. Which implies complicity. The Trafficking Unit loves that strategy. They just used it to convict some antiquities dealer, and a judge gave him seven years."

"He went to jail?" I ask incredulously, in part out of genuine surprise and in part out of the ping of dread the term *willful ignorance* precipitates in my stomach.

"Yep," Emmanuel says.

The natural conclusion, then, is that a hefty prison sentence isn't out of the question for Caroline. "But what did they say about Filippo Dalmasso and his ties to organized crime? I mean, isn't he far and away more guilty than she is?"

Emmanuel nods. "So the dealer with the Polaroids—and I would have been able to find this on a quick internet search if I'd tried—" He exhales, shaking his head. "But the dealer was some notorious Mafia boss. Valerio Piromalli, he's called."

My mouth goes dry. Valerio Piromalli is—must be—Giamma's father. But strangely, a few seconds later, a wave of validation floods my system. I knew this. I knew the warehouse Si mentioned was the same warehouse I visited with Giamma. For as alarming as this revelation is, it corroborates that the mounting danger I've been picking up on is not just in my head. I'm getting closer to understanding how and why my past and present are intersecting. I blink rapidly in an attempt to relax the muscles in my forehead.

"The working assumption, according to the DA's office," Emmanuel continues, "is that Dalmasso obtained the cup either directly from Piromalli or his American business partner."

In my mind, I'm transported to that cavernous warehouse in Chiasso, trailing behind Giamma and Quentin as I take in the metal shelves crowded with objects. *I don't know how he did it, but he did it,* Quentin says as he examines what we've brought him.

"I feel like I'm missing something," I say, tuning back in. "So Filippo Dalmasso buys something from a sketchy dealer—don't lots of people do that? How does a purchase equate to 'ties' to organized crime?"

"Valerio Piromalli owned twenty percent of Creon until he died," Emmanuel clarifies. "He also sat on the board of directors."

My chin juts forward uncontrollably. The first thing my mind goes to is inheritance—who inherited the 20 percent when Valerio died? Unless Creon bought him out of his shares, they most likely passed to Giamma. It's entirely possible that Giamma owns 20 percent of Creon. "You're joking."

"This is interesting too." He hands me a piece of paper. "Caroline had a courier drop it off earlier today."

The document is formatted like an over-designed résumé. I skim a physical description of the Cupid and Psyche cup underneath a new, high-resolution image. Then my eyes float down to a section with the header *Appraisal History:* the cup is insured for ten million dollars.

"Caroline's new provenance," Emmanuel says, setting the original typewritten one next to it. "Take a look at the dates."

"What is this," I murmur, noticing that the date the cup entered Filippo's collection has been changed from 1992 to 2004, the year I was in Orbagne. Prior to Filippo, the cup is documented as having been in an unnamed private collection since 1938. But Caroline is not stupid enough to think that the Italians won't see right through a doctored provenance document—so what is she thinking?

"It's printed off the new platform Fordham has been migrating their art records to, apparently. Some blockchain thing. Wherever the objects end up, from here on out there will be no way to tamper with the provenance."

My eyes slide from the documents in front of me to the window on my right. Outside, beyond the neighboring buildings, the Hudson is undulating indifferently. *We can't go back, but we can do better now,* Si said when we met at their studio. This document has Si written all over it. I rise to my feet. "Can I make a copy?" I ask.

Emmanuel motions for me to sit down. "There's more. Filippo Dalmasso's daughter has apparently come forward—"

"His *daughter*?" I blurt. Benedetta's name is on the tip of my tongue, but I stop myself from saying it aloud.

"She apparently has information that she's willing to trade to protect him."

I shake my head. "Information that he himself doesn't have? Why can't he make a deal on his own?"

"I don't know," Emmanuel says. "I don't know what she knows."

"So what does it mean for Caroline if Filippo gets protection?"

"I don't think it's a done deal." He grins. "Oh, *and*—the denouement. Caroline is announcing her retirement next week."

"Was that her decision or Fordham's?" I ask, wondering whether this development is tantamount to an admission of guilt, or if she's just fed up with the case and wants to stop the bleeding.

Emmanuel shrugs. "She's retiring to Kennebunkport, Maine. Long overdue, she told me. Anyway. That part doesn't change anything for us. She's on board with the recommendation to repatriate everything. I thought you'd be amused by the intrigue of it all."

I cross my arms and lean back in my chair. "But what's with this new provenance document? Or platform, or whatever?" I pick it up and read the conservation history section. *Extensive cleaning and restoration completed in 2012*, it says. *Silver encasing, 1820–1830 hallmark. Silicate accretions removed with 12% sodium hydroxide; approximately forty glass pieces reassembled with archival adhesive* . . .

"Hold on," I say, grabbing the original provenance document and scanning it. "This one doesn't say anything about restoration. Or a nineteenth-century silver encasing."

Emmanuel shrugs.

"That's a bigger deal than the date change, don't you think?" I ask, my voice jumping an octave. "Si implied that the cup was in pristine condition when Fordham got it."

Emmanuel studies me as he clicks his pen. "Who is Si?" he asks slowly.

I lock my vision on the pen, realizing my misstep. I'm still holding the two provenance documents. I grasp for an out. "Si is—" I say, weighing the risk of coming clean at this particular moment, of telling Emmanuel that I've had an informal, off-the-record conversation about the case with someone I said I would speak to formally. Someone I first met eighteen years ago. "Si is the conservator Caroline mentioned the first time we met. I was still planning on sitting down with them for a deposition, like we talked about."

Emmanuel nods, seemingly satisfied with my response. But the panic rising in my chest does not recede. Si lied; they definitely said the cup was whole when Filippo Dalmasso donated it to Fordham.

"There's one other thing," Emmanuel says, glancing over at the closed door of his office. "Nothing to do with Caroline or Dalmasso."

I shut my eyes. This is going to be about Giamma. It has to be. And I don't have the heart to attempt to wriggle out of it, because if the cup—or anything from Filippo Dalmasso's collection, for that matter—was looted, Giamma knows something about it. Of that I am sure. What I'm not sure of, is the extent to which I myself am complicit in what he knows. Maybe it would be a relief for Emmanuel to ask me about Giamma, I realize—because at this point I can't rule out the possibility that I might be in not just professional danger but actual physical danger.

"I'm thinking about starting my own firm," Emmanuel says.

"Oh," I say, opening my eyes in surprise. This is the last way I could have predicted that Emmanuel would sum up this unexpectedly harrowing conversation. "Your own law firm?"

"We'd focus on this kind of thing—repatriation, looted art—but we could expand to other areas of art law. Copyright, trusts and estates, like the kind of stuff you've been doing for your clients. Which is pretty entrepreneurial, by the way. I mean, no one told you to start advising clients on how to maximize the benefits of art donations. It's exactly how a partner should be thinking."

I nod slowly. I can infer where he's going, and I'm fighting the urge not to see this conversation as a threat to my carefully constructed professional world.

"Lena, would you ever consider joining me? I'd make you a founding partner."

But when he says these words, I'm not threatened at all; I'm elated. Emmanuel thinks I'm good enough—not only to make partner here, but to recruit away as a founding partner in his own firm. For the first time in a long time, I feel like someone is seeing me the way I want to be seen. "Yes," I say energetically, surprising myself. "Count me in. I'm in."

Emmanuel holds up his hands like he's surrendering, and after a beat I understand that he is offering me a high five. I smile and reach across the table to acquiesce.

We talk about his plan for a few more minutes, and when I stand to go, I text Si and ask to see them as soon as possible. Then I head downstairs and hail a taxi.

THE DOOR TO CAROLINE'S OFFICE at the Fordham Museum is camouflaged into a wood-paneled gallery wall. After the wide-eyed administrator who brought me here pushes the door open, she genuflects and backs away.

Caroline does not appear to be caught off guard by my visit; if anything, she's happy to see me.

"Congratulations on your retirement," I offer, perching on the wingback chair in front of her desk.

Her chest rises and falls. "I've been at this a long time," she finally says.

The unforgiving gray light from the room's two paned windows would seem to corroborate this statement—her marionette lines are cast in sharp relief, and the spines on her bookshelves are faded. My eyes drift to a set of framed drawings on the wall closest to us, each depicting a single all-caps word written in hurried, desperate pencil strokes: VENUS on one, TURAN on the other.

"He gave them to me," she says, nodding at the drawings.

An image of Cyrille enters my mind, but she can't possibly be talking about Cyrille—can she?

"Nineteen seventy-eight. That was my first dig season. I was twenty-two."

I do the math. It feels exceedingly unlikely that she knew Cyrille then, even if these drawings look like they could have been made by a child. "Where was the dig?"

"Outside Siena. Etruscan. It was founded by my undergraduate advisor at Bryn Mawr. Me and a bunch of graduate students, all men. They only let me participate because I was on my way out. Headed to Yale to start my PhD."

I sit forward, suppressing the desire to relate to her—to share that I was on a nearly all-male dig as an undergrad too.

She motions to the drawings again. "Twombly had a summer house near Tuscany. He knew my advisor—they were in the army together. When he visited the dig, we got to talking. I was bored out of my mind. Pottery, pottery, pottery. He asked me what I planned to specialize in, and in that moment—I'd never said it aloud before then—I told him papyrus. Words were what had gotten me interested in ancient objects in the first place—all those years translating Virgil and Homer. It made no sense to just abandon all of that linguistic knowledge for the sake of an object, that's what I realized that first dig season. He was interested in words too. And he invited me to come see what he was working on."

One of my eyebrows instinctively arches up.

Caroline lets out a chuckle. "Nothing like that. Even then, everyone knew he was gay." She pauses, inviting a rejoinder, maybe—but I know almost nothing about Cy Twombly. I've always found his work to be impenetrable, and therefore vaguely threatening.

"So the next weekend I get on a bus and visit him at his summer house. It's filled to the brim—I mean, the *brim*—with Etruscan and Roman antiquities from flea markets. Looting in Tuscany was rampant then. And he brought me to his studio, where he was finishing up the *Fifty Days at Iliam* cycle. Which as you probably know, ended up at the Philadelphia Museum of Art."

I'm not at all familiar with the artworks she's referencing, but I nod—I want her to keep going.

"When I saw those paintings—even though they were new, it was the first time I understood the concept of an ancient palimpsest. The layers, the erasure. The idea that every new thing belies something old."

"I was on a dig too," I blurt. "That's how I met Si. We were on a dig together."

Caroline pushes back from her desk, an awestruck look on her face. "*You* knew Cy?"

I nod.

She blinks at me slowly. "How old are you?"

"Thirty-seven. I was nineteen then."

"What was he doing on a dig at his age?" she says, mostly to herself. "He really was—"

"Oh," I interject, registering her misunderstanding. "I'm not—"

She cuts me off. "He was a mystery, wasn't he? And a genius. What did you think?"

I nod in an effort to mirror her enthusiasm. "I, uh—"

"I think that yes, he was brilliant, and yes, he loved the Classics. But I think he also wanted to see what he could get away with, you know? *Iliam* is tongue-in-cheek, even the way he misspelled it. He's championing and challenging the canon at the same time. Anyway, tell me about your dig."

"It was in Italy," I manage. "That's how I got assigned to your case.

I speak some Italian." I pause, then add, truthfully, "I didn't actually know him."

"That's right; I remember the Italian now," Caroline says. "*Un mondo piccolo,* huh?"

I draw in a deep breath. "Yeah."

"*Iliam* is actually relevant to the case, I'd say. If Twombly hadn't been commercially minded—if he hadn't gotten those paintings out of Italy back then, they probably would have gotten trapped there. It's almost impossible to get an export license for anything now. If the artist is deceased and the artwork is more than fifty years old, Italy can legally claim cultural heritage. Even if the artist isn't Italian. It's ridiculous, actually. It's almost starting to feel like a form of nationalism."

An export license. Caroline implied that she first saw the objects Creon donated in Torino on a donor trip in 2006. Which means Creon would have needed an export license to take them out of the country. But we don't have one in the file, and Emmanuel has never mentioned its absence.

"Why did you agree to return everything, even the cup?"

Caroline sighs. "I'm not going to take the stand in Italy, that's for sure. Remember Amanda Knox?"

"I hear you, but—"

She motions to the drawings. "I could probably get a million dollars for these, given their significance. I think it's the only time he used the Etruscan word for Venus. And yet I bequeathed them to the museum, even though they'll never put them on public display. Know why?"

I flash back to the Aphrodite exhibition opening last month—Oliver said he helped facilitate a different bequest on Caroline's behalf, a collection of Limoges snuffboxes promised to Fordham's library. "Because . . . they're safe here?"

"Because the museum is legally required to do what I ask. The market is not. I put these drawings up for sale at Christie's and they could end up in the wrong person's hands. And yes, I will benefit from the write-off. For some people, the write-off is an important motivator. But it all comes out in the wash. The financial benefits of donating versus selling, I mean."

A museum is legally required to do what a donor asks—this is true. And it dawns on me: I never actually saw the gift agreement between Creon and the Fordham Museum. Could this be related to the missing export license? Could the museum be covering something up? I open my mouth to say this, but Caroline keeps going.

"What everyone is dancing around in these restitution conversations is money. Right? The rare, high-value objects are simply worth more—to a collector, to a country. To an institution. Money corrupts. But money isn't the vehicle for wrongdoing. Money is the fuel. Without fuel, the car stops running. And then it rusts and degrades and becomes unrecognizable. You get what I'm saying. *Donors* are not the bad guys here. On the other hand, if American museums turned away every white-collar criminal who came knocking, they'd cease to exist."

As her words sink in, a bilious feeling comes over me—Caroline is wrong. The person who provides the fuel to keep an engine running is complicit in what the engine does. And moreover: when I facilitate my clients' museum donations; *I* am complicit in what the museums do. Emmanuel and I, by defending Caroline, are complicit in what she has done.

On my way out of the museum, I pause in front of the Cupid and Psyche cup. When I look closely I can make out a long, delicate crack, painstakingly restored, unfurling from Psyche's hand like Ariadne's thread.

XIV.

JULY 11, 2004

ORBAGNE

On Sunday night, when Simone and I returned to the palazzo from our dinner at the Botti vineyard, I went straight to the phone room—but this time I wasn't dreading the conversation. The envelope from Giamma was safely in my purse; if Jinny or my mother picked up, I wouldn't have to beg them for help.

Jinny picked up on the third ring. "Lena," she said. "I'm so sorry I keep missing you."

My first reaction was relief at the sound of Jinny's voice—everything was okay. Nothing was wrong. But this feeling was quickly replaced by a sharp pang in the center of my chest. "You said you would get their tax return to Columbia."

"I'm sorry, it's just—"

"You promised. If I lose my financial aid—"

"Lena, it's in the mail. If they don't already have it, they'll have it soon."

"Oh." This was gratifying, but resentment still flooded my system as I contemplated the amount of time I had wasted worrying for no reason. When I tuned back in, I heard voices in the background on the other end of the line. "Is someone over?" I asked.

"I don't know how to even say this—" First Jinny's voice cracked, and then she let out a sob.

"What's wrong?" I asked urgently, caught off guard by her distress. "What happened?"

Jinny breathed in and out a few times. And then, "She died. She's dead."

"How?" I asked instinctively, my body flooding with an abstract shock I didn't recognize. It didn't seem possible that my mother could be dead. She had lived recklessly for so long; she was indestructible. If she really was dead, some part of her must have willed it—this was my initial assessment of the situation.

"It was a car accident," Jinny managed to get out. "The night before the Fourth of July. I got the call a few hours after I talked to you. They had trouble identifying her body because she didn't have her license on her."

On July third, I'd been in Torino with Giamma. Probably it had been the middle of the night in Italy when my mother had died, or early in the morning. I couldn't recall any dreams I'd had at Giamma's apartment in Torino, or any other cosmic signals that might have clued me in to what had happened.

I felt comforted by the idea that I wasn't as psychically connected to my mother as I imagined I was. I couldn't even picture her dead body. A series of fictional deaths flashed through my mind: Ophelia in the river under the willow tree, Dido pierced through the side with Aeneas's sword, Antigone hanging from a veil in her cave-tomb. Each of those women had been betrayed by men they loved. My father, too, had betrayed my mother. He'd left her with two children she was unfit to parent and a life she didn't want.

This was the first time, in my memory, that I had ever come close to sympathizing with my mother. And it was too much for me to bear, the sense that she might have been deserving of my sympathy.

"Do you want me to book your plane ticket home?" Jinny asked.

I winced, not yet having considered the logistical implications of this news. In a few days I was headed to Sicily to visit Lakshmi at the

Selinunte dig. The idea of flying to Chicago instead, for my mother's funeral, made my stomach turn. "I can't," I heard myself say.

"You can't what?"

"I'm staying here," I said as firmly as I could, thinking of the high school years I spent alone with my mother. Jinny hadn't been required to move into the dorms—she could have lived at home and commuted to class. But she'd chosen to live separately. I, too, could choose to be separate.

Jinny was silent on the other end of the line. Maybe I was waiting for her to convince me, to explain to me why I should come back. I probably could have been persuaded. But she didn't.

"I get it," she said eventually.

After we hung up, I sat there for a while with my eyes closed. Then I opened them and looked around the room. It was exactly the same as when I'd entered just a few minutes prior. Later, when I looked in the bathroom mirror upstairs, my smile was the same—same overbite, same gap in my bottom teeth. *I am exactly the same,* I said to my reflection.

XV.

JULY 14, 2004

ORBAGNE

It was Benedetta's idea to invite us to the hot springs, Pietro said. "The bathhouse is under construction, but they stop work at five," he told Simone and me at breakfast on Wednesday. "We can leave when Lena returns from the site."

Simone hesitated, uttering something about the last hour of working daylight; but after a little encouragement, she acquiesced. I nodded too. Marco had said the hot springs brought droves of French and Italian tourists to this part of the Aosta Valley, and I was interested in seeing them—but more than that, I was intrigued by the idea of spending more time with Benedetta.

At five o'clock, Benedetta walked into the kitchen, where I was silently devouring a Nutella sandwich. "*Pronto?*" she said, opening her oversized blue oxford to reveal a black bikini underneath.

I held up one finger and ran up to the bedroom to grab my swimsuit, a striped one-piece I'd bought on sale at J.Crew in high school. When I came back down, Martha looked up from chopping carrots and said everyone was waiting in the car.

Twenty minutes later, we arrived in Pré-Saint-Didier. The "bathhouse" Pietro had referred to was in fact a sprawling historic complex that had been built as a casino in the second half of the nineteenth century. When the renovation was complete, he explained, it would reopen as a day spa.

"It looks closed," Simone said uneasily, nodding at the caution tape and construction trucks and a sign that said PROPRIETÀ PRIVATA.

Benedetta turned around and winked at us in the back seat. "*Non vi preoccupare.*" She explained that her father was an investor in the project and that the construction workers were gone for the day. If anyone gave us trouble—well, they wouldn't, because everyone in the area knew whose daughter she was.

Simone and I changed into our suits behind a cluster of oak trees near Pietro's parked car, while Benedetta finished her cigarette. I could only hear her voice, not Pietro's. She was repeating the word *esame* over and over.

As we walked around to the back of the building, I asked her if she was in school.

"*Sempre,*" she said, exchanging a smile with Pietro.

"It's true," he said in English. "She is an eternal student." He hugged her into him and kissed the top of her head.

"Now I am studying jurisprudence," she said. It was the first time I'd heard her speak English, but I had no idea what the word *jurisprudence* meant.

Pietro saw the blank expressions on our faces. "Law school," he clarified.

Benedetta nodded. "I finish my exams next year."

Before I could formulate any follow-up questions, my attention was captured by the scene we'd come upon. Behind the construction trucks and piles of rubble were three pristine pools, steam coming off them in the cool air. I couldn't figure out how the water was so clear and clean, especially in the context of an active construction site.

"What—how—"

"If we stay quiet, we can hear—" Benedetta stopped walking and gestured to the forest at the edge of the far end of the lawn. "Do you hear the *cascata*?"

I looked over at where she was pointing. The mountain in the distance was verdant and precipitous, its white peak like a thumb raised to the sky. It was numinous, godlike. The most godlike thing I'd ever seen. This was Mont Blanc, Benedetta would tell me shortly. But for the moment I closed my eyes and let the faint sound of rushing water wash over me.

When I opened my eyes, everyone was at the edge of the large pool in the center of the lawn. "The water comes out of the grotto very hot and flows through underground channels into the pools," Benedetta said when I joined the group.

"The Romans built them," Pietro added. He'd removed his T-shirt and was easing his way into the water. "The channels. Pliny wrote about the healing powers of the hot springs here."

I eyed the marble tile of the pool's edge. "But the pools themselves aren't ancient, are they?"

Pietro shook his head. "Any evidence of how the Romans used the hot springs, apart from the channels, is gone. Probably destroyed when they built the casino. Or maybe it was never more than a wood structure and some holes in the ground."

I lowered myself into the pool, amazed by the idea that I was now part of the millennia-long line of people who had enjoyed these alpine springs. It had been a hot day, but the air was still cooler than the water. I felt good—I couldn't remember ever feeling that good.

"Though there's always a chance they'll find something interesting in the renovation," he added after a beat.

"You will be the first to know if they do," Benedetta said.

You okay? I mouthed to Simone, who had been quiet this whole time.

She snapped out of her trance and nodded. "I was just thinking about channels. And about how far the Duria is from the villa."

I could guess where she was going with this—aqueducts. Cyrille had implied more than once that there was an underground aqueduct bringing water to the villa in Orbagne.

Simone continued: "And there was a vineyard there. I mean, there *is* a vineyard there. So they needed water, and a lot of it—a hundred dolia means it was a huge vineyard. I didn't think to ask when we were at your place the other night—how is the irrigation system set up now?"

Pietro looked away, noticeably uncomfortable. Simone and I exchanged a glance. "Is it built on what the Romans used?" I asked. And then, thinking of Cyrille, "Or what the Salassi used before them?"

"You can't excavate an active vineyard," he said.

I flinched at the certainty in his tone.

"But think about it," Simone pressed. "Think about these hot springs. Orbagne is in a region with tons of water—glaciers, rivers, tributaries, hot springs—but a grand villa gets built in this isolated place? It doesn't make sense."

"Orbagne's altitude made it advantageous," Pietro said defensively. "Probably we will find fortification walls. And water sources dry up all the time."

Cyrille had helped uncover a dried-up river basin while he was working in Ostia Antica, I suddenly remembered. He'd shown me a map of what it had looked like before and after his team's fieldwork there. My mind turned to the interview with Valenti at Pietro's apartment a week prior—he'd asked me about computer-generated maps. Was it possible that Cyrille was doing—or wanted to do—the same work he'd done in Ostia Antica in Orbagne?

"I imagine Orbagne's water source will emerge as we go," he added.

It was the repetition of the word *Orbagne* combined with the bath that we were sitting in that made me wonder suddenly if the *-bagne* in Orbagne might be derived from the word for baths. I wasn't certain of the French, but I knew the Italian word for bath was *bagno*, which came from the Latin word *balneum*. And if the Duria River was considered holy by the Salassi like Cyrille had said, was it possible that it connected somewhere underground to a grotto like the one that fed these hot springs?

"Could there have been baths like these near the villa?" I asked, laying out my etymological reasoning, but keeping what Cyrille said about the Salassi and their reverence for the Duria out of it.

"I have always wondered about that," Pietro said. "But there is no evidence of thermal springs at all in Orbagne."

"What about gold?" Simone asked. "*Or* is gold. The Salassi mined gold. Farther south, obviously. Could they have mined it somewhere else and rinsed it in Orbagne?"

Benedetta gave me a knowing look, like she either wanted to say something herself or expected me to speak up.

"You studied archeology, too, right?" I asked her.

She nodded.

"Why didn't you pursue it?"

She shrugged and told us that archeology was a man's world, that she could have a much greater impact on the field in Italy as a lawyer. She was studying cultural heritage law, she explained, and could use her father's connections to eventually get a job in Rome.

"A man's world—and I'm here with three women?" Pietro said.

Benedetta nuzzled him.

We stayed like that for another half hour, talking and laughing. I kept looking up at Mont Blanc. The white and green summit against the orange sky was painfully beautiful. Up until that point I'd managed to compartmentalize my mother's death; but now my eyes stung with the realization that my mother had invented a world to inhabit because the one she was living in—the one we were all living in—was too painful. Even moments of beauty could induce pain.

ON FRIDAY, JULY 16TH, I did a half day at the site, grabbed a prosciutto sandwich from Martha at the palazzo, and caught the train to Aosta. From the Aosta train station, there was a shuttle, and by three in the afternoon, I was at the airport for my 4:15 flight to Sicily.

The air-conditioning blasted as I walked through the glass doors of the airport. At the Ryanair desk, a dark-haired woman extended her hand and barked, "*Passaporto*"; I gave it over obediently.

Lakshmi was waiting for me at Arrivals in Trapani in an old Jeep with no doors. She looked even more golden than usual, her hair longer and tied back in a ponytail. She spotted me and waved as I approached. "Who is this?"

I hadn't had time to change out of my cargo shorts and dirt-caked T-shirt. "Do you like my look?" I said.

"It suits you," she said. "Archeology suits you."

I threw my backpack in the back of the Jeep and climbed in.

"The scenic route takes an hour," she said.

There was something different about her voice, but her face looked the same as always: amused, kind.

"Sound okay?" she asked.

I clicked in my seat belt. "*Perfetto.*"

As we taxied out of the airport, which resembled the suburban glass and concrete shopping mall of my adolescence, Lakshmi asked about the flight. I told her about the melee at boarding time, the shameless line-cutting as passengers pushed up to get to the good seats, which were apparently at the front and back of the plane. Having never taken a low-cost flight, I'd gone in with no strategy and had ended up between two large men with just a thin layer of pleather separating my body from the seat's metal frame.

The wind got louder, and I relaxed into the noise. The sun was sinking down toward the dry grass on the shoulder of the road. "We can drop off your bag at the apartment before dinner," Lakshmi said, glancing at her watch.

"Wait, what is this?" I asked, smelling the salt in the air and realizing that we were driving along the coast.

Lakshmi looked over at me. "Aren't they magical?"

What we were seeing was the sea—I was almost certain it was the sea—gridded off in square lagoons of green and red, punctuated by crumbling windmills. As we drove, the colors brightened—the red turned to hot pink, the green to neon aloe. I saw little mounds of white in between the squares and along the road. "Seriously, where are we?"

"The Marsala salt flats," she said. "They date back to the Phoenicians." Cars zoomed around us as I craned my neck.

"They're so pretty," I said dumbly. "What's with the windmills?"

"The Arabs built them in the Middle Ages. You know *marsala* means 'God's harbor' in Arabic? *Marsa Allah.*"

I squinted. "How do you know that?"

"Come on, Lena." She gave me a playful glare. "Basic Arabic? I get by."

I rolled my eyes. "Are there any languages you don't know?"

She smiled broadly. "Euskara."

"What's that?"

She raised her eyebrows. "I have a—oh my god, I can't even say it. A boyfriend. A Basque boyfriend."

I mirrored her smile, but I felt a pang—not of jealousy exactly, but anxiety. What would it mean for our friendship if Lakshmi had a boyfriend? "I don't even know what Basque is."

"It's a region in the north of Spain on the French border. But he doesn't identify as Spanish. He speaks Spanish, of course. And Euskara. Which is the only language isolate in Europe."

"What does that mean?"

"It means that basically they never fully Romanized. The language developed before the Gauls or the Romans were there, and then it somehow stuck around."

I thought about the Romansh from the menu in Lugano, but it wasn't the right analogue. "That reminds me," I said. "I've been kind of dating someone too."

"What's his name?"

"Giamma."

"Last name?"

I thought it over. "I don't actually know. Is that bad? What's yours called?"

"Iñigo!"

"Is he a PhD student?"

She glanced at me. "He's a GIS specialist assigned to the dig through a government contract. He's twenty-four."

"What's GIS?"

"Geographic Information Systems," she said. "It's the study of the spatial dimension of human behavior over time."

I was intrigued, but I didn't understand. It occurred to me, based on her mechanical explanation, that she herself might not understand what GIS was either. "What do you use it for?"

"You can use it to analyze stratigraphy."

I logged this as another nonanswer.

"Okay, you know how Cyrille's site was looted?" she attempted. "Iñigo, in theory, could look at a satellite image of the site post-looting, analyze it, and understand the damage done by comparing it to a pre-looting satellite image. You can see minute changes to the topography, especially when the changes are man-made, even when people try to cover their tracks. It's surprisingly detailed."

"Speaking of Cyrille's looting," I said, pulling my leg up onto the seat and turning toward her. "There is something sketchy about the dig."

"What do you mean?" Lakshmi asked, raising her eyebrows.

"My roommate overheard Cyrille's co-director, this guy Pietro, saying to him that the looters didn't take anything *else*, something like that. When I tried to talk to him about it, he told me 'not to give Cyrille any crazy ideas' because he is 'completely paranoid.'"

"Whatever they took is probably in a basement or warehouse in some random place," Lakshmi said. "Unless some idiot collector buys something and turns around to try to sell it at an auction house, or a museum acquires something and puts it on display—even then, how do they trace things back to a given site? Especially an unknown one like Cyrille's."

I felt weirdly dazed as I looked out at the rocky shoulder of the road. A warehouse. The bronze shield. I felt a thud in my stomach and thought about the BlackBerry in my back pocket, and resolved to ask Giamma directly about the looting when I got back to Orbagne.

"So, am I going to meet Iñigo tonight?" I asked, trying to keep my tone light, hoping Lakshmi wouldn't notice the subject change.

"Of course," she said, glancing over her shoulder to merge onto a faster road. The wind roared around us, and I sat there and took it all in—run-down buildings, dead grass, the pebbled road shoulders, the sinking sun, the drooping palm trees. "To have seen Italy without having seen Sicily is not to have seen Italy at all, for Sicily is the clue to everything," Goethe wrote in *Italian Journey*. I was skeptical, but I decided to suspend my disbelief.

LAKSHMI PULLED INTO A PARKING SPOT in front of a nondescript cinder block apartment building.

"Well, this is it, beautiful Selinunte!" she said, unbuckling her seat belt. "What do you think?"

There was nothing beautiful about where we were, I thought, eyeing the trash on the sidewalks, a convenience store with an outdoor soda machine, a soulless laundromat. "I mean—"

"I'm just joking," she said with a wink. "I'll take you to the site tomorrow."

I followed her into the apartment building and up a single flight of stairs in a dark corridor. "The accommodations are not great. But they're clean, and they're safe, and most importantly, free."

The apartment was empty. "Hello?" she called. There was no answer.

Lakshmi looked at her watch. "They might be at the restaurant already." She pulled her phone out of her tote. "Shit. Four missed calls."

I put my backpack in Lakshmi's room and changed my outfit. "I thought you didn't have a phone here," she said as she noticed me sliding the BlackBerry into my crossbody purse.

"It's not mine," I said. "I'm just borrowing it."

Lakshmi shrugged, and I was thankful that she didn't ask me to elaborate. "You ready?"

The restaurant was a fifteen-minute walk from the apartment on the patio of a nearby hotel. For the second time that day I underestimated our proximity to the ocean—a block into our walk, there it was, an undulating mass of steel green, the sun casting purple shadows on sparse clouds above it.

"This is our go-to weekend place," she explained as we walked through a hot lobby to get to the patio in the back. I gasped as soon as we got outside, because I hadn't expected them: the temples, and so many of them, at the edge of the ocean. They were totally at odds to where we stood, on the patio of a touristy hotel with faux shell centerpieces.

I understood then why so many students wanted to come to Selinunte. The site was much bigger than I'd expected—it looked like a whole city, with an acropolis, temples, and a visible layout. The dig in Orbagne—a single villa—was minuscule by comparison.

"There they are," Lakshmi said. I followed her to the other side of the patio and recognized a few of the grad students from our seminar. "That one is Iñigo," she said as we approached the table, pointing to a skinny young man with dark hair and skin so pale it was almost blue.

"He's cute," I whispered.

Iñigo smiled self-deprecatingly as he noticed us, then stood up to shake my hand. After we exchanged niceties, I turned to wave hello to everyone.

"How was the trip?" James from Cyrille's seminar asked.

"Not bad," I said. "I just—" I said, pointing off at the view.

"Yeah, yeah, the temples," James said, rolling his eyes. "We don't even see them anymore; they're like wallpaper."

I nodded absently, sat down, grabbed a thick slice of bread, and watched as Lakshmi poured olive oil into a little dish. "Dip," she instructed. I'd never tasted anything like that olive oil; it was peppery and fruity and rich—it was one of the best things I'd ever tasted.

After a dinner of grilled fish, eggplant caponata, and several carafes of the house white wine, we walked to a discotheque in the center of town. The heat hadn't abated, and I was glad to have changed out of my dig clothes and into a loose cotton dress.

We paid for our admission to the disco and claimed a couch at the periphery of the outdoor dance floor.

I looked out at the scene: it was mostly sweaty teenagers, clumped in packs of three and four. "Let's go," Lakshmi said, pulling Iñigo and me onto the dance floor.

James brought over a round of mojitos in plastic cups, and I smiled, remembering a party Lakshmi and I had attended in the spring at his apartment, white balloons pulsing to the bass of a Weezer song, the way the grad students "danced" by shrugging their shoulders and nodding their heads, swirling cheap red wine in Solo cups. Lakshmi and I had left after an hour, laughing as we descended the crumbling stoop and ducked into the Duane Reade to buy candy and Diet Coke.

It seemed impossible that that had only been a few months prior. So much had changed since: Lakshmi and I had both managed to avoid a summer at home; we were in Sicily; my mother was dead.

Lakshmi was really dancing now, putting her whole body into it, throwing her head back in laughter, and Iñigo was trying to keep up with her, unselfconsciously sliding around the dance floor and twirling her when they made contact. Eventually they stopped making an effort to include me and started holding each other and kissing.

I made my way to a lightless corner of the patio and called Giamma. I was planning on leaving him a *squillo* so he'd know I was thinking about him. But he picked up on the first ring. "Lena," he said. "Where are you?"

"I'm at a disco in Sicily," I said, smiling at the novelty of this statement.

"Yes, but who are you with," he said, a command, not a question.

"My friends from Columbia." I looked over to the dance floor, where Lakshmi and Iñigo were still dancing. Giamma didn't say anything. "What's wrong?" I asked.

"You sound drunk."

"Maybe I am." There was more silence. "Hey," I said. "I miss you."

He sighed audibly. "I'm coming to get you," he said.

I burst out laughing. "I just got here! My flight is on Sunday. I'll be back soon."

"I'm coming to get you," he repeated.

"I haven't even seen the temples yet!" I protested. "How about you pick me up at the airport in Torino on Sunday?"

I waited for him to respond. Giamma was terrible on the phone; too many silences.

"Okay," he finally said. "*Ci sentiamo allora.*"

I hated this phrase, *ci sentiamo,* which means something like, "let's be in touch." Pietro said it all the time. Magister Rizzi had said it the summer I house-sat for him, but he'd never reached out to me. It was only when he returned from his summer in Rimini that we'd had a halting conversation about his well-behaved cat and thriving plants.

But to Giamma I said okay, and when he came back with, "*Ciao amore,*" I sensed I'd be the one to hear from him.

I SAW THE TEMPLES FROM the back of a golf cart the next morning. Lakshmi was behind the wheel, Iñigo was next to her, and James was in the back with me, each of us clutching a plastic liter-sized water bottle. I squinted through the glaring sunlight, my head pounding from the previous night's mojitos.

I'd slept on a futon in the living room of Lakshmi's apartment and had awoken to the sound of running water. When I sat up and looked over at the kitchen, Iñigo was cracking eggs into a large silver bowl. "Good morning," he whispered. I waved and shuffled to the bathroom, where I splashed cold water on my face.

I'd only ever seen Greek temples in projected slides and textbook photos. In those images, even as they crumbled, the temples always had a pristine, exact quality to them. And they'd all blurred together: Selinunte, Segesta, Agrigento. I wouldn't have been able to distinguish one Magna Graecia site from another.

But in real life and close up, there was nothing pristine about Selinunte—the only temple that had been rebuilt at the site was the Temple of Hera, and it was tenuous and cracked. I lost count of the fluted Doric columns and metopes from the temples' friezes that littered the dusty ground. These, I understood, were ruins in the most literal sense. But Lakshmi had told me that the city was named for *selinus*, the wild celery that grew there, and I swore I could smell it.

We got out of the golf cart and stood in what remained of the market, one of the largest of its kind in ancient Greece, whose vendors had sold flour ground from Carthaginian wheat, local spices and herbs, wine, and garum. Lakshmi caught me looking over toward the ocean. "That was part of the city wall," she said, pointing toward a mass of stone bricks about a meter thick.

Iñigo shaded his eyes and smiled.

"So you work on GIS, Lakshmi told me?" I said to him. "I don't totally understand it."

He nodded thoughtfully. "Think about it like this: archeology is concerned with objects and buildings that tell a story about the past. But there is no consistency in the field in terms of methodology—the way the story is crafted. When we map a site using GIS, a logic is revealed, which is not subject to human fallibility."

I nodded, trying to process what he was saying. "What kind of logic?"

He pulled a device out of his pocket and tapped the screen with a stylus. "So—"

"Here he goes with the PalmPilot," James said.

"Oh calm down," Lakshmi said, elbowing him and smiling.

Iñigo showed me a grid of icons. "Do you know what is GPS?"

I shook my head.

"It's a way to track location," he said. "So if I hit this command here, and we walk toward the wall, the device will track our path." We started walking toward the wall, and he showed me the screen. "See?"

A line was forming on a map, whose features moved as we moved.

"Archeologists have been working here at Selinunte since the nineteenth century, but there are likely more structures to be uncovered. And so every time I use the GPS, we are building the geo-database that gives us a clearer picture of the site."

Cyrille had described something similar when he told me about the new technology he'd used in Ostia Antica. "Now, for example, we're near the outer limit of the site. I can take this information and compare it with maps and satellite images from decades ago and determine the threat of coastal deterioration."

"But what does that have to do with overriding human fallibility? Or whatever you said earlier?"

His eyes brightened. "Oh yes, well. For example. Someone could have drawn a map a century ago which was—biased. That tells a false story about what existed at the site. With this technology that won't happen."

"Do you remember those maps from Cyrille's packet?" I asked Lakshmi.

"Yes!" she exclaimed. "That's what I meant to say yesterday in the car. Those were made with GIS. And now he can use them to analyze the damage done by the looters, in theory. Here, there was documented Mafia looting in the seventies. The GIS work Iñigo is doing was actually commissioned by the Italian Ministry of Cultural Heritage. None of us know exactly what they want to do with it, but they could theoretically analyze looting patterns."

I squinted. If Cyrille was doing this kind of work in Orbagne—if he had a contract with the Italian Ministry of Cultural Heritage—that seemed like a justifiable reason for Pietro to feel threatened by him. Maybe Cyrille deserved more credit for procuring dig permits than Pietro, an actual Italian with a politician father, wanted to admit.

"Looting isn't a problem at Selinunte anymore, though," Lakshmi added. "This is basically how the Carthaginians left it—they sacked the whole place. Plus or minus a few earthquakes over the centuries. Coins from this site have turned up in Tunisia."

James looked amused. "The ancient need for destruction. You take everything. You burn it down."

I looked at James and saw him not as the academic I knew him to be, but as the gamer he was. It was all over his face, the time he'd spent building and destroying empires as a virtual soldier in a dark room. Probably there were hundreds of archeologists like him, man-boys who loved antiquity because they loved violence.

I'D MESSAGED MY FLIGHT INFO TO GIAMMA, and when I got off the plane he was waiting for me at the gate in a button-down, suit pants, and red-brown leather loafers.

I was happy to see him. "What are you doing all the way in here?" I asked. Jinny had been the one to pick me up from the airport the few times I'd arrived at O'Hare alone, and she'd always waited in the car at the curb for me at Arrivals.

"I'm picking up my girlfriend," he said, and he took my backpack, dropped it gently on the floor, and hugged me. I inhaled the scent of cedar and Marlboros as I sank into his body.

He put one arm around me and shouldered my backpack with the other while we walked up the white echoey concourse. At the exit, he nodded at a man at the security desk.

"Did you tip them or something?" I asked in a joking voice, feeling proud of myself for thinking I might have understood something about the world, about bribery.

"The guys know me," was all he said.

I looked up at him, showing him my whole face. "Do *I* know you?" Consciously, I meant this as a flirt, a sweet nothing, rhetorical banter. But in retrospect, I wonder if my mind was pushing back on my body, the subconscious force that drew me to Giamma. In which case, my body had won—Giamma took it like I meant it, and he smiled and bent down to kiss me.

* * *

WE'D BEEN DRIVING FOR A little over an hour when Giamma took an exit for Aosta instead of continuing farther into the mountains for Orbagne. I glanced at the gas meter—the tank was almost full—and then at the clock on the dashboard. It was six. "Where are we going?" I asked.

"There is a party for Andrea. Pietro's father. To support his election to the Italian Senate."

I frowned. Shouldn't he have given me a chance to weigh in about attending this party, and sooner than right now? I shifted in my seat, trying not to feel betrayed by this unforeseen turn of events.

"You don't have to come in," he said. "You can wait for me in the car."

I looked down at my cutoffs and stretched-out gray tank top, remembering a phrase Giamma had taught me about making a good impression, *fare la bella figura.* It had something to do with the notion that dressing well conveyed respect and good manners. My hair was clean after showering that morning at Lakshmi's, but I certainly wouldn't make a *bella figura* at an election party if I went like this.

The black dress Giamma had bought me in Torino—I'd brought it with me to Sicily but hadn't ended up wearing it. "I can change," I offered. "Unless you don't want me to come in?"

He squeezed my left knee gently. "I want you to come."

I shimmied out of my shorts, dug the dress from my backpack, and pulled it on. As we drove through Aosta's city center, I combed my hair and applied lip gloss.

Giamma parked in a lot near a traffic circle. "I want to show you something," he said, opening his car door after he'd zipped up my dress.

We crossed the street and stood on a patch of grass in front of a massive stone arch. "It is the Arco di Agosto," he said.

I nodded, searching for evidence of Augustus on the crumbling monument, to no avail. Other than the flora crowning its ten Corinthian columns, the arch bore no decoration whatsoever.

"It was constructed by a man named Aulus Terentius Varro Murena," he said, enunciating each syllable.

When I only shrugged slightly, he asked me if I knew who Murena was. I admitted that I did not.

"Augustus deployed him from Rome to conquer the Salassi. When Murena was successful, he erected this triumphal arch in honor of Augustus, at the same time that he built the villa you are working on in Orbagne." He glanced at me.

Though the broad strokes of this story were consistent with what Cyrille had always said about the villa, I couldn't remember him explicitly mentioning anyone named Murena.

"A year later, Augustus made him Consul," Giamma continued. "But he died right before his term began. Before the villa was fully built."

"So who finished it?"

"His adoptive brother. Another Murena. Who had just served as legate in Provincia Syria. That's what I believe. But then he died too."

"Cyrille never said anything about either Murena," I said.

Giamma smirked. "This is something your professor and I have in common. Neither of us think Murena is important. For him, the important part is what came before them. For me, it's what happened after."

"What happened after?"

"It likely passed to their sister Terentia, who was married to Maecenas."

I nodded in appreciation—finally, a name I not only recognized but revered. Maecenas had been the most important patron of the arts during the age of Augustus; he'd commissioned *The Aeneid* and

Horace's *Odes.* "So you're saying that Maecenas lived at the villa in Orbagne?"

"It's a theory."

I looked up at him. In Lugano, Giamma had said he'd only been up at the dig site when there was nothing to see; now he was admitting not only that he'd discussed the dig directly with Cyrille, but that he had his own theory on it.

"Pietro and Cyrille have a difficult time trusting each other because they are interested in different things," he said after a long moment. "And they come from very different backgrounds. But if they can figure out how to work together, they will uncover one of the most important archeological sites in Italy."

I thought back to my morning at Selinunte's sprawling ruins—to say nothing of Pompeii, Herculaneum, or the Roman Forum. Orbagne was nothing compared to the actual ancient cities other people were digging up elsewhere in Italy. Maecenas was a big deal, yes. But there had to be more to the story. What else did Giamma know about the dig in Orbagne that I didn't?

"There is a lot more to excavate," he added, perhaps reading the disbelief on my face.

We stood there for a while, looking at the arch. The sun was descending behind us. Giamma was a full foot taller than me, but the sun was positioned in such a way that my shadow loomed over his.

He gestured to the top of the arch. "Inside was an attic, built in the Middle Ages. To house soldiers. It was removed later, but a small compartment remains—you see?" He pointed to an aperture on the right side of the monument's barrel vault.

"Once, when I was little—five or six years old, something like this—my father woke me up in the middle of the night. It was summertime, we were staying in Orbagne. And he drove us here, to the arch, and—my father is tall like me—he hoisted me onto that ledge and told me to get up into the compartment."

"In the dark?"

Giamma nodded. "I was small enough to fit inside, to retrieve some—things. Things that had been stored there."

I crossed my arms over my middle, against the hollowed-out feeling that gave me the sense that I knew where he was going with this. I didn't ask him what was inside.

"When we got back to the house, my mother was up, pacing around, worried sick. And she screamed at him when she saw what was in the car, the firearms I must have thought were toys. It was a game, I'd thought, until I saw the horror on her face. And he hit her—he hit her so hard she lost consciousness."

I had no idea how to respond to this anecdote, which sounded like more of a witness story—a confession—than a childhood memory. "I'm so sorry, Giamma," was all I could think to say.

"My father's face—I will never forget the darkness in his eyes. He was unrecognizable to me."

"I can't even imagine," I said, and I meant it. I tried to picture myself as a five-year-old—my father had moved to California when I was five—witnessing something like that. My parents had argued when we were kids, but they'd never been physically aggressive, ever. "Is that why your mom is in New York?"

"He has three more years on his prison sentence. And then—I don't know."

"What do you mean?"

"The one thing I know for certain is that when he gets out, I will be gone from Italy. As long as he is alive, I will not return."

THE PARTY TURNED OUT TO be at Benedetta's childhood home, which was a ten-minute walk from the arch on the other side of a bridge arcing above a river formed by a melting glacier. It was an imposing stand-alone A-frame that reminded me of a house in the

Storybook ride at Disneyland, which Jinny and I rode during childhood visits to our father in San Diego.

"Come and find me in twenty minutes," Giamma said in a low voice as we approached the front door. "And we can leave."

Before I could react, we were swept into a silent entryway by a man in a black suit, who motioned to a tray of champagne flutes on a sideboard. "The others are upstairs," he said to us in Italian. He gestured to a closet under the stairs where I was to leave my backpack.

Giamma's hand floated on the small of my back as we ascended a wide oak staircase. I didn't hear any noise until we got near the top. We walked through a double door and into a large room with a vaulted ceiling and teeth-like windows that framed a perfect view of the Arco di Agosto.

The room was more crowded than I'd initially perceived, and when Giamma whispered that he'd see me soon and then disappeared, I scanned for familiar faces. Almost all the guests, men and women alike, were in suits and dress shoes. Uniformed waiters circulated, offering up bites of food on silver trays. I tried to disappear along the periphery of the room.

Eventually I found myself at the wall opposite the windows, face-to-face with a series of human-scale sculptures on pedestals.

Pietro appeared at my side. "They're from there," he said, gesturing to the windows.

"There?" I echoed.

"The Arch of Augustus. This one was on the right niche," he said, gesturing to a marble caryatid with swept-back hair and a drapey toga. "And that's Augustus himself; he was on the top."

Yes, this was Augustus—he always looked the same, with his wide forehead and awkward bangs. I pressed my lips together, not wanting to say aloud the one-word question reverberating in my mind: Why? As in, why are these here, when there is an archeological museum within walking distance of this house?

"They take good care of them," Pietro said.

I turned and scanned the crowd for Giamma, who emerged easily thanks to his height. He was deep in conversation with Pietro's father. Benedetta was nearby, chatting with a man in a navy suit who looked to be about Pietro's father's age.

"*Buona fortuna* to your dad," I said.

Pietro smirked. "You can say *in bocca al lupo.* Tell him yourself."

Andrea Botti entered my peripheral vision. "Maddalena," he beamed, holding me firmly by the shoulders and kissing both of my cheeks. "*L'amore di Goethe.*"

I glanced at Pietro. If his arms hadn't been crossed so tightly over his chest, I might have mistaken him for feeling at ease.

"*Hai visto?*" Andrea said to Pietro. "*È arrivata.*"

Someone had arrived, he was saying—was he talking about me?

"*Allora,*" he continued, making intense eye contact. "My English—it is not so good. But I need to make an important conversation with an American. On the phone. I would like that you translate."

I looked at Pietro again. Now his lips were clenched in a straight line.

"Not Pietro?" I said. "His English is very good."

"Let me tell you one thing about my son." Switching to Italian, Andrea Botti described the phone calls he'd received from Pietro's teachers at the start of every school year. He can't control the volume of his voice, they said. Instead of talking, he shouts. Every year, Pietro's hearing was checked, and every year, it was deemed normal. It was a nervous condition, the doctors hypothesized, one that was exacerbated by stress. "He cannot embarrass me tonight," he concluded.

The tips of Pietro's ears were bright red, and he looked like he might be close to tears. "Okay, sure," I said, in an attempt to halt the interaction. "When is the call?"

As he consulted his gold watch, the bearded man in the navy suit I'd seen talking with Benedetta moments earlier approached and clapped him on the back. Andrea Botti smiled. "*Ecco,*" he said to the man. "*Ti presento la mia tradutrice.*" And to me, "I am please to present the host of the party."

So this was Benedetta's father. He extended his hand, but did not introduce himself by name.

I cleared my throat. "Thank you for having me. You have a beautiful home."

Andrea Botti beamed. "*Hai visto come parla? Americanissima,*" he said to the man.

Though I'd never identified as particularly American, he had a point—here, at this party, among these upper-class Italians, I was more American than I'd ever been. As I was contemplating this, I noticed that Pietro had vanished, leaving me alone with the two men.

Andrea Botti told me to meet him in an office on the first floor in thirty minutes. We would be placing a long-distance call to Washington, DC, to the private residence of a man named Scooter Libby—*Scoot-air Lee-bee,* he pronounced it.

Italy was the United States' most important European ally in the Iraq War, he explained. President Bush had just been to see Prime Minister Berlusconi in Rome; thousands of Italians had taken the opportunity to protest Italy's involvement in the war, which Andrea Botti found to be both absurd and hypocritical, given how the Americans had come to the aid of the Italians during and after World War Two.

I nodded silently, feeling nonplussed, then excused myself to the bathroom. As I was walking away, I could have sworn I heard, "*Carthago delenda est,*" followed by peals of laughter.

I had no idea who Scooter Libby was, nor did I know anything about the relationship between Italy and the United States as it concerned the Iraq War. But even in my ignorance I understood Botti's strategy—by bolstering the Bush and Berlusconi relationship with his own American liaisons, he would ingratiate himself to Berlusconi and raise his own political profile.

In the powder room, I caught sight of my tension-filled face in an antique mirror above a tiny sink. Between my tan and the new faint lines in my forehead, I looked older. I'd been in Italy for six weeks and would go home in three. It was hard to fathom leaving, even if part of me longed for the familiarity of New York, for meals in the dining hall with Lakshmi. Suddenly something flashed in the corner of the mirror, and I turned around to examine what appeared to be a large, wall-mounted sculpture. It was a double-sided axe, I realized—a real one, with five bronze tubes encircling its long handle.

There was a knock at the door. "One minute," I said, flushing the toilet and running the water in the sink. *Fasces*, I remembered. That was the word for it.

"It's me," Giamma said.

"Oh." I opened the door, exhaling in relief.

"Andrea said I'd find you here."

I nodded. My eyes must have slipped over to the *fasces*, because Giamma cleared his throat and led me out of the bathroom. "I know," he said. "It's a joke."

The *fasces* was not a joke, or shouldn't have been. On some level, Benedetta's father liked the message that it conveyed, and so did the people at this party.

"I need to stay longer than I thought," he said. "And then I need to get back to Torino tonight. But Pietro can give you a ride back to Orbagne. He's leaving shortly." He slipped his hands around my waist and bent down to kiss my cheek. "I'm sorry."

"Okay," I said, my heart pounding in my ears. Something felt off about this whole series of events: Giamma demanding to know where I was when we talked in Sicily, then insisting on picking me up, only to strand me with Pietro at an election party for his father in Aosta.

Pietro appeared at the end of the corridor and jangled his keys. "*Andiamo*?" he called.

I waved goodbye to Giamma and walked over to Pietro. "What about your dad's phone call?"

He rolled his eyes. "That's why we're leaving now."

"Won't he be mad?"

"He's fine."

I eyed him.

"You're welcome," he added. "It's getting late anyway."

"This is late?" I asked as we descended the front stairs.

"I try to go to sleep by nine."

We were expected up at the site by seven thirty on weekdays, and Pietro was often the last to arrive; I'd assumed this was because he slept late. "What time do you wake up?" I asked.

He shrugged. "Almost every night I wake up at three. Most of the time I stay awake."

I understood what he meant, at least partially. Back at Columbia, I'd been startled awake before dawn every morning, on high alert. No matter how hard I tried, I could never fall back asleep.

In the car, Pietro handed me his book of CDs. I flipped past the death metal and inserted Rage Against the Machine, remembering how in high school, the captain of the debate team had blasted this album on his boom box in the bus en route to a tournament right around Bush's election. And now Bush was campaigning for his second term—November would be my first time voting in a presidential election.

As I listened to the music, my thoughts turned to what Giamma had said about Pietro, how he was the only person he knew who truly believed in God. This made me think of my mother, and Jinny, and the funeral that was happening at this very moment. I was filled with relief to be in a car in Italy, even one with Pietro, instead of Wilmette.

Twenty minutes later we arrived in Orbagne. But just like the night he'd ambushed me with the Valenti interview, Pietro continued past the palazzo, saying something about a quick detour. I tugged nervously at my seat belt. A minute later, he pulled over and killed the engine. We were on the outskirts of town on the shoulder of the road that led to and from the villa, near the dirt road you turned down to get to the Botti vineyard. I braced myself.

In my peripheral vision I saw him turn toward me. If he attacked me verbally and accused me once more of stoking Cyrille's paranoia, I could get out and walk away. Slowly, I moved my hand to the door handle.

"He knows where you are," he said, nodding at my backpack on the floor between my legs. "You don't have to worry."

I looked over at him. He was tense but smiling. "The BlackBerry," he added. "It tracks your location."

There was an unmistakable ring of truth to this statement. Giamma *had* seemed to have already known where I was when I called him from the disco in Selinunte. But if Pietro was right, and if Giamma had been hiding this information from me—it was for a reason. Maybe—probably—he wanted to know where I was so he could keep me safe.

"It's nice of you to help him," he said. "You should help me too."

Then he launched into an earnest appeal for my support in helping him garner American interest in the villa when I got back to New York. If he could get an American university to sponsor the dig, he said, he wouldn't have to continue pursuing Italian funding.

"What's wrong with Italian funding?" I asked.

"It's . . ." he trailed off, maybe considering the best way to formulate his response. "It's slow. And complicated," he concluded.

I narrowed my eyes.

"You saw the winery. This is one of the difficulties. My family."

"You mean, your father?" I said quietly, recalling the way Andrea Botti had humiliated Pietro an hour earlier.

Pietro sighed. "My father will spend more time in Rome now, with more pressing concerns than the site."

I told him I would think about it. Only later, as I sat in the kitchen eating focaccia with cultured butter, watching Martha load the moka pots with coffee grounds for the following morning, did I realize that Pietro had explicitly accused me of helping Giamma, but he hadn't said what I was helping Giamma with.

XVI.

APRIL 3, 2022

NEW YORK CITY

Si suggested we meet in Central Park, and on Sunday, I follow a pin they dropped to a spot between a baseball diamond and a playground. After a few minutes of searching, I see them perched at the top of a rock outcrop, shading their eyes and waving at me.

"I've never climbed up," I tell Si, who stays seated as I stumble toward them.

"Five hundred million years," they say. I perch on the flat surface next to Si and look at them expectantly. "That's how long these have been here."

"Huh," I say, weighing whether Si is radiating apprehension or openness. Openness, I decide. "So—" I start.

Si cuts me off. "Is this about Caroline's announcement?"

I pull my knees into my chest. "No," I say quickly. "No."

Ever since Si finally got back to me—a week after I texted them—I've been mentally shuffling the different potential shapes this conversation could take. Ultimately, I have decided that anything Si admits or withholds relating to the Fordham case could knock me even further from the already-precarious professional situation I have found myself in. And so this conversation has to be about Orbagne, and about what Si knows.

"Did you hear who's replacing her?" Si adds.

I shake my head.

"Eva Reilly. They just announced."

I release my legs and pull at the funnel of my black cotton turtleneck. The dominant feeling pushing to the surface of my consciousness is envy. But it's unfounded—I'm not a curator; I've never aspired to be a curator. "Wow," I manage.

"I knew it was in the works, but it would have been nice to get a heads-up that it was going to be official. Anyway, fuck that place," Si says.

"What do you mean?"

"They should have stood behind her. After everything she did for them."

"What did she do for them?"

I follow Si's gaze to a group of kids playing catch on the nearby baseball diamond. "Let's just say that Caroline's interests and the museum's interests were one hundred percent aligned."

"Are a curator's interests ever not aligned with a museum's?"

Si seems to ponder this. "Museums are broken," they finally say. "The model is archaic. In the US, most of them are ninety-nine percent privately funded. Which makes it—challenging, let's say—for them to do the right thing."

When I went to see Caroline at the Fordham Museum, she said something similar—museums are the bad actors, not donors. Still, she trusted the Fordham Museum enough to donate her Twomblys to it. "But where else are ancient things safe? Where else can you put valuable art for people to see?"

"That's the issue, right there," Si says. "Not everyone needs—deserves, rather—access. Kill the museum, as far as I'm concerned."

"But—but—" I stammer, feeling somewhat threatened by this assertion. "But how else are people supposed to learn?"

Si doesn't miss a beat: "Museums are mausoleums built to house the spoils of a bunch of rich people, most of them dead. And now, they're catching themselves in the mirror, looking all noble for returning things to their countries of origin. Meanwhile, thousands of important objects are languishing in storage. In the US and everywhere. Even Italy, with its 'Museum of Rescued Art' in Rome—it's kind of noble, but it's mostly performative. Museums are literal power structures."

I think about all the art appraisals I've reviewed, the museum donations I've facilitated; without the values dictated by the market, collectors have no incentive to donate. And museums in turn elevate and guarantee the prices of other works by the artists they collect. If there's a problem with museums, it's because museums are in league with the market. "If you kill the museum, you also have to kill the market."

"Exactly," Si says, smiling genuinely. "They're completely intertwined. For a single valuable ancient object to reach the market, countless others are destroyed. Priceless scientific evidence is lost. To buy anything ancient—legally or illegally—from the market is a crime against science, and a crime against cultural heritage."

"Wow," I say. "You would have made a really good lawyer."

Si elbows me playfully and relaxes.

"Will you continue to work with the museum?"

Si shrugs. "We'll see. Eva's not bad. She gets it, to an extent."

"Speaking of Eva. Giamma gave me something a few weeks ago," I say, reaching into my crossbody bag to procure the photo of Si with Pietro, Benedetta, and Filippo Dalmasso.

Si gazes at it for a long moment, then hands it back to me, apparently unperturbed. "Yeah?"

In light of the ease between us, and after what Si just said about museums, I decide to be direct. "I think Pietro's dad is behind the restitution request."

Si raises their hands defensively, then lowers them. They scrunch up their face. "No. Just—no."

"How do you know?"

"How do I know," they parrot slowly, keeping their eyes down.

"Si," I say, my neck prickling with anxiety. "Where did the cup come from?"

Silence, except for the sound of popping joints as Si tilts their head from side to side.

"Did it come from Orbagne?" I ask with a flash of dread.

"Did it—"

My chest is burning now. "Did the Cupid and Psyche cup come from Orbagne, Si?"

Si nods yes, but simultaneously says, "I can't tell you. I don't know."

I stare at them in disbelief. "Wait, really?"

"You asked me a question, and I answered. Anyway, I don't think anyone can prove the cup came from Orbagne."

"*I* can prove it," I say, louder than I mean to. "You just told me."

The corners of Si's mouth twitch up, and then down. "You asked to meet and talk off-the-record. I agreed. This is off-the-record."

Over on the baseball diamond, one of the kids starts wailing.

"Speaking of records. I saw the new provenance record for the cup. It's different. The first one didn't say anything about a restoration. Plus, in the Polaroid from the warehouse in Chiasso, the cup is intact," I say.

"Okay."

"So when Caroline got it, it was broken? Or when did it break?"

"All right," Si says. "Let's say that Pietro was right all along, and the villa in Orbagne was abandoned by Melania the Younger. That means it would have been previously owned by Melania the Elder, her grandmother. Who spent a lot of time at her primary residence in the suburbs of Rome. We know the cup was probably made in Rome either at the end of the third century or the beginning of the fourth. So Melania the Elder—who was also a Christian, by the way—buys the cup and displays it in her house in Rome. Rome gets sacked a million times between the fourth century and 1861, when the Italian Republic was founded. Anyone could have taken it between then and now. Or she could have brought it up to her country house in the Alps, which her granddaughter inherited. The provenance is literally anyone's guess. That's what I'm saying."

I nod slowly, taking this in. And suddenly it dawns on me: the timing. This is why the doctored provenance matters so much: because the cup couldn't have been looted from Orbagne in 2004 if it was in the warehouse in Chiasso in 1995. "But when did the cup enter Filippo's collection? Was it in 1992 or 2004?"

"It doesn't matter, Lena. Think about how many object histories have been composed by privileged old white dudes in the past two hundred years. And we take them as facts. But they're not facts. They're guesses. They're fictions."

"So—you made it up? The Cupid and Psyche cup provenance?"

Si is quiet for a long moment. "I'm not sorry," they eventually say. "I'm really not."

"Okay," I say, reeling from this confession. "But in this case the timing matters. A lot, actually."

Si looks away. "I have good reason to believe that Filippo acquired the cup in 2004."

"But in the photo from the Chiasso warehouse raid, it was intact. In 1995."

Si makes a rolling motion with their hands.

"What does that mean?"

"Look, things break all the time. In transit, or by someone's stupid mistake. I've seen art handlers destroy objects in the middle of an installation. And I've seen reputable archeologists with legal permits mishandle things they're pulling out of the ground."

"But you said something this delicate couldn't have come out of the ground intact."

"Sure it could. It could have been in a box."

I raise my eyebrows incredulously. "A box?"

"Yeah, or a sarcophagus."

An image of the Cupid and Psyche sarcophagus from the Met flashes in my mind. But that was discovered in the 1800s in modern-day Turkey—nowhere near Italy. 1800s—the encasing. Si's new provenance also describes a nineteenth-century metal encasing, which would seem to validate that the cup was unearthed long before 1939, as Caroline initially said. "*Was* it in a sarcophagus?"

"Lena, what do you want from me? She took the plea. She's sending everything back. This conversation is moot."

Benedetta told me, at the *aperitivo* in Torino, that her father was a collector of antiquities, and that he was friends with Giamma's father. It seems indisputable now, when I lay out the chain of connections, that Filippo bought the Cupid and Psyche cup from Valerio and Quentin.

The Chiasso warehouse. I close my eyes hard. "Giamma's dad ran that warehouse," I say. "I was there. The summer I was in Orbagne. Giamma took me there."

Si recoils. "Lena, *what*?"

I nod meekly, suddenly on the verge of tears.

"What—how—" Si attempts, looking like they want to run as far away from me as possible. "I don't even know what to say."

"I'm scared," I hear myself say.

"You should be."

"What do I—"

"You need to lay low, okay? For the next week. Just—don't work on the case. Don't talk to anyone about it."

"You mean Giamma?"

"Anyone. Don't talk to anyone about it."

I nod slowly, and we part ways. As Si descends the rock, I wait for them to look back at me; they don't.

* * *

IT'S ELEVEN O'CLOCK—eight a.m. in Malibu—when I get back to my apartment. I lean against my kitchen counter for a good five minutes, staring at my phone. It's early there, but if I wait any longer, I'll lose my nerve. I call Jinny.

She picks up on the first ring. "Lena," she says, sounding relieved. "I've been trying to reach you for weeks."

In the background, a muffled, familiar voice says, "All good?"

I have to swallow hard to keep my throat from constricting. "Nick. I just heard Nick."

Jinny exhales slowly and audibly, and when she speaks, her voice is thick. "I don't really want to get into it."

"Are you back together with him?"

There's a long silence. "Honestly, Lena, your judgment is the last thing I need right now."

I clear my throat and try to maintain my composure. "I just don't understand."

"I agree."

"No—I don't understand why you didn't tell me."

There's a pause. "Look, Lena. The reality is that you don't show very much interest in my life."

I walk over to my window and look down at all the pedestrians walking with determination, like they know exactly where they're going. "You were here less than a month ago. We talked all weekend."

"Yeah, we talked. We talked about what you wanted to talk about."

My cheeks get warm, and I stammer for a few seconds before I manage to find the words to defend myself. "I *asked* you if you were dating anyone. I even asked you if you'd talked to Nick lately. You said no. You lied."

"Okay, yes—I lied."

This admission stuns me into silence.

"*Why* did you lie?" I demand after a long pause. I need to know; I've never needed to know anything more than I need to know why Jinny lied to me.

"You're trying to make this something it's not, Lena—" she hesitates, then continues: "It has nothing to do with you."

"How does lying to me have nothing to do with me?"

"Me having a child has nothing to do with you, I'm saying."

Silently, I walk to my bedroom, switch on the bedside lamp, and climb under my duvet.

"The reason I didn't tell you is because of how you're acting right now," Jinny continues, her voice breaking. "When I told you I was pregnant, you just stared at me. It's the most important thing I'll ever do, and you basically treated me like a stranger. I was *planning* to tell you about Nick, and about everything, but you just stood there and stared at me like I should have asked your permission to get pregnant."

"That's not at all what I was thinking."

After what feels like several moments, Jinny says, "What, then?"

A wave of indignance gathers behind my eyes. "I was thinking about Mom, okay? I was thinking about Mom."

She clears her throat, then goes quiet. Eventually she says, "Anyway, they are putting me on bed rest. I'm fine but I wanted you to know. Dad came up to visit the other day. He told me a theory of his. About Mom."

My jaw clenches at the mention of my father, but I let my curiosity win out. "What is it?"

"He thinks she had postpartum after me, undiagnosed. And that they missed it because it wasn't depression, it was more like this manic anxiety. She didn't sleep, she never let me out of her sight, that kind of thing. And then with you, she didn't know until like fifteen weeks or something. She had these random horrible cramps and bleeding and when she went to the hospital they told her she was pregnant and put her on bed rest. Can you imagine?"

The idea of my mother as someone who never slept and never let her child out of her sight is so counter to my actual experience of her that I can't actually imagine it. "No," I say flatly.

"And so she had to live in the hospital that whole time," Jinny continues. "This was when I was three, I guess. Those are my earliest memories, going to see her in the hospital, crawling into her bed, lying there with her and watching *Sesame Street.* I would beg Dad to let me sleep over—he had to carry me out kicking and screaming. It was awful."

This is the first time in almost two decades that we've talked about our mother directly, and I feel uneasy, as if I'm willingly wading into a riptide just by listening to Jinny.

"And then you were born, and I kept waiting for her to get back to normal," she continues. "But she was this completely different person. And the hardest part was how Dad would tell me that you were my sister, *mine,* like I was the one responsible for you. I just wanted things to go back to the way they were, but they never did."

I try to summon my own early memories: Jinny and me playing in her room, running through the sprinkler together in the backyard, burrowing under our parents' comforter.

"The point is," Jinny says, and for the first time in this conversation I can hear resentment in her voice. "You got to have a childhood. I did not."

I close my eyes, and suddenly I'm in the passenger seat of my father's car at a curb in Departures at the San Diego airport. His forehead is crinkled, like he's empathizing with someone's sad story. *You remind me of her,* he says. *It scares me.* I open the car door and slam it behind me. He rolls down the window. *I just wish we could have caught it earlier. With your mom. I wish I could have helped her more.*

"He told me I reminded him of her," I say, feeling dazed. "The last time I saw him."

Jinny is silent on the other end of the line.

Pressure rises in my chest as I wait for her response, which doesn't come. But my voice is anguished, not angry, when I say: "Why aren't you saying anything?"

Jinny sighs. "Lena, I want to be honest with you. Can I be honest?"

"I don't know." I mean it; I don't know if I can handle hearing what she has to say.

Jinny hesitates, then says: "It's been really lonely as an adult. You not talking to Dad—believe me, I get it. I understand if you don't want anything to do with him. But it's lonely for *me*. And I *have* asked myself whether you're even capable of seeing it from my side. Because I think Mom lacked that ability. You know, to see things from our side, as kids."

It's excruciating to absorb what Jinny's saying. And yet strangely, for the first time, I don't feel the urge to defend myself.

"I guess I wish I could understand how much of it was her personality and how much of it was her illness. I wish I had understood her better," Jinny says, sounding a little shaky, like she might be close to tears. "The summer she died was the lowest I've ever been in my life. And you were nowhere to be found. Physically, emotionally—I mean, you didn't even come to her funeral, Lena."

After Orbagne, Lakshmi and I crashed on James's pull-out couch for two weeks. I didn't tell anyone about my mother's death, not until the fall. If I'd gone to the funeral, I would have had to pretend—and I couldn't pretend that there was any part of me that was capable of forgiving my mother.

"You can say a lot about how Dad fell short as a parent when we were little," Jinny continues, "but he was there for me after Mom died, he's here for me now. I feel like he's the only reason I ended up kind of okay. And I've let go of the stuff from the past so I can feel good about having him in my life."

I want to ask Jinny: Did *I* end up kind of okay? Am I okay? And am I even capable of knowing? That Jinny could understand me better than I can understand myself is at once comforting and terrifying—but more than anything it's painfully vulnerable. When I was learning Latin, *vulnerable* was how I remembered that *vulnus* is *vulnera* in its irregular nominative plural form. To be vulnerable is to have many wounds, not just one wound.

"I'm always going to be here for you," she says gently. "Even when I have the baby."

I want to believe her. I almost do.

XVII.

JULY 19, 2004

ORBAGNE

The morning after Andrea Botti's campaign party, I was in the kitchen drinking coffee with Martha when Pietro marched in with a stack of newspapers and a look of pure elation on his face. Valenti's article had been printed, he informed us.

I took a paper from his stack and examined the small black-and-white photo on the bottom right of the front page. It was Pietro in profile leaning on a pickax, bandana around his forehead, surveying the dig in a calm, inquisitive way that was the complete opposite of his actual frantic comportment at the site. The headline: ROMAN VILLA EMERGES FROM ANCIENT . . . something. *Frana* was the word.

I skimmed the article right there in the kitchen, most of which I was able to get—the Augustan-age frescoes in the *triclinium* and storage area we'd uncovered, all of which confirmed that the site had been built following Augustus's triumph over the Salassi and was continuously inhabited until the late Roman empire. But there was nothing about the black marks we'd seen on the walls in the storage rooms, and the entire dark layer that had seemed to indicate that a fire had led to the eventual abandonment of the site.

Every single quote was attributed to Pietro; none were from Cyrille. Valenti seemingly hadn't used anything from me or anyone else he'd interviewed.

Upstairs, Simone was lounging on her bed with a book, fully ready for the day, boots and all. "Hey," I said.

"What's up?"

"The article came out," I told her, and showed her the inside of the newspaper where there was a photo of the shelving system in her shed.

As she looked it over, I grabbed my Italian-to-English dictionary from the armoire. My bed creaked when I sat down. "Did you know the site was buried in a mudslide?" I asked, having looked up *frana.*

"That's not true," Simone said, flipping back to the front page of the paper. "Wait, who said that?"

"It's in the headline. And then he talks about it at the end too." I got up and showed her. "I guess a mudslide is an act of God."

She shook her head in confusion. "It's just not true. If it were a mudslide we would have found bones—like, human bones of the people trapped there, or at least animal bones that the mud captured in its path."

"And then there's this whole weird part about Cyrille's 'secret' GIS database?"

Her eyes flicked back and forth. *No,* she mouthed, her eyes darting over the page. Red splotches appeared on her collarbone.

"It's right here," I said, pointing to the middle of one of the paper's interior pages. "It says 'Dottore DuPuy was analyzing the site *illegally* with satellite imagery from an unapproved custom-built geographic information system—'"

Simone closed her eyes and shook her head. She exhaled. "It's not secret; it's not even password protected. It's on the shared drive."

"What is?"

"His database. I'm the one who found it."

"Are you sure it was about Orbagne? He worked on another dig before this, near Rome—"

"Of course I'm sure. I'm the one cataloguing the finds."

"And it's illegal?"

"How the fuck should I know, Lena? It's mostly spatial data and density mapping, but it's all surface stuff. It's the same thing we're already doing manually. I don't know what would be illegal about it."

I told her my theory about Cyrille working for the Italian Ministry of Cultural Heritage. "Pietro is threatened by him, clearly," I said. "Threatened enough to sabotage the dig. Because the only one quoted in the whole article is Pietro. So that must be something he said, right?"

Simone gave me a sharp look. "What is it with you and him?" she asked.

I glanced over at the open window, then back at Simone, who was still regarding me with wide, exasperated eyes. "I just think it's weird that he acts like this is his site. It's not."

"It's on his family's property. So Cyrille can't just show up in Italy and start digging. And frankly, if what Cyrille was doing with his GIS is illegal, that's also not okay. That's how archeology works, you have to follow the *rules*, Lena. Without Pietro, there wouldn't be anything to tell."

"I get it," I told her, understanding that I wasn't going to change her mind. "I really do."

I don't think Simone was expecting me to capitulate like that. She made a small, almost imperceptible nod and scanned me, the same way she had throughout our first days as roommates on the dig, like she was trying to figure something out.

She put down her book, and I caught a glimpse of the cover. It was *The Magic Mountain,* which I'd never read because Jinny and my mother had tried so hard to convince me I should. And in that moment, I realized that I knew nothing about Simone's family situation, and she knew nothing about mine. We'd kept so much from each other. It never crossed my mind that she might have seen *me* as the betrayer, the unsafe one, the neglecter of fledgling friendships.

* * *

CYRILLE ARRIVED AT THE SITE after lunch and made his trench rounds. I was working in the storage area, where we hadn't turned up anything except fragments of clay vessels. When he stopped at my trench, he kept his eyes on the dirt, lifting them only when one of my trench-mates brought him a shard to examine.

And so at the end of the day, as we were walking back to the palazzo, I caught up with him and asked him directly how he was.

"Not so bad," he said.

"I saw the article," I said.

He winced. "Yes."

"Why did it say there was a mudslide?"

He fixed his eyes on the path ahead. "Mudslides are common in this area."

I wanted to ask him about his GIS database, but I didn't know how to do it without offending him. "Remember Lakshmi, from your seminar?" I ventured.

He nodded.

"I was just in Sicily visiting her, and she was telling me about the GIS mapping they're doing in Selinunte. I don't totally understand it, but one of the guys has this thing he uses—it's like a tracker—"

Cyrille gave me a quizzical, focused look that threw me off. If it was true that he had a contract with the Italian government like Iñigo did, I wasn't supposed to know about it. Had Pietro outed Cyrille, not to sabotage the dig, but to somehow alienate him from it?

"Never mind," I backtracked. "I just—do you need help with anything?"

"I need to go back to Lyon for a few weeks," he said.

"But there's only a few weeks left here."

He glanced over his shoulder. The Frenchies were trailing behind us, but everyone else was back at the palazzo. "Just keep working and keep quiet."

We walked for a few minutes in silence. Near the edge of town, we passed the spot where Pietro had stopped the car the night before. I replayed our conversation in my head. He'd seemed sincerely concerned about the site's funding. This was what was driving his behavior, I realized—the fear that he would lose the funding he depended on to do his job. It was not unlike the way I'd felt when I thought my financial aid was in jeopardy. Then it occurred to me: the money from Giamma. It was hidden in an interior compartment of my suitcase. "Is this about the funding for the site?"

Cyrille expelled a long breath. "In some ways, yes. Probably."

"And if you were able to secure funding—would it make it easier for you?"

He stopped walking and stepped aside to let the Frenchies pass us. When they'd sufficiently receded into the distance, he placed his hands on his hips and met my eyes. His shoulders were still hunched in a withered, resigned way, but now a jolt of energy inflected his face. He didn't say anything, but some inner barometer compelled me to nod my head yes.

We resumed our walk. "Do you want me to watch out for anything?" I asked. "While you're gone?"

He was silent for so long that I wasn't sure he had heard me. "Keep your head down, Lena," he finally said. "Please."

TWO WEEKS LATER, I thought I was dreaming when I awoke to Cyrille at the foot of my bed. I sat up, alarmed. "What's wrong?"

He seemed to be doing better than the last time I'd seen him—more upbeat, like the version of him I'd met the previous winter in New York.

"Shhhh," he said, moving toward the door. I looked over at Simone, who was snoring softly, then got up and put on a hoodie over my pajamas.

"Shoes," he whispered.

"Wait," I said. I made my way to my suitcase at the foot of my bed and unzipped it as quietly as possible, grabbing the envelope of euros and stashing it in the kangaroo pocket of my hoodie. I plucked the BlackBerry from its charger—I always did my best to keep it out of Simone's sight—and put it in there too.

I followed him down the stairs and through the front door. Outside, the sky was navy and the air was brisk. Giamma's car was gone; he'd left for Torino the night before. When I looked up, I saw that a light was on in one window in the building next to the palazzo, and I remembered what Pietro said about waking up early to think. I felt for the BlackBerry in the front pocket of my hoodie and glanced at the screen: it was 5:02 a.m.

"What's going on?" I asked.

He handed me a flashlight. "Here."

"But where are we going?"

"To the villa," he said.

"In the dark?" I asked, twisting the sleep out of my eyes.

He gestured at the flashlight, and I flicked it on.

A full moon shone as we walked the now familiar route to the dig site. Cyrille pointed it out and described the moonbow he'd seen arc across the valley below the dig site an hour earlier. He'd never seen one before. It was a sign, he said, that he was on the right track.

"Cyrille, are you okay?" I asked him when we got to the steep part of the path. He seemed wired, practically vibrating with energy.

"Of course," he said.

When we arrived at the site, the sky had lightened somewhat. "Look," he said, pointing his flashlight at a tangle of yellowish leaves among the branches of an enormous oak tree. "Mistletoe."

Now that I could see him better, I realized that my initial read on Cyrille—that he was back to normal—was wrong. He was gaunt, with hollow, dark crescents under his eyes, like the addicts I used to see slumped over on Broadway near the north part of Columbia's campus.

I tried to placate him. "And that's what made this a—" I grasped for the term he'd used up at the summit but couldn't call it up. "A sacred grove, or whatever?"

"*Nemeton. Oui.*"

He knelt down under the tree and pressed his ear to the ground. "The mountains react to the draw of the moon, just as the ocean does."

"What are you trying to hear?" I attempted, not understanding.

"Not hear," he said. "Feel."

Flattened now on the ground, Cyrille motioned for me to join him. I lay down on my stomach next to him, making a pillow for my forehead with my hands. I closed my eyes. And to my surprise, I did feel something—a quickening. A murmur of life.

"What—"

"Shhhh." He lifted his head but kept his chin resting on the ground. I propped myself up on my elbows. "Do you see the mist?" he whispered.

I followed his eyes through the opening in the trees, which gave way to a view of the valley below us. The Botti vineyard was on the other side of that valley, mostly obscured by the trees. When I squinted, I thought I could make out a cloudlike haze in the distance, just beyond the Mary Magdalene chapel.

"There is a stream underneath us. Which is part of a sanctuary to the goddess of the Duria."

Before I could fully absorb what he was now explicitly telling me—that there was a subterranean body of water underneath where we had been digging all summer—the BlackBerry pinged inside my sweatshirt.

Cyrille's body tensed up. "What was that?" he asked urgently.

"Nothing," I lied in confusion, sitting up with my back to him so I could check the message. Giamma never texted early in the morning; something must be wrong.

What are you doing? was all it said. I closed the message and returned the BlackBerry to my pocket, exchanging it for the envelope from Giamma.

I stood up and handed it to Cyrille, who had gotten to his feet. "Here," I said, in an effort to divert the conversation away from the BlackBerry, and Giamma. "You should use it to do whatever you need to do to protect the dig. From Pietro, or whoever else."

He opened the flap and peered inside, then handed it back to me. "Where did you get this?"

I passed it back to him decisively. I couldn't bring myself to make something up about where the money came from, but I also understood that I could not tell him the truth. "Just take it," I said.

He nodded his head minutely and carefully slid it in between the open leather seams at the top of his tool belt, the part that wrapped around his torso.

"Come," Cyrille said, then hesitated. "Actually, stay here."

I followed his eyes to the valley where we'd seen the mist. "Where are you going?"

"I'll be right back."

I watched him disappear into the pines, basking in my magnanimity for having given him the money I no longer needed. He wouldn't tell Pietro about the money, was my sense; but either way, I'd placed my bet. I'd chosen Cyrille's side.

Then I reopened Giamma's message, remembering his reaction when I'd confronted him this past weekend with Pietro's assertion that his BlackBerry tracked my location. He'd laughed and said if that were true, it was news to him. I'd decided to take his answer at face value, because I wanted my read on him to be true; that he was a safe person, and that I was safe with him. *I'm up at the villa with Cyrille,* I wrote. *Early start. ;)*

I sat down and watched the sun come up, recalling my first day at the site, the countless wheelbarrows of back dirt we'd dumped into the forest. It was astonishing how much progress we had made in such a short span of time. I could see the villa's outline; I could picture people living their lives there. And I still hadn't gotten over the colors in the frescoes we'd discovered, the shock of red and inky black framed by geometric-patterned borders.

Around six, Cyrille still hadn't returned, and I started to get impatient. I rose to my feet and traced the perimeter of the site. But there was no sign of him anywhere.

I went back to the main path, calling his name at five-second intervals as I descended the wooded hill. There was nothing to worry about, I told myself—probably, in his exhaustion, he'd returned to his apartment, or to the palazzo for breakfast. Maybe he'd even told me to meet him back there; I'd been half-asleep during the hike up.

By the time I arrived back at the palazzo, it was nearly seven, and breakfast was laid out on the dining table. I went into the kitchen, where Martha was smoking a cigarette next to an open window. "Was Cyrille here?" I asked her.

"He's in Lyon," she said. I stared at her but didn't say anything. I was bewildered by what had just happened. My sweaty armpits confirmed that I'd just been up to the site and back—but had I imagined the Cyrille part? Had he really been with me? Yes—he was wearing a white T-shirt and cargo shorts; his eyes had brightened reluctantly in his gaunt face when I'd handed him the envelope of euros.

I found Simone at the dining table. "Where were you?" she asked.

Simone had noticed my empty bed—so I hadn't dreamed it. "Did you see him this morning?" I asked.

She unwrapped a packaged *cornetto.* "See who?"

"Never mind," I said, observing Pietro on the other side of the table silently mixing honey into his yogurt. When I got up, I felt his eyes on me. It was an expression that shot through me like a bullet, collapsing my posture.

I understood then, for the first time in my life, my mother's frequent assertion that someone or another was out to get her. It was a sickening feeling that I wanted to banish from my mind, my body; in fact, I wanted to be outside my body, because I hated the danger signals it was sending me. Or maybe I just hated that I didn't know what to do about them.

Suddenly the life I'd left behind in the States seemed like a refuge. But there was no reliable reality to return to; my mother was dead. Jinny hated me, I felt, for missing the funeral. It was possible that I'd never see the house I'd grown up in again.

I looked over at Simone, who averted her eyes. For the umpteenth time I asked myself why I seemed to be the only one at the dig vexed by Pietro's contradictions.

"Where is he?" I heard myself ask Pietro pointedly.

Now he was rueful, smirking. "Cyrille? He's in France."

I clenched my jaw and kept my mouth shut. Later that day, up at the site, I kept expecting Cyrille to appear at the edge of my trench. But he didn't. That was the day we unearthed a two-handed scythe. Pietro hardly skipped a beat; he just told us to keep going. He was insatiable. And I noticed, as he made his rounds, that he was asserting himself even more aggressively than usual. His voice had a different tenor, a newfound and disconcerting confidence.

WHEN WE FINISHED AT FOUR THIRTY, instead of returning to the palazzo with the others, I jogged over to the bed-and-breakfast in search of Marco.

"I need your advice," I said in Italian when I found him in the kitchen on the second floor, helping his grandmother with dinner prep. He nodded and led me to the sitting room downstairs.

"What do I do if I lost someone?" I asked, constructing the question that way because I didn't know how to translate *missing person* into Italian—it was the word *missing* that tripped me up. "Do I call the police or do I go talk to them in person?"

"Who did you lose?"

I told him the story of what had happened that morning at the site, how I'd followed Cyrille up to the villa in the dark.

"What were you doing up there?"

I hesitated. I didn't want whatever Cyrille was doing with the PalmPilot and GIS database to get back to Giamma, lest he relay it to Pietro. "All I know is that he said he would be right back"—*subito* was the Italian word I used—"but he never came back."

Marco's expression was skeptical. "Are you sure you want to talk to the police?"

I nodded vigorously. "Yes. It's important."

He nodded back at me but sounded oddly exasperated when he asked if I had talked to Giamma. I told him I hadn't yet.

If Giamma wanted him to drive me to the police, he would. "Call him," he said.

I dialed Giamma with the BlackBerry, but the line rang and rang. I turned away from Marco and hung up the call with my thumb. "Hi," I said in English. "Cyrille disappeared this morning from the dig site, after I texted you," I said to no one. "Yes, I'm really worried." I allowed a few seconds for a response, then continued: "I came over to the inn to ask Marco for advice. I told him I need to talk to the police." I paused again. "He should drive me there?" I looked over at Marco and gave him a thumbs-up. "Great, okay. *Un bacio. Ciao.*"

"*Allora,*" I said. "He thinks you should take me."

Marco shrugged agreeably and called up to his *nonna* in the kitchen that he would be back in an hour.

* * *

THE POLICE STATION WAS A ten-minute drive from Orbagne in Toulet. "Are you sure you want the police?" Marco asked me again as we pulled up to a beige building with a big round window below a sign that read POLIZIA MUNICIPALE. "Because here there is also the Carabinieri."

His attempts to dissuade me from talking to the police only made me more determined. I nodded and got out of the car. "I'll wait here," he said.

Inside, the small space was populated by folding tables and old desktop computers. Two men in blue uniforms gaped at me as I walked through the door. "Hello," I said in English. The older man raised his gray eyebrows. I hesitated. "English?"

The younger of the two stepped forward. He was sunburned, with curly hair and a kind expression on his face. "How can we help you?"

I relaxed my shoulders in relief. "I need to file a missing person report."

He glanced back at his colleague. "We can't help you with that here."

"Why not?"

He hesitated, taken aback by my intensity, I guessed. "Okay," he conceded. "Who is missing?"

"It's my professor. His name is Cyrille DuPuy, he's from Lyon. I work on the dig in Orbagne, and this morning we were at the site, and he vanished."

"Orbagne?"

"Do you have a form I could fill out or something?" I asked, turning around to make sure Marco was still out there waiting for me.

The police officer looked completely miffed by the whole thing. "There is no form," he said eventually.

"What am I supposed to do?" I burst out, exasperated at his apparent confusion.

The older police officer came over and launched into an explanation, in Italian, of why they couldn't help me. Their department dealt with traffic violations, not missing person reports. He asked me what Cyrille's family was doing to look for him.

"He is French," I said in English, my frustration rising. "I don't know how to contact his family. But he's gone, do you understand?"

The police officers exchanged a glance. "Someone needs to look for him," I continued. "He probably passed out somewhere near the dig site. He was really tired. He wasn't well."

"*Signorina,*" the older one said slowly. "*Devi parlare con—*"

"You should talk to the French authorities," the young one cut in. "The Carabinieri will say the same thing."

"I want to file a report," I insisted. "There must be something you can do."

They both shook their heads, looking genuinely, almost mournfully confused. "I'm sorry," the young one said.

BACK AT THE PALAZZO, I pulled aside one of the Frenchies and told him what had happened. "The Italian police said I need to get in touch with Cyrille's family. Or the French authorities. Can you help me?"

"Of course," he said, looking appropriately worried.

But the next day, he came to find me at breakfast, his countenance transformed. He wanted to help me, he said—but Pietro had advised him to stay out of "whatever was going on with Cyrille and Lena." In response, I wiped the expression from my face, nodded tersely, and shrugged as he backed away.

XVIII.

APRIL 4, 2022

NEW YORK CITY

On Monday afternoon at the office, I log in to my video call with Oliver Clive, who is working remotely from his weekend place in Kingston.

"Everything okay?" he asks. "My assistant said this was urgent."

I'm impatient too, so I get right to the point. "I need to see the gift agreement you guys executed for the Creon donation."

Oliver takes a sip from his coffee mug. "And?"

"That's it."

He gives me a half smile. "You could have emailed."

This feels like a stall tactic. "Is there a reason we don't already have it in hand?"

"Not that I'm aware of," he says, typing on his keyboard without breaking eye contact. "I can have one of the assistants at the office scan it in."

"I thought you said we could have done this over email."

"All the agreements from back then required a wet signature. They're filed. Check your email in a few minutes."

"Is it going to match the provenance?"

I hold my breath, awaiting his response. For a moment I fear his screen is frozen, but then I see a cat leap up onto the arm of the couch behind him.

"I'm not sure what you're implying—"

"I had an interesting conversation with Caroline the other day. We talked a little bit about the personal bequests you helped her with."

He leans back into his chair and nods politely.

"She got me thinking," I continue. "We got a chance to see the new provenance for the Cupid and Psyche cup. But we never saw the gift agreement."

"As you said."

"Or an updated appraisal. Or an export license."

"Lena, I work in the development office. This is above my pay grade—"

"The gift agreement would have been filed along with the original appraisal in Creon's 2017 US tax return. Which I can't access, since it's a privately held company."

I pause. When he doesn't say anything, I continue. "Caroline said you helped convince Filippo Dalmasso to donate to the museum through Creon. When you were on a patron trip to Italy in 2006."

Oliver makes a face. "Other way around."

"What do you mean?"

He exhales loudly. "The annual ten thousand they give is difficult enough. So much paperwork for such little money. I told him the only way we could talk about a corporate gift of art would be if it came from an *American* company, not an Italian one."

"He donated through the American office, right?"

He nods. "The gift agreement just came through, by the way."

I consult my inbox and download the PDF. The donor is listed not as Creon S.p.A., but as Museum Glass LLC. "I'll let you go," I say with a tight smile. "Thanks for your help."

I log in to DonorScan and look up Filippo Dalmasso. Under charitable contributions, there are just three entries, all to the Getty

Museum. Back-to-back in-kind donations, one in 1994, one in 1995, and one in 1996. I look away from my screen, processing this—that Filippo donated to the Getty as an individual, and to Fordham as a corporate entity. He was distancing himself from the donation. Under *business affiliations,* I find Creon S.p.A.'s linked profile, where there is an annual ten-thousand dollar donation to Fordham University—every year since 2004. I go back to the search results, reminding myself that what I'm seeing in this database isn't the whole picture—the richest museum in the world doesn't need to rely on donations. Whatever Filippo donated to the Getty benefitted *him* just as much as it benefitted the museum.

Now I look up Museum Glass LLC and find a single charitable contribution: $18 million to Fordham University in 2007. Then I search for the LLC on the California Secretary of State business database—no results.

"Surprise," Lakshmi says, interrupting my thoughts as she leans on the doorframe of my office. I look up at her in dismay.

She laughs uneasily. "You okay? You look like you've just seen a ghost."

I can't seem to stop blinking. "What are you doing here?"

"I'm picking you up for our last hurrah," she says. "Remember?"

I glance at the time in the upper right corner of my laptop. "It's only four thirty."

"Exactly. Come on, you can get back to work after dinner, I need to head to the airport by eight anyway. But right now I have a surprise for you."

"What is it?"

"Just—hurry up. You'll see."

"Okay," I say, trying to collect myself. I scan my desk for—what? I close my eyes and shake my head. "Sorry. It's been a really weird afternoon."

Lakshmi nods toward the door. "Tell me when we're walking."

"Where are we going?"

Lakshmi grins. "Lena, it's *a surprise.* But I'll give you a hint: it's something you've been wanting to do that has not been legally possible for the past several months."

I close my laptop and swoop on my blazer, desperate to tell Lakshmi what's going on but unsure of where I'd even begin.

"How'd you get up here anyway?" I ask as we wait for the elevator. "Security didn't call me."

"I charmed my way up," she says. "Just kidding. I called Emmanuel's assistant and told her I wanted to surprise you. She actually asked me if you were okay. She sounded a little concerned."

I look straight ahead, but my voice cracks when I say, "I don't know why she would be."

"Hey," Lakshmi says. "Hey. *Are* you okay?"

I look up at the fluorescent lights, and my eye catches the security camera. "I'm just feeling down, I guess."

"Oh, Lena," she says, looking genuinely upset. "I'm sorry, babe."

The elevator stops and two men in suits walk in and nod at us.

"What is it?" Lakshmi asks as we walk across the glass lobby. "What's bothering you?"

So much, I don't say. "I just—can't believe it's your last night in New York," I tell her honestly.

She puts her arm around me outside on the sidewalk. "I'll be a five-hour flight away. Closer than Jinny, even!"

As we walk toward the river, I direct the conversation to Lakshmi's new apartment in London and try to get her talking about the new furniture she plans to buy.

"Does Iñigo have any idea?" I ask when she tells me she's only bringing two suitcases with her.

She shrugs. "He's been in Spain for a week now and he's reached out to me once, with a text. I mean, there's a part of me that wants to tell him, to give him the chance to convince me not to leave. It wouldn't change my mind, because he's been lying to me—being in this relationship but not actually *being* in it. I guess we've been lying to each other. I just had the nerve to do something about it."

I nod, thinking of a moment at the end of our sophomore year, before we left for our summer in Italy. We were in Lakshmi's dorm room, and I was sitting on the bare mattress watching her pack up her closet. I'd asked her what her dad thought about Selinunte; I knew she'd waited until the very last minute to tell him. At first he was angry, she'd said. And then when that didn't have the desired effect, he told her he was disappointed.

Her wide amber eyes were amused, not fearful as she relayed this to me. And though it was hot in the room, the dark feathery hair along the edge of her forehead was dry.

The thing about authority, she continued, which clearly my father does not understand, is that for it to work, it has to be provisional. Or at least have the illusion of being provisional.

I remember not knowing what provisional meant, exactly, even if I could guess it was related to the Latin verb *providere*, "to look ahead." She gave me an expectant look, turning out one of her thin legs like a ballerina; she must have seen my gears turning.

I'm saying that if you accept authority, you have to eventually outgrow it, she concluded.

At the time, I wasn't sure if I agreed. But now I think I understand what she was trying to tell me—which is maybe that ultimately, we can only really be accountable to ourselves.

Now we're standing in front of *Vessel*, the staircase-laden sculpture that was erected a few years ago when Hudson Yards was first developed. It's visible from several conference rooms in my office; I hardly even notice it anymore when I look out the window.

"Here we are," Lakshmi says, glancing at her watch.

"It's still closed."

"I called in a favor."

A statuesque woman in a khaki trench coat approaches us and hugs Lakshmi warmly. "I work with the team that commissioned the sculpture," she explains to me.

"Oh," I say. "How do you two . . . ?"

"We know each other from Columbia," Lakshmi says.

I narrow my eyes. The idea of Lakshmi having had another—separate—friend from Columbia for all these years unnerves me. I try to determine if I've ever seen this woman before. No, I decide. There's nothing familiar about her.

"Okay, let's do it," she says, unlocking a padlock. "I need to get back to the office by five thirty. No photos."

When *Vessel* opened a few years ago, the lines to walk it went on for blocks. Also, I was skeptical—it was trying too hard to be an enormous piece of avant-garde jewelry, and there was something contrived and pretentious about even the title. But then, despite the thousands of buildings in New York City, the thousands of roofs, people started climbing to the top of the sculpture and jumping. The most recent incident involved a fourteen-year-old boy who had been seen laughing with his sister and parents just moments before he jumped to his death.

I became fixated on this story, wondering whether the boy's decision had been premeditated or an impulse. Had he been putting on a charade with his family that whole time, just waiting for his opening, for the exact right moment? Or had he felt the pull Cyrille mentioned at the summit of the Little St. Bernard Pass, *l'appel du vide*? Was there something about simply being at the apex of the sculpture that instilled in a visitor the impulse to die? I had to see for myself. But by then, it had been closed to the public.

We're almost at the top of *Vessel* now, and when I look out at the gray Hudson River, I'm surprised and maybe a bit relieved at what I feel: not suicidal. I'm actually inclined to turn away from the river and back to the city. I look up at my office, behind us, which is arguably more of a vessel than *Vessel.* My hair whips around as I survey the honeycomb stairs we've just ascended, and suddenly I'm transported to a moment at the beginning of my law career, when I was sent to Chicago for a meeting with a financial services company that my law firm was courting for new estate-planning clients. "They'll love it," the chair of trusts and estates had said, justifying my travel and expense budget to the other partners. "A fellow Midwesterner." I didn't tell them that I hadn't been back since I was nineteen; that no one in my family still lived there, that in no way, shape, or form did I view Chicago as home.

I went to the Art Institute and found Mao right where he'd always been. The O'Keeffe skyscape Jinny and I loved was still in the same spot over the staircase near the entrance. But the museum was deserted, and it didn't smell like wood anymore—now it smelled sterile and lifeless. I didn't feel even a glimmer of nostalgia.

Deflated, I wandered over to Millennium Park, where a crowd had gathered around an enormous, mirrored sculpture, digital cameras in hand. *Cloud Gate,* it was called. I approached the piece and gazed up at my warped reflection. What was it that people found so compelling about this thing? I wondered. Was it the fact of literally seeing themselves in the work? Was that what people were looking for in art—themselves?

Later that night, I had Enterprise bring a rental car to my hotel in the Loop—which had gentrified considerably in the eight years since I'd been there—and drove up to Wilmette. I took Sheridan and tried to imagine my mother on the night she died. The Bahá'í temple was humming with white light. What messages was she getting from God? Had *he* told her to drive off the road? I turned on my brights, unnerved by the blind turns, the way oncoming cars appeared out of nowhere—and alternated between hunching over the steering wheel, squinting, and sitting up ramrod straight. Maybe it wouldn't be a terrible way to die, I thought fleetingly. Letting go of the intense instinct to control and just letting the car do its thing. Probably it was a relief for my mother, the letting go.

"WE'VE GOT AN HOUR," Lakshmi says as we slide onto stools at Rubirosa.

She cranes her neck looking for a server. "Do you want to share the Fresca pizza?" she asks without consulting the menu. "Arugula salad and the garlic knots to start?"

"Sure," I say, following her gaze around the restaurant. This is the emptiest I've ever seen Rubirosa—it's about half-full; the other high-tops around us are occupied by older couples and tourists with shopping bags. Then again, I've never been here on a Monday.

"So, who was that?" I ask after Lakshmi puts in our order. "The woman who let us in?"

Lakshmi shrugs. "You don't remember her? She was in our dorm."

I think about it; no, I don't remember her at all. "So did you reconnect or something?"

Lakshmi gives me a puzzled look. "She's a friend. I don't know. I see her once every few months or so."

"I've just never heard you talk about her."

She sits back, a resigned look on her face. "What's wrong, Lena?"

I eye her warily. "I talked to Jinny. Do you remember Nick?"

"Should I?" she says.

"Jinny's ex-fiancé. Who left his wife for her."

A petite server with a pixie cut and a black T-shirt appears next to our table with a notepad. Lakshmi orders for us.

"—and then she broke up with him," I continue. "But they're back together now, or something. *He's* the father. They'd been trying for a really long time, I guess.

"Except apparently there were complications, and now she's on bed rest—I don't know, I just feel so betrayed. I can't explain it." I'm close to tears, but not from sadness; out of frustration at not having the words to express the depths of my anger toward Jinny.

Lakshmi nods sympathetically. "I can't even imagine," she says. "How strange it must be to watch your sibling go through something like this."

I shake my head no; that's not it.

"Is it the baby thing? Do you feel . . . ?"

"No," I say definitively, and truthfully. "I do not want a baby." But maybe there is an element of envy in what I'm feeling, I realize. Not for the child itself, but for the fact of Jinny having made a decision to fundamentally change her life. Lakshmi is doing the same thing with her move to London. My life, on the other hand, doesn't feel like a choice so much as it is a very long series of reactions. I've been on a track, and it's getting dark, and now a custodian is coming around to lock up. Either I'll be locked in or locked out.

"Here's what I think," Lakshmi says, misinterpreting the distress that must be showing on my face. "You've got one sibling. You don't have a relationship with your dad, and your mom's dead. It's worth working through it."

I'm startled by the directness of Lakshmi's words, but the anguish on her face prevents me from feeling offended. She inhales and closes her eyes. "I had a brother. *Have.*" She clears her throat. "I have a brother," she repeats.

Her eyes are still closed, and I'm thankful that she can't see the incredulous look on my face.

"He was in an accident," she says. "It was summer vacation. I was eight, he was almost three. I went inside to get something—no idea what—and when I came back out, he'd taken off his floaties, and he was just limp in the water. I was so scared, and I was even more scared to tell my parents, but if I'd done that, if we'd called for help right away—" She shakes her head.

"I'm so sorry—" I attempt, caught off guard by the gravity of what she's telling me. I reach across the table for her hand.

She tells me about how the paramedics pulled him out of the water and resuscitated him—too late—and how after months of rehab he eventually learned how to walk again, and to talk, and to live. But he never grew into a person who possessed anything that resembled independence.

Thinking of the pain that Lakshmi has been living with all these years—it's overwhelming. And yet, I understand. I understand the instinct to keep an entire part of your life private.

The appetizers come, and we stare at them. Lakshmi plucks a garlic knot and chews it apathetically.

"It wasn't your fault," I say finally, firmly.

"I know," she says after a moment. "I've only had two decades of therapy." She forces out a laugh and sips her water.

"I didn't know you were in therapy," I say, thinking of the therapist Jinny and I saw together after our parents separated. I hated sitting on that scratchy couch opposite a middle-aged woman who nodded while Jinny talked. I'd gaze at her lip liner and French manicure, trying to say as little as possible as she repeated the same vexing question: *How did that make you feel?* And Jinny would answer honestly. But I refused to say anything; I let Jinny speak for me.

She nods. "On and off."

I think back to the night Lakshmi and I first met in Cyrille's seminar. I would never have guessed, back then, that she had a whole hidden compartment of pain inside her. But maybe, subconsciously, we recognized that in each other, the need to conceal part of ourselves. I let her keep her secrets, and she let me keep mine.

"The summer we were in Italy was when my mom died," I suddenly feel compelled to tell her.

Lakshmi furrows her eyebrows. "Didn't I know that?"

"I didn't tell you until the fall. When I came to visit you in Sicily I had just found out."

Lakshmi nods, and we're both quiet for a while. It's a comfortable silence, the kind that can only happen when you feel deeply known by the person you're with.

"You know what I hated about archeology?" she asks. "It's a bait and switch. You're led to believe that you're going to understand people—the way they lived, why they did the things they did with the objects they had—but in practice it was all so rote and mechanical, so impersonal."

"Unless you're in charge," I say, thinking of what Cyrille's villa became under Pietro's leadership.

"Even then. There's a limit to what you can conclusively say about any of it. Like when I was in Selinunte, I remember how I kept thinking about Pyrrhus—" She stops and smiles sheepishly. "I haven't thought about any of this stuff in so long."

I nod in encouragement, not telling her that for me it's been the opposite—I haven't been able to *stop* thinking about that summer.

"I just kept thinking about how Pyrrhus had Sicily. Even after everything he lost in the war with the Romans, he was victorious in the sense that he had ultimately won, *and* he had Sicily. But he messed up the negotiations with Carthage so badly that all the Greek cities in Sicily turned against him and allied themselves with the Carthaginians—their enemies. And yes, the Carthaginians later went on to destroy Selinunte—but who says the Selinuntines didn't help them do it?"

I nod, trying to follow what she's saying. "What's the point?"

"The point is volition. Everything everyone said when I was there was that the city was sacked, destroyed—these people are victims. But what if they weren't victims? What if they *wanted* to burn everything down because they were descended from the Selinuntines who hated Pyrrhus? What if they inherited their predecessors' grudge?"

Volition. Pietro's theory—his original one, not the one that was published by Valenti—was that the villa in Orbagne had been abandoned by Melania the Younger and destroyed by a lightning fire. But Cyrille didn't buy it, and neither did Si. Si thought Melania's freed slaves burned the villa down on their own volition.

"What are you thinking about?" Lakshmi asks. "You look tense."

"Nothing," I murmur, taking a sip of water.

"What I'm trying to say is that archeological authority is a fallacy. But also, I understand why you didn't tell me at the time about your mom. And I get that you're mad at Jinny, and I know why you're mad at her. It's self-preservation. You're afraid you're going to lose her. I don't think you will. But if you mess up the negotiations, you might."

I can't help but grin at this logic, which is something only Lakshmi could come up with. "So you're saying I'm Pyrrhus?"

"I'm saying, don't be Pyrrhus."

"And just to clarify, who are my negotiations with?"

"It's not a perfect analogy, all right? But you get my point."

I nod, thinking how much I'm going to miss being in the same city as Lakshmi, sitting across from her at a restaurant on a random weeknight. "So what's going on with your case? Did you hand it off to someone?"

She shakes her head. "I can manage it from London. I finally got something I could submit as evidence."

The server places our pizza down on the metal stand in the middle of the table. "What'd you get?" I ask.

"Submarines. And submersibles," Lakshmi says, helping herself to a slice. "Of all things. These flimsy, jury-rigged submersibles. That's how they're getting cocaine into the States. Apparently this has been happening for years in the Caribbean, but now they're using entry points on Long Island. They're just smuggling tons, literally tons, of cocaine in these submersibles. Which are practically undetectable on any radar because they're so small. Half the time the people driving them are dead by the time they reach their location."

"What does that have to do with human rights? I mean, with the women in your case?"

"These subs are like human coffins. But also, the people running the 'ndrangheta—they kill people for what they know. That's the problem for these women. They know too much. And now, hopefully, we can actually help. I already got one of them into witness protection."

I drop my pizza on my plate, processing what she's saying. *They kill people for what they know.* And it dawns on me: *I* know too much. "Was it hard? Getting her into witness protection?"

"I mean, it's always a process. It will take a while to get it all done. But this woman randomly had US citizenship, so we were able to expedite hers."

I choke down another slice of pizza, and when the check comes, I swat Lakshmi's hand away, fingers trembling as I take my credit card out of my wallet. Giamma never said the word '*ndrangheta.* But at Fordham, on the night of the patron opening, he told me to be careful. And on Sunday in Central Park, Si told me I was right to be afraid. Pietro's face flashes in my mind, that enigmatic look he gave me at breakfast on the morning Cyrille disappeared. Even then, I knew too much. Cyrille too. And Giamma—Giamma knew the most. He still does.

"Did you ever come across the name Valerio Piromalli?"

Lakshmi hesitates. "Why do you ask?"

"That was Giamma's dad."

She pushes away her plate and stares down at the table. Eventually, she breathes in and meets my eyes. "Lena, he's legendary. There were literal parades in the streets of Turin when he died two years ago—" She pauses, clears her throat. "Your ex-boyfriend is 'ndrangheta."

I blink rapidly. "Not anymore, I don't think," I blurt. "He changed his—" He came to the States, he changed his name. Did he change his name to distance himself from his father or to disguise his actual identity? Or both?

"'Not anymore?' Did you—"

"No. I mean, there were some sketchy things—"

"Like what?"

I consider my response, remembering Si's reaction in Central Park when I told them I went to the warehouse in Chiasso. They reacted that way, I now realize, for the same reason I've never been able to shake Cyrille's disappearance—because he's dead. *They kill people for what they know.* But what did Cyrille know?

"Actually, it's better if you don't tell me. But Lena—" Lakshmi stops herself.

The more they know, the more vulnerable the site is. So Cyrille told me the morning he took me up to the summit of the Little St. Bernard Pass. At the time, I didn't know what he meant by "they"—but now it dawns on me. He was talking about Giamma and his father, Valerio. He was talking about the 'ndrangheta.

"You don't get to leave the 'ndrangheta," Lakshmi concludes. "If you want to leave, you have to die."

"What is her name?" I ask urgently.

"Whose name?"

"The 'ndrangheta wife with US citizenship. The one you got into witness protection. What is her name?"

Lakshmi studies me. "You know I can't tell you that."

An image of Si sitting on the rocks in Central Park on Sunday comes into my mind. "You don't have to say anything. Just nod yes or no."

"Lena—"

I never forgot Giamma's mother's name, because of the part in *The Aeneid* when Iris, the messenger goddess of rainbows, is dispatched by Juno to Sicily, where she stirs up discontent among the Trojan wives, inciting them to set fire to Aeneas's fleet of ships. Also, it was an unusual name for an Italian woman. Quentin had pronounced it *ee-rees* when he asked Giamma about her at the grotto in Lugano. "Is it Iris?"

Lakshmi's head is still—but there is clear affirmation in her eyes. Then she clears her throat and changes the subject to London, but her voice is shaky. And I'm not paying attention to anything she's saying, because my mind keeps turning over the phrase she used earlier: *You don't get to leave the 'ndrangheta. To leave, you have to die.*

When we finish, I climb down from my stool, and my knees give out slightly. But I breathe in and stand up straight, fortifying myself against Quentin, Caroline, Giamma, and any other unseen forces threatening my existence. I need to go back to the office; I need to warn Emmanuel. And then I probably need to resign from my job.

I walk Lakshmi back to her apartment and give her a long hug, trying to suppress my internal hellscape: broken pottery in trenches, a flash of Quentin and Giamma sitting across from me at the grotto in Lugano—interspersed with snippets of the past month's revelations—Caroline talking on her cell phone in Italian on the fifteenth floor, Si not looking back as they retreat from the rocks in Central Park.

"You have to let this go," Lakshmi says as she releases me. "All this stuff with Giamma, and Cyrille. Orbagne. Let it go."

I get in a cab just as my phone pings with a text from Si—a link. I tap through to an article posted two days ago on a British tabloid's website titled THE WARRIORS GET THEIR SHIELD BACK. I scroll down and inhale sharply when I see an image of the shield that Giamma and I brought to Switzerland all those years ago. "The Riace Warriors?" I whisper as I scan the article. There's an image of two enormous bronze figures standing in contrapposto, which I recognize from one of my old ancient civ textbooks. A warning. And it dawns on me—when Italy came after the Fordham Museum, they could have gone with a firm that specialized in cultural heritage law. But they chose us. They chose me.

BY SEVEN THIRTY, I'm back at work, marching straight through the labyrinth of cubicles to Emmanuel's office. His assistant has left for the day, but he's sitting at his desk with his noise-canceling headphones on.

"I need to talk to you," I say firmly.

He puts his headphones around his neck and his face changes as he registers my intensity.

"Everything all right?"

"I need to speak to the Manhattan DA team working on the Fordham case."

"What?" he says, motioning for me to close the door.

My eyes dart around the office. Though this building is surrounded by other high-rises, I feel weirdly exposed under fluorescent lights right in front of Emmanuel's floor-to-ceiling windows. I back away from his desk and lean against the shelving unit opposite it.

"I don't even know where to start," I say, searching for the right way to articulate the danger of our association with the Fordham Museum, and of the firm's association with me.

"Emmanuel, this is a setup. I have been *set up.* Because I knew about the warehouse in Chiasso, and the bronze shield, and—"

"Whoa," he says. "Let's slow down here. Let's take a deep breath."

I cross my arms tightly over my chest. "We need to act now. I need to talk to the police. Now, tonight."

"Why don't you take a seat?" he asks, gesturing to the round table next to his windows.

I ignore this suggestion and press forward. "Emmanuel, it's not random. None of this is random. These guys know who I am. And they're dangerous. Remember how you were saying the Italians dropped previous charges against Filippo because he had ties to organized crime?"

"Lena, who are you talking about? Who are 'these guys'?"

I exhale loudly. "I have information for the police."

Emmanuel regards me with a pained expression on his face. "What information, Lena?"

"I don't want to implicate you in this."

He walks over and examines my face. "You doing okay, kid?"

"I will be fine, once I talk to the DA," I say shakily. "Or the police."

"Sure," he says. "Sure. We'll get you connected. But in the meantime, I think you should go home and get some rest. Take the rest of the week off."

I shake my head. "I don't need time off. I need—"

"I gotcha, I know. But go home, take it easy—don't think about work for a few days. How's that?"

It takes every ounce of my self-control not to explode at him, but I somehow manage to regain my composure: I need him on my side.

As I head back to my desk to gather my things, I observe that the firm has mostly emptied out. When I was in my twenties, we were all still working at this hour. But this new generation is different. They're not willing to give all of themselves to their jobs. And they're probably onto something—I gave all of myself to this firm and look where it landed me. Right back where I was before I ever even considered becoming a lawyer, mired in my past mistakes.

Going off Emmanuel's reaction just now, the police probably won't take my story seriously unless I have something to show them—something that corroborates my memories, that proves I am in danger.

My hands are sweating so profusely that I have to wipe them on my pants before grabbing my phone out of my jacket pocket. I dial Si.

"Yeah?" they answer.

"It's Lena," I say as nonchalantly as possible. "Thanks for the article."

"No problem," they say. Music crackles in the background, which is promising; they might not be at home.

"It's a little loud," I say. "Where are you?"

"Italy."

I breathe in and out a few times; this is an unexpected twist. "Where in Italy?"

"Yes."

"Huh? I said *where* in Italy."

"Yes."

I stare down at the floor, understanding: yes or no questions only. "Okay. Are you in Torino?"

"No."

"Are you in . . . Orbagne?"

"No."

I change gears. "Are you coming back soon?"

"Yes."

"When? I mean, tomorrow?"

"I gotta run."

"Wait—are you safe?"

When they don't respond right away, a knot clenches in my stomach. "Si," I say. "Yes or no. Are you in danger?"

"No," they say, finally. "Talk soon."

I try to relax my face and keep breathing. Talk soon is promising; talk soon means that Si doesn't know of any immediate plan to eliminate me. Or maybe it's the opposite—maybe Si is going to *help* eliminate me.

Si and Giamma knew Caroline back then, when Cyrille was working in Orbagne; both of them know her now. Giamma was caught off guard when I told him I was one of Caroline's lawyers. Si, on the other hand, who Caroline went out of her way to introduce to me that night, was serene. Si, who is meticulous and deliberate and calculating. Si, who said they looked me up on LinkedIn a few years ago. Si, who was unfazed when I eventually tracked them down.

They expected me to find them, I realize, because they had something to do with me getting put on this case.

Even if Si isn't actually signaling for me to meet them in Orbagne, it's worth going: if I could get into Giamma's house there, I'd have a trove of physical evidence that I could trade in to protect myself.

I need to take this into my own hands—I need to go to Orbagne. No more confiding in anyone; no more protection-seeking.

I pull up flights. There's a direct one from JFK to Milan leaving tonight at 10:40 with open seats. I glance at my watch. It's eight o'clock now. I launch Uber and check the wait time for a black car—forty minutes to JFK, it says. I'd need to stop home and grab my passport and a few things. I concentrate, trying to figure out if I can do this. I can make it, I decide. I book the flight, call the car, and shove my laptop into my bag.

XIX.

APRIL 6, 2022

ORBAGNE

It's just after six in the morning when I land in Milan. I rent a car and commence my two-and-a-half-hour drive northwest. On the highway, I don't marvel at the scenery. I am focused on the roads, and on not running myself off them.

I have a license, but I never drive in New York; I walk, I take the subway, I rideshare. And even though I'm behind the wheel, and even though I'm on the other side of the Atlantic, I don't feel transported. I feel enclosed. Driving to Orbagne right now is the closest to tunnel vision I've ever felt, but it doesn't feel limiting—it's freeing. For once, I'm not scanning for threats.

Somewhere around Ivrea, the road starts to incline sharply, and I notice the vast quantities of snow covering the mountains despite the April sun. I have thought so often of the patches of snow at the summit of the Little St. Bernard Pass the summer I was in Orbagne, and Cyrille's response when I asked him why the snow didn't melt in the heat. "But it is melting," he replied. "It takes the whole summer to finish."

And I remember how it was for me—how I was—when I first came here. It was my first and only time out of the United States. The farthest I've ventured from New York since then is California to visit Jinny.

The GPS is draining my cell phone battery, and when a 10 percent notification pops up on the screen, I realize with a slow-spreading dread that I have failed to bring a European converter for my charger. Mercifully, a sign for Orbagne with an accompanying *Parco Archeologico* icon appears, and I take the next exit.

Following the *Parco Archeologico* signs, I turn off the paved road and onto cobblestones, processing that what was once at best a *comune* is now a full-on town with gas stations, stoplights, and restaurants. It's not that I was expecting Orbagne to have decayed; but I wasn't quite expecting it to have flourished so extensively. The Villa del Frutteto has apparently achieved theme park status.

Near the church, I find a place to leave my rental Audi—the only automatic option at the Hertz in the Milan airport—and I become aware of an insistent mantra echoing in my head: *I am different too.*

I get out of the car and walk down a familiar narrow street, scanning for signs of life. Lines of laundry stretch above me from one building to the next. Somewhere in the distance, children are playing. The street gives way to a piazza, and I stand at its periphery for a long moment, trying to figure out what's different. The old well is gone, I finally realize. It's been replaced by a bronze statue of a man in a suit, one hand in a pocket, a distant smile glinting under his mustache. I approach the statue and locate a placard at the base—*Andrea Botti,* it says. Underneath the name is a quote from Suetonius: *Marmoream se relinquere, quam latericiam accepisse.* "He left it of marble, that which he found of . . ." something. I don't know *latericiam.*

I reach into my back pocket to look up the word on my phone. But the screen is black, the battery dead. I continue past the piazza and am relieved to discover the palazzo that served as our dig dorm has not been demolished. On the contrary, it's been power-washed or white-washed, I can't tell which; but what was once a dingy pewter is now a bright white, and the wooden shutters have been replaced with glass windows. I locate the one on the second floor through which I first saw Giamma loading his car, a cigarette between his lips, the little boys circling him on their bikes. How would my life have turned out if I hadn't seen him that morning from my window, I wonder? Would I have returned to Orbagne year after year like Si? Would Cyrille still be alive?

Opposite the palazzo is Giamma's summer house, which, unlike seemingly everything else in Orbagne, is faded and decrepit. The stone walls around the garden are mossy and unkempt; there's a detached gutter dangling from the edge of one side of the roof.

I walk right up to the outer door, which still doesn't have a bell, only the same old pointless bestial brass knocker that was always there. I test the doorknob; it's locked.

My heart rate speeds up as I scan the wall for the loose stone where Giamma kept his spare key. It was to the left of the door, I'm sure of it. But as I start testing them, I realize that almost all the stones are loose.

I look over my shoulder and around me, the rapid warming of the air making me feel certain that people are opening their windows, that someone from some building somewhere is watching me. But the street is deserted. I tie my sweatshirt around my waist and run my shaky hand over the stones as nonchalantly as possible. 6:10, my watch says. Italy is six hours ahead of New York, which makes it 12:10 here.

After several minutes, I stop expecting to find the key—but I keep going. I lose myself in the search for long enough for the light to really change, for the sun to beat down on my face. And then, to my shock and fascination, I do find it. I find the old iron key. Some things are as I remember them.

In disbelief, I let myself into the courtyard, gently closing the outer door behind me. The lemon trees at the four corners of the garden are withered and bare, with no buds. The path that led up to the house is covered in dirt and slime, and two of the house's windows are boarded up. The place is very clearly abandoned.

At the front door, I glance behind me and push. "Hello?" I call.

The house is silent save for the steady stream of melted snow pouring into the drains along the periphery of the atrium. Down this hall was the kitchen; up the stairs were the bedrooms.

The galleries. I need to go to the galleries. The atrium has not been winterized in any way, and I step around the pile of melting snow in the center of the space as I make my way to the other side of the house.

But the whole place, including the galleries, is empty. There's not even an outline where the Flemish tapestries once hung. Everything feels damp, and utterly deserted.

I WALK BACK TO MY rental car and grab my duffel, then head toward the building which stands in the place of Marco's old inn. There is a sidewalk in front of it, which definitely wasn't here before, and a burgundy welcome mat with four gold stars under the name Parc Hotel Orbagne. Enormous glass windows emerge from the original stone edifice. When I step onto the welcome mat, the doors slide open automatically.

Inside, the floors are a polished black tile, and a woman in a starched white button-down behind a glass desk looks up.

"*Prego,*" she says as I approach.

"Hi—" I say, reshouldering my duffel.

"English?" she offers.

"Thank you—I'm, um—do you have any rooms available for tonight?"

She types into her computer. "Just yourself?"

"Just me," I say, looking around at the lobby's smooth surfaces and seeing no remnants of the old inn.

"We have a mountain view or a village view," the receptionist says.

I turn back to her. "Village view is good," I say.

She types some more. "The rate for the evening is three hundred and ten euros."

I hand her my AMEX and passport. "I remember when it was thirty euros a night for a room," I say. "Things have changed, huh?"

She narrows her eyes slightly.

"I guess it wasn't the same," I say, backtracking. "It was much smaller."

"And what brings you back to Orbagne?" she asks.

I think about the signs on the Autostrada indicating the archeological park, and the feeling of being watched outside Giamma's house. "I'm just here to see the villa."

I nod vigorously, proud of myself for having come up with this believable explanation on the spot. But the woman only shifts her stance, nods remotely, and goes back to typing.

A door behind the reception desk opens and a stocky man in a wool sweater emerges. When he meets my eyes, I recognize him immediately: Marco. He recognizes me too.

"Maddalena?" he says. "*Non ci credo.*" His smile animates his whole face.

I return his smile, but inside, I'm uneasy—his tone doesn't suggest disbelief. On the contrary: it almost feels like he was expecting me. I'm reminded that he was—is—Giamma's friend. Has Giamma been in touch with him? Could Giamma have somehow known I was headed to Orbagne?

"I really like what you've done with the place," I offer.

He laughs genuinely. "Thank you very much," he says in perfect English. The woman looks at him again. "Oh. This is my wife, Flavia," he says, reaching an arm around her shoulders.

"Nice to meet you," she says tightly, handing back my credit card and passport. "Your room will be ready at three o'clock."

Marco looks at the computer screen and says something quietly. She shakes her head.

"*Ecco,*" he says to me, smoothing his sweater and walking around the desk. "Can I offer you a coffee? Some lunch?"

I glance at Flavia, who is back to typing on her computer. "Sure," I say. Marco gestures for me to follow him.

We walk to the other end of the lobby and down a corridor, which merges with an interior glass-walled arcade. As we approach a large set of oak doors, Marco trots ahead of me and opens one of them. Eyes bright, he motions for me to look inside.

It's a ballroom of sorts, with wood paneling, high ceilings, and two mounted screens on either side of a low stage. "Wow," I say.

"We can do weddings here, business conferences, et cetera. Whatever you want. Friday there is a press conference."

I nod, feeling a wave of abstract pride for Marco, who became the person he wanted to become, who built the thing he wanted to build.

We continue on until we reach a host stand at the end of the corridor. A woman in a snug black dress scoops up two menus and leads us through a busy restaurant to a table in the back corner.

Marco pulls out a bistro chair for me and sits down himself. We regard each other. He has the same dark curly hair he had the summer we met, and deep smile lines around his mouth.

"Are you still in touch with Giamma?" I ask, attempting to sound casual.

He gives me an inexplicably weary look, but a waitress comes over to the table before he can answer me. He orders an espresso. "*Anch'io,*" I say to the waitress, and I open the menu, which is in Italian, English, French, and German. When I look back up, Marco is scrolling through his Apple watch.

I clear my throat.

“I haven’t spoken to Giamma in a long time,” he says.

I scan the restaurant. An exhausted man drinks espresso while a mother—I presume she’s the mother—bounces a baby on her lap.

Marco looks past me. “I haven’t seen any of them in probably ten years. *Anzi*—more than that, I think.”

He is being truthful, I decide. “Any of them?” I ask.

“Giamma, his mother. The house sits empty, even after his father died.”

I nod, hoping it doesn’t show on my face that I already knew that the house was abandoned. That I broke into it this morning.

The waitress brings our coffee and asks if we want anything from the menu. Marco looks at me. I order a plain omelet.

“What brings you to Orbagne?” he asks me after she nods and turns away from the table.

“I wanted to see it again,” I say.

Marco studies me. “The villa?”

I sip my espresso and nod.

He gestures behind him. I can’t read his expression. “That’s why everyone comes to Orbagne.”

I press forward. “What about Pietro? Do you see him a lot?”

Marco sits back in his seat. “You mean *Dottore* Botti?”

I mirror the look of amused reproach on Marco’s face. “I saw the statue. Of his father.”

“They never let us forget how important they are,” he says. He’s quiet for a moment, seemingly pondering this statement. “Despite the fact that neither of them lives here.”

I lean forward. “Really? Where do they live?”

“Andrea is here a few months out of the year, otherwise he is in Rome. Pietro moved to Aosta. His father-in-law gave him a house. Nice for him, right?”

An image of the A-frame house near the Arco di Agosto—

Benedetta's father's house—where Giamma brought me to celebrate Andrea Botti's Senate campaign, flashes in my mind. "Filippo Dalmasso," I say without thinking.

Marco tilts his head. "You know him?"

"I knew Benedetta the summer I was here," I say, truthfully.

He nods.

"So who runs the vineyard then?"

"Pietro's sister."

I nod, remembering the one time Pietro mentioned his older sister to me. Their relationship was complicated, I'd understood, sympathizing with him at the time. And then an image of Jinny comes into my mind, pregnant and bed-ridden. I push it away.

"*Comunque*, the Botti family are happy. The vineyard does well, the villa brings in tourists. For now."

"For now?"

He hesitates then motions for me to lean in. "The Carabinieri closed the site on Monday for an investigation. They said it would be open again in twenty-four hours, but today is Wednesday, and it is not reopened."

My eyes widen. "What are they investigating?"

Marco looks energized by my reaction. But he's not smiling.

Though he's not answering me, I sense he knows something, that he wants to tell me what he knows. Just like the summer I was here. On the night I met him, he was open with the details of what he remembered about the looting.

"Hey, remember the other professor, the one who went missing?" I hear myself ask. "And you drove me to the police station?"

"The French guy?"

"Before he disappeared, I told him to come talk to you," I say, squinting, feeling for something just out of reach. "Did he ever ask you about the looting?"

Marco drinks the last of his espresso and frowns into his little porcelain cup. "I don't know. I don't remember."

I clear my throat. "The night we met—do you remember that? I asked you about it. About the looting. And you told me—do you remember what you told me?"

"I'm sure I had a theory," he says, searching my face.

"You said: 'Italians would never dig holes like that.' And that it could have been the Albanian mafia."

Marco winces. "A ridiculous thing to say."

"But I remember the little boys on bikes. Giamma was kind to them. He told me that everyone else treated them badly."

"That was a long time ago."

He looks like he wants to say more, so I keep quiet and let him talk.

"A few years after you were here," he continues, "Andrea Botti—Pietro's father—initiated a campaign. Now he's a *senatore a vita*, a senator for life." He pauses. "Do you know the Lega Nord?"

"A little," I say, remembering Andrea Botti's Wikipedia page.

"*Practicamente*, they're fascists," he says. "*Italians first*, is what they say. But in reality they don't want *any* immigrants here. Meanwhile, almost all of my staff were Eastern European refugees. But Pietro's father, back then, having the power he had, mounted his campaign—billboards, television commercials, strikes—to get all the immigrants in Orbagne out. They cannot live here, they cannot work here."

I shake my head and mirror the dismay on Marco's face. "Just in Orbagne?"

"*Just* in Orbagne," he says. "Something about the archeological park and the tourists and the way we need to represent Italy now. It's crazy. And for us at the hotel, it's been impossible. We can't keep up with the demand."

I nod. "So the campaign worked."

"It worked. And so you see my disapproval of myself as a young man with my little theories. There was so much I didn't understand."

"What else?" I ask, on instinct.

When Marco finally speaks, his voice is low. "That place—La villa del frutteto—should be called La villa del *sfruttato.* Everyone knows that Andrea Botti is *in combutta con*—I don't know in English. Everyone knows Andrea Botti was bought by the 'ndrangheta. Everyone in Orbagne."

I gape.

"I am not telling you a secret," he says. "We all know it."

"Is that what the Carabinieri are investigating?" And what I want to know, but decide not to ask—does the 'ndrangheta own Pietro too?

Marco raises his eyebrows and shrugs.

But then it occurs to me: Pietro hated his father. I recognized this, even if he never expressed it. And Si said they had a falling-out with Pietro because of his father, who had his own interpretation of the site. *Glory of Rome,* Si said. That's why Si stopped working at the dig: because of Pietro's father.

I force myself to refocus. "I need to ask you about someone."

"I'm sorry?"

I look up at Marco, my heart pounding. "Do you remember my friend from the summer I was here? Blond, American, walked really fast?"

He looks blank.

"Here every summer for a long time," I add.

He gestures to his head. "Ah, yes. Short hair?"

"Yes, yes. Have you seen them recently?"

The waitress presents me with my omelet, and I take my eyes off Marco to thank her.

When I look back at him, he's rising from his chair. "I don't think so," he says conclusively. "Excuse me."

I'm not sure what to make of the fact that Marco is ending this conversation so abruptly, but I eat and watch him walk out of the restaurant.

I could go to Aosta, to Filippo's house. It was near the Arco di Agosto. I remember it clearly; it looked like one of the houses in the Disney Storybook ride. I could find the house and try to talk to Pietro and Benedetta. Si might even be with them.

When I'm finished I return to the lobby, where Marco and Flavia seem to be bickering, quietly. "Sorry," I say. "My phone is completely dead. Do you have a charger I can use for a half hour?"

"Of course," Marco says. "Flavia can charge it."

I hand my phone to Flavia. "*Grazie,*" I say to both of them.

Then I repair to a collection of low furniture next to the windows and take a seat, gazing out at the cobbled streets, the stony Baroque church, the edge of the mountains. This is nearly the same view I had on the evening I first spoke to Giamma, at the tables outside Marco's inn. And the last evening I spoke to him in Orbagne too—the sky was darker, but the view was the same.

IT WAS A SUNDAY, the eve of my twentieth birthday. Cyrille had been missing for a week, and Giamma had been distant, physically and emotionally. We'd only spoken once in the days leading up to my departure from Orbagne, when I called to tell him about Cyrille's disappearance after I filed the missing person report. He'd been silent for a full minute, and eventually stammered out an awkward, bewildered response, something to do with climbing accidents and tree roots. I changed the subject, furious at myself for initiating the conversation over the phone instead of face-to-face. Because I needed to see his face. I knew Giamma well by then, and I knew that there were some things he couldn't say, that he could only convey without words.

And so on Saturday, my last weekend in Italy, when I heard his car tires snapping over the stones outside my bedroom window, I shut off the BlackBerry and closed the shutters. A few minutes later, Martha called up for me. Reluctantly, I descended the back staircase.

It was strange to see Giamma in the palazzo's kitchen; he looked too big for it. The wheeled prep tables hit him mid-thigh. I breathed in his cedar-and-cigarette smell as Martha looked back and forth at us. We both stood our ground.

Martha believed that Cyrille was still in Lyon, engulfed in research that kept him from contacting her. She clung to this version of things, no matter how many different ways I explained the sequence of what happened the morning Cyrille went missing. I didn't know what led to my diminished credibility in her eyes; I still don't. The only thing I could think at the time was that Pietro could have helped me convince her otherwise. He knew more than he was willing to admit.

It was because I didn't want to upset Martha that I eventually followed Giamma out of the palazzo and back to his villa, where we sat in the kitchen sipping espresso. I waited for him to bring up our conversation from earlier that week, but he didn't. And there was something repentant in his eyes when he leaned forward on his stool to squeeze my thigh, so I let him lead me up to the bedroom, and I let him undress me, and though I'd only ever fleetingly thought of Cyrille in a sexual way, I imagined that it was Cyrille I was kissing; that it was Cyrille who was pulling me toward his body with tentative tenderness. Suddenly there were tears streaming down my face, and when I reentered the scene I saw that Giamma was frightened. "Did I hurt you?" he asked.

"Yes," I said, on instinct. I told him about Pietro, and how I was certain he knew something about what had happened to Cyrille. And I explained to him about Martha and Simone, and about the lies in the *Corriere* article, and how no one believed me about the morning Cyrille disappeared.

"I believe you," he said, tucking a strand of hair behind my left ear.

And in that moment, I believed that he had nothing to do with it. Or rather, I chose to believe that we were both innocent, both doing our best. We passed the rest of the day and night in a détente of sorts: me saying no more about Pietro, or Cyrille, or about what would become of our relationship after I returned to New York. He would drive me to the Torino airport on Monday morning on his way to work; that was as far as we got.

Sunday afternoon we wandered over to the inn, where Marco made us two pirlo cocktails that we brought outside to one of the picnic tables facing the church. It was the hottest it had been all summer, and though I'd never acquired a taste for Genetrix, I liked the cinnamon aftertaste of Campari, and I drank my pirlo down fast. But then an image of Cyrille's gaunt face with its patchy beard came into my head.

"You have to help me," I said abruptly.

"Help you with what?"

I hesitated for a moment, then came out with the words that had formed in my head. "I saw the gun in your glove compartment."

Giamma reddened. But to his credit, he didn't lunge at me; he didn't even tell me to keep my voice down. What he did—and this is what I felt I could never forgive him for—he laughed.

I doubled down. "I need you to find out what Pietro knows about Cyrille."

Giamma shook his head in dismay.

"Did you *help* him or something? Why can't you just do this for me?"

"Did I help Pietro with what?"

"With—" I started. But I couldn't articulate what I was getting at. "Are you friends with Valenti too?"

"Who is Valenti?"

"The journalist, the one who wrote those lies—"

And Giamma lost his composure then. He hissed that he had

nothing to do with the site, that he wasn't an archeologist, that whatever Pietro did or didn't do was his own business.

"What are we?" I interjected. "I mean, what is this? What am I to you?" I was insinuating that as his *fidanzata*—or so he'd called me—he should be loyal to me. He should take my side.

Anger flashed in his eyes, and then he shook his head and wiped his face of all expression.

"I am going to gather my things at your place," I told him. "And tomorrow I'll take the train to Torino. To catch my flight home." I felt my throat close around that word, *home.* I wasn't going back to Wilmette; Lakshmi and I were headed to New York, where we would crash on the sofa bed at James's off-campus apartment until the dorms opened.

"Safe travels," was all Giamma said as I handed him his BlackBerry and walked away.

Mystified by Giamma's immediate and complete capitulation of our relationship, I cleared out my drawer at the villa, then returned to the palazzo, where Simone was up in our room packing. "When is your flight?" I asked her.

She glanced up at me from the floor, where she was folding clothes in front of her open suitcase. "Martha and I are going to travel in Tuscany for a few weeks. And then I'll go to New York."

"Oh," I said, processing the fact that the two of them had made a plan without me.

"I figured you were planning something with Giamma," Simone said neutrally.

"No. I think we just broke up."

She stopped folding and looked up, presumably waiting for me to elaborate. I didn't have anything to tell her, because I couldn't make sense of what had just transpired. I could only think of a poem by Horace that Cyrille had recited in Latin to us back in New York. It was from the fourth volume of *Odes*, commissioned by Maecenas, written in celebration of Augustus's military successes over the Sygambri. Cyrille had contended that the Sygambri in the poem stood in for Augustus's broader domination of northern "barbarians" and Gauls. But I could hardly pay attention to the military part, because I was fixated on the first stanza, ostensibly a non sequitur, when Horace says that any poet who tries to rival Pindar—anyone who tries to be greater than he is—will end up falling to his death like Icarus, whose wax wings melted when he flew too close to the sun.

I DON'T THINK I WOULD have been able to vocalize my feelings at the time, but I remember what I felt then. I can even revive the feeling, sitting here in Marco's hotel lobby: an abstract understanding of my own self-delusion; a sense of power being relinquished.

If Giamma had the Cupid and Psyche cup—if he, rather than Valerio or Quentin, sold it to Filippo and orchestrated the Fordham donation behind the scenes—all of his actions were intentional. As in, he is the reason that the cup left Italy. And if it's true that the cup came from Orbagne—is it possible that this was why Cyrille mentioned Giamma the day he took me to the summit? He knew Giamma had something valuable that had been looted from the dig, and he suspected that I might know too?

Suddenly I am seized by the conviction that the Cupid and Psyche cup was not indirectly, but directly related to Cyrille's disappearance. Cyrille had a GIS containing extensive spatial data about the site in Orbagne. A GIS could analyze the damage done by looters. Cyrille must have had solid evidence that the villa, which was on Andrea Botti's property, had been illegally looted. With those images he would have been able to make the case that the Cupid and Psyche cup, and perhaps other valuable things, had been taken from Orbagne at some point *before* he started surveying the site with Pietro in 2000—yes. This is it. This explains the timing of the Polaroids confiscated in the 1995 Chiasso warehouse raid. Cyrille knew that the site had been looted long before he started working on it. *They kill people for what they know.* He not only knew the terrain, but he had a digital, visual representation of it. A visual representation that was probably destroyed in the wake of the *Corriere* article that slandered him.

Marco just told me that Andrea Botti was bought by the 'ndrangheta. The villa is on his vineyard. Andrea must have let the 'ndrangheta loot the site long before Cyrille and Pietro started working on it—and Cyrille either knew this or suspected it.

In the summer of 2004, Andrea was the *sindaco* of a small alpine town with outsized political connections, campaigning for a seat in the Italian Senate. Based on everything Lakshmi has told me about the way the 'ndrangheta works, it wouldn't come as a shock if the 'ndrangheta got Andrea elected, in exchange for government contracts and political protection. In which case, Andrea would have had a lot to lose—more than Giamma did.

I breathe in and out, taking stock of things. I have nothing except my memories to convey to the authorities, American or Italian. My only move is to locate either Pietro or Si, to tell them what I know: Giamma had the cup.

It's only been thirty minutes, but I grab my phone from Flavia and thank her for charging it. I stalk back to my chair and navigate to Si's number, but right as I'm about to call, the sound of a fist hitting the counter prompts me to look over at the reception desk, where Flavia and Marco are whisper-fighting again. I catch the word *Venerdi* a few times—Friday. The days of the week in Italian are so close to their Latin antecedents. *Venerdi* routes back to *Veneris Dies,* the day of Venus.

Friday—Marco said the hotel was hosting a press conference on Friday. Si said that objects repatriated to Italy usually go to the regional museum closest to their origin sites. Could it be some kind of homecoming for the Cupid and Psyche cup? And if so, what exactly is Si's role in all of this? Si told me Italy would never get the cup back. They also told me to lie low for the next week. Lie low until after the press conference, in other words.

Pietro. I need to find Pietro. I pocket my phone, rise to my feet, and walk out the hotel's automatic glass doors.

XX.

The sun is high in the sky as I thumb Arco di Agosto into my GPS and head east toward Aosta in my rental Audi.

The roads: I can't stop thinking about the roads. The Little St. Bernard Pass, the Great St. Bernard Pass; the road to the Villa del Frutteto. The Romans wanted Aosta for the roads the Gauls were blocking—so Cyrille said, the day I first met him.

Suddenly I'm nineteen again, sitting on the arm of a couch in the Classics Department at Columbia, waiting for the professor overseeing my independent study on spoken Latin. Cyrille comes in, but he doesn't notice me at first. He's distracted by someone else: a tall man with copper hair and a fitted blazer, emerging from the copy room.

Of all the memories my mind houses, this one has somehow eluded me. But now it comes into focus. The roads; they talked about the roads. The Gauls were blocking the roads the Romans wanted. Cyrille was standing in the way of a dig the Italians wanted.

Giamma looked familiar when we first met in Orbagne because I *had* seen him before. The day I met Cyrille. Giamma and Cyrille were both in New York, at Columbia, when the villa in Orbagne was looted.

According to Fordham's new provenance document, the Cupid and Psyche cup entered Filippo Dalmasso's collection in 2004, the same year I went with Giamma to his father's warehouse in Chiasso. That day, Giamma told me he owed an American curator—Caroline—a favor for helping get him into Columbia. The Cupid and Psyche cup must have been that favor.

It scared the shit out of Caroline when Italy came after the Getty, Si said. And yet the Getty accepted a final donation from Filippo Dalmasso in 1996, the same year Caroline left, at a time when it would have been very risky to do so—the Chiasso raid had happened the year before, and Italy was actively prosecuting the Getty. Did Caroline somehow "purchase" Valerio Piromalli's protection when she helped facilitate gifts of looted art to the Getty in the nineties? Art that Valerio got paid for when he sold it to Filippo, and for which Filippo got a tax write-off? And is it possible that *Caroline* was the one who wanted Filippo to donate the objects through Creon instead of as an individual? To make it more difficult to link her directly to Valerio Piromalli, a known 'ndrangheta boss?

Si said Caroline was blacklisted in the wake of the Marianne Flynn scandal—that no museum was ever going to hire her again. But she still gained something from her time at the Getty—access. Access that initially threatened but ultimately saved her career. Because she did return to the museum world, when Fordham hired her in 2004, the year the Cupid and Psyche cup entered Filippo's collection. She must have leveraged her former dealer network to get that job. Giamma was her tether to that network.

Caroline had proposed global exchange initiatives in the nineties designed to weaken the black market for looted antiquities. And if I'm right about Cyrille, it was the machinations of the black market that led to his death. Is there a world in which Caroline was working from within the system to try to change it? Could she have been some kind of informant for what was happening at the Getty while maintaining her black-market relationships over the long term?

Caroline probably didn't know enough to make her dangerous

to the 'ndrangheta. But she knew enough—she did enough—to go to jail. This must be why she accepted Emmanuel's recommendation to give everything back to Italy. At the same time, even if Caroline was complicit, she's not to blame. She can't be blamed for the system of tax loopholes that enabled Filippo Dalmasso to distance himself from his art collection. Everything he did—including donating through shell companies—was technically legal.

Now, tuning back into my actual physical surroundings as I drive through Aosta's city center, I realize that Giamma never answered any of my emails in my twenties because he knew what I knew. He knew I knew he worked for his father, and that I understood, however abstractly, that he was connected to a powerful network. I told him as much, when I confronted him on my last night in Orbagne. And again a few weeks ago when I asked him if he was still an art dealer. He was protecting me by ignoring me. He is still protecting me by ignoring me.

I park my car at the lot near the Arco di Agosto, which looks the same: hulking, imperial, austere. And everything from the night I was here eighteen years ago comes back: Giamma telling me about his father's prison sentence, and about climbing up into the arch's barrel vault as his father's assistant. His father had three more years in prison. *After he gets out, I'll never come back here,* Giamma said.

Giamma said something else that night: *Se vogliamo che tutto rimanga come è, bisogna che tutto cambi.* If we want things to stay the way they are, everything has to change. It was from *The Leopard.* I'd turned the quote over and over in my head, confounded by it. But now, eighteen years later, back in front of the arch, its significance clicks into place. Without change, there is no life—that's what he meant.

The external will decay. Ancient sculptures break, papyri disintegrate, humans age; but the internal, the intangible, can persist. The soul of a thing can stay the same. This is why ancient objects have value. This is why people care about them, and why countries fight over them. Because the soul of them persists. We sense this, as humans, even if we can't see it with our eyes.

When I was in Orbagne, handling the objects in Giamma's art collection, inspecting the bronze shield we brought to Chiasso—this is what I was experiencing, this paradox. The immutable concealed by the mutable. Maybe archeologists think they're looking for evidence of how people lived, or how they experienced the world. But what they're really looking for is a feeling. Cyrille told me that the morning he disappeared. I experienced the feeling that morning, when he had me put my ear to the ground. Archeologists are following their instincts, trusting that immutable part of themselves. Which requires bravery; it requires faith. I wouldn't have been able to express it back then, but this is why I was drawn to archeology in the first place. I wasn't brave, or faithful—but I wanted to be.

Standing tall, I back away slowly from the Arco di Agosto and cross the bridge, heading away from Aosta's city center. I locate and approach the A-frame house where Andrea Botti's campaign party took place, which looks exactly as I remember it, with the exception of the Nest Cam doorbell to the right of the old oak door. I draw in a breath and ring the bell, thinking that it's actually a good safeguard. If something happens here, there will be a record of me having approached and entered the house.

A little girl with blond curls and huge eyes—a miniature, fairer version of Benedetta—answers the door. She stares at me plainly, and without judgment. She's five or six years old, if I were to guess. Her wise little eyes betray nothing. "Papa," she calls behind her eventually.

The sound of footsteps bounding down the stairs.

Pietro takes her place. Curious, confused. Aquiline nose, sharp blue eyes. There's a hint of gray in his hair, but he otherwise looks the same. He searches my face, maybe trying to place me. Then he draws his pale brows together in recognition.

"Is it Lena?" comes a voice from behind him.

Pietro opens the door wider, and Si is behind him, grinning incredulously. "You made it."

TEN MINUTES LATER WE'RE SEATED under the vaulted ceiling of the great hall upstairs. Pietro's daughter is in the corner working on a puzzle. Outside, the sun is setting between the snow-covered mountains through the room's panoramic windows. The statues from the arch are gone. The only work of art in the room is a Modigliani-esque painting that's undeniably contemporary.

"It started with the sanctuary," Pietro opens. "Which we found last season."

He tells me about the enigmatic underground sanctuary—possibly a Mithraeum, based on the white bulls painted on the walls and its subterranean location—that he and his team unearthed below the storage room, right near one of the trenches I had worked on.

"The point is," Si interjects, "he finally denounced the mudslide theory."

"It was always a guess," Pietro says defensively. "And I maintain that it was a good guess. There was no other evidence of a fire outside that area, so it didn't make sense that the whole complex would have burned down. But a Mithraeum would explain the fire. The ceremonial feasts, the sacrifices—all of them involved fire, burning things."

The main thing I remember learning about the cult of Mithras was that it was secret, and for men only—women were strictly forbidden from participating. "But why Mithras? Why not Apollo?"

I glance at Si, who swats Pietro. "Tell her the rest."

"What we know about the cult of Mithras is largely derived from the writing of Porphyry. So I return to the epithalamium that brought Cyrille to Orbagne. And I see it differently. It was not porphyry the material that was being mentioned, it was Porphyry the person. The epithalamium was commemorating his marriage to Marcella, a young widow he married at the end of his life."

"Who is Porphyry?"

"The philosopher who basically popularized Neoplatonism in Rome, Plotinus—Porphyry was his best student. He got married at the villa. We don't have enough physical evidence to fully corroborate this, but I believe he owned it. At the end of the third century.

"The villa could have then passed from Porphyry to the family of Melania the Younger after Mithraism gave way to Christianity," he continues. "We know the estate was valuable to Rome, because of the wine and fruit that was being produced there. Melania's father was a powerful senator. It makes sense that Melania's family would have been among the few wealthy Roman families who could have afforded it at that time."

"Your original theory," I say.

"Tell her the other part," Si says to Pietro.

"There was a mention in the poem of *vasa diatreta.* Dichroic glass."

I look back and forth at them, understanding that this is the reason why Si confirmed that the cup came from the Villa del Frutetto—because of the poem. Not necessarily because of Giamma, or because of what I think I know about the history of looting in Orbagne.

"Inside the temple, there are the wall paintings of the bulls, and there are several shallow figurative sculptures and niches carved into the walls. One of which is an image of Psyche holding up a torch to Cupid's face. Which is unusual for a Mithraeum. Not completely unprecedented—"

"Just like in the cup," I interject.

"It matches almost exactly," Si says.

"But how—you said you stopped working here—"

"He sent me photos when he found it. About a year ago."

My mind spins with the dizzying revelation that this makes *Pietro* the origin of the investigation into Fordham's collection. "Had you seen the cup in Filippo's collection?" I ask him.

Pietro shoots Si a confused look.

"As you have so relentlessly insisted, Lena," Si rushes to say, "the cup was in fragments when it was donated to Fordham. I'm the one who told him about it."

I process this. "So *you* started this whole thing?"

"I don't know if it's fair to say I *started* it—"

"But the poem was part of Caroline's research. Right? How did she miss it? Wouldn't she have connected the cup to that epithalamium?"

"She didn't necessarily miss it."

"But she was the curator of that Aphrodite exhibition. She even talked about primary sources at that opening last month. It's not like she would have forgotten her own research."

"That's not the only dichroic glass in the world. Pietro hadn't publicized the discovery of the Mithraeum yet. He still hasn't. She couldn't have linked it back to the site."

"Why didn't you publicize—"

Si interrupts me. "Pietro also pointed out that she could have been translating it figuratively," Si continues. "Like in—what was it, Pietro, Corinthians?"

"First Corinthians," Pietro says, his voice strangely pained. "'Now we see through a glass darkly; but then face-to-face: now I know in part; but then shall I know even as I am known.'"

Just then, Benedetta walks through the door. Their daughter, who has somehow been quiet this whole time, runs over and flings herself into her mother's arms.

"Wow," Benedetta says when she sees me, and collapses onto the sofa without removing her coat, the girl perched on her lap now. And to Si, "*Non stavi scherzando.*"

I look at Si expectantly—what does Benedetta mean by that, that Si wasn't kidding?

"I told them how we reconnected," Si says. "And that you were probably going to be back here at some point to see the site, given your involvement in the restitution case and what we know about the cup's provenance." Si widens their eyes and nods at me. "Right?"

They are trying to signal nonverbally that I should play along with this explanation, but I'm too distracted to do that, because this is too glib, too presumptuous—*your involvement in the restitution case.* It's a tell.

"Did you tell Caroline to hire my firm?" I blurt.

Si breathes in and out, maybe weighing their response. But they don't break eye contact. "Yes. And I told her to make sure someone who knew international tax law and Italian was put on the team. I figured I'd take my chances that you didn't have too many Italian-speaking colleagues."

This admission should be validating, but it only unnerves me further. "But why—why—" I stammer. "I mean, what was your end game?"

Si relaxes their shoulders down and leans forward. "I wasn't trying to fuck with you, Lena. I thought you could help. None of this was Caroline's fault. She deserved to get off. And I figured you would protect her, because you knew. I genuinely did not think Fordham would send it back. I still don't think they should have to."

She was far more complicit in this than she has led anyone to believe, I want to say. But I hold off for now, because the phrase *willful ignorance* is echoing in my mind. I was complicit in what Giamma and Caroline were doing too. And so instead I say quietly, "You thought I knew Giamma had it. That he sold it to—"

"My dad," Benedetta says flatly, exchanging a look with Si.

"Something like that," says Si.

"Is that why you sent me the article about the shield?"

Si exhales through their nose. "Quentin Mathieson is a client of mine. I asked him about you after you said you were at the warehouse. He told me about your visit. If I'd known about that before—to be honest, I wouldn't have roped you into this."

A sudden wave of anguish comes over me. I did try to stand up to Emmanuel; I did try to tell him we should push harder to keep the objects in the US. I understood, if abstractly, that I needed to protect Caroline. Because by protecting Caroline, I was protecting myself. But Emmanuel overruled me. "I couldn't help you, because I have no power." My voice breaks.

"Hey," Si says, coming over and sitting next to me on the couch. "Stop. That is not true."

I can't look at them; I can only look away, out the windows at the mountains where Cyrille disappeared on my watch. "She shouldn't have taken the plea," I say quietly.

"I agree," Si says. "But hey, I know how your mind works. You were asking all the right questions. You did what you could. And it's going to be fine. Caroline is fine."

Si knows me. It's a comforting thought. But then again, I don't really know them. Si has a BlackBerry; Si just said Quentin was a client of theirs. And Marco had a strange reaction earlier when I asked him about Si. It's entirely possible Si is working for the 'ndrangheta.

Pietro shifts restlessly, motioning to his daughter, who is dozing in Benedetta's arms.

"When can I see the Mithraeum?" I ask him.

"The villa is closed, unfortunately."

I play dumb—I want to see what Pietro has to say about the shutdown. "Why?"

Pietro closes his eyes, shakes his head. "I've spent the past forty-eight hours trying to understand why this is happening. Or rather, why now." He breathes in deeply. "The Carabinieri say they suspect the site of 'ndrangheta involvement. And—there is truth to this suspicion."

Si and Benedetta look horrified, as if they can't believe he's saying this out loud.

"Twenty years ago, Cyrille and I used an 'ndrangheta guarantor to establish the terms of our partnership," Pietro continues, looking down at the floor, "and to accelerate the excavation permitting process. This is one of the biggest regrets of my life."

The room is utterly silent. I find I can't look at Pietro straight-on, so I watch the shock wash over Si's face. Benedetta looks shocked, too, but it's the shock of betrayal. Whatever he's confessing to now, she already knows.

I know it too. All of a sudden I'm transported in my mind to a windowless office in the Classics Department at Columbia at the end of August, less than a month after Cyrille disappeared, searching for remnants of him. In the filing cabinet, empty folders dangle on metal tracks. I pull the drawer all the way open, registering that one of the folders in the back is slightly ajar. Inside I find a thin notebook with thread binding the size of my hand. I take a seat at the rolling desk chair and page through dozens of sketches labeled with coordinates. The word *Orbagne* appears several times. All of the dates are from the summer of 2003, and everything is in French. It's a dig log, not unlike the one Cyrille kept in his tool belt, jotting down notes up at the site whenever we found something worth documenting.

Wedged into the back flap are two folded papers—photocopies of printed scans, it looks like. I squint to make out the loopy cursive underneath a CARIBINIERI TPC header on the first one, along with a street address in Monza. It's dated March 31, 2004. The words *nessuna prova* are underlined twice.

At first glance, the second document appears to be a letter, but when I look closer I see that although there is a date at the top of it, it's not addressed to anyone. There are four short paragraphs of text and three signatures at the bottom, accompanied by fingerprints.

Instinct draws me to my feet, and I shut the door of the office, hands trembling as I read and reread the names at the bottom of the document: Cyrille DuPuy, Pietro Botti, and Giamma Piromalli. I sit back down and study the paper, written in such abstract and stilted Italian that I can hardly make sense of it. All the verbs are conjugated in the *passato remoto,* which I haven't come close to mastering. But I understand the words *sangue,* and *spirito,* and conclude that the document represents some kind of oath-grounded pact.

Puzzled to the point of frustration, I make my way to the department lounge, locate Cyrille's name on the wall of mail slots, and slide the notebook inside. A week later, when I stop by the administrator's office on my way to class, it's gone.

All these years, I have held on to the possibility that Cyrille made his way back to New York and took that notebook. But it was a ridiculous hope, an impossible one. *Giamma* was the one who went back to New York. Giamma took the notebook. He must have known I put it there, that only I could have done it. He took it as a signal that I was willing to keep his secret. This is the key to my protection now.

Si breaks the thick silence that's settled over us. "What are you saying?" they ask. "What guarantor?"

Pietro shifts his elbows onto his knees and holds his head in his hands. "One year later, the dig was looted in the off-season. Investigators—friends of my father—determined that nothing of obvious importance had gone missing, and that it was likely a failed attempt at looting an inhospitable and nascent dig site.

"In reality, the looting was ordered by Valerio Piromalli. We had agreed that objects looted from the dig would serve as payment for the services his associate had provided to us. But the situation became difficult when Cyrille started to suspect that the looters had taken more than was fair, and that the looters had seriously compromised the integrity of the excavation. He started asking around and threatening to go to the Carabinieri. He had no idea how dangerous these guys were, how powerful. No idea." Pietro pauses and looks up at the lights.

I fix my gaze on Si. They give me a single nod. Yes—this is in reference to the conversation they overheard between Cyrille and Pietro. *They didn't take anything else,* Si heard Pietro say to Cyrille. But they took things. Pietro is admitting now that he knew the looters took things, valuable things.

Absurdly, the little girl is still dozing in Benedetta's arms. Benedetta's face is pained, her eyebrows drawn together. Outside, the sun is low in the sky.

"And so I decided to teach him a lesson," Pietro continues, his voice cracking. "I brought him to a cave in the mountains. Growing up here, I played often in the mountains; I knew the caves well. Cyrille was convinced that there were gold mines near the villa, that it was a place where the Salassi had rinsed the gold they found in the mines. And I lied and told him I had a new idea about where the mines could be. But when we got to the cave, I told him that this was the kind of place the 'ndrangheta would bring him if he didn't stop what he was doing. And I left with my flashlight. I left him in the dark and ran. But when I went back later that night, he was—it appeared he was gone."

An image of Cyrille standing at the foot of my bed the morning he disappeared floats back to me. He was gaunt and radiating an intensity I'd never observed in him. But I recognized it, because I had seen it before in someone else: my mother. My mother had been convinced that God was transmitting messages to her through the lights emanating from the Bahá'í Temple on Sheridan Drive. She had believed it with every fiber of her being. Cyrille had believed that there were hidden truths to uncover at the site, and that he was the one to uncover them. He'd told me to press my ear to the earth. He'd said there was a stream under the ground. And then Giamma had texted me, asking where I was, breaking the spell.

"Was this the morning I was up at the site with him?" I ask. "The day he disappeared?"

Pietro nods.

"Giamma told you."

He narrows his eyes. "Giamma?"

"He texted me that morning, asking where I was. I told him. And I told him I was with Cyrille."

Now Pietro recoils, leaning back into his armchair, a mix of horror and confusion overtaking his face. "No. *No.* I heard Cyrille getting back to Orbagne in the middle of the night—he woke me up. And I watched out the window, and I saw you two walking with your flashlights—"

"*Basta,* Pietro," Benedetta says sharply, waking the child, who starts to whimper that she's hungry. "*Dai, andiamo,*" Benedetta says to the girl brightly, vanishing the anger that was in her voice just seconds ago. I watch as the girl takes her mother's hand and leads her out of the room.

"This is the truth about Giamma," Pietro says quietly. "He was our guarantor. That's it."

Si looks like they've seen a ghost. "But this doesn't make sense. What was it he paid with? What did the looters take?"

"It couldn't have been the Cupid and Psyche cup," I say to Si. "This is why I was saying the timing was important. This is why I was asking you why you changed the dates in the provenance from 1992 to 2004. Because the cup was in Chiasso in or before 1995. So someone knew about the site back then, right?"

Pietro looks stung by my words. "Everyone in Orbagne knew about the site. I was born knowing. I just didn't have the right to excavate."

Why aren't either of them getting the significance of this? Is Pietro trying to protect his father, or keep something from Si—or both? "What I'm saying is that site must have been looted before. Right?"

"I honestly thought he would turn up at some point," Pietro says, more to himself than to Si and me. "I did. And then at a certain point I understood—he was dead."

I think of how *Antigone* ends, how as she was being led into the cave to be buried alive, the Chorus sang to her about Danaë, and the way Zeus still reached her in the form of golden rain while she was being held captive in the basement by her father. Nothing escapes fate, was the point.

"Pietro, why are you saying all of this now?" Si asks, their tone measured.

"I was afraid before. I couldn't say it. But now the site is closed. I don't know why. I don't know what's going on."

Si gives me a pointed look.

"What?" I say. "You think *I* had something to do with this?"

"What's the latest with the case? Did you tell anyone you thought the cup came from Orbagne?"

"Of course not," I say. But as soon as these words leave my mouth, I remember that I did share details of the case with Lakshmi. I told her I thought Andrea Botti might be behind the restitution request. I told her Si was my roommate in Orbagne; I told her Giamma knew more about the looting at the dig than he admitted. Lakshmi, who is defending Giamma's mother in an international human rights case against the 'ndrangheta.

All the energy leaves my body, because I am guilty—not only of sharing my theories about the Cupid and Psyche cup with Lakshmi, but of messaging Giamma that I was up at the dig site with Cyrille, the morning he vanished. The morning Pietro brought him to an alpine cave, abandoning him to the darkness. *You were the last one to see your professor before he disappeared.*

I need to get out of here. As I stand, I barely register the question when Si asks me where I'm going. I tell them the truth, that I'm headed to the hotel in Orbagne.

"Let's meet for breakfast," Si says as they walk me down the stairs to the front door.

I cross my arms and regard them coolly. "What's going on at the hotel on Friday?"

Si's face brightens, then darkens. "I'll tell you tomorrow."

ONCE I GET ON THE ROAD, adrenaline takes over. The last light of the sun, a pink glow at the horizon. But I have no bandwidth for this beauty; I need to pay attention to the roads, their hairpin turns, the bright lights of oncoming traffic. When I arrive back in Orbagne, my cheeks are hot, and my armpits are damp as I park near the church.

I stumble into the hotel restaurant and force myself to eat a bowl of pesto gnocchi and gulp down a large bottle of mineral water. Then I race up to my room and pull the drapes in my room closed. I should call Lakshmi. I want to call Lakshmi. But when I sit down on the bed, I'm overcome by a wave of exhaustion and I fall into a dreamless sleep. When I wake up, it's five in the morning.

The room is freezing, and I lie in bed thinking about yesterday's revelatory conversation. Pietro's strange confession, Si saying they told Caroline to hire my firm because I knew. They thought I knew Giamma had sold the cup to Filippo, and that in order to protect myself—to avoid implicating myself—I would protect Caroline. The trouble was, Si didn't know everything I knew. They still don't.

Finally, I throw back the covers, turn up the thermostat, take a long shower, and watch the façade of the church out my window start to get light.

At seven I bring my laptop downstairs to find coffee. The lobby is empty. I continue down the corridor and into the restaurant, where a handful of people in business clothes are eating fruit and drinking coffee. I take a seat next to the fireplace and order a cappuccino.

I'm just opening my laptop when Si appears.

"It's so early," I say.

Si runs a hand through their hair. "I couldn't sleep. Yesterday was crazy. *Crazy*. But you always said you thought Pietro knew something about Cyrille. You were totally right."

I eye Si suspiciously, thinking but not saying: I don't want to be right about this.

"I swear to God I had no idea. I still feel like I have no idea what he was talking about. But at the same time, why would he make something like that up?"

I tell Si about the document I found inside Cyrille's old dig log in his office back at Columbia. "I think Pietro's being honest."

Si breathes in and out, reeling from what I've told them. "I knew Giamma was— I knew about him. But I didn't know about Cyrille and Pietro. I swear. I didn't even know why the site got shut down until Pietro said that thing about organized crime yesterday."

Si's pleading eyes would seem to indicate that they're telling the truth. But this can't possibly be true.

"Okay, but who do you really work for?"

Si looks amused by this question. "I work for myself."

"But you have a BlackBerry. Which is what Giamma had me use the summer I was here."

They snort a laugh. "That's not an 'ndrangheta thing. They use burners, obviously. Giamma is one of the only people in the world who still uses a BlackBerry. He says Apple is spying on him, but I think he's just too lazy to learn how to use an iPhone. He's the only one I talk to on it."

"So he doesn't still work with—"

"No," Si says, waving their hands. "He never went back."

"But Giamma—not Quentin—sold the cup to Filippo, right?"

"Right. Quentin thinks that the Italian police took it in 1995 as part of the raid, that it ended up back on the black market somehow and was sold to Filippo, that it's a big conspiracy. But I don't think Valerio kept him in the loop on everything. Quentin was never 'ndrangheta.

"At the end of the day, Giamma got the cup out of that warehouse and into Filippo's collection. And then he made sure it got out of Italy. He hadn't connected all the dots, but he knew it was important, and he took it upon himself to save it. He did the right thing."

"To save it from what?"

"That thing is insanely rare. And valuable. It would have made for a highly useful piece of collateral. Which is sadly what happens to a lot of these black-market antiquities."

If Giamma's primary motivation was getting valuable antiquities out of the 'ndrangheta's hands, then it seems entirely possible that Pietro was telling the truth: that Giamma had nothing to do with Cyrille's disappearance.

"Okay," I reason. "Obviously Andrea Botti's link to the 'ndrangheta is Giamma's father. What if the same kind of agreement that Giamma had with Pietro and Cyrille also happened decades earlier between Andrea and Valerio? Say it was the eighties. Andrea was mayor of Toulet before he became a senator, right? Maybe it goes all the way back to that election. And weren't you the one who told me that the vineyard was decimated during World War Two because they didn't have pesticide or something like that? Their wine used to be as popular as Barolo, isn't that what Martha said? And by the time we were here, it was back to being popular—right?"

"Lena—"

"And the vineyard belonged to Pietro's mother's family, remember? Andrea bought it from them—when, and why? And with what money?"

"Yes, but—"

"Let me finish. What I'm saying is that if it comes out that the cup—or anything—was looted from the villa, Andrea Botti looks terrible. He had—and still has—the most to lose if this gets out."

Si nods thoughtfully. "That does make some sense."

"Pietro said he was scared. What if it was because Andrea didn't know that Pietro had executed this agreement with Giamma and Cyrille? And what if Pietro was, at the end of the day, more afraid of his father finding out what he'd done than of the 'ndrangheta or the Carabinieri?"

"But what would that mean?"

"It means that Pietro wouldn't have given Cyrille up to the 'ndrangheta, even indirectly. He had too much to lose."

We sit in silence. The restaurant is starting to fill up with tourists.

"The thing I don't get," Si says, "is the gold mines. Okay, fine, Cyrille wanted the etymology of Orbagne to mean something. Same. But there are no gold mines anywhere near here. They're much farther south. That's been studied extensively. Silver mines, yes, gold, no. Not to say there couldn't have been some kind of workshop here—"

"*That's* what you're fixated on?"

Si shrugs. "I specialize in metals. The idea of rinsing metals here is intriguing."

Rinsing metals. The fountain near the dig dorm in the piazza—it's not there anymore. "What happened to the fountain? The fountain in the center of town, the one where the Andrea Botti statue is now?"

"No idea."

"Can you call Pietro and find out?"

"I kinda don't think we should bother him right now."

"Si, Cyrille was looking for the water source. He told me there was an underground stream. Like a secret water source that was also some Gallic sanctuary, that made the Romans think the farm was magic."

Si's face reddens as they look around the restaurant to make sure no one is watching us. "I need to show you."

AS WE START OFF IN the direction of the dig site, the cold air stinging my ears, I lose my breath almost immediately. But I don't lose heart, because if the mountain is pushing me back, it's also raising me up. Cyrille was pushing against the mountain's resistance too. And in the end, he had something of an apotheosis, at least in my mind.

The old, inclined forest trail we had to hike to get to the dig site is now a concrete staircase with railings, and at the top of the stairs there is a box office in a wood cabin, hemmed by vinyl line keepers. I see a sign for toilets and a Lavazza vending machine. The air feels thin and smells like nothing.

A CHIUSO sign in the plexi window of the box office catches my eye. But there is no blockade, no locked door. A security camera glares down at us, but we keep going. "They probably don't start actively guarding the site until ten in the morning," Si says.

When we arrive at the site, I blink hard and refocus my gaze. This is not a villa; this is a compound built to accommodate the slope of the land. The villa is a U-shaped structure with a reconstructed tile roof and a fully landscaped garden. The garden is filled, improbably, with red roses. *If they can figure out how to work together,* Giamma said, *they will uncover one of the most important sites in Italy.*

Si gestures to a building adjacent to the villa and leads me through an arched doorway into a half-room with a dirt floor. Black plumes climb the walls—yes, this was the storage area I helped excavate all those years ago, where we found the scythe.

"Down here," they say, starting down a set of shallow stone stairs.

The only source of light is from the stairwell, but it's enough to illuminate the procession of white bulls painted onto the far wall, and the marble niches flanking it. I am so overcome with awe that I have the sensation of sinking down into the earth. All I can do is shake my head in amazement. *This was here the whole time*, are the words that come into my mind. Cyrille was right. He said he thought there was a *fanum* in the villa—this is the *fanum*.

After a long moment, I notice the rest of the room: the stone benches on either side of the nave, and off to the side, behind one of the benches, another white marble relief. I step closer to it and point my own phone's flashlight at the two figures. Before I can even process what I'm looking at—Psyche with her butterfly wings and her torch, Cupid's perfect sleeping face—my eyes start to sting with emotion. It's the exact same image from the Cupid and Psyche cage cup.

And on the opposite wall, the myth's inverse moment: Cupid waking a sleeping Psyche with one of his arrows. For Psyche's last punishment, Venus sent her to the underworld to fill a box with Proserpina's beauty. On the way back up, Psyche's curiosity got the best of her, and she opened the box. It contained not beauty, but Phrygian sleep. Cupid came to the rescue, rousing her and helping to complete her task; when it was all over, Venus and Jupiter gave them permission to wed, just in time for Psyche to give birth to their daughter.

It occurs to me now that what happened to Psyche was awful, but it wasn't really anyone's fault. She couldn't help being born. And her parents were rightfully afraid of Venus, which is why they yielded to the gods' request to offer her up as a sacrifice in the first place. Psyche's pregnancy had to happen in order for the story to make sense. Without it, there would have been no inciting incident, and no final redemption.

I examine the niche below the relief. There are two rough

patches, where a sculpture would have been attached. "What do you think was here?"

Si shrugs. "Probably some kind of figurine. Like the ones over here."

We walk over to the niches in each of the corners of the bull wall. In one is a small sculpture of a woman riding sidesaddle on a seahorse, a key in one hand and an overflowing cornucopia in the other. And in the other niche is Venus, emerging from a cloud of sea-foam, backed by a fluted shell. "They're fountains," I say in awe.

"And look at this," Si says, motioning to the altar in the center of the wall.

I step closer to it, taking in the menacing face carved into the stone. He's surrounded by laurels, bunches of grapes, and rosettes. Two waves, cresting toward each other, frame all of this in. "It's the same face from the fountain that used to be in the piazza."

"And the collection basin at the Botti vineyard—remember? I think it might be Silenus," Si says.

"Who was he again?"

"He was a satyr, Bacchus's tutor. Sometimes he has little horns like these. Makes sense for a vineyard."

"So then why is Pietro calling it a Mithraeum?"

"It might have been built as a nymphaeum or something, but at some point I think it was used as a Mithraeum. That explains the fire, and the benches. The altar in the middle of the bull wall—that face confuses me. Normally there would be a relief of Mithras plunging his knife into a bull. But this is the layout of a Mithraeum. And it's underground."

"The white bulls could be in reference to Gallic rituals, right? Could he be a Gallic god, not Silenus?"

Si winces. "Could be, I guess."

"Because this has to be Epona," I say, indicating the wide-eyed, regal figure in the left corner of the room. The only Gallic goddess to be fully Romanized, Cyrille said. Epona Augusta. She was associated with horses, and the Roman cavalry. Lucius prayed to an effigy of Epona in *The Golden Ass*, the night he turned into a donkey.

I approach the other fountain and reach out to stroke Venus's cheek. She's bigger than the figurine from Giamma's apartment in Torino, and she's not missing her head—but her body is the same. She's holding something in her hand. An apple, like the golden apple Paris gave her in *The Aeneid*—like the apples that grew here. I return to the altar and realize that the fruit I mistook for grapes on the Cupid and Psyche cup must be the white berries produced by mistletoe. The mistletoe, which was used in the production of Genetrix.

Cyrille thought there was an underground sanctuary devoted to a Gallic river goddess beneath the villa. He was right. The Romans merged her with Venus, who was born from the water.

Cyrille was looking for the water—the magic. These are the magic, once-flowing fountains that were continuously replenished and drained. Now, they're bone-dry. When did they dry up? And what did I hear the morning Cyrille disappeared, when he had me press my ear to the ground?

"They ran out of water," I say in bewilderment.

"Well, yeah," Si says. "Clearly."

"No, I'm saying—that's why the site was abandoned. They ran out of water."

Si stares at me, calculating. "But what about the vineyard? How could it have survived?"

"Someone at some point must have diverted the water source with an aqueduct. Or it went fallow, and someone got it going again later."

"I don't think—"

Suddenly something occurs to me. "Remember when we were at the hot springs with Pietro and Benedetta, and you asked Pietro about the vineyard's irrigation? Because the villa was so far from the Duria? And all he said was 'you can't excavate an active vineyard,' or something like that?"

Si nods hesitantly.

The words rush out of me. "Which is obviously bullshit, right? Of course you can excavate a vineyard—but his father didn't want him to. Because of *what they might find* if they started digging. Which would also explain why Andrea got rid of the fountain in the piazza, because it was linked to the one up here, and everything is connected—"

Everything is connected. "We need to go back to town," I conclude, my heart pounding in my chest. "Now I need to show *you* something."

TWENTY MINUTES LATER I GRAB the key from behind the stone and let us into Giamma's abandoned summer home. Breathlessly, I lead us into the atrium.

"I always wondered what this place looked like inside," Si says, taking it all in. The snow pile in the atrium is smaller than it was yesterday, and instead of a stream of water rushing down the gutters, there is only a quiet, steady drip.

"The first time I was here, Giamma pointed out the drainage system. He told me the design of the house was 'completely inappropriate for the Alps.' And I thought nothing of it."

"Yeah, this is like a house you'd build in the south."

I bend down and jostle one of the grates, then point my phone's flashlight down. "We've gotta get down there."

Si looks skeptical. "Not sure a human can fit in that thing."

I wrench the grate off finally and stick my leg into the opening. I might be able to get both legs in here, but my hips would prevent me from lowering myself down.

"You'd have to be a small child to fit through that," Si says.

A small child. Giamma was a child when his father hoisted him up into the chamber inside the Arco di Agosto. Giamma befriended the Albanian refugee boys who followed him around Orbagne. This is why. "We need a kid. Should we call Pietro?"

"You're joking, right?"

I'm already on the other side of the atrium where there is a different configuration of drains—one of them, at the corner, is bigger than the rest. "You're skinnier than me," I say, yanking the grate up from its frame. "Can you try to fit?"

"What do you think we're even going to find down there?"

I tell them about Lakshmi's clients, and the inventive ways the 'ndrangheta hides cocaine—inside statues of the Virgin Mary, shipping containers of coffee cans, and coffin-like submersibles. And then I tell them about what I saw with my own eyes, in the bathroom walls of Giamma's Torino apartment. Finally, I tell them what Marco told me yesterday at the hotel—that Andrea Botti was bought by the 'ndrangheta.

"Oh my god." Si covers their eyes. "What else have you not told me?"

"That's everything. And this is why I think that what Pietro said yesterday—" I search for the right way to express what I'm thinking. "You said a provenance is a story about an object that adds up, that makes sense. Pietro made up a narrative to try to understand what happened to Cyrille. He probably knew about his father, and obviously he knew about Giamma. But I don't think he knew everything."

"So you think that what, there's coke down there?"

I shine my phone's flashlight into the drain. "I think this leads to a tunnel. Inside the tunnel could be anything. And I think Cyrille was getting too close to figuring this out—because he was fixated on the water source. And the water source connects everything in Orbagne—including 'ndrangheta activity."

I run my hand along the perimeter of the drain, feeling for a way to make the opening bigger. On the left side, my hand catches on something—some kind of metal ridge. "Can you give me some light?" I ask Si.

I peer inside—it's a mounted ladder. A large, flat flange is holding it in place—and I release it, sending the ladder swinging down into the darkness. I sit back on my heels. Si and I look at each other in silence for a long time.

"We need to tell the Carabinieri," Si finally says. "They can figure out how to get down there and look."

"It can't be me," I say.

"It has to be you. I need to go and do damage control with Benedetta."

"What does she have to do with any of this?"

Si gets to their feet and brushes off their knees. "She's my business partner."

"Your *business partner*?"

"We're hosting a press conference tomorrow morning in the hotel to announce a project we've been working on."

"I thought you weren't working here anymore," I say as we walk out of the house and into the courtyard.

"My work with Bene has nothing to do with the villa," Si whispers. "I just don't want her to be blindsided. And I'll give Pietro a heads-up too. You just—I think you should go back to your hotel room and call from there."

"And then what?"

"And then—I don't know. I guess it depends on what they find, right?"

We part ways, and I speedwalk back to Marco's hotel. Up in my room, I sit on the bed and stare at the phone. I'm not ready to call the Carabinieri yet. I open up my laptop and FaceTime Lakshmi in London. "Pick up, pick up," I murmur as the line beeps.

Miraculously, she does. She appears to be sitting at a table in front of a window. "You want a tour of my new place?" she asks.

"No," I say, suddenly on the verge of tears. "I mean, yes. But not right now."

Lakshmi looks horrified as I recount the sequence of events that brought me to Orbagne, what Marco told me about Andrea Botti, Pietro's stilted confession last night, and the villa, which is not really a villa but a massive ancient compound with a mysterious underground sanctuary. "This goes way deeper than I thought," I tell her. "Literally."

Lakshmi's blinking, anxious face disappears momentarily, and then returns. "You need to get out of there."

"What did you just do?"

"I just wanted to see exactly where you were so I could figure out the nearest airport."

"Like, where Orbagne is on the map?"

"You share your location with me."

"Oh," I say, deflating slightly as I recall the date with a socially awkward Google engineer a few months back that prompted me to share my location with Lakshmi in case he turned out to be a serial killer. Apparently I never turned it off.

"Lena, you've got to get out of there. Come to me in London, I don't start work until Monday. Or go back to New York. Let me look at flights—"

"I just need one more day," I say, thinking of the press conference that's happening tomorrow. "And Si said I should call the Carabinieri."

"Yes, call them. But don't mention the curator, or your theories about Cyrille. Just tell them you're working with the Manhattan DA. And as soon as you're done, book the soonest flight out of Milan or Torino, whichever is closer. Promise me."

We hang up, and I navigate to my FindMy app. I'm only sharing my location with Lakshmi, no one else. I can see hers, too, in a neighborhood called Mayfair in London. And I can see the pulsing orb of Jinny's location—she's in Thousand Oaks, at home, pregnant with my niece. I love her. I miss her.

THE NEXT MORNING I ENTER the hotel ballroom, which is packed with press conference attendees. Walking down a makeshift aisle, I scan the two sections of folding chairs for Pietro. But I don't see him anywhere. Eventually I take a seat on the right side, behind a three-camera setup. I crane my neck toward the back of the space, just in time to see Andrea Botti walk in. His face is open and smiling as a few attendees rush up to him. Politics haven't taken much of a toll on his physical appearance, it seems—he looks almost the same as he did in 2004. Slightly more bronzed, maybe.

I turn my attention back to the stage, where Marco is plugging cords into outlets with a look of determination on his face. *Everyone knows,* he said yesterday. *Everyone knows that Andrea Botti was bought by the 'ndrangheta.* It doesn't seem like everyone in this room knows.

At ten o'clock exactly, the lighting in the room changes, and everyone quiets down. Si and Benedetta walk to the center of the stage and stand in front of a double-wide podium.

"Thanks for being here today," Si opens briefly, turning their attention to Benedetta.

"We are so pleased to announce the launch of an important new initiative," Benedetta says. "Conceived and realized with the collaboration of the Italian Ministry of Cultural Heritage."

Benedetta does most of the talking, and in perfect, practiced English. "The battle to keep the black market for Italian antiquities in check has long been a losing one," she says. "Thousands of objects are still being smuggled out of the country on an annual basis, and those that stay in the country are being used as collateral to further local crimes and schemes."

Then she transitions to counterterrorism, and disrupting the stream of antiquities sales that benefit organized crime groups in Italy and abroad. The problem isn't the monetary value of the objects, she asserts—it's what they represent. And what they stand in the way of: precious metals, development of infrastructure, and distribution of resources. In order to keep the objects safe, we need to disrupt the market. And the way to do that is by giving amnesty to the owners of illicit objects, be they institutions or individuals. Under this new initiative, owners who come forward with the true histories of an object will receive a long-term lease on the object; Italy will technically own them, but whoever possesses them will get to hold on to them for one hundred years, or until the owner dies.

"We are all guardians of ancient civilization," she concludes. "And now Italy will formalize a global network of protectors of our unique cultural heritage."

Si thanks Benedetta and clears their throat. "You all may be wondering how this will work in a practical sense," they say, going on to describe the blockchain-backed inventory management system they have been developing for the past ten years. "Regardless of where these objects have been, once owners of these objects start coming forward, Artemis—which will eventually be a publicly accessible platform—will track the whereabouts of the objects in real time."

Artemis is the platform Si migrated Fordham's art inventory to. *We can't go back*, they said. *But we can do better now.*

Reporters fling up their hands, and I look around for Filippo Dalmasso, wondering how he fits into all this. But he's nowhere to be found. Neither is Pietro. I only see Andrea Botti a few rows back, looking oddly smug.

A man a few seats down from me stands up and projects his voice. It's familiar, I realize, the *r* in the back of his throat. He's Valenti, the reporter who interviewed me the summer I was in Orbagne. "How will this impact active archeological sites vulnerable to looting?" he asks. "Couldn't someone knowingly buy something illegal and come forward to get the lease?"

"The owners of the objects will have to supply information about the object in order to obtain the lease—who they bought it from, where it may have come from—and eventually we will have enough information to prosecute all of the major players involved," Benedetta says.

Benedetta and Si field a few more questions, and then stand to leave. Benedetta makes her way off the stage as Si lingers to flick off the microphones.

When the lights go up, I walk over to Valenti. "Do you remember me?" I ask him.

He clears his throat nervously.

"You interviewed me about my professor. And then you published an article about him that was full of lies."

"I—"

"You know he died, right?"

Si appears at my side. "We need to talk," they say to me, tugging on my arm. "Privately."

They lead me out of the ballroom and toward the elevator bank. "Why didn't you tell me about this Artemis thing?" I ask.

"That's the least of your worries right now. Go up to your room and turn on Rai."

I TURN ON THE TELEVISION and find a news station. The word *PENTITO* is emblazoned under a photograph of Pietro. Pietro is collaborating with authorities to find the French professor who disappeared in a *lupara bianca* almost two decades ago, a reporter says.

I watch in silent awe as she segues into a segment on Valerio Piromalli, who built the San Bernardo ski resort in the 1980s, having first immigrated to Bardonecchia in the 1970s on a *soggiorno obbligato* with other Calabrians suspected of ‘ndrangheta involvement. But he never left the ‘ndrangheta; he grew it, rising to prominence in the organization through the lucrative construction contracts he shepherded. The Carabinieri were after him for years, the reporter says. They never got him on racketeering or money laundering, though—after decades of trying to file charges against him, he was ultimately arrested for antiquities smuggling during a Swiss warehouse raid connected to a high-profile Italian lawsuit against the Getty Center in the United States in the nineties.

Her words speed up, and now she's speaking so quickly that I can hardly get any of it, but I watch anyway, mesmerized, as she describes the tunnel that was discovered under Valerio Piromalli's country house in Orbagne. *800 kilo di cocaina,* she says. The biggest drug bust in the history of the Aosta Valley. An image of Cyrille's tool belt flashes on the screen. *Una busta contenente diciottomila euro,* I catch. An envelope containing eighteen thousand euros was discovered in a fold of an old tool belt, which Pietro Botti, the son of Senator Andrea Botti, identified as having belonged to the French professor who disappeared. We can never really know another person, she says, adding something about how the ‘ndrangheta is everywhere and nowhere.

I open my laptop and look for flights, fully convinced now that I need to get out of here—I need to go home. There are no more flights to the US today, but I book one for tomorrow morning out of Milan. Then I shut my laptop, pull the blackout curtains closed, and climb under the covers.

WHEN I DOZE OFF, I dream of a mountain—a man-made one. I'm climbing to its summit, shaking, clutching the edges of my jacket sleeves as I breathe in the exhaust from the cars idling nearby. I've never been more physically terrified in my short life. The treads on Jinny's hand-me-down boots are worn down. In Chicago, snow never fully melts on anomalous warm days the way it does in New York—there's too much of it. It may soften in the day, but then freezes overnight, and soon it snows again. Parking-lot mountains are therefore terrifyingly vertiginous. "I'm right behind you," Jinny says. Her voice is a net, and I summon the strength to keep climbing.

I jolt awake to the sound of banging at my door. It's Si, hiking boots on, parka zipped all the way up to their chin. "What time is it?" I murmur, glancing down at my watch. Nine o'clock, it says, which makes it three o'clock in the afternoon here.

"He's dead," Si says, panting.

"What—who?"

"Pietro. Pietro is dead. Shot in the back of the head. At a safe house in Courmayeur."

I rub the sleep out of my eyes, squinting at the brightness of the hallway. "*What?* What happened?"

"I don't know," Si says, their voice high. "Bene got a call. I just know he's dead."

"Come here," I say, pulling them into my room.

Si lets me hug them as they let out heaving sobs. After the initial shock wears off, their sorrow seeps into me. Just two days ago I was sitting across from Pietro in Aosta. Eighteen years ago he carried my suitcase up the dig dorm's front stairs when I first arrived in Orbagne. And now he's gone. I'll never see him again. Just like I'll never see Cyrille again.

Now I'm crying too—at the injustice of all of this, and for Benedetta and her daughter, who will have to figure out how to live without him. I hug Si tighter.

Eventually my double breathing subsides, and I call Lakshmi on speakerphone.

"It's an 'ndrangheta hit, definitely. The bullet in the back of the head—he was playing both sides. Doesn't get to see his murderer."

Si and I exchange glances. I tell Lakshmi about Cyrille's tool belt. "The reporter said he died in a *lupara bianca.*"

Si fixes their attention on me. And as I scan their face, I see that there is no danger, no disapproval; only kindness, and maybe even a glint of admiration. "You knew something weird went down with him."

"It's true," Lakshmi agrees.

For the moment, this is enough—this validation from two people who have known me since the summer Cyrille disappeared. And to be fully here, physically and mentally, in this moment.

"You both need to get out of there," Lakshmi says before she hangs up. "Get back to the US."

"I can't leave yet," Si says. "I need to see the villa one more time."

"I'll go with you," I say, half expecting Si to protest. But they nod, gratefully.

"Someone will have to take over the site, right?" I say as I throw on my jacket and step into my sneakers.

Si shrugs. "It's too soon to say."

They're right; there is nothing to figure out right now. And more than that: this place where I started to become the person I now am, where I thought I lost the person I used to be—I can move on now, because I've found her. Or maybe, more accurately, I've acknowledged her.

We head out of the hotel and walk in comfortable silence, in the orange light of the late afternoon, along the Little St. Bernard Pass. The Mary Magdelene chapel in the distance is boarded up—and when I squint, I can make out a narrow stream of snowmelt rushing down the mountain toward it.

"I looked up Porphyry earlier," I tell Si in an effort to take their mind off Pietro. "And you know, I don't think he was necessarily a follower of Mithras."

"Really?"

"Everything he wrote about Mithraism is from some exegesis of a passage from *The Odyssey*. 'The Cave of the Nymphs.' I skimmed it this morning. Didn't you say you thought the sanctuary at the villa might have been a nymphaeum?"

"I mean, it's not an original idea. Any sanctuary with a fountain is a nymphaeum."

"I just feel like Mithraism is so—I don't know, male? And that sanctuary feels very feminine. Like, divine feminine."

Si looks amused. "Okay, keep going."

"Porphyry wrote about how what matters most in life is learning to free the soul from the body. Because the soul is part of the intelligible world, and the body is part of the profane world, or something like that? Psyche is the soul, so the soul is feminine."

"Sounds . . . Neoplatonic."

"I just kept reading the word *soul* over and over in every article about him. The cosmos is the expression of the soul, the soul is connected to nature, soul this, soul that. Oh, and the souls of embryos come from the mother, never the father." I pause and glance at Si. They're listening. "I'm just saying, he commissioned the cup to commemorate his marriage to Marcella. He wouldn't have excluded her from his religion. I mean, Pietro said they didn't have enough evidence to prove that Porphyry owned the estate. I read that Marcella was a wealthy widow. What if Marcella bought it? What if *Marcella* commissioned the cup?"

"It's possible."

"By the way, I think I finally understand the Cupid and Psyche myth."

Si smiles. "Tell me."

"Only love—Cupid—can wake up a soul—Psyche—that's sleeping. Psyche went to sleep after she made the mistake of opening that box from Proserpina. She'd suffered so much, but she never learned from her mistakes. She just kept making them. And Cupid didn't save her, exactly—he woke her up. The soul can be awakened, basically. By love. Amorous love, or platonic love. Neoplatonic love, I should say."

Si nods thoughtfully. "I like that."

We walk in silence for a few minutes.

"What's going to happen to the cup, do you think?" I ask.

"They haven't decided yet. Either the museum in Aosta, or the Museo dell'arte salvata in Rome. It doesn't really matter."

Si's right, I realize—it doesn't matter. We can't go back. But we can do better now. I can do better now.

We fall into silence again, walking in lockstep. And I think about what I'll do after this, after I see the villa one last time with Si.

I'll drive back to Milan and fly to LAX and rent a car and drive up the Pacific Coast Highway. I'll approach the Getty Villa, and I'll remember the one time I was there—it was with Jinny, right around the time she started teaching at Pepperdine.

We wandered around Getty's simulacrum of the Villa of the Papyri from Herculaneum for hours, tracing the peristyle, gazing at ourselves in the reflecting pool. We stared at a perplexing engraved gem from the second century, in which Psyche as a butterfly flitted among multiple Cupids. Jinny told me it made her think of a German essay she'd just read by Herman Hesse about butterflies—which was really about nature, and the elusiveness of language, she'd said—and he'd invoked a quote by Goethe: "I am here, that I may wonder!" And we'd laughed about our mother, and her obsession with Goethe, and things were easy between us.

When I get to Thousand Oaks, Jinny will be on top of the covers in bed, propped up with pillows. Nick will be working from the spare room on the other end of her single-story ranch. He will have greeted me warmly, and then he will have left us alone.

I'll tell Jinny about my summer in Italy: about Giamma, and Cyrille, and Pietro; about Si and Benedetta; and about the Cupid and

Psyche cage cup. It can be claimed, but it can't be possessed; not really. It may have come from Orbagne, but it doesn't really belong to anyone, or any place. I'll tell her that maybe the only way to respect an object—to respect anything—is to not look for it in the first place. To let it find you.

"But sometimes you have to dig things up in order to understand," she'll say.

"It doesn't matter if you understand," I'll reply, because understanding is not the same as knowing. More than anything this is what I want from Jinny: to be known unconditionally. And for her to be known to me. I will tell her this.

She'll disagree: "You can't know me, Lena."

"Why not?" I'll ask, rubbing the quilt on her bed between my thumb and index finger.

"Because you want me to be who I was to you back then. But who I was to you then was not, and is not, who I am."

As soon as she says it, pressure will gather behind my eyes because I'll finally understand my problem, but I'll be too ashamed to say it aloud. "No, that's not it."

It's not a lie, not exactly. I don't want her to be who she was back then. It's that I don't want to be the person *I* was then, to her.

Our relationship will never be equal, I will understand. It will always be weighted toward her. I will always need her more.

"Then what is it?" she'll ask.

I won't be able to verbalize the emotional truth, so I'll get at it indirectly. "My Latin teacher wrote the word *sincere* on the chalkboard once," I'll say. And I'll tell her how he drew a box around *sin* and a circle around *cere*. Underneath, he wrote *sine-cere*. *Sine* was easy; *sine* is "without." None of us knew *cere*. Wax, he explained. If an object is without wax, it hasn't been broken, and it hasn't been repaired. A sculpture for sale at an ancient market was *sincere* if it was whole.

From that moment on I would find myself preoccupied—

haunted, really—by an apposite image, that of a broken vessel. But I was so fixated on its network of wax veins that I failed to acknowledge the fact of its utility: the vessel still held water.

BACK ON THE ROAD UP TO THE VILLA, my phone buzzes. I pull it out of my pocket and look at the face, glowing with a message from Lakshmi: *You're still there.* In Italy, she means. Warmth floods my body as I heart her message. I'll call her later.

I am here, that I may wonder, I say to myself as Si and I walk through the woods. I hear the rush of a stream; I smell the leather of the oak trees. For the first time, I really feel the aleatory magic of this place, its mingling facts and fictions. And suddenly something Cyrille murmured the morning he disappeared comes back to me: water cannot be created or destroyed—it can only change forms.

That's true of many things, I think.

ACKNOWLEDGMENTS

Thank you to Olivia Taylor Smith, whose insights, dedication, and encouragement brought this book to its fullest potential. I am so grateful for the time we spent working on *Artifacts.*

Thank you to Sabrina Taitz, for championing this book and believing in me as a writer. Also to Ty Anania, Cashen Conroy, and everyone at WME who has guided and supported me throughout this process.

Thank you to the rest of my amazing team at Simon & Schuster: Brittany Adames, Danielle Prielipp, Stacey Sakal, Maggie Southard Gladstone, Amanda Mulholland, Lauren Gomez, Olivia Perrault, Rachael DeShano, Carly Loman, Meryll Preposi, Beth Maglione, Samantha Cohen, Mikaela Bielawski, Paul Dippolito, Jackie Seow, David Fassett, Emma Shaw, Tom Spain, Ray Chokov, Nicole Moran, Michael Nardullo, Mabel Taveras, Lyndsay Brueggemann, Sean Manning, and Irene Kheradi.

Thank you to Giovanna Centeno Barbalho, for seeing beyond what was on the page in early drafts and for our many energizing conversations. I am so lucky to have crossed paths with you.

Thank you to Ella Weston and Cheryl Bosnak for reading and discussing early drafts, and to Jessie Trudeau, for sharing your expertise on organized crime and pointing me to the important work of Anna Sergi.

Thank you to my community at Emerson, especially Raquel Pidal, Dan Weaver, Steve Himmer, Steve Yarbrough, Rick Reiken, and Novuyo Tshuma.

Thank you to my undergrad Classics and archeology professors, especially David Proctor, Anne Mahoney, and Maxence Segard.

For the practical (and moral) support that made it possible for me to find time to write, thank you to Mallory Ruymann, Zuleyma Guzman, Emma Tamer, and Sophie Phillips.

For well-timed advice and/or encouragement, thank you to Betsy Groban, Sara Freeman, Lauren Stein, Courtney Maum, Rebecca Petchenik, Lynette Widder, Kristen Arnett, Laura Zigman, Adelle Chang, Jamie Staples, Adam Harris Levine, Nicole Baas, and Vanessa Miceli Janes.

And for giving me the best reason to get out of my head and live in the real world, thank you to Emilia, Sylvie, and Jake. I love you.

ABOUT THE AUTHOR

NATALIE LEMLE is a writer and visual art advisor with a BA in Classics and art history from Tufts University and an MFA in creative writing from Emerson College. She lives outside of Boston with her husband and two children. *Artifacts* is her first novel.